The Lie

HILARY BOYD

PENGUIN BOOKS

PENGUIN BOOKS

UK | USA | Canada | Ireland | Australia
India | New Zealand | South Africa

Penguin Books is part of the Penguin Random House group of companies
whose addresses can be found at global.penguinrandomhouse.com.

First published 2020
001

Set in 12.5/14.75 pt Garamond MT Std
by Integra Software Services Pvt. Ltd, Pondicherry
Printed and bound in Great Britain by Clays Ltd, Elcograf S.p.A.

A CIP catalogue record for this book is available from the British Library

ISBN: 978–1–405–93483–1

www.greenpenguin.co.uk

To my sister, Judie, with love

Just as ripples spread out when a single pebble is dropped into water, the actions of individuals can have far-reaching effects.

Dalai Lama

I

Romy stood and eyed the large cardboard box lying on the patio. It was a new garden table, the old one so rotten she could almost push her finger through the wood. Summer was only a few months away and – just possibly – she might feel like having someone over for a meal by then, if the weather was good enough. But she made no move to open the box, just closed her eyes for a moment, slowly breathing in the soft air of early spring, and felt a delicious peace wash over her.

This was new, the sensation of letting go, and she realized she'd been strung so tight in the little over a year since she'd left Michael – strung tight and closed down – her feelings swirling in a tepid soup beneath the surface. As if she had been hibernating.

It was only in the past couple of months that she'd sensed a lightening around her heart, the dreary plod through each day replaced by a small, burgeoning enjoyment in even the most mundane of tasks, as if she were coming to life, like the tight pink buds blossoming on the cherry tree in her neighbour's garden.

As she stood there, contemplating the morning ahead, she heard a knock at the front door. She was still in her pyjamas and froze, then reminded herself she wasn't in the London flat now – where she would no more have opened the door in her nightclothes than flown to the moon – but in the garden of her small fisherman's cottage, overlooking the Sussex harbour.

'Hi, Maureen.' Romy greeted her new friend with pleasure. 'Sorry, caught me on the hop.'

The old lady gave a throaty chuckle, her worn, weather-beaten face lighting up with amusement. She was Romy's height – and Romy was tall – ramrod-straight, with thick white hair cut like a man's and fierce blue eyes that missed nothing. She waved away Romy's apology as she entered the house, bending surprisingly nimbly for someone of her age to pick up the post from the mat. She handed it to Romy. 'I forget the rest of the world doesn't get up at five.'

Romy had met Maureen a few weeks ago, when they'd got chatting in the village deli. Keith, who owned the shop with his wife, had given them both some goat's cheese from a nearby farm to taste. And when Romy professed an interest in local organic produce, Maureen had suggested Romy come with her to the farmers' market the following Saturday.

Even a couple of months ago, Romy would not have got involved in chatting to anyone – in fact, she chose the anonymous supermarket by the big roundabout into town over the deli for that very reason. Nor would she have agreed so readily to Maureen's plan. But the old lady was straightforward and funny – and didn't ask prying questions. Romy found herself looking forward to seeing her again, after months of avoiding the world.

'Coffee?' Romy asked now.

'If you're making it. I won't stay long. I just have a proposition to put to you.'

Intrigued, Romy went over to her new pod machine. Michael came unwillingly to mind as she waited for the cup to fill. He had refused to have one, saying they were a waste of space, that the coffee was lukewarm and there wasn't enough of it. But she was thrilled with her purchase – as she was with so much else in her new life.

Now, taking the milk from the fridge, she caught sight of the letters Maureen had handed her, which she'd slung onto the counter. The top one was handwritten – unusual, these days. She knew it came from Uncle Geoff, an old friend of her parents, now in his nineties. But the cream envelope and black ink reminded her of another, much more significant one. Immediately she felt a spike of unease, unable to prevent the familiar words from flashing through her mind: *This is a difficult letter to write . . .*

Brushing away the thought, she carried the cups of coffee outside. Nothing was going to spoil her mood of optimism this morning.

'So,' said Maureen, when they were settled on the rickety wooden bench on the patio, toes brushing the unopened box, 'I thought from what you said – and now that you're here full time – you might be interested in doing some conservation work.'

Romy waited for her to go on.

'It's voluntary, of course. But there's a group of us meet up at Ebernoe Common on Mondays – do you know it? North of Petworth, a wildlife reserve. We do coppicing and clearing bracken, monitoring wildlife, that sort of thing. But we also bring picnics and put the world to rights.' She gave her an appraising look, amusement in her eyes. 'It's hard work, but you don't look like a wimp.'

Romy grinned. 'I would absolutely *love* to join you, Maureen. What a wonderful idea.'

When her guest had eventually gone, Romy hugged her arms round herself. This was exactly what she wanted to do. Conservation – the environment – was her passion. And there was no Michael to scoff at her now, mock her for wanting a cleaner planet.

Leaving the flat-pack on the patio – the thought of managing to slot the correct widget into the correct hole the correct way round made her sigh – Romy decided to go for a run, before the changeable March weather turned.

Out along the harbour road she went, trying to beat the clock on the incoming tide. The sailing boats would start to go back into the water soon, the huge crane on the quay churning away most days as, inch by inch, it lifted the vessels – smallish, mostly, the bigger yachts moored in the larger marina along the coast – then lowered them gently into the sea.

For a moment she stopped and looked out towards the Norman tower of the church on the far side of the bay. She was sweating in the spring sunshine so she ripped off her hooded running jacket and tied it round her waist, securing her curls in a thick ponytail with a band she kept around her wrist. She had a black vest underneath and the breeze felt delicious on her bare skin.

But as she started running again, her trainers dancing over the many potholes in the crumbly asphalt, the smooth rhythm of her stride could not prevent the sudden intrusion of another flash: *I just thought you should know who you're married to, Mrs Claire.*

2

The good weather had been short-lived and rain dripped off the hood of Romy's anorak, darkening her jeans. She was grateful for the race marshal's hi-vis jacket, which added extra warmth on such a miserable day. But despite the vile conditions – and the hours she had agreed to spend handing out water bottles and directing the runners left, not right, along the lane – she found herself enjoying being involved, being part of something again.

It was an hour and a whole slew of runners later that a slight, older man with a grey buzz-cut – arms flailing, race number flapping loose on his singlet, his rasping breath leaving vapour trails in the cold air – came struggling up the hill on his third lap. But as he swerved left, ignoring the outstretched water, he suddenly pulled up, letting out a roar of pain as he hopped on his left leg and clutched his right thigh with both hands.

Romy hurried to his side. Groaning and swearing under his breath, he leant heavily on her shoulder.

'Not again,' he muttered, through clenched teeth, to himself rather than Romy.

'Sit down while I get help,' she said, opening the battered wooden camping stool that had belonged to her father but was still perfectly functional.

He winced, then nodded. She lowered him gingerly onto the damp canvas seat. Crouching beside him as she alerted the medical team, she was aware that a panting figure had drawn up alongside them.

'Can I help?' asked a breathless male voice.

She looked up, pushing back her hood and her damp, unruly curls to see who had spoken. The eyes she met were brown and kind and she held his gaze for a second before replying. 'Thanks, but I think we're OK. They're sending someone.'

'Morning, Finch.' The older runner's face was set in a pained grimace.

The man called Finch laid a hand on his shoulder. 'Not really the weather for sitting about in your vest, Terry, my friend,' he said affectionately. 'What have you gone and done to yourself?' He looked at Romy again. 'I can take him down, if you like. Better than waiting in the freezing rain for help to arrive.'

Romy hesitated. 'I'd come with you, but I'm not supposed to leave my post.'

He grinned, his eyes lighting in amusement. 'Best not, or they'll all go the wrong way and end up in Hull. He's not heavy . . . are you, Terence? I can manage.'

And Romy thought that he probably could. He was broad-shouldered, muscled and clearly fit. Terry seemed to think so too. He seemed reassured by Finch's suggestion and grasped the outstretched hand, which dragged him gently to his feet.

'Robert Fincham, by the way – although I prefer Finch,' the runner said, nodding to her as he practically lifted Terry off the ground, his arm clamped firmly round the older man's skinny waist.

6

'Romy,' she replied, reluctant, for some reason, to tell him her surname.

'See you in the Bell?' Finch threw out, as he turned down the lane to the village hall.

He was gone before Romy could reply. She knew who Robert Fincham was by reputation. A few years back the retired soldier – her neighbour had proudly told her this fact as if Finch were her own son – had taken on almost saintly status with the older women in the village as he cared for his wife while she died a painful and untimely death from recurring breast cancer. Since then, Romy had seen him about occasionally, running around the harbour or striding through the village. She had wondered about him; he cut a lonely figure.

Maybe I will go to the pub after the race, she thought later, as she packed up the drinks station, her feet and hands numb with cold. She felt a tiny flutter of anticipation at the prospect.

The low-ceilinged pub was rammed and booming with the hyped-up chatter of people coming down from a successful physical challenge. Romy gazed over the heads of the crowd.

'What are you having?' The chief marshal suddenly had his arm around her shoulders, his deep voice rumbling in her ear above the hubbub.

'Very kind of you, Stuart, but I should get my own,' Romy said. She barely knew the retired mountaineer.

'Don't be daft. Least I can do. You rescued the indomitable Terence. Silly old sod would probably have run on regardless, if you and Finch hadn't been on hand to stop him.'

Cradling the glass of red wine Stuart insisted on buying her, Romy hovered by the bar. There was no sign of Finch – as everyone seemed to call him. She decided he must have already left and felt a small, ridiculous stab of disappointment.

But she found she was enjoying being out. The runners were a friendly bunch and seemed to welcome her into their group as they stood dissecting the race. She knew none of them and they wouldn't be aware of her recent circumstances, for which she was grateful. Being part of a couple for decades and then not being was an ongoing adjustment for Romy.

It wasn't till a while later, when the pub had thinned out somewhat, that Romy caught sight of Robert Fincham, sitting in a corner with a much younger man she didn't recognize. As she watched, he glanced up and caught her eye. She gave a brief smile and looked away quickly. But a moment later he was by her side. 'Come and join us?'

Romy peered over at his companion. 'I don't want to interrupt.'

Dropping his voice, Finch said, 'Oh, please . . . Jason's been bending my ear about his exploits in Nepal last summer and there's only so much I can hear about the queue of blonde Australians he lured to his tent at Base Camp.'

Romy couldn't help laughing as she accompanied him to the corner table.

'I've just filled Romy in about your adventures,' Finch said, straight-faced.

She saw Jason's eyes widen in alarm. Barely out of his teens, he flushed, looking as if he wished the earth would swallow him. Shifting uncomfortably on his stool, he picked up his phone and studied it intently. 'Think I'll be heading home,' he said, nodding to Romy and giving Finch's shoulder a reproving cuff in parting.

When he was safely out of earshot, Romy and Finch laughed. Then a silence fell. Romy searched around for something to say, unused to her sudden awkwardness. She, who had entertained the great and the good – from judges to politicians and media notables – during the thirty years of her marriage and never been short of conversation. And this was despite not really feeling part of the inner circle, as Michael – star that he was – had become.

'I've seen you around,' Romy said, bold now. 'You have a bit of a reputation in the village.'

Finch raised his eyebrows. 'A "reputation"? Sounds sinister.'

'Depends . . . My neighbour calls you saintly.'

'Oh.' His smile fell away.

Romy cringed, wishing she could take back her glib remark. 'I'm sorry, that was so crass . . .'

'No.' Finch held up his hand. 'It's been four years. I'm fine with it.'

He didn't seem particularly fine to Romy, but as she was worrying how to reply without putting her foot in it even more firmly, Finch saved her by asking, 'What's your story?'

'I'm not with anyone,' Romy said quickly, her tone unintentionally fierce. She wasn't even sure it had been what Finch's question implied, but he would ask eventually, and she might as well get it out of the way.

He looked a bit startled. 'OK . . .' he said, and his wry expression made her laugh.

'Sorry.' She took a deep breath. 'I'm separated, not actually divorced yet. Just getting going on a new life down here.'

Finch was regarding her with his steady brown eyes. She could not decide what he was thinking, but she was aware of relaxing under his gaze, as if she were letting something go – but also, at the same time, stirring something up. The feeling took her completely by surprise. She had not thought herself capable, not after what had happened.

Finch was a handsome man. Not in a chiselled, classical way, but his regular features were open and appealing, his brown hair and eyes, the healthy glow to his skin, those of a much younger man than someone in their late fifties – another fact dropped into her lap, unsolicited, by her gossipy neighbour.

'I'm off to my bed.' Stuart was looming over them, pulling on his purple North Face jacket and fiddling, head bent, with the zip.

'I suppose I ought to go, too,' Romy said reluctantly.

Finch yawned. 'Yeah, I'm knackered.'

Outside the rain had stopped, but the March night was chilly and damp. Romy shivered after the warmth of the pub as they made their way along the lane towards the village-hall car park. She suddenly realized how tired she was, too, even though she hadn't run the race.

Finch hesitated. He wasn't looking at her as he clicked his key fob towards a silver Toyota parked along the fence, flashing on the orange indicator lights.

'Maybe we could go for a walk or something, when the weather improves?' He stared down at her in the half-light of the single security lamp high up on the bricks of the hall, his expression uncertain.

She smiled her agreement, but felt the panic rising. *Do I want to see him again?* The brief banter with an amusing man had been fun – more than fun – but way out of her recent comfort zone. So far out, indeed, that part of her hoped he wouldn't get in touch. Because that would be simplest. She wasn't sure she was ready . . . or would ever be. Men were not on her to-do list.

Maureen was as good as her word and regularly took Romy under her wing on the Mondays that followed. There were around twelve volunteers, mostly middle-aged, more men than women, all of them in weathered anoraks and beanies, boots that had seen considerable action. Romy was self-conscious with her brand-new gardening gloves and squeaky boots. But they welcomed her enthusiastically, happy for an extra hand to tackle the bracken and bramble, or coppice the hazels straying onto the path. It was sweaty and exhausting, but Romy loved every minute – she lost herself in the work.

Later, when they were all perched on a damp log with lukewarm Thermos tea and squares of Maureen's deliciously sticky gingerbread, the chat was all about the rewilding of Knepp – the estate down the road. For a glorious few hours, Romy felt as if she'd been untethered from her past. It was like a soft spring breeze blowing through her body.

She had left her phone in the car while she worked, not wanting any interruptions. When she checked it again, before driving home, she saw a text. *About that walk*, it said. *Saturday is supposed to be fine, if you're still up for it? Finch*

'Do you fancy a drink, maybe a bite to eat?' Finch's question was tentative as he and Romy rounded the corner and saw the car park up ahead. It was a beautiful day, hot for April, and Romy had struggled to keep up as they strode the two-hour route round the Roman villa, although she was sure he was modifying his pace to suit her own.

She had been nervous the day might be awkward – she barely knew the man and they hadn't seen each other since that night in the pub, nearly a month ago now. But her fears melted away as they walked. Conversation was so easy with Finch, as if they were tuned to the same wavelength. She couldn't say exactly what they talked about, except neither ventured into very personal territory. But he made her laugh and she forgot, for a while, the thoughts that regularly tormented her. At times Romy sensed the weight of their pasts in the unsaid, but it was so enjoyable to walk with a companion for a change – especially someone as personable as Robert Fincham.

She hesitated before replying to his suggestion. Part of her would have loved to sit with him and a glass of cold white wine, somewhere outdoors on this stunning spring evening, but another part clung to her default position. Before she had given herself time to think, the wariness won out. 'That would have been lovely, but I've got someone coming over later,' she blurted, before she could change her mind. She was sure her words rang false and she quickly regretted her lie.

But Finch did not look discomposed in the slightest. He merely smiled. 'Shame. Another time, perhaps.'

The following morning, Romy woke up disappointed with herself. But the past few years had been so confusing, she wasn't sure she could trust her instincts any more. *It happened on Thursday, 13 June 2002 . . .*

As she lay there, uncomfortably catapulted back into the past, her phone rang. It was barely seven and she knew it would be Rex – it was the best time to talk from Australia.

'Hey, Mum. How's it going over there?'

He sounded upbeat, as always. Her laidback son – now twenty-seven – seldom showed signs of stress, unlike his elder brother, Leo. Rex had deliberately chosen a lifestyle for himself that didn't include it: a barista job in a trendy coffee shop in Sydney, blue skies and a nicely waxed surfboard, the stunning beach a stone's throw away.

She listened for a while to Rex's account of a spectacular wave the previous weekend, and caught up with news of her brother, Blake – who had emigrated with his family to Sydney twenty years ago – before her son stopped mid-flow, his tone suddenly serious: 'Tell me how *you* are, Mum.'

'Well, I'm OK, actually. Better than I've been for a while.' She went on to tell him about Maureen and the conservation group, Keith in the deli and his wife, Cathy. She didn't mention Finch, although she wasn't sure why not.

'Go for it,' Rex said, when she stopped talking. 'Love it that you're into Thermos tea again. Remember those sausage and fruitcake picnics in Scotland? And that day Dad swam in his Y-fronts across the freezing loch?' She heard Rex chuckle. 'I wished I'd been brave enough to go with him.'

Rex and Leo had rarely spoken of Michael since their parents had split up. Romy didn't know how to articulate what had happened between them to her sons, and they clearly didn't know how to ask.

But she couldn't help laughing as she remembered the Scottish holiday. Those had been the best times. 'Your father never does anything by halves.'

Her son was silent for a moment. Then: 'It's good you're sounding happier, Mum. You've got to go for things in life, you know.'

She lay back against the pillows after they'd said good-bye. That last phrase ran through her mind, like a banner fluttering behind a plane. *Go for it*, she thought. And before she'd had a chance to change her mind, she texted Finch.

I'll cook you supper one night, if you like. R

3

Later that day she was in the kitchen, flicking through some paint charts on her iPad, when Michael rang. 'Hello?' Romy knew she sounded unintentionally wary. Until recently – when her growing optimism about life had opened up a welcome space between them – she'd still felt so tightly bound to Michael, even though they no longer lived together. And meeting Finch felt like another small degree of space.

So now, speaking to Michael, she noticed herself becoming tense, convinced he would make some demand and impinge on her hatching independence. He tended to ring every few days, usually on some pretext, such as the boiler playing up or the windows needing cleaning, which he had to share with her because, he kept reminding her, she still owned half of the Chelsea flat.

Or it might be to relay some gossip about one of their friends, a chat he'd had with Leo or Rex. It was almost, Romy thought, as if he hadn't quite grasped that she'd left him, despite his spending the past year in the arms of the lovely Anezka, the Czech maître d' at a restaurant off Fleet Street where many of the legal profession gathered.

'Just checking in,' Michael said. 'Haven't heard from you in a while.'

'I'm fine. Nothing to report,' she said, not choosing to point out that four days wasn't exactly 'a while', but making it clear she was not in the mood for a gossip. She wondered, ridiculously, if her husband had somehow got wind of the text she'd sent Finch earlier, or yesterday's walk. Michael always seemed to nose things out before anyone else – a useful knack in his line of work.

'It must be lovely down there,' Michael went on.

'It is. Michael, I'm just about to go out. Is there something you want?'

'Well . . .' He seemed unusually hesitant. 'I was hoping we could get together, have a talk.'

'About what?'

'Perhaps it's time to consider our position, Romy.'

Heart fluttering anxiously, she asked, 'What do you mean, "our position"?'

Michael was silent for a minute, then he said, 'I was thinking about maybe getting on with a divorce.'

Romy was taken aback. It was fourteen months now since she'd left and even then there had been no official statement that they were separating. She had just moved out of the flat and not come back. More to the point, Michael had been brought up a Catholic – altar boy, First Communion – and, although lapsed since his twenties, he was, in principle, against divorce. Romy couldn't imagine wanting to marry again, so it wasn't a priority. And she had her sons to think of. But the word gave her a jolt, nonetheless.

'Are you thinking of marrying Anezka?'

'Heavens, no!' Michael exclaimed, with convincing horror. Then he gave a short laugh. 'Sorry, that sounded rude.' He paused. 'I suppose I just want to be clear about what's going on between us.' His voice was soft, uncharacteristically tentative.

Now Romy felt the full weight of what seemed like a lifetime with Michael fall on her, like a heavy cloak. Their two boys, all the experiences they'd shared: the fun they'd had, the problems they'd weathered, the powerful love she had undoubtedly felt for her husband. No part of her wanted to go back, but she couldn't help feeling the burden of the unfinished business between them. Unfinished business that – although Michael claimed to want clarity – continued to sit like a box stuffed in the attic. Ignored, but a constant presence above their heads.

'If you want to go ahead, I'm fine with it,' she said, her voice restrained.

Michael did not immediately reply and she wondered if he'd heard. When he did speak, she thought he sounded distinctly disappointed. 'Oh, right . . . Well, we can talk about it when we meet. I'll send some dates.'

After they'd said goodbye, Romy was slightly shaken. *Was he testing me?* she wondered. *Trying to stun me with the reality of divorce – see if I still care for him?* If he was happy in his relationship with Anezka – which her sons seemed to imply he was – then he should have sounded pleased, rather than disappointed. Whatever he'd meant, Michael, she realized, still had the power to unsettle her. She took a shaky breath as she silently mouthed those ink-black words: *Even now, I sometimes have flashbacks that make me tremble and sweat.*

4

'That was superb.' Finch sat back in his chair and gave her a grin of satisfaction.

'It's all you're getting, I'm afraid,' she said, smiling at his compliment – it had only been a modest pasta: spinach and mascarpone fusilli. 'There's Brighton Blue and grapes. I don't do puddings.'

It was liberating not to feel the need to wade through complicated recipes for Finch and just do something she could cook with her eyes closed. Not because he wasn't worth it. The evening had been so comfortable – really lovely, in fact – and Finch so appreciative of her efforts. But she remembered all those formal dinner parties she'd thrown for Michael, how they'd taken her all day to organize and cook and left her exhausted, with little appetite for being sparkling and witty with his clever colleagues from the judiciary.

Finch's eyes widened in horror. 'What? No chocolate and hazelnut roulade? No tarte Tatin? What will the village say when I spread the word?'

Romy started to laugh. 'Probably confirm their worst suspicions that Michael left me because there weren't three puddings on the table every night.' Her face fell, his name casting a shadow. 'Although it was me who left him,' she added softly.

'Cheese is perfect,' Finch said diplomatically, as she reached across to clear his bowl. 'Is it all right to ask why?' he said after a minute, his tone cautious.

Romy didn't answer until she had placed the cheese and fruit on the table and sat down again. She knew she had to give him some kind of response, but she found she couldn't meet his eye as she eventually spoke. 'We were married such a long time. I think we just ran out of steam. Michael is a barrister. His first love has always been his work.' She didn't want to lie to Finch, but her deliberately evasive reply was playing with the truth.

Finch nodded, but she could tell he had noticed her equivocation from the puzzlement she saw flash across his eyes. 'Must have been a difficult decision.'

'I didn't feel I had a choice,' she said, contradicting her previous statement, but realizing, for the first time, that this was probably true. The actual moment of leaving had been almost an anticlimax, as if she'd just wandered off to the cottage and could, at any time, wander straight back to Michael. It was certainly how her husband saw it – or, at least, he had, until he'd requested a divorce the other day. But it was, in truth, more defined than that: she had reached a tipping point, the letter changing everything.

'How about you? It can't have been easy since you lost your wife,' she asked, hoping her question wouldn't feel too intrusive. Finch's wife had died before Romy was living full-time in the village. She vaguely remembered a pretty, gamine blonde – sort of Mia Farrow-ish, with a wide, slightly crazy smile.

'Not easy at all. You're right. It's quite hard to describe it,' Finch began, looking away. Romy saw his mouth working. Then he turned to her, the gaze from his expressive brown eyes seeming to hold hers with almost fierce determination. She guessed he didn't talk about Nell's death to many people and she felt honoured that he should trust her. 'Nothing is what you expect. It's like you're standing on the edge of a deep, dark pit and constantly having to stop yourself falling in. But gradually you get better and better at negotiating the edge.' He gave her a self-conscious smile. 'I'm sure that makes no sense to you.'

Romy smiled her understanding, because oddly, although it wasn't a death for her, Finch's analogy rang a powerful bell. She dared not show this too readily, though, for fear he would ask more questions. But it pained her that she couldn't be equally open with this sensitive, empathic man.

'At first I kept judging myself for not recovering quickly enough. A pull-yourself-together type of thing,' Finch was saying. 'Now I just feel what I feel.' He smiled. 'But I'm getting there. I think I can see ahead in a way that was impossible till recently.'

Like me, Romy thought. But she wondered whether, also like her, Finch was ready for anything more than friendship.

It was almost dark when they went through to the sitting room, where Romy had lit the wood-burner. Finch had to duck to avoid the lintel above the door.

She had tidied up earlier, and the clutter littering the surfaces had been shoved unceremoniously into the cupboard under the stairs. All that remained were three framed photos of Leo and Rex as children – the one of her and Michael, windswept and laughing on a friend's boat, she had moved to the spare room, unwilling, as yet, to hide it away in a drawer.

The room – which had been extended into the garden – contained a faded rose-linen sofa piled with cushions and a small wingback chair in oatmeal tweed, two slim bookcases on either side of the fireplace and a coffee table made from reclaimed barn boards.

Finch had settled on the sofa when Romy came back with coffee and the box of chocolates he'd brought with the Merlot. She wondered whether she should sit in the armchair across from him, or be bold and choose the sofa, too. After a moment's hesitation, she followed her instincts and opted for the latter.

The atmosphere in the room was warm and intimate, the flames from the wood-burner hypnotic. Glancing at the clock Romy realized it was nearly eleven – she and Finch had been talking non-stop for hours. The evening had gone in a flash.

With Michael, Romy had often got the feeling that he was busy forming his next sentence while she was talking – keen to get his views across instead of really listening to what she said – so at first she'd been almost reticent with Finch. But as the evening had worn on, she'd felt as if they were old friends who had known each other all their lives – at the same time as being exciting new ones.

Romy was acutely aware of Finch so close, the clean, orangey smell of soap, the strong hands with the long fingers curled around the stoneware mug, his thigh – clad in charcoal chinos – only inches from her own. It was as if she had been gathered up into a softly vibrating lacuna, where there was no need to go forward or to look back: she could just bask in that single moment. A log cracked loudly against the glass door of the stove and she jumped.

Finch smiled at her. 'What a lovely evening,' he said, looking at his watch. 'Thanks for the delicious supper.' After a pause, he added, 'I suppose I should get going.' Although he did not immediately make a move.

Hearing the reluctance in his voice, which so exactly mirrored her own, she smiled. When he did get up, she followed him through to the hall, watched as he shrugged his broad shoulders into his navy peacoat and patted his pockets for his phone and keys.

For a moment they were trapped close in the confined space as she reached past him to open the front door. Their eyes met. Neither moved. She held her breath, aware of the quickening of her heartbeat. For what seemed like a lifetime to Romy, they were anchored, only centimetres apart. Then they both drew back, looking at each other with a degree of embarrassed surprise.

Finch raised his eyebrows at her. 'These narrow hallways . . .' he said, with a wide grin. She nodded, unable to suppress her own smile of relief that he'd defused the tension. Finch seemed to shake himself. 'Night, Romy,' he said, leaning down to give her a decorous peck on the cheek. Then he ducked his head to accommodate the low doorway and was gone.

For a moment Romy stood at the door and took deep breaths of the cold night air, feeling the sea breeze caress her hot cheeks. She gave a quiet chuckle of disbelief. *I think he nearly kissed me.*

But, as she went back inside and double-locked the front door, disbelief quickly turned to panic. *Suppose he had?* It had been such a wonderful evening. Finch had taken her out of herself, beyond the confusion and pain of the recent past. But the near kiss had brought it all back.

Like the demand of a jealous lover, she heard the siren call. Unable to resist, Romy found herself slowly climbing the stairs to her bedroom and unlocking the top drawer of her dressing table. The letter she drew from the envelope was creased and thumbed, but the handwritten words were still as clear as the day it had dropped through the letter box of the Claires' Chelsea flat two and a half years ago:

12 October 2015

Dear Mrs Claire,

We have never met.

This is a difficult letter to write, and will be difficult for you to read, I'm sure. But watching the news the other night and seeing the triumph on your husband's face on the steps of the Old Bailey – after successfully defending that creepy TV presenter accused of rape – made me feel physically sick. And furious with myself for keeping silent all these years.

Because Michael Claire sexually assaulted me.

I was sixteen years old.

23

It happened on Thursday, 13 June 2002. I'd just finished my GCSEs and my mother had arranged for me to do a week's work experience in your husband's chambers.

Michael was working late that night. All the others had gone home. He asked me to stay behind to help him sort out a ton of papers he had to read for court the next morning. It was almost my last day, and I'd had such a good week. Everyone had been incredibly kind to me.

When I finished sorting the papers, he gave me a glass of red wine and had one himself. He didn't have proper wine glasses, I remember, just Duralex tumblers. He was friendly and funny. There was a small button-back leather sofa in the corner of his room and he told me to have a seat. Then a few minutes later he came and sat beside me. I was uncomfortable and really shy; Michael was seen as a bit of a god in the chambers. I saw him as a bit of a god.

He put his hand on my thigh first. I was wearing a red cotton dress, no tights — it was very hot that week. I froze. I didn't know what to do. Then he moved my dress up and began stroking my bare skin, squeezing my thigh. I pushed him off, but he just laughed and took my glass from me, putting it on the desk. He seemed to think I'd given him some sort of message that this was what I wanted, because he said, 'You're such a tease.'

He was trying to banter with me, not threatening me as such, but physically pinning me to the sofa with his arm so I couldn't move. Then he started kissing me really hard, pushing his tongue into my mouth, squeezing my breasts, forcing me back against the end of the sofa so I was pinned under him.

I started to struggle, but he was so strong and determined. I didn't scream, I didn't dare . . . I couldn't really believe what was happening. I know I was telling him to stop, but I don't think he even heard me, he was so intent on his own pleasure – if it could be called 'pleasure', forcing someone like that, against their will.

Then the phone rang on his desk – maybe it was you? It caught him off guard. He pulled back just long enough for me to push him away and run.

I didn't have a coat, because it was so hot. My dress was torn at the shoulder, so I borrowed the beige cardigan Wendy, the office manager, had left on the back of her chair. My mother and I lived in Sussex at the time, and I was staying the week with a school friend. She was out with her boyfriend, and her parents were at the theatre, so I was able to sneak in and never tell a living soul – not my friend, not her parents, not my mother – what had happened. In the morning, I rang Micky, the senior clerk, who'd taken me under his wing, and said I was ill and couldn't come in.

I have spent so many hours thinking about that night in the thirteen years since it happened. I've wondered if I did lead Michael on, if I was giving him mixed messages. I blame myself, of course I do. I shouldn't have stayed in the first place, shouldn't have accepted the wine. Was my dress too short? Why didn't I scream? Why didn't I get up and leave as soon as he put his hand on my thigh? I still don't know. I suppose I never believed he would do that to me.

That night still regularly haunts my dreams. Even now, I sometimes have flashbacks that make me tremble and sweat. I probably drink too much and suffer bouts of anxiety. But it didn't kill me. I cope; no one would ever guess.

I'm not intending to go to the police or the media or anything. There was no way I could have told someone at the time and it's too late now. I don't have the courage, anyway. And I won't sign

*this letter — it's much too small a world. I saw red, though, the
other night, watching Michael Claire, QC, crowing so smugly
about getting a man off who everyone says is as guilty as sin.
I just thought you should know who you're married to, Mrs Claire
— assuming you don't already.*

Romy read it from beginning to end — although she
pretty much knew the nightmare words by heart, so
often had she studied the letter, both in fact and in her
mind. For a moment, as she sat on the edge of her bed,
she had a strong desire to tear it up, burn it — as
Michael had begged her to back then. But even with
the future beckoning with such promise, she could not
quite bring herself to destroy what she still considered
unfinished business. By doing so, she felt she would be
abdicating all responsibility — finally and for ever — for
the unnamed girl.

5

Finch walked the seven minutes home from Romy's in a daze. It was pitch dark, and breezy, but he was unaware of anything except the frisson he'd felt just now, in Romy's hall, her face almost touching his.

Arriving home, he slung his house keys onto the hall table and went through to the kitchen, turning the lights on as he went. All around him on the walls were photographs of Nell, some with her daughter, Grace, some with just himself, some of the three of them together. One photograph, in particular, framed in pale wood next to the oven, was his favourite. It was a headshot of Nell, taken on the beach at Climping on a glorious, shimmering-blue summer day. Her head was back, her short blonde hair ruffled by the breeze, her wide grey eyes squinting against the sun as she smiled exuberantly into the camera. It was the image Finch talked to – every day, after he'd first lost her – when he wanted to tell Nell something.

Finch had met Nell – a professional dancer who taught at a Brighton dance centre – on a train. She had lost her ticket and the whole carriage, especially Finch, became involved in the drama. By the time a volatile and dramatic Nell had dug it out of the zippered pocket of her bag – where she'd already looked for it a thousand times – Finch was completely hooked.

Now he went straight over to the photograph and stood, hands planted on the work surface, and stared at his wife.

'OK.' He took a deep breath. 'This is serious, Nell.' As he spoke, he could suddenly feel her all around him, hear her crazy laugh, her lively teasing, see her fluid dancer's walk. 'I very nearly kissed someone tonight,' he said, almost as if he thought the woman – frozen for ever in time on the wall in front of him – might actually reply.

Hesitating, not comfortable with what he was saying, he added, 'Her name's Romy. You might have seen her around the village, but we didn't know her to speak to. Tall, sort of wiry and energetic, wild dark curls . . . She used to be married to a barrister, but I can't put a face to him now. They were weekenders back then.' He paused. 'Anyway, I'm hoping to see her again . . . I really like her.'

It was four years since Nell, fading in front of his eyes to a frightening echo of herself, had clasped his hand weakly as he sat beside her hospice bed. She had reached that point where she'd become almost ethereal, already not of this world, and was no longer fearful of what lay ahead.

She'd smiled at him. 'Don't be miserable for too long, Robert,' she'd said, through struggling breaths, her eyes shining with tears. 'Find happiness. Help Gracie, too . . .'

The thought of another woman – unimaginable at the time, of course – had never even crossed his mind until Romy.

But on that draughty, damp corner of the 10K course, with Terry in pieces between them, he had sensed a connection with her, which excited and confused him in equal measure. It was why he had held off calling her. But he had amazed himself tonight. He'd truly wanted to kiss her.

The following morning Finch had a meeting in the garden-centre café with Jenny Tully – the woman in charge of fundraising for the hospice where Nell had died – to discuss his next marathon. He had worked for them tirelessly since his wife's death, helping to raise hundreds of thousands, either from his own marathons or from coaxing companies and wealthy individuals to donate. His thirty-two-year military career, including postings to most of the world's hot spots, such as Iraq and Afghanistan, was a major asset, both of them agreed.

'I'll get these,' Finch said now, as he and Jenny queued for their coffee.

'You're our number-one fundraiser, Finch. I can at least buy you the odd coffee.' Jenny nudged his hand from his wallet. She had a lively, pretty face set off by a feathery grey pixie cut and the most beautiful grey-blue eyes – marred by a wary sadness lurking in their depths.

They talked for a while about his next run, which Finch had decided to do along the west coast of Ireland in the early autumn. But he was finding it hard to concentrate. He hadn't slept last night, his whole being churned up about Romy. He yawned.

Jenny raised her eyebrows. 'Late night?'

To his horror, Finch felt heat flooding across his cheeks.

Jenny had scooped him up after Nell died, as if he were a lost child. She was endlessly on the phone, on his doorstep, asking him if he was all right and if there was anything she could do to help. Her kindness had seemed almost excessive at times, and he worried that he would never be able to repay it.

'I'm not saying a word, Jenny. It'll be all around the county before lunchtime if I do.'

She chuckled mischievously. 'Ah, so there is something to tell.'

Finch didn't want to talk about Romy to anyone yet. It felt too new, too delicate for gossip. For so long the only name on his lips had been Nell's. But Jenny's stare was insistent and he gave in, surprising himself with the flutter of pleasure he felt as he said her name.

When he'd finished, Jenny was frowning. '"Claire" . . . I know that name.'

'They used to be weekenders, but she lives here full-time now,' he said. 'She's separated, used to be married to a barrister.'

'Well, you must introduce me,' Jenny said brightly, but Finch sensed a distinct lack of enthusiasm, which he thought stemmed from her general cynicism about relationships, her own having gone south around the time Nell died; her husband had announced he had a two-year-old child with a much younger work colleague.

'Way too soon to think it might go anywhere.'

Jenny seemed to pull herself together. 'It's been a long time since Nell, Finch. You shouldn't be alone.'

'It's the hardest thing, letting her go. I've been sort of OK, living with her spirit . . . but Romy has a good spirit too.' He stopped, embarrassed at his ramblings in front of his friend. It would have been simpler if he didn't feel so much for Romy. Then he could have walked away and stayed in the safe zone – however lonely – of his past with Nell.

But Jenny didn't appear to be listening. 'Got it! I knew the name Claire rang a bell. Michael shares chambers with my old friend James Bregman who used to weekend here. It was the Claires he sold his cottage on the harbour to, about fifteen years ago, I think.' She stopped. 'James was a close friend of Nell's, as I'm sure you know.' Her mouth twitched almost imperceptibly.

Finch was puzzled. No, he didn't. Nell had always told him everything, but he'd never heard of James Bregman.

'Hope I haven't spoken out of turn?' Jenny said, a concerned frown on her face, which didn't seem entirely genuine to Finch.

6

October 2015

Romy glanced quickly at the post, which held nothing of any interest except one handwritten letter, addressed to 'Mrs Claire'. The envelope was cream and good quality, her name and address handwritten in italics and black ink, a script she did not recognize. It was addressed to Michael's chambers, 'Private. Please Forward' in the top left-hand corner, Wendy's neat redirection sticker sitting beside the crossed-out black ink.

Intrigued, but with no time to waste – she was due in Barnes, at the London Wetlands Centre, where she volunteered one day a week, taking groups of school children around the park – she stuffed the letter into her handbag, dumped the rest of the mail on the ledge above the hall radiator, then hurried down the stairs and out into the gusty autumn day, pulling the hood of her parka over her head to prevent the drizzle playing havoc with her already chaotic curls.

It wasn't until Romy was seated on the Tube, trundling along the District Line to Hammersmith, that she remembered the letter and took it out of her bag. At first she couldn't understand what she was reading. She stared at the words, but they made no sense. She glanced furtively at the man sitting next to her – the contents seemed to be shouting at her, and she worried he could somehow hear too. But he was deep in the yellowing pages of a John Updike novel.

The carefully scripted words swam before her eyes as she read and reread the text. The woman – as she would be now – said it was 'too small a world' to identify herself, whatever that meant. *Is she implying she knows us?* she wondered. Stations came and went, passengers ebbing and flowing around her. The sun pierced the grimy window in a blinding shaft as the train came overground and Romy shook her head in shock, quickly followed by bewilderment. *There must be some mistake*, she thought. *She can't be talking about Michael*. Romy's husband.

But it was clear that she was. She had seen him on the television, named him specifically. Romy's thoughts were a jumble as she tried to work out what it meant, who this woman might be. She was so explicit. The sofa in Michael's office; Wendy's beige cardigan. Her stomach twisted. For one horrible split second she couldn't prevent the thought that the letter might be telling the truth: that her husband might actually have done such an appalling thing.

Then she pictured Michael – her intense, charismatic, workaholic star of a husband. His dark eyes were always sharp with intelligence, but also vulnerable and fiercely honest.

There's no way on this planet Michael would attack anyone, let alone a sixteen-year-old girl, for heaven's sake, Romy told herself sternly. *I would have known. He wouldn't have been able to hide such a terrible thing from me*. She tried to pinpoint the date in the letter, to recall what was happening at that time, but her mind was spinning.

As the minutes passed, Romy's heart still pounding in disbelief, she felt a flare of anger. *How dare she write such vile things about Michael?* And, what's more, imply that she, Romy, knew what he'd done. Imply she was somehow complicit . . . 'assuming you don't already [know].' *How bloody dare she?* Michael was not perfect, not by a long chalk, but he was certainly no sexual predator.

Who is this woman? Romy wondered. She had been around the justice system long enough as Michael's wife to know that there were people out there with a skewed version of reality, which they nonetheless clung to wholeheartedly . . . although the contents of the letter seemed perfectly rational. And so detailed.

The train drew into Hammersmith station, the doors opening, life going on for all the other people in the carriage. This was her stop, but Romy was paralysed. She sat with her bag clutched to her body, the letter singeing a hole in the tan leather, like a hot coal, as the train trundled on to Ravenscourt Park, where she managed to lurch from her seat and step out onto the platform.

'Gemma, it's me.' She called her friend, who organized the school trips around the Wetlands Centre. 'I'm so sorry, I'm on the Tube, but I'm not feeling well. I think I'd better go home.'

Gemma was sympathetic – although Romy barely registered what she said. She quickly crossed to the eastbound platform. As she waited for the train, she wanted desperately to call Michael, then and there, to have him instantly confirm the absurdity of the whole thing. But it felt too exposing to read the letter over the phone in a public place.

The journey home seemed to take an age, each rattle of the train and brush of a passenger almost painful in her state of suspense. Because she knew she wouldn't get any clarity until she could speak to her husband face to face.

Michael was late home that night. He looked exhausted, dropping his briefcase in the hall with a thud and slinging his dark overcoat – glistening wet from the day-long drizzle – onto the hall chair. Romy stood and watched him from the entrance to the kitchen. She wanted to look hard into his face and find proof of innocence there. Reassure herself that he was the man she thought him to be, the man she had trusted for nearly three decades, before the waters were potentially muddied with denials and justifications, accusations and rage.

He sniffed the air. 'Mmm . . . Smells good,' he said, with a tired smile.

'Pork belly,' she said. 'Do you want a drink? There's the remains of the Bordeaux from last night.'

'Love some,' Michael said. 'Sorry I couldn't get back earlier.'

She nodded. After so many years as his wife, she didn't need yet another explanation about the pressures of being a top silk. She turned away. 'I'll bring it through.' The letter was in her bag. She had read it on and off throughout the afternoon. But she'd put it away before Michael got home – like her own dirty secret.

As she poured red wine into the long-stemmed glasses, she realized she was almost shaking with nerves. The letter had taken on gargantuan proportions, acquiring a physical presence way beyond the single sheet of paper on which it was written.

Their sitting room was an elegant space, high-ceilinged and wide. Long windows gave onto a balcony that fronted the red-brick block of flats, the view looking down the length of the street opposite. Romy had kept the décor simple: a long sofa, lined with cushions, in pale tweed; two tapestry-chintz armchairs either side of the gas log fire; a heavy black lacquer coffee table on which stood a vase of yellow tulips; books on the wall by the door and ochre and blue curtains. Michael had seated himself in his chair to the right of the fireplace, head resting back on the cushion, eyes shut.

Romy placed his glass on the coffee table, keeping her own in her hands. *Should I wait till after supper?* she asked herself. But she knew she was just being cowardly. She turned abruptly and went to retrieve the letter. Arm outstretched, she handed the sheet of paper – no longer in its envelope – to her husband. 'This came in the post today.'

Michael raised his eyebrows as he grasped the letter and began to read. It seemed to take him a very long time, longer by far than the short text allowed for. His expression did not change, remaining almost mask-like in its stillness, but she thought his olive skin paled.

Then he waved the sheet of paper in the air, shaking his head in apparent bewilderment. 'This is ludicrous. I don't understand. Who is this woman?'

'I thought you'd know.' Romy saw him blink rapidly, then his eyes returned to the page.

He looked up at her. 'We have hundreds of kids doing work experience in chambers. How am I supposed to know which one this is?' His tone was aggrieved.

'Well, she gives the date.'

'The date is irrelevant, Romy, because this is all complete nonsense. I'd never attack anyone.' Michael flapped the letter angrily. 'Thirteen years ago? I can't remember that far back, for God's sake, with all the people who trail through the place every day.'

Romy thought this was probably true. An insignificant teenager about chambers . . . Although she knew her husband had a razor-sharp memory, almost photographic in its recall. *But why should he remember someone who wasn't important to him?* she asked herself.

Her husband reached for his wine and took a long gulp. Romy didn't know what to say. But obviously she couldn't leave it there.

'Can you try to remember, Michael? It's important you do.'

He frowned. 'Why? Sounds like she had a bit of a thing for me . . . She almost admits she did. And now her life's gone to the dogs and she's looking for someone to blame.' He shrugged.

Romy had retreated to her chair, but she was sitting on the edge of the cushion, leaning towards her husband. 'So you don't remember any incident where you gave a girl some wine in your office and she sat on the sofa . . .' She paused. 'She seems to know a lot of detail.'

'Romy?' Michael stared at her, a wounded look in his eye as his glass clunked down on the table. He seemed to be waiting for her to respond, but she didn't know what to say. 'You don't honestly think I did this, do you?' He jumped up, still clutching the letter, and began pacing back and forth across the window bay. 'Of course she knows details. She was probably in and out of my office all week.'

Neither spoke for a moment. Then Romy said. '2002 was when you were doing the Charlie Brigham case, wasn't it?'

Brigham was a music promoter accused of grooming an underage fan. It had been a long drawn-out case, because more victims had come forward pre-trial, with a lot of publicity attached. Michael lost and Brigham had gone to gaol. Romy had been working back to the date since she read the letter.

It was a summer she would not forget. She had fractured her right tibia falling off a bike and careering down a steep bank when they were staying with friends in the New Forest during the boys' half-term. She was in plaster, couldn't drive for the rest of the summer, and Michael was hopelessly unreliable in helping out with the boys, then aged twelve and nine. She remembered him being tense and bad-tempered for weeks, which she felt was more *her* prerogative.

'It was the summer I broke my leg.'

Her husband nodded as he threw the letter onto the table, a frown of concentration on his face as he began pacing again. Then his expression cleared slightly, although the frown remained. 'There was one girl around that time . . . Emily? Emma?' He shook his head. 'But I'm sure she was older . . . already at college.'

Romy sighed. 'What was she like?' she asked. 'Did you do stuff with her?'

Michael rounded on her. 'What do you mean by "stuff", Romy? Are *you* accusing me of molesting her now?'

'Of course not. I meant did she help you sort documents – as she said in the letter? Did she . . . I don't know . . . Were you friendly with her? *Did* you offer her wine?'

He threw his arms into the air. 'I offer lots of people wine, but I haven't attacked a single one of them. I told you, I *don't know who this person is*,' he almost shouted, thrusting his head towards her, dark eyes blazing.

'OK, OK. Calm down. I'm just trying to get a picture of the girl, trying to work out why she would accuse you like this.'

'This is insane,' he muttered, throwing himself into his chair again and covering his face with his hands. 'And really upsetting.'

There was a long silence.

'You could ask James?' Romy suggested. 'Or Wendy? She's bound to remember. Nothing goes on in the place that gets past Wendy.' Romy paused. 'And she said she borrowed a cardigan from –'

Before she could go on, her husband's head flew up. 'Seriously? You want me to bring this ludicrous accusation up with my colleagues? How do you think that will play?' His look was scornful, but he also seemed hurt by her reaction.

Romy waited for him to say more, but he remained stubbornly silent. 'So what are you going to do, Michael?'

Her husband shrugged. 'What do you expect me to do?'

'I don't know . . . but don't you want to find out who she is?'

'Nope,' he snapped.

'Well, I'd like to, even if you don't,' Romy said. 'We should work out who she is and why she's written a letter out of the blue like this. Even though she says she's not going public, we don't know she'll stick to that, now she's made the first move. Shouldn't we at least be prepared?'

Michael frowned. 'So you want me to find her? Confront her? That's probably exactly what she's after.' He shook his head. 'I feel sorry for her. She's obviously got issues.'

Romy wondered if Michael could be right. That the girl – *woman* – was some sort of attention-seeker, perhaps, and had fixated on him because he'd meant something to her when she was young?

'I'm amazed you feel sorry for her, Michael, making false accusations like that. She could cause you a lot of trouble.'

'Which is my point, exactly. It's not a can of worms worth opening.' His voice was calm now, almost matter-of-fact, and Romy, not a little puzzled by his reaction, sat without speaking. She didn't know what he should do, either. But he didn't seem angry with the anonymous girl, didn't seem to find her significant at all.

'Are you just going to leave it, then?'

'Well, what else do you suggest?'

'I don't know . . .'

Before she'd had a chance to say any more, Michael seemed to shake himself. 'I'm starving,' he said. 'What about that pork belly?'

7

'Maybe we should arrive separately,' Finch joked. They were sitting round the oak central island in his kitchen. He'd poured her a glass of white wine and pushed a bowl of pistachios towards her.

Romy laughed. 'We were invited separately and nobody's aware we even know each other. So if we arrive together won't it just seem like coincidence?'

'Hmm, well, almost nobody.' He looked a bit sheepish. 'I did tell my friend Jenny. But I don't think she'll have told anyone.' He gave a wry laugh. 'Although who am I kidding?'

Romy was enjoying herself, her eyes drawn to the many photographs on the walls of Finch's family. 'That's Nell?' she asked, pointing to a frame with an attractive blonde and a girl of about twelve, with a cheeky smile and wheat-coloured hair in a thick plait.

'Yes, and Gracie, my stepdaughter. She lives in Manchester with her husband, Sam. I adore her.' Romy noted the tenderness in Finch's voice as he gazed at the photograph. 'She's the only family I have.'

Cathy and Keith's home was above the delicatessen on the main street of the village. The place wasn't smart – the walls could have done with a freshen-up, the furniture had seen better days – but Romy instantly felt at home as she sank into the huge sofa and accepted a large glass of wine from their host. Keith was loud and overweight, with a manic, laughing energy. He never talked about anything but food, never did anything that wasn't food-related – it was his lifelong obsession. Cathy was quiet and blonde and well organized, the perfect foil for her husband.

Supper consisted of a huge home-cooked ham with baked potatoes and numerous salads. Finch sat across the wooden table from her, flanked by Jenny and Cathy. Romy had Keith to her left and their teenage son, Louie, on her right. It was impossible not to catch Finch's eye over the candles. She felt suddenly lighthearted from the wine and their innocent secret as the conversation flowed and laughter rang out above John Denver on Keith's Bose stereo.

Jenny was talking to her. 'How are you finding village life, Romy? Don't you miss the bright lights of London?'

Romy thought her smile a little forced. 'Not at all,' she replied. 'I needed a change of scene, a new direction to my life.'

Jenny nodded, clearly unconvinced. 'You won't get bored with all us bumpkins and run back to the excitements of the city?'

Romy couldn't resist giving Finch a grin. Life in the country was far more exciting than she'd previously imagined.

But Jenny must have clocked the look, because she added, rather sharply, 'It's very different from weekending, you know. That lot never involve themselves, just invite their London mates to stay, bring their own fancy food instead of buying locally, then bugger off back to

42

the Smoke.' Although she'd spoken lightly, Romy sensed the simmering anger behind her words and thought it might be about more than weekend visitors and second homes. 'I hope you're going to be a proper part of our community.' It was as if she were throwing down the gauntlet.

'I fully intend to,' Romy said, drawing herself up and giving Jenny her very best smile. When she glanced at Finch again, she saw his eyes widen in mock-alarm. 'I was brought up in the country, Jenny. I know how it works.'

It was true: her parents had been hippies – before hippies were invented. Her father, Alan, was part of what would now be called the 'gig economy' – a part-time gardener, handyman, painter and decorator – while her mother, Peggy, baked cakes for the village shop, looked after their extensive vegetable garden and chickens, and smoked the trout Alan regularly pulled from the local river.

Romy and her brother Blake lived a wild, unsupervised childhood, roaming the fields and woods around the village with glorious freedom. They never wanted for anything, although their clothes and every single thing in the house were secondhand, picked up from goodness knows where by her father on one of his mysterious forays with his bicycle and trailer. They didn't have a fridge, a Hoover, heating or pocket money and certainly not a television. It was Michael's party piece, to recount her parents' eccentricities – he seemed almost proud of them – but she wondered with amusement how Jenny would view the way in which she'd been brought up.

*

'Game, set and match,' Finch joked, as they walked home later that evening.

'Is Jenny always that fierce?' Romy asked.

'I'm not sure she appreciates a city interloper on her patch, however much she claims to want you to join in.'

'It was such a fun evening, despite Jenny giving me the third degree,' she said, as they stood on the corner where their paths diverged, Finch going north, she south across the village. And it had been. Although she barely knew any of those present, she'd found herself oddly relaxed in their company. She felt she'd been heard, that they were interested in what she had to say. She was not just making conversation, as she had so often in the high-octane social gatherings of her past.

'So you don't think Jenny has a point?' he teased. 'You must have hung out with some pretty interesting people through Michael's work.'

'Sometimes,' she acknowledged. 'But, on the whole, the networking dinners I gave for Michael bored me to tears,' she told him. 'I much preferred tonight.' As she spoke, she imagined turning up to Cathy and Keith's supper with Michael. He would have stolen the show, been so charming and magnetic that the other guests would have gone home feeling privileged to have met him. But she would have got barely a word in as she listened to all of his stories for the thousandth time. She sighed unconsciously.

'Everything OK?' Finch asked, laying a hand on her arm. It was late and he spoke quietly as they stood outside the silent row of houses – all in darkness at this time of night.

Romy noted his curious glance. He had the sort of eyes that invited confession, and she wanted to say more, didn't want to leave Finch on this note. But thoughts of Michael among her new-found friends left her scarcely able to speak.

She looked up at him, her expression clouded. 'I'm sorry . . . Sometimes . . .'

Finch seemed to understand, because he just pulled her into his arms and held her close for a moment. 'Tell me about it one day,' he said into her hair.

Watching him walk slowly away, Romy let out a slow breath. She dreaded the prospect that one day she might, indeed, have to tell him – or keep her disturbing secret for ever.

8

December 2015

In the weeks since Romy had read the letter, she had been in a quandary. She had promised Michael she would not talk about it to anyone, but the words ran round and round her brain whenever there was a quiet moment, such as at three o'clock in the morning when she couldn't sleep.

Finally, despite her promise, one miserable December day she found herself confiding in her best friend, Bettina.

Sitting at a window table in the fifth-floor café of the local department store, with a view over the rooftops of Chelsea, Bettina had listened carefully to Romy's précis of the letter. 'God,' she said, 'how awful.' She let out a long breath. 'That's just horrible.'

'I don't know what to do,' Romy said.

Her friend frowned. 'You don't think it's true, do you?'

'No,' she said hurriedly, feeling almost ashamed it was her husband they were talking about. 'Of course not. Michael wouldn't attack anyone, not in a million years. He's not even a ladies' man. You know that. He only has eyes for his beloved work.'

Bettina gazed at her. 'I'm sure he wouldn't . . .' She stopped, and Romy, sensing a 'but', waited for her to go on. 'It's just such a strange thing for someone to do, write an accusing letter like that. Especially since she says she's not going to the police. I mean, what does she gain from it?'

'Satisfaction in telling me, I suppose.'

Her friend looked puzzled. 'But that's implying Michael did it.' Her Australian intonation — modified after decades in England — was heightened when she was making a serious point.

'I'm not.' Romy was shocked to hear the waver in her voice. She wanted so badly to allay her own niggling fears. In telling Bettina, she had thought her friend would laugh at the letter, dismiss it as simply the ramblings of a sad, deluded person. And she needed to share the burden with someone. 'But he won't talk about it at all, Bet. He gets hurt and upset when I mention it, as if he's surprised I should want to. Like the letter only exists in *my* head. He seems to think that just by bringing it up I believe he's guilty. Which I don't understand.'

'Wendy organizes the work-experience kids. Knowing how meticulous she is, there'll be a spreadsheet somewhere with all the names stretching back to the year dot,' Michael had stated, with deceptive equanimity, one morning over breakfast, not long after the letter's arrival, when Romy had brought up the subject yet again. 'If you're so desperate to know, why not ask her?'

Romy was amazed. He'd been furious when she'd made the same suggestion before. Was he testing her? But while she hesitated, wondering whether she might actually do so, Michael had erupted.

'For heaven's sake, Romy, you seriously think it's a good idea to draw attention to someone possibly hell-bent on destroying me . . . *us, our family*?' He'd shaken his head, as if she, Romy, were the madwoman here.

Then he'd scraped his chair back and dropped his napkin on his empty toast plate, his mouth clamped shut in a resentful line. 'Drop it, Romy. Just drop it. She's had her say. Hopefully she'll leave it at that.' He stood above her, fixing her with a hurt stare. 'Because you realize if you do *anything*, say *anything* to *anyone*, you'll be opening up a whole nightmare scenario. Which, despite the fact I've done absolutely nothing wrong, could finish me.' His voice broke and he cleared his throat, his gaze softening somewhat. 'You do realize that?'

Romy, taken aback by the emotion in his voice, had nonetheless persisted. 'Don't treat me as if I'm stupid, Michael. I just can't understand why you're not even a bit curious as to who she is and why she's doing this.'

'Change the record,' her husband had muttered wearily, turning to leave the room.

Bettina was nodding. 'Tricky to say what I'd do in the same circumstances. I don't have so much to lose, obviously. It's a bit different for a pillar of the justice system, like Michael.' She eyed her friend. 'So are you saying him not talking about it is making you suspicious, Romes?'

Not suspicious, exactly, she thought. *More baffled*. But she couldn't bring herself to voice – even to her closest friend – the vaguest notion that maybe something did happen . . . like a kiss or something. And this woman, for whatever reason, had inflated the situation. Or she and Michael had had a consensual affair at some stage. When it didn't work out, this was her sinister revenge.

Bettina was watching her again, waiting for her to respond. Romy shrugged. 'He spends all day every day with people accused of things they might not have done. Perhaps he's right to be cautious.'

'As long as *you* believe he's innocent, Romy, and this woman shuts up . . .' she paused '. . . saying nothing, doing nothing is probably the best plan.'

But do I believe him? Romy asked herself, as she walked slowly home. Bettina's momentary doubt had made her realize she wasn't as completely certain of Michael's innocence as she kept telling herself she was.

9

Romy had agreed to meet Finch at the station at five. She had dressed up a little – so far Finch had only seen her in jeans or joggers. Although those were her comfort zone, she didn't feel the black trousers and soft blue linen jacket with the mandarin collar would frighten the horses. Clothes had always been a thorn in Romy's side: her not very extensive wardrobe ranged with stuff that never seemed quite right on the night. She blamed her mother, who, as far as she could make out, had worn the same jeans and bobbly pink sweater for Romy's entire childhood.

He was already there when she arrived, pacing up and down the almost empty platform. He looked scrubbed and handsome in his white shirt and dark jacket – and slightly nervous, she thought.

'Hey,' she said, smiling up at him. 'This is fun. I haven't been to a play in ages.'

He grinned back, making no effort to hide his pleasure at seeing her. 'It's had pretty good reviews.'

Romy wasn't really concerned about the merits of the play, but she'd been looking forward to the evening with Finch in a quiet hum of excitement. It was cosy, sitting side by side as the train slid through the beautiful coastal wetlands in the fading light. Just Finch's proximity, the warm bulk of him, was enough for Romy. They didn't say much – she had never been one for entertaining the entire carriage with her life story – but it was a comfortable silence she didn't feel the need to fill.

'Oh . . .' Finch stopped beside her, halfway up the steps at the Regent Street exit to Piccadilly Circus, where there was still some shelter. It was not just raining, it was absolutely bucketing down, the streets awash, people pressed against the sides of the buildings, desperate to get out of the downpour. Their planned stroll to the theatre was barely ten minutes, but without an umbrella – and absolutely no chance of a taxi – it would leave them drenched.

'We're late already. We'll have to make a run for it,' she said dubiously, glancing up at the blackened sky and finding no joy.

'Here, have my jacket,' Finch said, beginning to pull it from his shoulders. But she stopped him, pressing her hand to his chest.

'Thanks, but it's coming down too hard to make much difference.'

For another moment, they stood there in silence. Then they gave each other a resolute smile as Finch grabbed her hand and they ran, sploshing through the puddles, waiting impatiently for the lights to change and dodging the crowds of tourists – many in emergency waterproof ponchos – as best they could until they arrived breathless at the theatre entrance.

Even in the few minutes it had taken, they had been soaked through and stood – arms held out from their wet clothes – looking at each other in amused dismay. Finch's hair was plastered to his head, face slick with rain, white shirt stuck to his chest, his tan brogues now mahogany from the puddles.

Romy began to laugh. 'We can squelch through the first half and hope we dry off by the second. It's probably warm inside.'

Finch didn't reply. He seemed to be considering something as they stood dripping in the milling foyer. 'Or . . .' he began '. . . radical suggestion . . .'

Romy heard the urgent clang of the three-minute warning bell.

'I'm a member of this place around the corner, for when I need to stay in London – two minutes away. It's definitely warm there.'

'You mean miss the play? Seems a terrible waste.' But she was already beginning to shiver, the wet linen of her jacket clinging heavily against her skin. Plus she had been up to the common the previous day, where Phil, the group leader, had introduced her to coppicing. She had thrown herself enthusiastically into the task, but as a result every muscle in her body had stiffened achingly overnight.

Finch held out his hands, palms up. 'Decision time.' He raised first his right like a scale. 'Sit in wet clothes for two hours, get pneumonia and quite possibly die?' Then he lowered his right and raised his left. 'Or . . . get warm and have a large martini and a steaming bowl of chips?' He was grinning mischievously as the rest of the audience filed past to find their seats.

'It's clear where your allegiance lies,' Romy said, laughing, as he took her hand again and they went back out into the rain.

*

The martini went straight to her head. They were sitting in the third-floor bar, in the corner of a black button-back banquette. It wasn't a particularly stylish room, the decor modern but more functional than pretty. Romy didn't care. It was toasty warm, the alcohol had loosened her tongue – loosened Finch's too – and the conversation buzzed and flowed between them. She sensed a difference in him tonight – as if he had let something go. It made him more expansive, the light in his eyes sparky and flirtatious.

They had munched their way through a large bowl of crunchy hot, salty potato wedges dipped in garlic mayonnaise and downed a couple of cocktails each, when Finch suddenly picked up her hand and held it lightly in his lap. It seemed like such an intimate gesture. More intimate than if he had reached down and kissed her.

'You know,' he said, not looking at her, 'being alone for a while, you forget how much fun it is, doing things with someone else.'

Romy squeezed his hand, letting out a long breath. She looked up and his eyes met hers. Neither spoke for a moment, then he whispered, 'I would love to kiss you, Romy. But I can't. Not here.'

Her breath caught in her throat. 'Against club rules?' She felt his finger gently stroking the back of her hand, the small movement almost unbearably seductive.

He gave a quiet groan. 'I wish I'd never suggested that stupid play. I wanted to impress you, Romy, do something special, something away from the village, so you wouldn't think me just this bumpkin colonel character. But here we are, stranded in the city, and I can't even kiss you.'

She began to laugh as he put his arm round her shoulders and they moved close together on the banquette.

'We mustn't miss the train,' he said, bringing his watch up to his face in the half-light. 'Ten thirty-six, isn't it?'

Romy automatically did the same. They both stared at each other.

'Oops,' said Romy.

It was already seventeen minutes past. There was no way they could make it to Victoria in time, even if they left this instant and by some miracle found a taxi. They hadn't yet paid the bill and they needed to collect their jackets from the downstairs cloakroom where they were hopefully drying off.

'We could see about staying here tonight,' he said, his voice tentative. 'That, or the milk train . . .'

Romy tried to think through the options, but the cocktails and the sexual frisson she felt for the man beside her weren't helping. Her look must have appeared doubtful to Finch, because he immediately held up his hands.

'I didn't mean . . . We'd get two rooms, of course.' He searched her face. 'I wasn't suggesting . . .' He frowned. 'Or we could go to Waterloo, get a train to Havant and a taxi from there. The trains go later on the Portsmouth line.'

The thought of a dreary journey stretching into the small hours, with aching limbs in still damp clothes, did not appeal to Romy. 'We'd be very late . . .'

Finch pushed the table away and stood up. 'Listen, I'll go and check if they've got any rooms first, before we make a decision.'

He left Romy feeling slightly apprehensive. Ten minutes before, her body had been on fire, aching to be alone with Finch. But suddenly being thrown together overnight, albeit in separate rooms . . .

When Finch came back, he was looking nervous, too. 'Well, the good news is, they have a free twin. The bad news is, that's all they have.'

'Right.' Romy didn't know what to say.

'So you take the room. I'll bunk off and find somewhere else.'

'Heavens, no, that's ridiculous, Finch. It's still chucking it down.' She could see the rain splashing in puddles on the outside terrace. 'Anywhere you find that's close will cost you a second mortgage.' She hesitated. 'We can manage. Two beds, take it in turns to use the bathroom. It'll be like a school trip.' She was trying to make light of the situation, trying to hide the nervous tingle she felt running through her body.

But as she watched Finch's face, she thought he didn't seem entirely on board with her analogy.

'I didn't mean . . .' She touched his arm. 'Let's give it a go,' she said encouragingly, inwardly squirming as she thought of the embarrassment of sharing with a man she barely knew. She didn't even have a clean pair of knickers and a toothbrush – the duo her mother insisted was all a girl needed for a night away from home. *Don't let me snore or dribble*, she prayed.

Finch was self-consciously twirling the room key in his hands. 'Shall we go up, or do you want another drink?'

Romy shook her head.

The bedroom was like the bar downstairs: clean, neat, functional . . . and chilly. Romy sat down on the end of one of the single beds, Finch on the other. She looked at him. He raised an eyebrow.

'So, come on, what *did* you get up to on school trips?' Finch asked, a mischievous smile on his face.

She grinned back. 'Oh, smoke, snog boys, the usual.'

He laughed loudly. 'OK. Well, that doesn't sound so bad.'

'I bet you got up to much worse.'

'I wish. No school trips for me . . . I was home-schooled by my mother until I was fourteen.'

'Wow, unusual. Where did you live?'

Finch didn't reply for a moment and Romy felt his change of mood as he said, with clear reluctance, 'The Painswick Valley, an old stone cottage miles from any-where. My dear old ma was paranoid about the outside world. Xenophobic, even . . . probably bordering on sur-vivalist.' He paused, as if deciding whether or not to go on. 'The basement was crammed with hundreds of cans of food. She owned three shotguns and a rifle. I could shoot and skin a rabbit by the time I was eight.' He gave a short laugh. 'She absolutely hated any kind of authority, which was why she wouldn't send me to school. She con-sidered all teachers lefty tyrannical morons.'

'And your father?' Romy felt almost rude asking, sensing a palpable reticence from the man on the bed next to her.

Finch shrugged. 'Married man. I only knew him by sight – a local landowner with a large family. He's dead now, but he never acknowledged me.' A wry smile formed on his lips. 'Probably suspected Ma just wanted his sperm – which might have been true, knowing my mother – and didn't want me getting my mitts on his estate.' For a moment he seemed miles away. Then he added, 'She was an extraordinary woman, but perhaps not the easiest of mothers.'

Romy was amazed. Robert Fincham seemed the epitome of middle-class conservatism. She had assumed he came from some tidy family in the Home Counties, with two nice parents – father a dentist or in insurance, perhaps – a handful of siblings, two golden retrievers, a Rover on the gravel drive, maybe even a horse in some nearby field. *We might have more in common than I thought*, she decided. 'Why on earth the army?'

He laughed. 'I know, sounds like an improbable choice of career for someone with my background. Nearly gave Ma a heart attack when I told her.' He hesitated and she noticed him wringing his hands together in his lap. 'Being used to guns, I suppose, being part of something . . . And I think I wanted to prove I wasn't a mummy's boy . . . which was what the boys at school called me, of course, when I eventually got there.'

Romy realized she needed to have a major rethink about Robert Fincham. He hadn't told her a single thing about his childhood before, always brushing off any tentative enquiries she'd made. Talking now, he seemed almost apologetic – embarrassed even – about his upbringing, yet she'd always had the sense that this was a man enviably at ease with himself.

'So,' she said brightly, feeling the atmosphere was getting way too thick with Finch's past and anxious not to start focusing on her own, 'I suppose we should get some sleep.'

Neither of them moved. 'I'm sorry, Romy,' Finch said. 'I wanted this to be a perfect evening, and it seems to have gone a bit pear-shaped.'

Romy began to laugh when she saw his stricken expression. He didn't immediately join in and she knew she should control herself, but it wasn't easy in her tired, slightly tipsy state. 'I've had a wonderful time! Eccentric, perhaps,' she managed to say through her giggles. 'But certainly not the stuff of disaster.'

He gave a rueful grin. 'I'm normally good at logistics.'

'You are good. You saved me from a life-threatening illness, remember? Made sure I was fed and watered, and now I have a cosy . . .' she looked askance at the sad, chilly singles '. . . bed for the night.' She got up. 'What more could a girl want?'

Finch was really laughing now, as he stood. For a moment they hesitated, watching each other in silence. Then he gently pulled her to him and wrapped her in his arms. She sighed with pleasure, knowing she was trembling slightly as she looked up to meet his eye. Then Finch kissed her.

His kisses were soft at first, but as he felt her respond, they grew more intense, their bodies pressed together in the narrow gap between the beds.

After a while they pulled back, a question on each of their faces. Romy was buzzing, aroused. But Finch seemed to be holding back.

'Maybe we shouldn't rush,' he said, his voice croaky with desire, at the same time holding his palm against her cheek. Her eyes met his and she took a steadying breath.

The desire she felt made Romy's head spin. But now she couldn't help projecting herself into the cold light of morning, waking in the club room scrunched, half dressed, beside Finch in the narrow single bed, make-up blotched on her face, mouth stale and no toothbrush, wondering what they'd done. That was the trouble with being older: you thought about these things.

She reached up and kissed him again. Not a come-on kiss, this time, but a holding one, which spoke of promise and looked forward to the next time they might be in each other's arms.

10

November 2016

Nothing was ever the same in Romy's marriage after the letter. It was as if a malign – and uninvited – guest permanently stalked the flat. Despite her outward support for Michael's position – as in going along with his determination to do nothing – those words had created a seismic shift in their relationship. She was almost afraid to be with Michael, reluctant to look him in the eye for fear of what she might see. And as the months went on, the distance between them seemed to become solid and increasingly unbreachable.

Until that point, her faith in her husband had been absolute. She had taken him at face value, warts and all, accepting his addiction to work, how little he was around when the boys were growing up, the way he took her for granted as his wingman, without ever questioning her feelings about being subordinate to his stellar career, because she loved him, because it hadn't always been like that between them . . . because, although she knew he wasn't perfect, she had always believed in his integrity. And his intrinsic love for his family.

They had grown up in the same village in the northeast, known each other only by sight – Michael was older by three years and considered inaccessibly cool by her and her friends. When their paths did eventually cross one hot, crazy June night in a Stockton pub, Romy sixteen and star-struck, there had been no turning back for either of them.

In those early days Michael's drive and charisma had created an exciting life. He had seemed to need her by his side, his pride in his northern roots also tinged with self-consciousness among the mainly public-school crowd his pupillage for the Bar threw him together with.

Now, when Michael was at work and she was alone in the flat, Romy, in an attempt to block out those stark words on the cream writing-paper, would summon up happier times, remind herself that it hadn't always been like this between them.

And as her birthday loomed – thirteen months after the letter's arrival – she recalled a long-ago celebration with a smile: Michael standing by the door of their shabby bedsit near Russell Square, grinning and wheeling his arms impatiently as she put on her coat. '*Hurry up*, we're going to be late.' He had woken her before six that morning, handing her an envelope: two plane tickets to Paris concealed in a birthday card.

Neither had ever been to the city before. 'We must have the full-on Paris experience,' Michael had said excitedly. 'Do everything: the Eiffel Tower, Notre Dame, the Louvre. Float down the Seine on a *bateau mouche*.' So they stayed in a chilly pension on the Left Bank, with brown tiles on the floor and no pillow, just a lumpy cylindrical bolster, which made them laugh till their sides ached. It was a raw, wet November, but Mona Lisa's smile, endless steak-frites and a great deal of cheap red wine kept them warm. When they made love, the iron feet of the bed screeched on the hideous tiles and reduced them to more tears of laughter.

They had been such a team back then. 'It's us against the world, Romy,' Michael would say, with a confident grin. She worked for a firm of architects in Islington – they called her a 'secretary' in those days – while Michael completed his pupillage in Gray's Inn. Most weekends they would throw spaghetti suppers in their tiny flat, with raucous, drink-fuelled rows about anything and nothing. Michael's increased pressure of work as he rose quickly through the system, and the birth of the boys, had begun to alter all that.

Romy's birthday this year, however, would be more momentous by far than the Paris trip had been – but with none of the innocent enjoyment that had accompanied it. Because it was the day when she first began to think seriously that she might leave Michael, despite the trigger being almost ludicrously insignificant.

Her husband had appeared agitated that morning. 'I'm really upset, Romy. I ordered your present weeks ago and the bloody thing hasn't arrived,' he said. 'I'm so sorry.'

When she'd assured him it didn't matter – which it didn't – he went through a whole charade. 'Were you in yesterday?' he asked, and when Romy said she wasn't, he went on, 'Maybe Mrs Ratti took it in. I'd better run down and check.' And he'd gone off to ask the Italian caretaker, who lived in the basement flat, if she'd seen the package. But when the present did arrive – an expensive Mulberry handbag in soft cerise leather – Romy noticed the order date was the actual day of her birthday.

It was such a small thing – in the past it might have been something they could laugh about. But his lie felt much more sinister to Romy than just a silly fib about forgetting her present. When she confronted him at breakfast that weekend, he initially denied it.

'Are you accusing me of lying?' he'd said, slamming his coffee mug onto the table, surprisingly full of aggression.

She'd laughed, tried to make light of it. 'Well, you did, Michael. I don't give a toss that you forgot – you know me better than that. But there's no need to lie.'

For a moment he had continued to eye her indignantly. Then his face had collapsed into a sheepish grin and he'd held up his hands. 'It's a fair cop, guv,' he said. 'I'm so sorry, Romy. I felt terrible when I realized I'd forgotten.'

But Romy had not been mollified. She'd totally believed the charade with the lost parcel. *If he can lie so convincingly about something as trivial as my birthday present . . .* she thought. Because the letter coloured almost every exchange she had with Michael these days, as if she were filtering all his utterances through the prism of the woman's words.

Romy hated herself for it, but she found she couldn't stop as the poison drip-dripped onto the fabric of their marriage, burning small holes at first, which soon joined up into huge jagged ones, until she felt there was nothing left but tatters. She had finally lost the strength to hold the fabric together.

And Michael obviously felt it. She'd sensed him pulling away from her over the previous thirteen months – spending ever more hours at work – at the same time as she had taken a step back from him. But distance only spawned more distance, with neither able to talk about it. The moment seemed to have passed when she might have spoken, Romy realized.

By tacit consent, they stopped entertaining – even for networking purposes – and he moved into the spare room: 'I don't want to wake you when I'm home late,' he said, although he'd never cared in the past. Romy, in turn, began to make social arrangements with her friends, leaving her husband out of the equation altogether. They became like polite strangers, gliding past each other with only the briefest of acknowledgement.

On the rare occasions when they sat round the table together as a family, Romy would search Michael's face, check how this uneasy domestic arrangement was affecting him. But all she saw was a guarded acceptance, and a titanic effort not to meet her eye – *Just in case I mention the unmentionable*, she thought sadly.

But it seemed as if there were light years between Romy's first thought that she might leave her husband and deciding actually to do so. The prospect – which daily tormented her – made her feel physically sick. It wasn't until six weeks after the incident with the Mulberry bag, on an icy January morning, that she finally plucked up the courage and confronted Michael.

The moment had been planned for – over and over – in the preceding weeks. She would lie in bed, stomach churning, telling herself, *Today's the day*, then for some reason – Michael would leave early, she would over-sleep or simply lose her nerve – he would be gone and she still hadn't said a word. Which proved both a temporary relief and a cause of weary frustration with her own cowardice.

The Wednesday in question she had no plan. She'd been up early, working on the mission statement for a friend's charity, which was raising money to save a large area of wasteland in East London that had been colonized by rare birds. When she heard Michael moving around, she had known this had to be the moment – it was days since they had spoken, she realized, even to say hello – but the tension remained. The shilly-shallying had to stop. She positioned herself in the hall, by the entrance to the kitchen and waited, holding her breath, her whole body rigid.

Normally he would speed through from his bedroom to swallow a cup of coffee, eat a slice of toast and marmalade – although since she'd stopped making it for him, he'd stuck to just coffee – before heading off for another long day. But that morning, almost as if he knew something was up, he had forgone even coffee and immediately grabbed his coat from the hook, keen to be away.

'I'm going to stay at the cottage for a while,' she began, hearing her voice tremble.

Michael stopped as he straightened his coat collar and frowned at her. 'What do you mean?'

'I love it down there,' was all she managed to reply, even though she had spent the previous six weeks preparing an elaborate speech for this moment.

'In January? Seriously? It'll be freezing . . . and fucking miserable.' Her husband turned away and picked up his bulging briefcase, as if that were the end of the conversation.

'I know, but I'm going anyway.' She heard her voice take on a resoluteness that had not been there before. And Michael heard it too.

'What are you on about, Romy?'

She took a breath, feeling her belly fluttering with anxiety. 'I think it's best we have a break, live separately for a while.' Michael's dark eyes narrowed, never leaving her face. 'We haven't spoken for days. It's not as if we spend any time together any more,' Romy added.

Her husband did a double-take. 'Wait . . . You're leaving me? Is that what you're trying to say?' He shook his head in apparent incomprehension. 'Listen, I'm late. Not the best time to drop a bombshell like this.' Opening the front door, he turned, a frown on his face. She didn't know if he was shocked, or puzzled, or simply annoyed. 'See you later,' Michael stated, as if she hadn't spoken.

And she found herself replying, 'OK,' because suddenly she felt ridiculous and small.

As soon as the door slammed behind him, she burst into tears. But as the day wore on and she began to anticipate how she would explain to Michael what she felt, she realized she wouldn't be able to. He would twist her words, make her feel she was overreacting, probably talk her out of her plan without making any concessions on his part – or even, she thought, properly acknowledging how bad things had become.

So after lunch she packed her clothes and drove down to the cottage by the sea. Once there, she didn't rest until she had unpacked her stuff, gone to the supermarket, made supper and opened a bottle of wine – settled in, in a very deliberate manner. But her eye was always on the clock as she waited for the time when Michael might come home and find her gone. The evening ticked by, her stomach churning, and there was no call.

It wasn't until early the following morning that he phoned.

'Where are you?' he demanded.

'In Sussex,' she said.

'Without any discussion?'

'I didn't see the point.'

There was silence at the other end.

'Romy,' Michael's voice, for the first time in months, sounded uncertain, 'this is silly. You can't just up sticks and leave like that, without even telling me why. I know we haven't been connecting much recently but . . . what's this really about?'

She didn't reply for a moment. Where to start, without disparaging the whole thirty years they'd been together – without blaming Michael? She wasn't even sure she was doing the right thing. All she knew was that she needed to get away from the stalemate, the deadness that shadowed the flat, the blank, disengaged stare of her husband.

'I don't understand,' he said.

She wondered why he didn't. *Is he being deliberately obtuse?* Or was he simply blind to what had been going on between them?

She heard him sigh. 'Well, I'm not going to beg.' More silence. Then, 'I've got to go, I'm due in court. But I'll come down at the weekend and we can talk properly. Sort things out.' When she didn't reply at once, he added, 'OK?'

Romy took a deep breath. 'Please don't come, Michael.' The line went dead.

11

Romy left Finch in the sitting room to go upstairs. She was tingling with the slow, tentative kisses that had begun soon after they were through the cottage door an hour ago, the wine and coffee she had promised entirely forgotten. She turned on the bedside light, surveyed the small bedroom and smoothed the duvet cover. She hadn't come up to 'slip into something more comfortable' – her blue rayon dressing gown, apart from needing a wash and being a bit moth-eaten at the cuffs, would be a serious passion-killer. She wanted a breather, just a moment alone.

They had met, early evening, on the back terrace of the pub looking out over the harbour. The tables were much sought after in the summer when the weather was good, but tonight they'd had the place almost to themselves. It was early in the season and not particularly warm, but there was no wind, the spring sky cloudless, and both wanted to watch the sun sink behind the masts of the boats floating gently on the water.

The plan was to have supper. But in the end they'd just finished a bottle of cold blush rosé and picked at a plate of whitebait. There had been a quiet buzz between them. They hadn't talked much, as if both were waiting. And finally she had got up and taken his hand. 'I've got wine and coffee at home . . .' she'd said.

Now, when she went through to the en suite and rinsed her mouth with cold water – resisting the telltale smell of toothpaste – she stared at herself in the mirror. Her cheeks were flushed with wine and arousal, her eyes sparkling, her hair framing her face in as flattering a way as was possible with her awkward curls. Was she really going to make love to the man sitting on the sofa downstairs? Let him see her body in all its nakedness? Let him . . . She stopped. *I haven't made love to anyone but Michael since I was sixteen.* The thought threatened to overwhelm her and she shook it off and hurried downstairs before she lost her nerve.

Finch glanced at her as she came into the room. 'Everything OK?' he asked. He was looking at her questioningly, but his smile was gentle and confident.

She went over to the sofa, standing quite still in front of him and holding his gaze, allowing herself to sink into those brown eyes until nothing else seemed to exist. The anxiety had gone, to be replaced by a patent desire. Her heartbeat quickened. Then she leant down and kissed him gently on the mouth. Finch took her hands and pulled her onto the cushions, returning her kisses with increasing intensity as he slid his hand beneath her shirt, making her gasp as she felt his thumb circle the smoothness of her naked breast. A moment later, his own shirt dispensed with, she was lying on his bare chest, delighting in the feel of his warm skin brushing against her nipples . . .

They never made it up to the freshly laundered sheets on the bed upstairs. Not till much later, that is, when they fell beneath the cool linen in a daze.

*

Finch turned on his side to face her, his hand across her body, tenderly stroking her thigh. It was early, the light beautiful as it came off the water, needle-bright against the white walls of her bedroom. The duvet felt cosy, his body warm as they relaxed against each other. Romy wanted to sing out with happiness.

'That wasn't as scary as I thought,' he said softly.

'You were as nervous as me? You didn't show it.'

'It's not like we're novices . . . but still . . .'

Finch didn't go on and instead she heard a pigeon's strident cooing from the ridge of her neighbour's roof where he perched and strutted all day long.

Finch gently tipped her chin up to look into her face. 'You were amazing, Romy.'

She blushed, bringing his hand to her lips for a kiss. It had been amazing.

'I could make scrambled eggs,' Romy said, when they had lain, for a while, in sleepy silence. 'Or we could go to the café for a bacon sandwich.'

Finch stretched, letting out a luxurious groan, his long body suddenly taut beside her. 'You don't want to cook. Let's do the café.' He grabbed her up and rained kisses down on her face until she pushed him away under protest.

Downstairs, she opened the doors to the garden and sucked in the spring sunshine. When she had left Michael, she had not been sure she would adjust to country living, after decades in the centre of the capital. But she had dreamt of moments such as these, on those days when, instead of breathing in the fresh salty tang of the estuary, she had opened the windows of the London flat to the metallic whiff of exhaust fumes.

They strolled the short distance to the café and chose one of the tables on the tiny balcony overlooking the sea. No one else was there yet; the coach parties who stopped by for tea and cake in this destination café would not arrive for another hour or so.

Two bacon sandwiches and coffee – cappuccino for him, a latte for her – were slapped on their table by the sullen middle-aged manager, who always succeeded in making Romy feel she was inconveniencing her by being in the café at all.

'What are your plans for the rest of the day?' Finch enquired, grabbing his sandwich, squashing it between his fingers and stuffing it into his mouth.

'Well . . . I've got to follow up on a job I saw advertised on the Sussex Wildlife Trust website, in the environmental education programme. I'm probably not qualified, but it might be a toe in the door. I volunteer on a nature reserve at the moment, but I'd like to find something I can really get my teeth into.'

'So this is part of the new life you talked about?'

Romy nodded. 'My parents were dyed-in-the-wool greens before greens were invented. It's in the blood.'

'I suppose Ma was green, too, in her own way, given that she never went anywhere or washed anything and the house was always freezing cold.'

Romy laughed. 'So was ours.'

They ate in silence for a minute or two.

'Maybe I could come with you to the nature reserve one day?' Finch asked tentatively. 'I'm interested . . . and I love a physical challenge, particularly outdoors.'

Persuaded for so long by Michael to consider her passion a sideline, almost a joke, she was surprised by Finch's interest and willingness to take her seriously.

She gave him a smile. 'OK, why not?' Glancing up at the sky, she noticed the clouds were white and unthreatening. 'Listen, I could do the job thing later . . . If you're free, maybe we could have a walk on the beach.'

But Finch didn't answer. He was cocking his head, listening to something. 'Is that your phone?'

Romy, now hearing the buzzing too, dug for the mobile in her bag by her feet.

'Mum, it's Leo.' Her son's voice wobbled alarmingly, as if he was about to cry. Before Romy had time to ask what was wrong, he went on, 'Where are you? I've called you a million times.'

'Why? What's happened?' Anxiety stabbed in the pit of her stomach.

'It's Dad. He's had a stroke.'

12

Romy stared at her screen. While she and Finch had been unbuttoning each other's clothes on the sofa, her husband had been ill and alone, knowing he was in trouble and crying out for her to rescue him. The thought brought her out in a cold sweat and her breath caught in her throat. *Where was Anezka?* she wondered, yet she knew from Rex that, although Anezka had been with Michael for the best part of a year, she didn't actually live with him yet.

'*What?*' Romy had gasped when she heard her son's words. 'Oh, my God . . .'

Leo gave a shaky breath. 'It's really bad, Mum. Theresa found him when she arrived at nine. Thank God she had a key. The doctor says she thinks it happened early last night and he was lying there for hours. He was really cold and weak.'

'Is he all right? I mean . . . how bad is he?' What her son was saying just didn't seem possible. *Suppose it hadn't been the day Theresa came in to clean?*

'They say he's critical, Mum.'

Romy's heart was racing. 'Where is he? Which hospital?'

'Chelsea and Westminster. I'm here now, in the ICU . . .'

She looked over at Finch and saw his concerned frown, his eyebrows raised in question. 'Have you told Rex?'

'I left messages, but it's the middle of the night in Sydney.' He paused. 'Please come, Mum. He might die and I don't know what to do.'

'I'll jump in the car right now.'

'OK. But hurry . . .'

She'd taken a steadying breath. 'Listen, Leo, I'm sure he'll be fine. He's in the right place and he's tough, your dad. Don't panic, I'll text you when I get close.' Her bullish assertion was very far from the image in her mind. She knew that the longer a stroke is left untreated, the worse the outcome. And if he'd been lying there all night . . .

When she'd clicked off, she saw that there were six text messages, three voicemails. Three of the texts were sent last night, each from Michael. They all contained a version of random letters: *Dddgi poiif.* As if he'd bashed his finger across the keypad in panic. The time stamp said they were all sent within a few minutes of each other, from 11.03 p.m.

Now she turned the phone to Finch, who squinted at it in the sun as she explained what had happened. 'He texted me,' she said. '*Three times.*'

'Last night? When we were . . .' He winced. 'God . . .'

She got up, the metal chair legs screeching on the stone terrace. 'I need to go.'

'You can't drive when you're in shock, Romy. I'll take you.'

'No . . . No, I'll be fine,' she said, although she didn't feel fine at all: her heart was thumping and she was slightly dizzy. It somehow didn't seem right, though, to drag Finch into a drama concerning Michael.

Finch had already risen from his chair, a determined look on his face. 'I'll fetch the car. Meet you at yours in fifteen,' he said. 'I can drop you off. It won't be easy to park near the hospital.'

Romy knew he was right and, after a brief hesitation, nodded. 'If you're sure.'

As she randomly threw clothes into an overnight bag and shut up the cottage, seeing reminders of those wonderful hours last night in the scattered cushions on the sitting-room floor, the rumpled bed, his jacket still on the peg by the front door, she felt the whole thing had happened a million years ago, in a totally different universe.

Romy stared down at the face on the pillow in the high hospital bed and heard her breath catch with distress. It was a face once as familiar to her as her own, but now it seemed like that of a stranger. Michael lay sunken, diminished, his normally animated features flat and pallid, like a clay mask. She placed her hand on his, as it lay on the sheet, gently squeezing it.

'Michael?'

She hadn't expected him to open his eyes, but he did, his gaze unfocused. Then they slowly closed again. She had seen him asleep a million times over the years – it was the only time his spirited, intelligent face seemed to find any peace. But now she wanted to shake him awake, jolt him out of this horrible stillness.

Romy turned to Leo. 'Has he said anything?' Her son, tall like her, dark like his father, but with her wide brown-gold eyes and mutinous curls, which he kept very short, looked haggard, blinking back tears that she rarely saw from her self-possessed boy. She took his arm and brought him close, but his body was rigid with tension and he did not respond, his eyes fixed on the figure on the bed.

'He looked at me earlier and tried to speak, but I couldn't understand what he said.'

Romy checked around the ward, light pouring in through the extensive windows. 'Who can I talk to?' There were medical staff everywhere, and a sense of professional calm, with enough room between each bed-station – she reckoned around twelve in all – to give a sense of privacy.

Leo pointed to a woman in blue scrubs with short mousy hair and a large bosom, a stethoscope slung round her neck, talking earnestly to a bespectacled man in a dark suit behind the nurses' desk. 'That's her, Dad's doctor.'

Michael's scan, so Linda Stott later informed Romy and Leo in the patients' waiting room, had shown a clot in the right carotid artery in his neck, which had reduced the blood flow to his brain.

'So what happens next?'

Linda pursed her lips. 'Well, there are a number of things, but the problem is that because it was quite a while after the stroke before your husband was brought in – judging by his deteriorated condition – we decided clot-busting drugs wouldn't be so effective and could make things worse.'

The doctor stopped and, for a ridiculous moment, Romy – her mind flashing back to the unanswered texts and the scene on the sofa – thought she was reproaching her. She might as well have done; Romy felt a crippling guilt that she hadn't responded to Michael's cry for help. She knew it could be the difference – those lost hours – between a good recovery and a not-so-good one. Between life and death, even.

'But there's a plan?' Romy asked urgently, when Linda didn't go on.

'Surgery to remove the clot is an option but, again, it carries risk. We feel the best thing to do is to monitor him and give him medication to prevent another potential stroke while we wait for the clot to disperse.'

Romy frowned. 'Do nothing?'

The doctor gave her a sympathetic smile. 'Not nothing, Mrs Claire. We're giving your husband the very best supportive care. But it's vital he has time to stabilize. We don't want to aggravate the situation.'

'He's going to be OK, isn't he?' This from Leo.

Dr Stott looked him straight in the eye. 'I won't lie to you. Your father's in a critical condition – there's a real danger that he might have another brain attack. The next forty-eight hours are crucial.'

Stunned, Romy stood by the bed, searching her husband's face for signs of life. It was unbearable, seeing him like that, and also witnessing the shock imprinted on her son's face. But there was nothing they could do, except this – the passive staring, the watching for any tiny twitch in the face on the pillow. After a while she dragged Leo out of the ward and down to the Costa café on the ground floor, where she got them both a strong coffee.

Finch had driven her expertly – at breakneck speed – to Fulham, then told her he would hang around for a while in London, in case she needed him. She glanced around to see if he was in the hospital reception area, but there was no sign of him. And while she longed for his comforting and capable presence, she did not relish explaining him to her son right now.

'Does Anezka know?' she asked, when they were sitting at a table covered with crumbs and coffee stains, which Leo impatiently wiped away with a wad of napkins.

'I left an urgent message, but she hasn't got back to me,' he said tiredly.

'Try her again. She should be here.'

Dr Stott referring to Michael as 'your husband' had been unsettling. Yes, he was technically that, but Anezka – whom Romy had yet to meet – was really the person they should be talking to about his treatment. Or Leo . . . Rex if he were in the country. Because by leaving Michael, she had pretty much abdicated all responsibility for him.

Leo pulled his phone from his pocket, punched in a contact. After a moment with the mobile pressed to his ear, he shook his head. 'It's Leo again, Anezka. Please ring me. It's really urgent.'

He clicked off, but his phone rang immediately.

'Hi . . .' He frowned, clearly taken aback by what he was hearing. 'OK, no, I understand . . . *No* . . . Anezka, *listen*, for God's sake. Dad's had a stroke. He's in hospital. They say he's critical.'

After a further short exchange, Leo clicked off and widened his eyes at his mother. 'Bloody hell.'

'What?'

'She and Dad had a terrible row yesterday evening, apparently. She says she dumped him. When she saw I'd called, she assumed Dad had asked me to mediate.'

'Like your father would ever do that,' Romy muttered. Then she realized what her son said. 'She *dumped* him?'

Leo nodded. 'Sounded really upset . . . But she's coming in now, anyway.'

Romy wasn't sure what to do. 'Maybe I should go, if Anezka's on her way.' She saw her son's look of alarm and hurried on, 'She's his partner now, Leo . . . This row they had, it's probably nothing. Won't it be a bit weird, both of us sitting by his bedside?'

'You can't leave us, Mum. Please. Don't you want to be here for Dad?'

'Yes, of course I do,' she said wretchedly. Which was true. She couldn't imagine leaving him when it wasn't certain he would live. And she would never leave her son to cope alone. But she was apprehensive.

'Anezka won't mind,' Leo was saying. 'She's cool . . . Well, she's very far from cool, actually. She's feisty and takes no prisoners – leads Dad a proper dance, is my guess. But I'm sure she won't mind you being here.'

Romy was not convinced, but she wasn't going to argue. 'We should get back,' she said, finishing her coffee.

Leo nodded and they rose to their feet.

'You like her?' she asked, as they made their way to the lift. This was the first time she had properly asked Leo about Michael's girlfriend. She hadn't thought it appropriate to question the boys and they hadn't volunteered much, although Rex – who liked a good gossip – had dropped the odd hint that he found it uncomfortable being around Anezka and his father in those months before he'd gone to Australia, because she was very physical and cuddled and kissed Michael openly.

'Yeah, she's OK. But she's closer to my generation than his, Mum. It's kind of weird.'

Romy pressed the lift button, avoiding the censure in her son's eyes. Neither of them could understand why she had left their father after a lifetime together. Soon after they had told the boys about the split, Rex had said, 'I don't get what the problem is, Mum. You and Dad never seem to argue.'

'That's because we never talk,' she'd replied.

He'd thought about this. 'You used to.'

'Not recently,' she said, holding back further comment.

He'd frowned. 'Has something happened, Mum?'

'No, nothing,' she'd insisted, ashamed of her lie.

Rex had nodded slowly, seeming to believe her. 'I remember you and Dad laughing together a lot when I was a kid . . . but, yeah, maybe not so much recently, I guess.'

Romy had realized that laughing with Michael seemed a distant memory now. Not since the letter, certainly – which she refused to mention to her sons – but before that too. Nor could she explain the intricacies of a long marriage, the grey area where dissatisfaction and resentment run alongside friendship and passion in the early days, but the steady contentment many of her friends had grown to feel with their spouse as they became older would now never take hold in Romy and Michael's relationship.

'I'll see how it goes with Anezka,' she said now. 'If I feel I'm in the way . . .'

But her son grabbed her hand. 'Mum, I'm telling you, I can't do this on my own. I don't think Anezka will be great in a situation like this. She might require as much support as Dad.' He stared at her. 'I need you . . . Please, *please* don't go.'

As the doors of the lift opened on the intensive-care floor, Romy experienced an unpleasant thud of premonition and a sick feeling in her stomach, as if a large hand were reaching out to clamp her and drag her unceremoniously away from her promising new life.

13

Romy woke to find herself in a strange bed: the spare room in the flat, which she had never slept in before last night. After she'd moved out, Michael had apparently gone back to the main bedroom, and Romy found herself reluctant to sleep in what was now his and Anezka's bed. And, anyway, the room was a mess. The bed had been pushed aside, the duvet balled and dumped in the corner by the window, the sheet half pulled from the mattress. There was a scrunched-up plastic hood of some sort littering the floor and a syringe cover – debris from the paramedics' equipment. *They must have been in a hurry*, she thought miserably, as she began to set the room to rights.

The flat no longer felt like her home, but there were disturbing echoes everywhere of her life with Michael. She had taken very little to the cottage. The photos of the family on the walls, all her kitchen gadgets, the books and even various bottles of self-tan and sachets of hair mask in the bathroom cupboard were exactly as she'd left them. There was very little sign of the Czech girlfriend, except for a scented candle in the bathroom – scented candles always made Romy sneeze – and a few random items of clothing in her side of the wardrobe.

Leo was right: Anezka was quite something. Romy and Leo were sitting on either side of Michael's bed when she'd arrived at the ICU the previous afternoon in a whirlwind of drama.

Tall, slim and very beautiful, she had a dramatic curtain of thick, brown hair, which she raked with her fingers, swishing it from side to side every two minutes as if she couldn't decide where it was most comfortable, huge blue eyes in a classically proportioned face and full, perfect lips that made Angelina Jolie's look amateur. Romy was taken aback. As Leo had observed, she seemed so young and so glamorous – for some reason she'd pictured a woman more like the tough, clever types Michael admired in his professional life.

She was dressed in jeans, a round-necked white T-shirt – which showed off her perfect breasts – and trainers with no socks. But she'd thrown over the simple ensemble an oversized grey and white checked duster coat that instantly lifted the outfit to supermodel status. Leo was clearly in awe, his youthful skin blushing under her enthusiastic hug.

'Oh, my God, darling. What has he done? I can't believe this is happening,' she exclaimed loudly, drawing the attention of most of the nursing staff and those patients who weren't actually in a coma.

Leo, recovering himself with effort, had introduced Romy and she'd seen the younger woman's gaze flick up and down in an uncomfortably appraising manner. Then Anezka came towards her and wrapped her in her arms. 'I am so happy to meet you at last,' she said, with such genuine warmth that Romy almost burst into tears, the strains of the morning finally overwhelming her in the face of this unexpected kindness.

Anezka drew back, her huge eyes also glistening. Then she turned to the bed and took a deep breath as she stared down at the man she loved, tentatively laying a hand on his forehead, her own creased in concern. It was obvious to Romy that she'd had little experience of illness and that it frightened her.

'Michael.' She bent close to him. 'Miláčku . . . can you hear me?'

Michael opened his eyes at the sound of her voice. He had been in and out of consciousness but so far had not said anything coherent to Romy or Leo. Now, however, he spoke, his words slow and very slurred.

'Annie . . . what is . . . what . . .' His eyes closed, but Romy saw him clinging to Anezka with his right hand. His left flopped uselessly on the sheet, grey and lifeless, like a dead fish. His eyes opened again and he almost smiled, although the left side of his face drooped severely, giving his expression an almost piratical air. 'So tired,' he added, then closed his eyes again, his grip loosening.

Anezka looked triumphantly at Leo, then Romy. 'He's talking! A good sign, no?' She sank onto the chair Leo had vacated and put her hands over her face. 'I thought he was dead and you weren't telling me,' she said, and began to cry softly behind her long fingers.

Romy had suffered a painful stab of jealousy when she first saw Anezka, but she found her heart going out to the woman. *Was the row serious?* she wondered. *Has she really dumped Michael?* If he recovered – and there was no guarantee he would – it would be a long road until he was fit again.

She remembered the last time Michael had been in hospital during their marriage, and that was only A&E, nearly fifteen years ago now. He had stood on a rusty nail in the Sussex garden and the wound became infected, his whole foot swelling to twice its normal size so he couldn't walk. He'd behaved like a bear with at least two sore heads until the swelling went down. He would not be an easy patient.

Now she got out of bed and went through to the kitchen, switched on the familiar kettle, got out one of her favourite mugs with a blue and white flower pattern and made herself a cup of tea. She half expected her husband to pop his head round the door on his way to work, but the flat was eerily silent.

What should I do? Obviously she would go back to the hospital this morning. Leo had finally spoken to Rex and he was on his way home from Australia. He wouldn't get in till tomorrow afternoon and she was dying to see her younger son, even in such grim circumstances.

She worried, though, that if she stuck around the medical staff would see her as Michael's closest relative. Yesterday, each time there was a development in his condition, it was to Romy that the nurses referred, not Leo or Anezka. And neither appeared to mind. It seemed churlish, though, when he was so ill, to quibble about who was his next of kin, so she didn't make a fuss. But she was being drawn inexorably into decisions about his care because technically she was still married to him.

She reached for her mobile. Leo had said he would stay over at a friend's place nearby in Battersea, his own being in Tottenham, near the old Spurs ground, and a long trek. Her son's phone went to voicemail and Romy didn't leave a message. *He's probably still asleep*, she thought.

She rang Finch. She had texted him the previous day to tell him to go home, not to wait for her. She had no idea when she would be able to get away.

'Hey.' He picked up immediately. 'How is he?'

'They aren't saying much. Or doing much, it seems. Just waiting. It's twenty-four hours now and he hasn't improved, but then he hasn't deteriorated either. They seem to think that's something.'

'And how are you, Romy?'

His voice was so tender that she found her eyes filling with tears. She swallowed hard. 'Don't be nice to me, Finch. I can't handle it.'

He laughed softly. 'Do my best.'

She smiled through her tears. 'The girlfriend, Anezka, pitched up yesterday. She's stunning . . . not that that's got anything to do with anything. But it's a ticklish situation, because apparently she dumped Michael just before he had his stroke. So there's me and her and Leo round the bed . . . Honestly, I don't know how to play it.'

'It must be very upsetting, seeing Michael like that.'

Romy felt her mouth wobble and no longer tried to hold back the tears. 'It is. It's horrible, really horrible. I know our marriage is over and all that, but I loved him once, Finch. I loved him for a long time. And he's just lying there . . . I'm not even sure he'll make it and Leo's in bits . . . What shall I do?' The question came out almost as a wail.

'I suppose the only thing you can do is wait, see how it goes.'

It was so good to talk to Finch. He didn't give her false hope. She didn't have to be strong, like she did with her son. 'You don't think I should walk away? Let Anezka take over?'

Finch didn't reply at once. 'You could. But would you feel comfortable leaving your son . . . leaving Michael, when you don't know if he'll come through?'

She sighed. 'No . . . No, you're right. I can't leave Leo. And Rex is coming in later today. I haven't seen him since Christmas.'

Finch did not reply immediately. She wanted to tell him that she was missing him already, but she couldn't quite say the words out loud.

When Romy arrived at the hospital, neither Leo nor Anezka was there. Michael looked no better. She thought he was asleep, but when she touched his hand, he opened his eyes. At first he seemed not to recognize her, his eyes still glazed and blank from the trauma.

'Romy . . .?' The word was a long time coming, distorted, dragged up from the damaged recesses of his brain.

'How are you?' she asked. Jasmine, Michael's nurse, had said he was still disoriented and not aware of what had happened.

'Am I . . .' his face clouded with confusion, '. . . am I . . .'

She wasn't sure what he was asking, but she told him anyway. 'You're in the Chelsea and Westminster, Michael. You've had a stroke.'

He frowned. 'I . . .' But the effort to think was obviously too much and he closed his eyes. 'Just . . . want to sleep.'

Romy went outside to call Leo.

'I'm on my way, Mum. I had to make some work calls.' Leo sounded flustered, and Romy knew the asset management company that was training her son put him under a lot of pressure. She felt so sorry for him, just at this stage in his life, having to stop everything to deal with this.

'I'm not hassling you. Take as long as you need. There's no real change in Dad, anyway.'

'I should be about half an hour. Is Anezka there?'

'No. Just me. He's sleeping most of the time. I'll talk to his nurse and ring you back.'

Romy watched Jasmine – so young, so eager – put on her reassuring face as she approached.

'OK . . . So he's not had a bad night,' she said. 'His swallow reflex is improving and he's been drinking little bits this morning. They're doing an ultrasound scan on his carotid artery later, to see if the blood clot has dispersed. The signs are encouraging, but he's not out of danger yet, Mrs Claire. We're still monitoring him very closely. We'll be able to tell you more after the tests.'

Romy nodded her thanks, but didn't feel particularly encouraged. Michael was obviously still far from out of the woods.

The hospital had a soporific effect on Romy. It felt like a separate world: overheated air, polished corridors and pleated blue curtains, frightening equipment and people talking a language that made her feel stupid and out of control. There was nothing to do except sit and watch as different elements of the medical team zoomed in on Michael, like bees to a flower, performed whatever service they were required to provide, then melted away.

She ate too many biscuits and crisps and drank too much coffee. She had brought her book and tried to read. But in the end she just sat vacantly, unwilling to analyse her presence beside Michael's bed or her feelings about the man lying in it.

In her mind's eye, an old memory sprang up, an event she hadn't thought of in years, triggered because it had taken place in a large house in one of the streets behind the hospital. It was a New Year's Eve party they'd been to before the boys were born, given by one of Michael's fellow trainee barristers in his parents' home. She'd had on a gorgeous strappy dress in deep raspberry. The band was top class, Michael a great dancer – like everything else in his life, he wanted to be the best – and she just followed his lead. She remembered his dark eyes flashing with pleasure as he whirled her expertly around, skirt swirling out from her long legs, remembered the exhilaration she felt just being in his arms.

Will he ever be able to dance again? The thought brought tears to her tired eyes.

14

Michael's condition had gone up and down in the five days since his stroke. It was Saturday now. Romy still felt scratchy and bone-tired from worry, but also cautiously optimistic. Michael was no longer considered critical and they had moved him out of the ICU to the stroke ward on the floor below – where, to Romy's guilty relief, visiting hours were limited to the afternoons.

He was definitely more compos mentis now, although his speech was still extremely slow and distorted and his whole left side hung uselessly from his body, making him horribly lopsided and incapable of balancing on his own when the nurses got him out of bed. But the danger of another stroke was still a real threat, according to the doctor.

Today he seemed pleased to see her, raising his good hand to take hers when she reached the bed. Someone had shaved him and put his pyjamas on, and he looked a bit more like his normal self. Her husband had always been striking rather than handsome. A lean man of average height, he had begun shaving his head decades ago, after he'd cut it open getting off a faulty ski lift, then decided he preferred the look. It accentuated his high cheekbones and large dark eyes, his Roman nose – inherited from his Venetian grandmother – and made him stand out among the more conservatively presented judiciary. But now his exposed skull just made him look ancient.

'Hey,' she said. 'I brought you some chicken broth.' She placed the Thermos on the bed table, moving aside the inevitable grapes and a pile of books brought in optimistically by Leo, none of which Michael had even glanced at. 'Bit of a cliché, but you've always been fond of my soup and I'm sure the food in here is shit.'

Michael nodded and smiled. 'I'm very fond of . . . things you cook,' he said slowly, obviously searching for words, the meaning hard to glean from his mangled speech. Then, to Romy's horror, she noticed a single tear course down his cheek. Then another.

'Michael?' She stroked his hand, finding a tissue in a box on his bedside locker and handing it to him. The tears stopped almost as soon as they'd started.

Michael gave her a weak smile. 'Not sure . . . why that . . . why I . . .' he mumbled, appearing bewildered rather than embarrassed. Romy had rarely seen him cry, not even when his beloved mother had died. It shocked her that he was so disarmed; it touched her heart.

'Shall I pour you some soup?' she asked, to cover her own emotion.

He shook his head, but she couldn't understand the words he was trying to articulate.

The afternoon wore on and there was no sign of the boys or Anezka. Michael's long-time colleague and friend, James Bregman, with whom he shared chambers, dropped in, clutching a lavish, dewy bunch of flowers, which he waved vaguely around, and finally laid on Michael's bed.

'Thanks, these are gorgeous,' Romy said, after she'd greeted James. 'But I'm not sure they allow flowers on the ward, these days.'

His expression fell and he looked ill at ease – although James was not someone easily discomposed – as he hopped from foot to foot in his expensively tailored suit, his plump, fair face flushed. 'Sorry, didn't think . . .' He stared at Michael's sleeping figure. 'Bit of bad luck this, eh?' As if his friend had just lost on the horses.

James, through all the guff and posturing, was actually a decent person, Romy knew – he would have done anything to help, had she asked – but he was not the easiest man to talk to, even though she'd known him for decades, unless the subject was the law.

'Are you and Michael –' James was interrupted by the arrival of the ward staff nurse at Michael's bedside. He looked relieved. 'Better leave you to it,' he said. 'I'll pop in another day.' And he was off, leaving the flowers on the bed, without having said a word to his ailing friend.

The nurse cleared her throat. 'Perhaps we could step outside for a moment,' she said in a low voice.

They stood in the corridor. Staff Nurse Weeks had her arms crossed over her uniform. She was dark-haired, neat and businesslike, her friendliness slightly forced as if she considered this part of her job a chore.

'It's early days, Mrs Claire, but I wanted to touch base with you about Michael's rehabilitation.' When Romy, caught off guard, did not instantly reply, she went on in her clipped voice, 'As I'm sure you're aware, there's a lot to organize. Obviously Michael's not ready to go home quite yet. But we try not to keep stroke patients in hospital any longer than necessary. We find they do much better in familiar surroundings, as long as they have proper support.'

Romy felt a shaft of panic. 'I'm not really the one responsible for that,' she said. 'Michael and I aren't together. We haven't been for a while.'

She seemed taken aback. 'Oh. No one mentioned this to me.' She paused. 'So will your son be responsible for Michael when he goes home? Because we need to check there's someone arranging his care package for when the time comes. Such as taking charge of his finances while he's incapacitated. I'm sure the family has thought of this, but he'll need his accounts monitoring, his bank informed and his bills paid until he can do it himself. Plus someone will have to oversee the various aids and equipment he'll need in his current situation and make sure there's always someone present – he can't be left alone. Is this something –'

'He has a partner,' Romy interrupted, although she knew as she said it that this might very well not be the case any more. But she was uneasy about steaming in and potentially treading on Anezka's toes. *Can she be totally sure about splitting up when Michael is too incapacitated to have a proper conversation about the row they had?* 'I think you should talk to her,' she added.

Weeks nodded. 'Is she coming in today?'

'She might be,' Romy replied uncertainly. Because Anezka hadn't visited in the last couple of days, only kept in touch with Leo on the mobile. But even if she did come in, Romy was having trouble imagining Anezka picking out which Zimmer frame would be most suitable for

Michael. As she stood watching the retreating figure of the staff nurse, she suddenly felt frighteningly alone, like a drowning person. The finger of responsibility seemed to be pointing directly, inexorably, at her.

15

It had been a tearful reunion with Rex on Thursday, the three of them hugging each other in mute bewilderment when he arrived, dazed from his twenty-four hours of travel. But being there to welcome her son in the place the boys still thought of as home felt strange without Michael, especially as now she considered the Sussex cottage her home. As a family they seemed disoriented, not sure what to do with themselves.

Later that day Rex and Leo took over from her at Michael's bedside. She needed to go to the flat to collect clean pyjamas and his shaving soap. 'Meet me at five thirty across the road?' she asked her sons. She needed to talk urgently to them – in the wake of the staff nurse's bombshell – and do it away from their father's hearing. At least they could get a decent cup of tea and a piece of cake in the café opposite the hospital.

Now her sons gazed at her expectantly from the other side of the rough wooden table. She had a sudden flashback to their youth, their faces barely changed, in her eyes, since they were small boys, and felt an overwhelming love for them both.

'OK, so Staff Nurse Weeks collared me earlier. She's already talking about the plan for when your dad gets out,' she said.

Rex glanced sideways at his brother. His hazel eyes – always with a slightly dreamy, faraway look – were underscored with dark circles from the jetlag. It was so lovely to see him again, although he seemed different, even in the six months he'd been gone, almost foreign with his surfer-style clothes, his tan and longer, salt-bleached waves. All of which were so out of place in the grey city light. She wondered how long he would stay: her heart was already steeling itself at the thought he would soon be gone again.

'Anezka has said she can't be involved,' Leo stated flatly.

Frowning, Romy asked, 'Already?'

Leo shrugged. 'We left her with Dad earlier because Rex needed a smoke. Then we grabbed a coffee so she could have some time alone with him. But on our way back in, she came flying out of the revolving doors, almost in tears. Apparently one of the nurses had tried to talk to her about Dad's rehab and she freaked, told them she had nothing to do with it. Said she was just a friend.' Leo raised his eyebrows.

'So . . .' Romy let out a long sigh. 'So she's saying it's really over with your dad?'

Rex spoke up. 'Certainly from her point of view, I reckon. Although she waves her arms about and shrieks so much, I can't make out what she's on about half the time. She kept saying, "I love him, I love him", but then she says something about Dad not wanting her any more.'

'And when I asked her if she was going to stop visiting,' Leo took up the story, 'I thought she was going to lynch me. She grabbed me by the arms and shook me. "*Of course I come,* Leo. Who do you think I am? I will not leave your father when he is like this. I told you, I *love him.*"' Leo did a terrible imitation of Anezka's accent, which might have made Romy laugh at any other time.

The three were silent. Then Leo said, 'Mum, what are we going to do? Anezka is obviously a lost cause.' He shook his head slowly. 'I mean, I guess I can take a bit of time off work, if they'll let me. But I'm not exactly sure . . . I hope I'm up to it. And Rex won't be any help. He has to get back to start his new job next week.'

Romy gave her youngest a sharp look. *Next week?* Her heart lurched. 'What new job? You didn't tell me.'

Rex sheepishly lowered his eyes and picked at the crumbs on the paper case that had held his chocolate muffin. 'I only just heard. It's not barista work this time. This is a proper global outfit. It's my dream job, Mum. If it works out, it means I'm set for life. I can travel all over the world.' There was a lengthy pause. 'But obviously I don't have to take the job. I wouldn't want to land Leo in it.' He gave a resigned sigh. 'I'll stay if you need me, of course . . . It's just . . .'

'Coding?' she asked. She'd hoped he would get bored with Australia and come home after a few months. But now he'd probably settle somewhere thousands of miles away from her, meet some girl and live a life she would only know about on Facebook.

'Yeah. Uncle Blake had a contact. They seem to think I'm pretty good.' He gave a shy grin.

'That's great.' Romy managed a smile in return. 'I'm pleased you'll be –'

'It's great for Rex, obviously,' Leo interrupted. 'But where does it leave Dad? I've got a job too, which I certainly don't want to lose.'

In the silence that followed, Romy felt that menacing finger pointing at her again. She winced, her mind whirring. Why didn't Michael have a convenient relative with nothing else to do? Some doting Cousin Mary who could ride in and take control. But Michael wasn't really in touch with his extended family. He spoke to his three brothers only when they called him – which wasn't often – and rarely travelled north to visit. He'd felt he had nothing in common with them since leaving home as a teenager.

When she didn't reply at once, she saw the boys give each other a look. *This is something they've already discussed*, she thought.

'Dad can afford nurses, can't he?' Leo asked tentatively.

Romy nodded. 'He's got insurance.'

Another glance between her sons, but neither spoke.

'Mum . . .' Leo looked her straight in the eye and took a long breath. 'If I see to Dad when he gets out, will you help me . . .? Just for a week or two, while I settle him, find good people to come in,' he added quickly, his look beseeching.

Rex took hold of her hand. 'I know you and Dad aren't together, Mum, but I can't easily stay and it's a lot for Leo to manage on his own.'

They both fell silent.

'Once we've got carers settled in and he's used to them, he'll be fine, won't he?' Leo asked, when Romy still couldn't find words to reply. 'I can drop in all the time to make sure things are going OK. And, anyway, it shouldn't be too long, the nurse said yesterday, before he can get round on his frame by himself.'

The image of Michael, staggering around the flat on a frame, dishevelled, dragging his leg, one arm completely useless, made Romy want to cry.

'I don't know which nurse you spoke to,' she finally said, 'but he's going to need a lot of help for quite a while, Leo. He won't be able to get to the loo, even wipe his bottom, take his medication, lift a plate – not for weeks.'

Both her sons looked embarrassed.

'Poor Dad,' Rex said.

'Yeah,' Leo agreed. 'But the carers can do all that, Mum. And he'll get physio . . .'

Romy didn't reply. They had absolutely no idea. She'd seen her friend Angie's husband, Barry, after his stroke. Angie had done every single thing for the man for months. Although she'd probably done too much, and made Barry even lazier than he already was. *Michael isn't lazy*, she thought. *He'll be really motivated to get better.*

Now it was Leo's turn to reach across the table and take her hand, his eyes filling with tears. 'Please, Mum. I know it's not fair to ask you, but will you help?' He took his hand from hers to brush away his tears. 'I'll do it all, I promise. I just need some moral support.'

Romy knew she didn't have a choice. 'I'm going home this evening,' she said, her tone painfully reluctant. 'I need to get clothes and stuff.' She took a slow breath, trying to quell the roiling in her gut. 'But I'll be back Sunday night . . . And, yes, of course I'll help you, Leo.'

As she said goodbye to her grateful sons and walked away from the café, she thought of the email she'd received earlier in the week, the request from the Wildlife Trust to come in and meet them. She thought of Finch. The prospect of going backwards – even for a short period – to tend a post-stroke Michael made her feel like throwing plates at the wall.

16

'I know it's late, but can I come over?' Romy's voice had sounded strained when she'd called earlier.

Finch was delighted. In the days since he'd dropped her off at the hospital, he'd become increasingly anxious. He'd begun to feel that the night they'd spent together would prove a grand finale to their relationship, not the opening ceremony, as he'd hoped.

She had started to cry as soon as she was through the door. He'd taken her in his arms and just held her, listening to her muffled, disjointed fears about helping out with Michael's rehabilitation.

'Glass of wine?' he asked later, when she was calmer and had flopped down tiredly on the sofa.

She nodded. 'Make it a large one.'

He came back with two glasses of red and a big bowl of crisps. Romy's eyes lit up and she helped herself to a handful.

'You won't be needed for too long, I imagine,' Finch said, settling beside her.

She met his eyes, her expression blank and exhausted. 'You must think I'm awful, being so reluctant. It's not that I don't want to make sure Michael's OK. And of course I'll be there for Leo. It's just . . . recently I've felt so excited about things . . .' She looked away. 'And this feels like . . .' She didn't finish, but her expression said it all.

'You don't think Leo could cope?'

Romy shrugged. 'I'm sure he could. He's nearly thirty, not a kid – although I still think of him as one. I'm sure people his age have to deal with much worse than this, all the time. But if I can help . . .'

Finch, who'd had to do just that when he was not even twenty and his mother had fallen seriously ill with congestive heart failure, did not comment. He didn't want Romy to think he was criticizing her sons because he wasn't. He wouldn't wish what he'd had to go through on anyone.

Romy went on, 'But both the boys are at the beginning of their careers. They can't easily take six months out to look after their father.' She gave an apologetic smile. 'I don't think I'm being too soft on them.'

Finch nodded. He understood.

'The thing that really worries me is that Leo's estimate of two weeks is way off. It could take much longer to settle things.'

'You don't know that. See how it goes,' Finch said, trying to be encouraging. But he felt he was swimming against the tide. Romy was too wound up to take in what he was saying.

'Michael doesn't trust people like normal people do,' Romy was saying. 'He's never been dependent on anyone.' She took a large gulp of wine. 'I've got to find a carer tough enough to withstand his will, but kind enough to look after him properly.'

Finch nodded, and decided that, much as he would love to save Romy from her fate, he knew, as clearly as he knew his own name, that she would end up managing her ex's rehab.

'Don't look at me like that,' she said, her face a picture of despair. 'I know what you're thinking.'

'Maybe you shouldn't fight it, Romy. From what you've said, you can't walk away – neither Michael nor Leo could manage if you did.' He paused. 'If we're being practical, perhaps you could set a time limit for yourself. Say, a month. So you move back into the flat and hire trust-worthy help, settle Michael with all the aids he needs to walk and feed and shower, get him started with physio, sort out his medication . . .'

Romy was staring at him, a small smile playing around her mouth. 'Impressive. Would you like to take over?'

Finch pulled a face, remembering the hassle of per-suading his fierce mother to give him power-of-attorney, having fights with her grouchy GP, getting his head round her daily medication, dealing with her clucking – albeit well-meaning – friends, who kept offering conflicting advice. He hadn't had a clue what he was doing but it had worked out all right in the end. And he'd managed to make the last months of his mother's life as comfortable as was possible, and worry-free.

He sipped some wine. 'Better to organize it like a cam-paign than fight it and end up feeling guilty.' He wondered, as he spoke, what on earth he was doing persuading the woman he thought he was falling for to spend such extended time with her ex. The newness of their relation-ship made it feel very fragile.

Romy stretched and yawned. 'God, I'm so tired,' she said.

'Shall I drive you home? Or you could stay here . . . No pressure,' he added, not wanting her to think he was expecting sex, or taking advantage of her when she was so upset.

She seemed to be considering his offers. Then she met his gaze. 'Would you mind if I stayed? Don't think I've even got the energy to make it home.'

Romy fell asleep as soon as her head touched the pillow. A person sleeping is so vulnerable that Finch almost felt guilty as he watched her. He had watched Nell sleeping when she was very ill, always convinced she wouldn't wake again. But this was different. It was as if he were being given special privileges in seeing her long lashes fluttering on her cheeks, her hair falling over her eyes, her lips twitching slightly – as if she was talking to someone in her dreams.

When she woke in the night, she cried out, and Finch took her in his arms. She was trembling. He stroked her head, kissed her hair, told her it would be all right – as if she were a child. And she fell asleep again almost immediately. But he did not. He was struggling with a childish jealousy. Yes, Romy had clearly been keen to see him last night. And it was understandable that her thoughts would be consumed with Michael at a time like this. But he was filled with foreboding. *Is she really doing this solely to protect her son?*

17

'Will you go back first thing?' Finch asked, as they sat at his kitchen table on Sunday night, dazed and pleasantly tired from an afternoon on the beach. He had made a cheese and parsley omelette, tossed some leaves in dressing and toasted chunks of stale baguette. Setting the plates on the table, he poured them some wine.

Romy nodded. She had thought she was hungry, but the food seemed to stick in her throat. She was dreading going back to the flat. It wasn't her home now, but it was obviously so familiar – especially with Rex in residence – that being there seemed to wipe out the months since she had left, negate the gains she had made without Michael in her life. Her gaze wandered round the room and settled on one of the many photos of Finch's pretty, smiling wife that seemed to surround them, reminding her that she was not the only one with a past that was, perhaps, hard to leave behind. 'Tell me about Nell,' she said, anxious to divert her painfully circular thoughts. 'What was she like?'

For a moment, Finch looked as if he might refuse. But then she saw his expression lighten. 'I don't know where to start. I've spent so much time since she died idealizing her that I've sort of lost the balance of who she really was.'

Romy had asked herself many times in the past week how she would feel if Michael died. She knew one thing:

she didn't want to remember him under the pervasive shadow of that letter. 'I'm not sure what's wrong with idealizing someone you love, especially when they can't disappoint you any more,' she said.

She noticed Finch's fleeting frown and realized she had sounded bitter. 'That didn't come out quite right.' She let out a long sigh. 'Michael and I are not like you and Nell, as I'm sure you've worked out.'

'But you loved him.'

Tears pricked behind her eyes. 'Of course I loved him.'

Neither spoke for a while.

Then Romy said, 'Your past is so pure and uncomplicated, however painful it was losing Nell.'

Finch's mouth tightened. 'What is it about your marriage that makes you so angry?' he asked, his brown eyes perplexed.

Romy flinched. 'I'm not angry,' she said, the lie making her flush.

Finch gave a small shrug and reached across the table, laying his hand over hers. Romy had to bite her lip hard to stop herself crying from frustration. She was not only upset about what had happened historically between her and Michael. She was also upset with his current – albeit unwitting – insinuation into her relationship with Finch. She'd been enjoying the feeling recently that this was *her* time to make decisions about how she spent her days, and with whom. Perhaps be a bit selfish. But the family she had thought was on the way to independence was once more calling . . .

*

Rex and Leo were in the kitchen when Romy returned to the flat on Monday morning. Rex was frying eggs, waving a spatula at Leo as he loudly made some point.

Their backs were to the door and they didn't hear their mother come in. For a moment she just stood and watched them, seeing them, almost for the first time, as grown men. Her mind went back to tea after school at the same kitchen table. She had always insisted on toast and jam, biscuits and fruit while they debriefed about their school day. That was the moment – fresh from the coalface – when she'd heard amusing vignettes of teachers, learnt about friendship conflicts, success or failure in tests and on the sports field before they disappeared into their bedrooms and became buried in their homework. She'd loved that time – the cosy, predictable routine, the knowledge she built up about her boys' lives. Knowledge she'd always felt sad that Michael didn't share.

'Hey, Mum.' Leo sprang up and came to give her a hug.

'Want a fried egg?' Rex asked, lifting the pan from the hob before coming to kiss her.

She shook her head, then made herself a cup of coffee and joined them at the table.

'Have a nice weekend?' Rex asked, mouth full of toast. Romy thought he looked a bit rough, his tan beginning to fade. *Suffering from too much alcohol and not enough sleep*, she decided, although she couldn't bring herself to disapprove. She could hardly talk.

'Lovely,' she said, unable to hide her pleasure. She quickly bent her head to take a sip from her cup. When she looked up, she saw Leo, his eyes quietly appraising. Rex was too busy with his breakfast to notice.

'How's Dad?'

'Much the same,' Rex said.

'Did you speak to the doctors?'

'No one's around at weekends. There's a meeting about him this morning, according to Super Nurse, with the stroke-management team. We'll find out more when we go in. But . . .' he glanced at Leo '. . . from what I understand, they seem to be saying he can be discharged soon.'

Romy's stomach flipped. She stared at her sons. 'I know there's been a lot of discussion about his rehab, but surely he's not ready to come home yet.' Although, through her panic, she vaguely remembered someone telling her that stroke patients did better at home.

Rex sighed. 'Honestly? You wouldn't think so to look at him, Mum,' he said. 'But they say there isn't anything wrong with him now – meaning he's not critically ill, I suppose.'

Nobody spoke.

'They basically told us that as soon as we've organized what Staff Nurse Weeks calls his "care package", he can be out – even as early as the end of the week.' Leo gave an anxious grimace.

'*This* week?' Romy shook her head. She couldn't think, couldn't focus, couldn't decide what she should worry about first. Because even while understanding perfectly well that Michael was coming home, being responsible for the care of such a damaged person still seemed a bit unreal, something that would happen eventually but not yet, not so soon. It reminded her of the terror of bringing Leo home, two days after he was born. She'd been convinced that without the nurses' reassuring support she would do something dreadful and the vulnerable little bundle in her arms would suffer. Michael wasn't a baby, obviously, but he was perhaps equally vulnerable.

'They're sending someone round to assess the flat, tell us what equipment we need,' Leo said. 'Like grab rails for the shower and a seat, so he can sit when he's washing.'

'And Anezka?'

Leo shrugged. 'I doubt she'll stick around once he's home.'

'So sad for your father,' Romy said.

For a moment they didn't speak. Rex messed with some spilt coffee and drew it across the table in a figure of eight. Romy wanted to slap his hand away, as she would have done when he was a child, but she stopped herself.

'Well, boys,' she said, straightening her shoulders and summoning every ounce of strength in her body, 'looks like it's down to us. So we'd better get on with it.' Finch's military master plan rang in her ears. She would do this. She would make it work for them all. And she would try not to think about all the things she was missing out on at home, try not to worry about how her defection would impact on her burgeoning relationship with Finch.

18

When Romy glanced at Bettina, she saw her friend shake her head slightly, her eyes narrowing with disapproval.

Romy didn't need her friend's help, though, when it came to Magda. The Hungarian woman, in her fifties, was charmless and tough. She would probably be very efficient – there was nothing she didn't know about strokes – but not necessarily kind.

When the woman had been dispatched, Romy flopped down next to Bettina and sighed.

'That's the fourth. They're all so . . .' She cast her mind back through the people she'd interviewed.

'Grim?' Bettina offered, pulling a face as she flicked her blonde fringe off her tanned face. She ran an upmarket bakery in Hastings with her Swiss husband, Jost, but she'd taken Thursday off to help choose a live-in carer for Michael.

'I'm trying to put myself in Michael's position, imagine myself in bed, feeling rough, and the door opens and in walks Magda.'

They started to giggle.

'It might motivate him to get out of bed really, really quickly.'

'Or send him straight back under the duvet.'

They fell into a subdued silence.

'Well, we've got Daniel next. I have high hopes for him,' Bettina said, 'even if I am biased.' Daniel, twenty-five, was the son of a friend of Jost. He'd just finished his master's in mental health and wanted a job in London for a while before going back to Switzerland. 'And he might be better with a man looking after him – a guy would be stronger, for a start, lugging Michael about. And it'll be less embarrassing for Michael.'

Romy nodded. She wasn't sure. 'He's a bit overqualified to be a carer.'

'He seems happy with the idea . . . and if you think he's suitable, you wouldn't need to stick around too long.'

Romy had told Bettina how cornered she felt by the situation. But since knowing the date for Michael's discharge – the following Monday – she had thrown all her energies into the task in hand. Finch was right: it made her feel calmer.

The final brick had fallen out of the wall of her resistance the other day, when she'd been sitting beside Michael in the blue hospital chair while he slept. She had been reading, when suddenly she'd felt his eyes on her.

For a moment he stared at her, as if he were trying to focus. Then he said, 'I'm finished, Romy,' as he unsuccessfully bit back the tears. With his good arm he had indicated his body beneath the sheet. 'Have you ever seen a one-armed, one-legged silk who can't remember the day of the week?'

When Romy didn't immediately reply, shocked he should see himself in such terms, Michael had given her one of his knowing smiles and turned away.

She quickly pulled herself together. 'Don't say that, Michael. You're improving every day, even if you can't see it.' She heard the false brightness in her tone, and finished more gently, 'It'll just take time.'

Michael nodded wearily. He'd heard it all before. Then he reached for her hand and clung to it, his eyes anguished as he met her gaze and a torrent of words came spilling out in his slow, compromised speech. 'I'm so frightened, Romy. For the first time in my life . . . I can't manage even the simplest thing. I don't know what I'm going to do. I don't know what the hell's going to happen to me.' He swallowed with effort, furiously rubbing the tears from his face.

Romy had found her heart breaking. Since Michael's stroke, all she had been able to think about was what this meant to *her*, what *she* would have to do and how much she didn't want to do it. But now she fully focused on Michael's predicament. How truly terrifying it must feel – for anybody, let alone a man as proud and independent as Michael – to be so reduced, so helpless.

'I'm going to help you, Michael,' she heard herself saying, as if the words came out of someone else's mouth. 'I'll stay with you for a while, and we'll get people in, organize things. Leo will be around too. You'll be managing without us in no time.' It sounded so simple as she said it. And so untrue.

Michael blinked, a slow frown forming on his forehead. 'You're going to be there?' he asked, as if he hadn't heard right.

She nodded.

'You'd do that for me?' he said, his face crumpling again.

Romy felt her own eyes pricking. This was a man she had loved so much, once. Really worshipped. *Part of me still does*, she admitted silently, reminding herself that the notion of leaving her marriage had never even crossed her mind – despite the common marital grouses – until that envelope had dropped through the letter box.

She patted his hand as it rested on the arm of her chair. 'Of course I will. Just concentrate on getting better, Michael. Things will seem much brighter when you're in your own bed again.'

Am I so selfish, she asked herself, as she left the ward to get a cup of tea, *that I can't give him a few weeks of my life in his hour of need?* What was she scared of? That she would never leave again? *My life will still be there, in Sussex, when Michael no longer needs me*, she told herself firmly.

The doorbell rang, startling both women, and they jumped up.

Daniel was of medium height and willow-slim, his dark-blond hair cut very short, his fair skin glowing with health. He had a pleasant face, the glance from his light blue eyes shy at first. He looked incredibly young to Romy – even younger than Rex, whom she would have hesitated to leave in sole charge of any sick person. *Will he really be able to cope with a cantankerous stroke patient 24/7?* she wondered, as she made more coffee and left Bettina chatting to Daniel.

But the boy seemed very confident as Romy filled him in on Michael's condition and what would be required of him – not that she really had a clue what to expect when her husband came home.

She hired Daniel on the spot, and she and Bettina went out for lunch round the corner to celebrate. He would start on Monday, Michael's first day home, the only catch being that he didn't want to move in for another two weeks, when Andreas, his boyfriend, went back to Denmark and they gave up their rented flat. But he agreed to work eight to eight, five days a week until then. Which meant Romy would have to be there during the night at first, and fill in at weekends – or get someone else, like Leo, to do it so she could go home, see Finch – but she was so grateful that she had found someone of his calibre that she didn't quibble.

When she got back to the flat to wait for the man who was going to install the grab rail in the shower, she called Finch. His phone went to voicemail and she wondered what he was doing. *Probably running*, she thought, with a smile, imagining his look of intense concentration, the flush on his cheeks as he splashed around the harbour road and wishing she could be there with him.

'I hope to be down tomorrow or Saturday,' she said in her message, not sure if she could expect Finch to drop everything for her flying visit. But as she sat on the edge of Michael's bed, remembering she had to get a super king-size waterproof mattress cover before Monday, her phone rang.

'Hi,' she said, so happy to hear his voice.

'I'm in town tomorrow night,' Finch said. 'Got a dinner in the City. So, we could meet up on Saturday morning. Or you could brave another chilly night in the sex-palace?'

Romy laughed. She very much wanted to see him. And she longed to get away from the flat. It felt as if the place were on tenterhooks, waiting for Michael's return in strained silence. 'Won't you be late back from your dinner?'

'They usually finish promptly at ten thirty – the old buffers have to get back to the shires. I could be there by eleven, but that's probably too late for you.'

'Eleven's fine,' she said quickly, having the uneasy sense that she should grab all the moments she could with Finch before she became trapped in the relentless cycle of Michael's care.

'Are you all going to be OK without me, Mum?' Rex had his backpack ready by the front door. He was just about to leave for Heathrow.

Romy gave a wry smile. It had been so strange, seeing him this time. Both of them had been on edge, neither committing to bonding with each other, as they would have done on a planned trip home. Michael had taken up all of their energy. Now, torn between disappointment at her son's only fleeting visit – she wanted to blurt out, 'Like you care!' – and sadness that it would be months before she saw him again, she felt bereft. Dragging him into her arms, she said, 'I hope the new job goes well, sweetheart. Let me know.'

Rex hugged her close. 'I'm really sorry I'm leaving you in the lurch.' He pulled away and looked intently into her face. 'You do understand, don't you? Leo's livid with me.'

'He'll get over it,' she said, hoping she was right. She didn't want this wretched situation, which was nobody's fault, to come between her sons. But recently she'd sensed

Leo had grown up, while Rex remained stubbornly teen-aged, clinging to a student-like existence, where he wandered from job to job – even though he claimed this one was different – and only worked because he had to.

'You've got Daniel, and I'm sure Dad'll come on in leaps and bounds once he gets out of that dreary ward,' Rex went on, his guilty conscience tidying things up neatly so he didn't have to worry. 'He's a tough old bastard, don't forget.'

'Let's hope so,' Romy said, kissing his cheek, her lips remembering the countless times they had performed the same act of love since the day he was born, her heart wanting to hold her boy tightly in her arms and prevent him from leaving her for the other side of the world.

'Whoa,' Romy whispered, as Finch entered the lobby. He looked so handsome, like James Bond in his dinner jacket and black tie. The taxi had dropped her only five minutes before and she felt like someone on a late-night illicit assignation, aware of the watchful eyes of the two staff members behind the reception desk. The thought made her smile and her body buzz with anticipation. There seemed something end-of-the-world-ish about tonight.

'What's so funny?' he asked, as he kissed her cheek, his breath wafting brandy.

'They probably think I'm a lady of the night, summoned on some dodgy app while your wife snores innocently in your Hampshire vicarage,' she whispered.

Finch grinned and took her arm. 'If so, you're a very classy one.'

The room was warm, the place much more welcoming than Romy remembered from that rainy April night. She sat on the bed and watched Finch take off his jacket and hang it up, stuff his black tie and cufflinks into a pocket.

'Fun dinner?'

'It was OK, predictable. The lady next to me was charming, but so deaf I don't think she heard a single word I said.'

Finch came and stood in front of her, his shirt cuffs dangling loose, and reached forward, stroking his fingers down her cheek. 'I'm so glad you're here, Romy . . . I know you're up against it at the moment.' He paused, and she sensed he wanted to say something more. But he just continued to gaze down at her, his expression unreadable.

Romy did not want to think about what she was 'up against'. She just wanted to be normal, to make love to this attractive man who had so quickly managed to invade her heart. She said nothing, hoping he wouldn't mention Michael's name, as she began to pull him down towards her, suddenly desperate to hold him in her arms. But Finch resisted and turned away from her embrace, sitting down beside her in silence, his hands clasped in his lap.

'How's the invalid?' he asked.

Romy frowned. Finch had asked after Michael many times since his stroke. But tonight there seemed a faintly sardonic edge to his enquiry. Their relationship was still so new – although it seemed much older than it was – but she had no idea what he really felt about the situation. 'You don't mind, do you? Me moving back to help Michael out?'

Finch was slow to answer. 'Should I?'

She shook her head, turning to him and sliding her hand through the gap where his shirt lay partly unbuttoned, her fingertips grazing his smooth skin. 'There'd be no need,' she said. 'I'm doing this for Leo as much as for Michael. And it's just a few weeks.'

Finch nodded and put his arm around her shoulders. But he still seemed preoccupied, not completely present as he had on previous occasions. Michael seemed to be hovering over them both, like a sad ghost. It was the first time Romy had been aware of Finch's unease about the situation. But she felt powerless to brush it away and, as they sat there in silence, she was aware of a small frisson of anxiety building in her own gut.

19

'I may not be able to move my left side very well,' Michael complained to Romy and the staff nurse, while they waited for the hospital transport, 'but I can still comprehend that you're talking about me as if I'm a halfwit . . . or not here at all.'

Romy was embarrassed. They *were* talking about him as if he wasn't there.

'I fully intend you to hear everything, Michael,' Staff Nurse Weeks said, giving him a glacial smile before turning back to her. 'It's tempting for family members to pander to stroke patients when they first get them home. But you won't be doing him any favours, Romy. Michael will just get lazy, won't you?' She shot him a severe look. 'And it'll take him much, much longer to recover.' She paused. 'The physios will be in every day. They'll tell you what he is and isn't capable of.'

'I can bloody well tell her that, myself,' Michael growled weakly.

The two ambulance care assistants carried the wheelchair, with Michael in it, up the curved staircase. The block had a lift, but it did not stop at the landing where his flat was situated. *Getting him out again is going to be a nightmare*, thought Romy, glancing back at the additional flight of steps outside the main front door, as if seeing them for the first time, despite having walked up and down them for years.

Leo opened the door and she could see the worry writ large across her son's face as he glanced at his father in the wheelchair. Daniel stood silently behind Leo, and she took comfort from the Swiss boy's calm presence. *He will know how to handle this*, she thought, as one of the ambulance assistants pressed the brake on the wheelchair with her foot and waved a cheery goodbye.

'This is Daniel.' Romy introduced the Swiss boy to Michael. 'He's going to be helping out till you're back on your feet.'

Michael seemed dazed. He nodded tiredly but made no move to shake Daniel's proffered hand. 'I need to lie down,' he said, addressing Romy.

This is worse than I thought. Romy stood looking down at the figure on the bed, his eyes closed, head resting on the linen pillowcase. Michael looked to be at death's door, his skin sweaty and tinged with blue, his breathing laboured – she worried he wouldn't even last the day. *Can he really recover from this?* she asked herself, as the three of them crept quietly away.

Romy made Leo and Daniel coffee. As they sat at the kitchen table, she saw Leo glancing at his phone and frowning as he began to type something with impressive speed.

She felt sympathy for him. 'Work?'

Her son nodded. 'Thirteen emails already. *Fuck*,' he muttered, under his breath, then added, 'I . . . sort of told them I'd be in later.'

'Today? You're going in today?'

Leo squirmed. 'I really should, Mum. Dickeson is taking a dim view of me having any more time off.'

Although Romy understood, she felt a spurt of irritation at his boss and at Leo – unfair, she knew – for being so compliant. Daniel, perhaps sensing the tension, got up and rinsed his cup, then left the room, muttering about checking on Michael.

'Shall I make a sandwich for you to take with you?' she said to Leo, her voice carefully controlled as she opened the fridge and stared at the contents. 'I've got some ham – the one you like – and cheese. There's salad . . .'

Leo looked panicky, running his fingers nervously through his short curls. 'I'm OK, thanks, Mum,' he said. 'In fact I should get going – if you think you can manage, that is. There's a really important meeting this afternoon.' He looked at her guiltily. 'But if you need me, of course I'll stay . . .'

Her son knew she would let him go. She'd always managed, as far as Leo was concerned. 'Go on, then,' she said, then added, 'But can you come back over the weekend? Daniel isn't working Saturdays or Sundays, as you know, until Andreas leaves and he moves in full time, when we can arrange his days off to suit us all. And I don't want to be on my own with your dad until he's stronger. I'm not sure if I could hold him if he topples.'

'Of course, Mum,' he replied distractedly, as he got up from the table. She could tell he was itching to be off and would probably have agreed to anything in that moment.

'Lucky old Rex, eh?' Leo said, as he gave her a quick kiss on her cheek. 'Bet he's on his surfboard right now, skimming through those waves on Bondi, soaking up the rays, not a care in the world.'

Romy laughed. 'Even surfing seems preferable?' She knew Leo was not a fan of his brother's passion, admitting at an early age, one summer holiday, that he was frightened of the comparatively tame waves at Newquay. A fear Romy respected and thought immensely sensible, although Michael had seen it as a sign of weakness. 'I know you're under pressure, sweetheart, but we need to pull together at the moment. I can't do this without you.'

'I know, I know. And I'll be here, Mum. Promise.' He was obviously trying to sound reassuring, although she heard only reluctance – but she loved him for making the effort.

'Great,' she said, letting out a small sigh. 'Thank you.'

Romy stood by the window, listening to him thumping down the carpeted stairs, the slam of the outside door and the faint sound of his shoes as he hurried along the covered walkway of glass and wrought iron that led to the pavement. Then she watched his retreating figure disappearing down the street, her mouth dry, her head aching from the morning's tension.

She heard Daniel approaching from the other end of the L-shaped flat and fled to the loo, where she leant against the locked door, hand towel pressed to her mouth, trying to stifle an overwhelming urge to scream. All she wanted to do in that moment was to sling on her trainers and take off round the harbour, gulping in great draughts of spring sunshine – run and run until her brain was empty of thought and every muscle in her body begged for mercy.

*

Romy slept in the room next to Michael in case he needed her. That first night back, she was dragged awake by the frantic ringing of the small brass hand-bell — her grandmother's — she'd placed on his bedside table. She didn't know what was happening, or where she was, and it took her a few minutes to orient herself before she shot out of bed and pulled on her dressing gown.

When she turned the light on, Michael was half out of bed, slumped on his back on the mattress, his weak leg dangling helplessly over the side. When he saw her he waved his good arm urgently at her.

'Need to pee,' he gasped.

The urine bottle was lying on the bed, where Daniel had left it, within easy reach of Michael's right hand. But he obviously hadn't seen it in the dark, or remembered it was there.

Romy hurried over and pulled him up against the pillows. She lifted his leg back onto the mattress and handed him the bottle, helping him position it so he could pee. But she saw that his pyjama bottoms were already wet, the sheet too.

Michael let out a relieved groan when he'd finished, and handed the bottle to Romy.

'That was close.'

'Got to get you out for a moment,' she said, not wanting to humiliate her husband by explaining why. But he didn't query her as she hauled him upright and swung him precariously round to sit in the armchair next to the bed she had brought through from Leo's room. It was some old thing she'd picked up from a junk shop, decades ago — shades of her father's penchant for anything secondhand – and the rusty-orange Dralon cover was stained in places, but the foam cushion and high back were perfect for Michael to sit in for short periods.

He smiled up at her. 'Thank you.' Then his face clouded. 'I'm cold, really cold.'

'I'll turn the heating up,' Romy promised.

After she'd settled him back in bed with clean pyjamas and a fresh sheet, Michael grabbed her hand.

'Sit with me for a while,' he begged.

She hesitated, then sat on the orange chair, but didn't know what to say.

Michael was looking at her. 'Does Anezka know I'm home? I don't want her going all the way over to the hospital . . .'

'Leo told her,' Romy said.

Michael nodded. 'Did she say she'd come?'

'I don't know. But you can have your mobile tomorrow and call her yourself.' She remembered the nurses' advice that they shouldn't mollycoddle Michael. He was right-handed, thank goodness, and he could surely work a phone now. She hoped Anezka would answer, for a change, and tell Michael the truth, dispel, once and for all, the notion he clung to that she still cared.

He frowned but said nothing as his eyes closed. Romy held her breath, hoping he would fall asleep. It was chilly, sitting there in her thin dressing gown. Her feet were freezing and she was dying to get back to bed. But as she waited, watching her husband's face, she realized she felt almost wary of the figure lying there. She had not watched Michael asleep in this bed for a long time. Not since he'd decided to move into the spare room in order – she was certain – to avoid seeing the words of the letter printed in her eyes. Now, as she sat on in the semi-darkness, her thoughts started to take an involuntary trawl through those months before she had left, eventually arriving at what had been – in her eyes – the last moment of their marriage.

It was a nervy, unresolved ending. Romy was so frightened of Michael's superior debating skills, his ability to twist what she said into something ridiculous, that she had made every effort to avoid any discussion about why she had gone, specifically asking him not to come down to the Sussex cottage in the weeks after she'd left.

But before nine one morning, as she walked slowly back from buying a croissant at the village deli – enjoying the warm spring sunshine, the peace and quiet around her – she'd seen his car parked in the lane. She had felt her heart squeeze and her breath trap somewhere high in her throat. *No.* She just wanted to run.

Michael was sitting calmly on the sofa. 'Thought I'd surprise you,' he said cheerily, as if there was nothing untoward between them, as if he'd arrived early for a planned weekend together. When he registered the lack of welcome on her face, however, the mask slipped. She saw hurt in his eyes as he pulled himself to his feet.

She didn't speak and, for a moment, neither did he. Then he'd said, 'I'm baffled, Romy. Thirty years of marriage and you just walk away without a single word? What am I supposed to do now?'

She had tried to control her thumping heart. His coiled energy was palpable, almost menacing in its restrained power.

'What you always do? Work,' she said eventually, hearing the crack in her voice.

He raised a sardonic eyebrow. 'And that's a bad thing?' He glanced around. 'It's paid for your lifestyle . . . this cottage.'

She didn't answer, stung by his jibe. She had been a dedicated mother, an accomplished hostess, a loyal wife and a valuable asset on his arm as he had climbed up through the network of the judiciary. The fact that none of these roles attracted an actual salary was not her fault.

She had done random office work in the early days, but the jobs she had been really interested in – and for which her environmental degree qualified her – involved working in the countryside, studying the natural world. But Michael had wanted to be in London and, as he frequently pointed out, he was the one earning the money to support the family.

Michael had covered his face with his hands – a familiar gesture when he was tense or upset. When he raised his eyes to hers, he said, 'Be honest, Romy. You owe me that at least.'

Romy had taken a deep breath. 'OK, well, we never talk. We don't eat together, or hang out. You work twenty-four/seven . . . The boys have gone.'

He nodded slowly, although she didn't know if this signified his agreement, or was just an acknowledgement that he'd heard her.

'That's the situation as it stands,' he said evenly, 'but I'm still waiting for the *reason* it became as bad as this between us.'

She felt like a rabbit in the headlights. The letter hung like a flashing neon sign between them. She wasn't going to be the one to mention it, but could he honestly pretend it wasn't a valid reason? *The* valid reason?

Michael turned away, his mouth set in a tight line. He looked strained, tired, Romy thought, as she watched and remained silent. The room seemed to freeze-frame as they faced each other, their bodies rigid with tension, their lives halted on the brink.

'OK,' he said, taking a deep breath, his energy apparently restored. 'I'll say it, if you won't.' He stood, legs apart, in a dominating stance, his arms crossed. *He only needs his wig and gown*, she thought. 'You believe the letter that woman sent you. You think I'm a sexual predator. You perhaps even worry that I've done it more than once. You no longer trust me.' He stopped, stared at her. 'Have I left anything out?'

Romy winced. The coldness in his voice was like a stab to her heart. *I want you not to be that man in the letter so badly it hurts, Michael*, she longed to say. *So why won't you at least try to make me believe?* But she knew, for whatever reason, that he would not.

What she actually said was, 'What am I supposed to think, when you won't talk about it?'

He lowered his eyes as she spoke and she couldn't see his expression. 'I shouldn't have to explain anything.' His eyes met hers again, his gaze level. 'You should be on my side, Romy, without question.'

Romy let out a tired sigh. *Stalemate.* She no longer had the energy or the desire to control herself, to protect him from the knowledge that there was, indeed, that tiny sliver of doubt in her mind.

'A woman writes to me to say you've molested her. You show no interest, not even much outrage. You don't even remember – *you say* – who she is. And apparently have no interest in finding out or even talking about it.' She paused. 'Look at it objectively, Michael. If this were one of your clients, wouldn't you find it all a little strange?'

His stare did not waver and he didn't move a muscle, as if he had suddenly been turned to stone. Romy felt a frisson of dread that he might be about to admit some level of guilt. But he gave a harsh laugh and his features returned to normal.

'Ha! If you're comparing me to my clients, Romy, then there's no reaction on earth I would find the slightest bit odd.'

'So you're not prepared to talk about it, even now?'

He leant forward, arms akimbo. 'Read my lips. *There is nothing to talk about.*' The last words were almost shouted across the coffee table, flecks of spit shooting from his mouth.

She wanted to bang his head against the wall, to knock some sense into him somehow, to dislodge the infuriating denial that had finally driven them apart. But she knew it was pointless.

'It's not just me who's been different since the letter,' she said. 'You completely shut me out. As if *I* was somehow to blame.'

Michael had paced up and down for a minute, then gone to lean against the mantelpiece, tapping the wood impatiently with his fingers. 'Only because you clearly thought I'd done it,' he said, his tone aggrieved. 'But how can I prove I didn't? I could say so till the cows come home, but you wouldn't necessarily believe me. So I wasn't going to waste my breath.' He sighed. 'And you wanted to talk about nothing else. Are you surprised I avoided your company?'

Why didn't you say this at the time? Romy had found she couldn't speak. Bubbling up inside her was a melting pot of emotions that made her feel almost nauseous. Doubt – of herself and him – fury at his intransigence, love for the man she thought she remembered, and finally bewilderment that they had got to a point at which the connection between them appeared so flimsy that his presence was like that of a stranger.

She'd just wanted him to leave, so she could go upstairs and cry out her frustrations in private. But before she could find her voice, her husband had slammed the door of the cottage, and she'd heard his car revving angrily in the lane outside.

Now, in Michael's darkened bedroom, she shivered at the memory. She had never been scared of him before that day, but his pent-up fury at being abandoned had felt explosive, almost dangerous in the small Sussex sitting room. As she shook out the patchwork counterpane and pulled it gently across the duvet, tucking his arms inside, she had to remind herself that the man before her was no longer capable of frightening anyone. He seemed like a child, like Leo and Rex when they were ill and fractious as boys, and she almost dropped a kiss on his forehead. But she stopped herself and walked away.

20

'That was a bit rubbish,' Jenny said, as Finch pushed open the heavy glass door of the cinema complex and they emerged into the warm May evening. 'Fun,' Jenny added, 'but rubbish.'

Finch laughed as they wandered across the paved courtyard towards the burger joint where they always ate after a movie.

'So, how's it going with Romy?' Jenny asked later, picking a long sweet-potato fry from the metal canister they were sharing and dipping it into a pot of mayonnaise.

Finch heard the same veiled snippiness from the supper with Cathy and Keith. He'd known Jenny might be jealous, from the flirtatious smiles she always gave him, the hand on his arm as she spoke, the way she took him about the village as if she owned him. But he had never been interested in her in that way. Never been interested in any woman since Nell, until Romy. As he took a bite of his burger, he knew he didn't want to talk to Jenny about her.

'You haven't answered my question,' Jenny was saying.

'It's going well.'

Jenny put her head on one side. 'Hmm . . .'

Finch sighed, realizing he wasn't going to be able to fob her off. 'There's been a bit of a glitch.'

Jenny waited for him to go on.

'Her ex had a stroke. Romy's gone back to look after him, just till the carer's settled in.'

'God, how awful. Poor man . . . poor Romy.' She thought for a moment then frowned. 'But why is *she* looking after him? I thought they were divorced.'

'Separated, not divorced.' He was reluctant to continue. 'It's complicated. There's nobody around, except one of her sons. I think she wanted to help him out . . . and I'm sure she feels sorry for Michael. Who wouldn't?'

Jenny gave a derisive snort. 'Ha! Depends on your ex. If Euan had a stroke I'd think it served him bloody well right. I wouldn't go within a hundred miles of him, except to gloat.'

The venom took Finch aback.

'She hasn't still got feelings for him, then?' Jenny was looking at him askance.

Finch felt a pinch to his heart. 'No,' he answered firmly. 'She's been very clear about that.'

'Aren't you just a teensy bit concerned?'

'About what?'

Jenny shrugged. 'Oh, I don't know . . . that she might go back to him, I suppose. Play happy families. But . . .' she put on a bright smile '. . . clearly you're not. Sorry. Euan's destroyed my faith in human nature. I think everyone is a two-faced liar these days.'

Finch, shaken, he had to admit, by his conversation with Jenny, rang Romy as soon as he was home. It was ten thirty, but he just wanted to hear her voice. She answered immediately.

'Finch!' She sounded so pleased, all his fears instantly evaporated. 'How are you? I'm missing you.'

'I'm missing you too,' he said happily.

'Hold on a minute . . .' He heard her footsteps, then her voice again, lowered now. 'Sorry, we were settling Michael down for the night.'

'How's he doing? Is he out of bed yet?'

'Oh, yes. Imogen, the physio, insists. She takes no nonsense from Michael,' Romy said.

'So he's walking?'

'Shuffling, more like. Only short distances – with a frame. He looks about a hundred, Finch, it's so sad.'

'It must be. Is Daniel working out?'

'Oh, my God, the boy's a miracle. When Michael grouches at him – which he does, a lot – he seems not to notice. And he's so strong, although you wouldn't think so to look at him. He's as narrow as a pipe-cleaner but he hauls Michael about like he's no heavier than a pound of butter. Which, I can assure you, he is. Lugging slippery branches across the common is a vicar's picnic by comparison.'

Conversation lapsed for a second. Their worlds were so different, these days, and Romy sounded so involved in hers. Then he said, 'Any chance you can get away soon?'

'Definitely.' She hesitated. 'Leo's coming over this weekend . . . tomorrow. I'll train him up so he can do next weekend. I could be home Saturday morning, stay till Sunday afternoon.'

Finch wanted to cheer. 'It's a date. You'll need a break by then.'

'I need one now,' she said, her voice suddenly heavy with tiredness. 'Michael often rings his bell in the middle of the night for something, then wants me to sit by his bed and chat. But he falls asleep like a baby, and I go back to bed and lie awake for the rest of the night.'

'What does he want to chat about?' Finch asked, his tone sharper than he intended. But Jenny's suspicious mind had proved contagious.

There was a long silence at the other end of the phone. Then Romy said, 'Oh, you know . . . just stuff from the past.'

Finch wondered at the delay in her reply. He was trying hard to put himself in Romy's position but, despite his obvious sympathy for her, was singularly failing to do so. He wondered why and realized it was because he couldn't get a proper handle on Romy's marriage or why it had broken up. Was he being played, as Jenny had almost suggested? And if so, why? *Why would she bother with me, if she wants to go back to her husband?* He took a deep breath, trying with all his might to fight off his jealousy.

'So his speech is improving then? That's a good sign, at least.' He cringed at his jokey response. But Romy didn't appear offended.

'Every cloud,' she said wearily. He waited for her to go on, but again it seemed a long time before she spoke. 'He's changed, Finch. He's not the man I was married to.'

Finch expected more exposition, but Romy added nothing, except to say, 'Anyway, see you in a week.'

They said goodbye and he clicked off, baffled. Was it good that Michael had changed? Or bad? And from whose perspective? He felt almost angry that he was

suddenly in this unsettling position, after years of plodding quietly along in Nell's reassuring shadow. Romy had
ignited his feelings again, brought him alive. But now she
seemed to be putting him on hold. He knew he should be
more grown-up, but it was painful, as if his insides were
twitching, vibrating, and there was nothing he could do
to calm himself . . . He just had to wait.

21

'God, Mum, it's stifling in here,' Leo muttered, fanning his face as he followed her down the corridor towards Michael's bedroom. Romy could tell he'd run from the Tube because he was out of breath and sweating when he arrived. But she was so glad to see him.

She glanced round with an apologetic smile. 'He's really feeling the cold – I can't crank the thermostat up high enough for him.' She stopped outside the bedroom door. 'I haven't got him up yet. I thought you could help me wash and dress him.'

Leo nodded and gave her a smile, but it was clear he was steeling himself and she sympathized. *Has he even seen his father naked?* she wondered, knowing how private Michael had always been.

Michael was sitting propped against the pillows, the duvet up around his chin, his eyes closed, as they entered the room.

'Hi, Dad,' Leo said, hovering by the bed, clearly not knowing if he should kiss his father – it wasn't really something the men in her family did. A brief cheek brush in the process of a hug was as physical as Michael got with his sons. In the end Leo just patted his father's arm.

Michael opened his eyes. 'Leo!' he said, a bemused smile on his face. 'What are you doing here?'

'We're going to give you a shower and get you up now,' Romy said brightly, knowing she sounded for all the world like Super Nurse on the stroke ward.

Much later, they were trying to pull Michael's boxers over his bum, but his skin was still damp from the shower and the cotton was wadding in a roll underneath him. Both Romy and Leo were red-faced and pouring sweat in the sweltering bedroom as they bent over the prostrate figure.

She caught Leo's eye and felt an uncontrollable giggle form in her chest, seeing a similarly suppressed grin on her son's hot face.

'Come on, Michael, make an effort and lift up,' she encouraged, resisting the mirth that was bubbling up despite her best efforts.

Michael looked up at her, then at Leo and, for a second, Romy worried he would think they were mocking him. But his face broke into a slow smile and she gave up trying to be serious, the laughter bursting out in an explosive snort.

'Sorry, Michael,' she spluttered. 'I know it's not funny but –' She couldn't speak for laughing.

'You should see . . . your faces,' Michael said, with his usual slowness, his dark eyes lighting up as he lay helplessly on his back, bare except for his boxers still bunched round his thighs. 'I shall sue for defamation. My reputation is in tatters.'

Romy was holding a hand to her mouth, her eyes filled with tears of laughter. Leo probably hadn't seen her laugh so much with his father in years – *which is ironic*, she thought.

'Let's worry about your knickers first and *then* your reputation.'

'Need both,' Michael retorted, with effort.

'Good to know you've still got some marbles skidding around in there,' she said.

'I had . . . more than my fair share . . . in the first place.' Michael's face contorted as he attempted to lift himself clear of the sheet.

'And clearly no damage to your arrogance, either,' Romy said, still grinning, then added, 'Phew!' as the boxers finally slid into place and the three of them did a collective high-five.

She realized she had almost enjoyed the process with them all pulling together for the first time. *Ever?* she asked herself, and decided, *Yes, ever.* Looking at Leo, she thought he had enjoyed it too, although his expression at times, when he was listening to his parents' banter, had seemed somewhat bemused.

They settled Michael in the sitting room, Romy hovering while Leo went off to make coffee, perhaps unwilling to watch as his father stuttered, 'Can I have my . . . my . . .' waving his arm and grunting in frustration until he took a deep breath. 'You know . . . the thing I read on. Can't remember its bloody name.'

'iPad,' she said, seeing it on the coffee table and handing it to him.

Glancing up at the kitchen clock a few minutes later, Romy said to Leo, 'Imogen'll be here in a minute. Michael's paying her double time to come at weekends – although he's not aware of this yet – because I'm told the early period after a stroke is vital.' She took the cup of coffee Leo offered her. 'And the good thing is that your father is in love with her.' She smiled as she settled at the kitchen table. 'She's all bouncy and blonde and bossy. It's late in the day to realize this, but I think your father quite likes a domineering woman.'

Leo laughed. 'Speaking of which . . .'

Romy shook her head. 'Not a peep – which is hardly a surprise. The snag is, your dad's damaged brain just won't seem to accept that she's gone – despite all the evidence.'

The previous night was a case in point. It was about one in the morning when she was dragged from a deep sleep to the sound of Michael's bell. But when she asked him what he needed, he'd responded, 'Nothing. I'm fine. I just wanted to find out if you've heard from Anezka. I keep leaving her messages but she doesn't get back to me.'

Romy had let out a long sigh. 'It's one in the morning and you want to talk about Anezka?'

Michael's face had fallen. She thought he seemed slightly disoriented. 'Oh . . . I'm sorry . . . I didn't realize it was so late.' His mouth twisted with anxiety. 'It's just I really need to talk to her. Did she ring you, Romy? You can tell me.'

'No, Michael, she didn't. Now go to sleep and we can discuss it in the morning.'

He'd nodded, but she could see he was still upset, so she sat down in the orange chair. 'Go to sleep,' she said, more gently this time, stroking his hand. He'd closed his eyes and was asleep within minutes, as usual, leaving Romy wondering what had gone on between him and Anezka to make him so desperate to speak to her.

She sat on in the darkness, wide awake now. Michael was muttering in his sleep, his head tossing from side to side as if he were trying desperately to shake something off.

'No . . . no, no, no . . . don't look at me like that . . . I didn't . . .' He threw his arm out violently, hitting the wall behind his head.

Romy laid a hand on his shoulder. 'Michael, it's OK,' she soothed. For a second he opened his eyes, then lapsed into sleep again. *Was that about Anezka? Or was it about something that happened much further back in his memory bank?* She'd shivered, the words of the letter once more in the forefront of her brain, and had taken herself off to bed.

None of which she would explain to her son. 'Listen,' she said now, 'could *you* talk to Anezka?'

'Me?' Leo looked instantly nervous. 'What would I say?'

She gave him one of her patient looks, which she knew had irritated both her boys in the past. 'Just meet for a coffee and explain that she needs to come round and tell your father face to face that it's over. I know she's made it clear enough to the rest of us, but she never answers his calls and the message just hasn't got through.'

Romy stood outside the Sussex cottage, breathing the clear sea air with relief. The house looked so welcoming – almost as if it were actually smiling at her – sitting in the neat row with its white walls and ash-blue window frames. She pushed aside a maverick tendril of the pale pink climber next to the front door and reminded herself she must cut it back later.

Her anticipation had been mounting over the past week, as she counted down the days before she was home again, before she could sleep in her own bed and not have to listen out for that damn bell, or hold her breath as she emptied the urine bottle or watch the man who had once been the centre of her life struggle in vain for his dignity.

She opened all the windows and doors, turned on the hot water and made herself a cup of tea. She would need to buy food, but that could wait. Now, she took her tea outside into the sunshine and sat at the new garden table – which looked almost too new, the wood glowing orange in the May sunshine – and let the heat of the sun warm through her.

Later, Finch brought round some lunch from the deli – sliced ham, big round beef tomatoes, potato salad dressed with olive oil, spring onions and lemon, and a triangle of Brie so ripe it looked as if it might wander off of its own accord, just how Romy liked it. They sat in her garden with a bottle of chilled Picpoul, talking with their usual ease, each enjoying digging out nuggets from the other's life. Romy found her head spinning pleasantly from the wine, the sunshine and Finch's diverting company.

It was such a contrast to the rest of the week that, as she closed her eyes for a moment, it seemed almost unreal that she was there. The invisible pall of London's pollution, the suffocating flat, the constant background noise, she had barely noticed it when she lived there. But now, sitting in blissful quiet, surrounded by blooms and bird-song, the cool wind off the sea, she appreciated what she'd been missing – appreciated what she had now.

But despite her unwillingness to talk about Michael, she found she could not so easily banish him from her thoughts even as she and Finch were chatting. The previous night he had rung the bell, as usual, at about one thirty. Since the night when she'd been so disturbed by his anxiety about Anezka and that strange dream, she'd been wary of sitting with him too long. She'd taken to going straight back to bed as soon as she'd sorted out what was bothering him. But last night he'd begged her to stay for a bit and she couldn't refuse.

'What is it, Michael?'

He was smiling, seemed almost playful as he began to ramble on in his halting speech. 'I've been lying here remembering. That night at the Metropole . . . we were only kids . . . well, barely more than kids.'

The warehouse-like bulk of the Stockton pub rose instantly to her mind. In those days there were pubs you went to and others you didn't, depending on alliances that were innate and almost tribal. The Metropole was her stamping ground. And his.

'You bought me and my friends vodkas and lime and they cost a fortune. I'll never forget.'

He grinned. 'I must have been trying to impress you, but you weren't impressed at all. You called me a pillock because I didn't know who Steely Dan was.'

She couldn't help smiling back. 'I wouldn't have dared. You were older than me and scarily cool back then.'

Michael chuckled quietly. 'God, you were magnificent, Romy. Tall and wild, those eyes of yours on fire. You weren't even remotely scared of me.'

He was right. She'd seen him as a challenge. Her friends all thought he was up himself – arrogant and superior – and she tended to agree. But she'd noticed something softer in those dark eyes – and, anyway, she fancied the pants off him, with his lean frame and intense stare, black hair brushing the collar of his denim jacket. 'You made me weak at the knees.' She laughed.

They both fell silent. Romy was remembering the sweeping rush of exhilaration as they'd walked away from the pub and their friends, hand in hand in the summer night, down the high street and over the bridge. She had literally felt she could fly. And fly she did, later, when Michael made love to her – quickly, urgently – in the back of his brother's worn-out Vauxhall, parked in a lane on the outskirts of the village.

When her thoughts returned to the bedroom, and Michael lying in the bed beside her, he was speaking again, his voice cracked and dull. 'I'm such an old crock, Romy. Who will want me now?' And Romy hadn't known how to reply.

Now, she realized Finch was talking. 'You're miles away,' he said, his eyes narrowed in the sunlight. 'What were you thinking?'

Romy gazed at him with a feeling almost of dread, because on Friday night she'd sensed the ties that bound her and Michael struggling to reassert themselves, felt the powerful pull of their history together. *It was probably the least contentious, most intimate exchange we'd had in years*, she thought. But she didn't want to be intimate with her husband. She didn't want to feel anything for him, except sympathy.

'Nothing. I'm sorry. Just tired,' she lied. But she saw from the cloud that flitted across Finch's face that he didn't entirely believe her. She shook herself and got up quickly, reaching for the wooden tray she'd propped against the wall. She wanted a moment to compose herself. 'I know it's utterly childish,' she said, as she folded the remains of the cheese back into the waxed paper, 'but I feel almost resentful that I have to witness what's happening to Michael.' It wasn't the whole truth, but it was at least true.

Finch, dangling the empty wine bottle in one hand, the pepper mill in the other, gazed at her sympathetically, the doubt clearing from his eyes. 'I imagine there's nothing more painful to watch than the slog of rehab, Romy. Don't beat yourself up for finding it hard.'

But Romy realized it wasn't really Michael's rehab she was objecting to – however hard. It was his dragging her back to memories of when they'd been happy together, when things had seemed so unambiguous between them. She worried that even touching on them, just allowing herself to remember, would trap her for ever, the past becoming her living present.

22

Daniel was standing beside Michael, holding him up, when Romy came into the bedroom on Monday morning. Leo had been almost pathetically pleased to see her the night before – disappearing from the flat, like a greyhound out of a trap, almost as soon as she got through the front door.

'Morning,' Michael said now. 'You're back.'

She nodded. He'd been asleep when she'd got in yesterday evening, and if he'd rung the bell in the night, she hadn't heard him. There had not been a great deal of sleep going on with Finch the night before and she'd been dead to the world.

'Yup.' She moved across the room. 'Can I help?'

Daniel – looking so fresh and clean and young in contrast to Michael's grizzled appearance – hesitated. 'I am going to shower him. But I think his medication is running out. I can go later to the surgery, if you will be here?'

'No,' Romy said quickly. 'I'll go. I'll do shopping and stuff while I'm out.' Any excuse to leave the flat. But she must have seemed too keen, because Michael gave her a quizzical look as Daniel began to walk him towards the bathroom.

'What?' she asked.

'Nothing,' he said, clearly amused. 'You seem a bit . . . skittish this morning, that's all.'

Romy tried to settle her features, but a sudden recollection of her and Finch on the bed, his fingers inside her, made her almost gasp, her mouth twisting as if she'd just sucked a lemon in her attempts to stop the colour beating a path to her cheeks.

Michael stopped in his tracks.

Blast, he knows me so well, she thought. Her face, she was sure, was now a picture of discomposure.

'How was the weekend?' he asked pointedly, the amusement gone from his face.

'Lovely,' she said, meeting his eye with determination.

Michael continued to stare at her, then turned and allowed Daniel to help him across the carpeted floor in silence.

That afternoon, Wendy Marsan paid a visit. She was around Romy's age and had been with Michael's chambers since the beginning. If asked, she still termed her job as 'receptionist', but what Wendy did was way beyond that: she ran the place. And she knew – probably documented in one of her many spreadsheets – where all of the bodies were buried, going back decades. Michael and James adored her. They always claimed chambers would collapse without her.

'Romy, dear,' Wendy said, brushing Romy's cheek with her own and shaking her hand in an awkward greeting, 'this must be so difficult for you all.' She was slim with thin dark hair to just above her shoulders and a straight fringe skimming her blue eyes. She wore little make-up, but her clothes were carefully chosen and classic. Today she looked especially smart, and Romy decided she must be going on somewhere. Her elegant navy dress with broderie anglaise edging the sleeves and neck was way too formal for tea with an invalid, even if he was still technically her boss.

Like many of Michael's visitors, she proffered a small bag. 'Just some little fancies from the patisserie. I know Michael likes them,' she said, peering round the door to the sitting room.

'Lovely, thank you,' Romy said. 'He's just getting up from his rest. Come into the kitchen and we'll get the tea on.'

Wendy leant against the worktop, arms crossed, while Romy filled the kettle. She had always liked Wendy for her efficiency and reserve. She'd never pretended to be Romy's friend, but was helpful if she wanted Michael corralled or dates synchronized, addresses found. Romy had no idea what she thought of the split in the Claire marriage, and she was sure Wendy would never dream of telling her.

'How is he?' Wendy asked, voice lowered.

Romy never knew how to answer that question. 'He's sticking in there. Prepare yourself, though. I'm not sure he looks much better than he did in the hospital.'

Wendy's face clouded. 'Poor man. It's so unfair. He always kept himself so fit with all that cycling.'

Michael's supposed obsession with cycling was old news. It was years since he'd biked to work every morning and spent weekends driving to the South Downs to ride with his friends. But Wendy clearly liked to cling to the myth, so Romy said, 'Well, hopefully it'll stand him in good stead now.'

There was silence. She listened out for Daniel and Michael in the corridor, but there was no sound, except for the dull pulsing of a drill somewhere in a neighbouring flat.

'We miss him,' Wendy said. 'Any idea when he might be back?' She gave an apologetic smile and added quickly, 'Probably too soon to ask.'

'Certainly not for a while.'

Wendy shook her head gloomily. 'That Andrew Marr fellow seems to have got back to normal,' she said. 'And his was a nasty one, by all accounts.'

'I'm sure Michael will too. But the doctors have warned us not to expect too much too soon.'

Silence again. Romy found she couldn't think of anything to say, because the only question that was burning on her tongue was the one that went, 'Do you remember a work-experience girl, about sixteen years ago, who came for a week in the summer?'

Instead, she said, 'I know you're always very busy at this time of year. It must be hard being one barrister down.'

Wendy laughed ruefully. 'It's been a nightmare, to be honest. Michael has such a stellar reputation that everyone and his dog wants his services.'

Romy took a breath. 'Do you still have all those work-experience teenagers helping out?'

'"Helping out"?' Wendy harrumphed. 'More like cluttering up the place.' She gave a long-suffering sigh. 'I'm not being unkind. They're usually very sweet and eager to please. But they nag me all day long. And it's always me they come to, because they're too scared to ask anyone else.'

Romy laughed. 'I was talking to someone the other day, and she thought the daughter of a friend of hers had done a week with you back in June 2002.'

Wendy shrugged. 'Could have. What was her name? I never forget a name, even if I can't remember what they look like.'

Romy pretended it was on the tip of her tongue. 'Umm, what was it now? Emma, or Emily? Something like that. She was James's connection, I think.'

Wendy thought for a moment. 'There was Emily Hay-hurst, but she was much later – more like 2011. I remember her because she was such a little minx, racked up a vast sum on the mobile I lent her to book taxis for court, ringing her boyfriend in France.'

'Teenagers, eh? Like herding cats,' Romy said sympathetically. 'It was the year I broke my leg falling off a bike,' she added, hoping to jog Wendy's memory. 'It was really hot that summer.'

'Oh, gosh, I remember. Such bad timing, with the boys out of school . . . I tried to get Michael to take time off, but he was so involved in that dreadful man's trial . . . Oops, shouldn't say that, should I? But he was a nasty piece of work.'

'So maybe the girl . . .'

Daniel's head appeared at the kitchen door. 'He's in the sitting room,' he said, and Wendy looked relieved, jumping away from the worktop to follow Daniel.

'I'll bring the tea through,' Romy said, feeling disappointed, but also thankful that she hadn't been able to get a name out of Wendy.

What would I have done if she had remembered her? she asked herself, laying the dainty iced cakes on a plate.

She couldn't imagine searching out the woman and confronting her now. It had been all she wanted to do three years ago, but Romy had gradually come to realize that nothing would be gained by it – at least for her. However convincing the writer of the letter might be, she would still be left with the excruciating dilemma of whom to believe. But what worried her most, as she filled the teapot with boiling water and stirred the leaves, was that she was even asking Wendy. Why was she still pursuing it – and still, in truth, itching to know – when she'd been doing everything in her power, until the stroke intervened, to refocus her life away from Michael and what had happened in her marriage?

23

'He seems to really like Daniel,' Romy said to Bettina, when she phoned the following morning. 'The boy's so good with him, and doesn't seem to notice Michael being snippy. I can't thank you enough for recommending him.'

'I'm just happy it's working out,' Bettina replied. 'And you? How are you surviving?'

'I'm fine,' Romy said. 'I'm just worried that Michael seems to be depending on me more and more. Not in a physical sense, so much – that's Daniel's territory. But he hates being on his own, doesn't want me to leave him for long . . . As if he's frightened.'

'He probably is frightened. I would be if I was him.'

'Me too.'

Yesterday evening, when she'd settled him in bed, Michael had snatched her hand and given it a quick kiss. 'Thanks for all you're doing for me, Romy. I know I'm a grumpy old sod most of the time, but that doesn't mean I don't appreciate your being here – more than anything else in the world.'

She was taken aback and hadn't known how to respond. To tell him it was a pleasure would be a lie he would never believe. But to tell him the truth – that she longed to get away so much sometimes that it hurt – would be plain cruel. She managed a smile and gently withdrew her hand.

It confused her that he was being so nice. Michael didn't do 'nice'. He abhorred sentimentality and favoured honesty over tact. He was so caught up in his own world that he didn't concern himself much with other people's feelings. But since the stroke, that had changed.

'I haven't told you enough in the past,' he was saying.

'Don't be silly.' She'd been embarrassed.

'No . . . Lying here, I've had time to think. I took advantage of you, Romy. I didn't appreciate just how much you meant to me, or how much you put up with, until you left.'

Michael's slow, ponderous speech gave a weight to his words that made Romy self-conscious. He was still staring at her, his eyes willing her to take him seriously.

'No, well . . .' She didn't want his apologies. But the moment felt dangerous, as if she were poised at a door, which, if opened, might lead her straight back to Michael's side.

He must have seen her reluctance because he turned away on the pillow and she heard him give a short laugh.

'Sorry, not the time for all this,' he said quietly. 'I'm a bit of a soppy old fool these days . . . but I meant what I said.'

Now Bettina was asking, 'So he's noticeably better?'

'Oh, yes, definitely. But, God, it's slow, Bet. I can't see an end to it.'

'Don't say that,' her friend said anxiously. 'He's not your responsibility any more, Romy. He's really not.' A pause. Romy knew what was coming and she knew Bettina was right. 'I think you should start finding someone else to help Daniel, if he needs it. You've done your bit. You need to go home.'

'Yeah,' she said, feeling too tired to speak. 'I know I do. And I will.' It should be simple, but the thought of telling Michael she was going back to Sussex made her falter. 'He's still very weak,' she added lamely.

Bettina was silent.

Romy took a deep breath. 'But I'm going out tonight.' She hadn't yet told her friend about Finch. There had been nothing to tell until recently, and then there had been Michael's stroke. So now she wanted to reassure her that she was not falling back into a relationship with a man Bettina had always been a bit wary of. Although she nearly hadn't agreed to Finch's invitation when he'd called.

'I'm coming up tomorrow,' Finch had said. 'Got a couple of meetings. I thought I might stay over and we could have supper together.'

Romy had not answered immediately. She'd felt almost panicky at his request, as if even the possibility were too much for her to process. All she had in her head was Michael, Michael, Michael. So when she'd eventually replied, she'd said, 'God, that would be lovely. But I'm not sure. It's such a long process getting Michael settled at night and I'm always so knackered afterwards.'

There had been a very long silence, during which Romy felt she could hear Finch's thoughts as if he had actually spoken them: *Too knackered to have supper with me?*

'Pity,' she'd heard him say, his voice determinedly light. 'Another time, then.'

She'd known he was about to hang up and her palm was sticky on the handset as she rushed out the next words: 'Oh, to hell with it,' she'd said. 'Of course I'll have dinner with you. I'm getting so one-track, these days, I can't see past the end of my nose . . . or Michael's nose, more like.' She heard him laugh dutifully. 'I'd really love to see you,' she'd added slowly, allowing her feelings for Finch to inhabit every word. And she knew he'd heard.

'Good,' said Bettina now. 'Who with?'

Romy suppressed a smile her friend couldn't see and replied casually, 'Just a man.'

There was silence at the other end of the line. 'Umm, what sort of just-a-man?'

'The sort you go out with.' Romy was enjoying herself; enjoying talking about Finch and not Michael; the future, not the past.

'Wait . . . Are we talking about what I think we're talking about?'

'We are, indeed.' Romy found herself giggling like a schoolgirl.

She heard her friend whoop. 'Oh . . . my . . . God. You dark horse, Romy Claire.' Bettina whistled softly. 'And you didn't think to mention it?'

'I am mentioning it.'

'Well, go on, then. Mention it some more.'

Unable to bear meeting Finch wearing either of the two pairs of jeans, or any of the tired old T-shirts she'd brought with her to the flat, Romy nipped out and wandered round the shops for half an hour. She came back with a wraparound jersey dress in green and gold. She very seldom wore anything except trousers these days – but it was

June, and she'd been inspired by Wendy in her fetching summer dress. She wanted to look good for Finch.

She helped Daniel get Michael settled for the night, then showered and changed into her new dress and a pair of pumps, which she dug out from a box at the back of her old wardrobe – neither she nor Michael had cleared it out.

Feeling nervous and guilty – it was almost as if she were having an affair, sneaking out behind Michael's back – she picked up her navy jacket, checked her image once more in the mirror, then opened her bedroom door. Finch had told her to meet him in Soho, at a trendy dim-sum restaurant she'd never been to. But as she began to walk down the corridor, the blasted bell sounded.

She hesitated. *Don't stop*, urged a voice in her head. She had told Michael she was going out, but she was sure he would have forgotten by now. If there was a problem, Daniel could deal with it, now he was living in the flat full time. But she knew she would worry if she didn't go to him.

Michael stared when Romy entered the room.

'Gracious,' he murmured. 'You look stunning.'

She gave an embarrassed laugh. 'Thanks . . . Do you want something?' She knew she sounded brisk, but she was late already.

'You're going out?' Michael raised his eyebrows.

'Of course not. I always dress up like this to watch *Murder She Wrote*,' she retorted, riled at his obvious assumption that she had no other life. 'I did tell you.'

'Who with?' he asked, ignoring her sarcasm.

'A friend.'

'What friend?'

'He's a neighbour, in Sussex.'

Michael frowned. 'Do I know him?'

'No . . . Listen, I've got to go, Michael. Is there something you need? I can get Daniel . . .'

Michael blinked hard, as if he couldn't believe what he was witnessing. 'Umm, no. I'm fine. Just felt like a chat.'

'Sorry about that.' She gave him a small wave. 'Night. Hope you get some sleep.'

'Don't stay out too late,' Michael called, as she turned away.

'You look completely gorgeous,' Finch said, as they took their seats in the restaurant, and Romy heard the uncomfortable echo of Michael's words. 'Love the dress.'

Romy couldn't stop smiling; she was so pleased to see him. She'd been tense on the journey there, holding onto herself tightly, unable to shake off Michael's expression when she'd referred to Finch. She'd felt an urgent need to put distance between herself and her knowing husband and had hurried to the restaurant as if she had the devil on her tail.

It was a long while later – a good many glasses of deliciously chilled white and an array of spicy dim sum consumed – that Finch gave her a level gaze across the table and said, 'I'm staying up tonight. Come back with me?'

Romy smiled awkwardly. She didn't want to ruin the evening, didn't want to explain again about Michael waking in the night and calling for her – Finch already knew. She watched his tense expression as he waited for her reply. An image swam before her eyes of Michael lying lonely in the semi-darkness of the boiling room, his eyes lighting up when she staggered in, half asleep. She had not told Daniel she might stay out. *Although*, she thought, *I could text him*. She could text Michael too, for that matter. *He isn't a child*, she reminded herself. *And I'm not one, either.*

'No pressure,' Finch was saying, his expression hard to read.

Romy gave herself a mental shake. 'We'd better get going,' she said, laying her napkin on the table and pushing back her chair. 'We don't want to keep the love-nest waiting.'

She was rewarded with a smile worthy of a child on Christmas morning. She realized she'd become so buried in Michael's life, she'd almost forgotten she had a right to her own pleasures. But as they made their way up the restaurant stairs and out into the cool summer night, Finch's hand firmly round her own, Romy felt Christmas morning had arrived for her, too.

24

Leo drummed his fingers on the table and checked his phone for the third time in two minutes. She was late. Maybe she wasn't coming. He thought he'd be partly relieved if she didn't. He was sitting outside the café at Somerset House, in front of the fountains hidden in the paving stones of the courtyard; they sprang up randomly, wetting any unsuspecting passer-by. He often came here, because it was a short walk from his Chancery Lane office and he liked the open space and the fresh wind from the river, especially on such a lovely summer day.

But he was nervous – reluctant to get involved in his father's affairs of the heart – as he caught sight of Anezka's tall figure at the entrance to the courtyard. She had on a sleeveless red dress and large sunglasses, her hair flowing out behind her in the breeze.

'I'm so sorry, Leo.' Anezka was slightly breathless. 'This is supposed to be my day off, but they still phone me with idiot questions.' She sat down in a billow of skirt, sweeping her shiny hair across her head in the familiar gesture. 'I have not much time,' she added, seeming almost impatient.

Leo took a steadying breath. 'Right, well, I'll get to the point. Mum asked me to see you.' He noted Anezka's slight raise of an eyebrow. 'I know you've finished with Dad. But he still asks after you . . . and I know he calls you.' She gave a wry nod at this. 'Like he hasn't got the message?'

Anezka looked away and didn't answer.

Leo ploughed on: 'So Mum wondered if you would come round – or just talk to him over the phone – and really sort out what's bothering him, once and for all.'

She stared at him with her large blue eyes, almost defiantly. 'Do you want to know what it is, this thing between us?'

'Umm . . . not really my business, Anezka.'

Ignoring his reply, she went on, 'I will tell you what we argue about.' She gave a heavy sigh. 'We have been seeing each other a long time, you know. I think we love each other. So, I suggest we move in together. Your father, he says yes,' she gave a short laugh, 'but he mean no.'

Leo had no idea how to respond, but before he had time to think, she was asking, 'You want to know why?'

He didn't, but he knew she was going to tell him.

'He is still in love with your mother.' She spoke slowly, emphasizing each word loudly and carefully, as she cast a wounded glance at Leo. 'All that time? He was just using me for sex.'

Leo was shocked. Was any of what she said true? His father 'using' someone for sex? His father in love with his mother throughout? Now he recalled Anezka implying, when they were in the hospital one day, that Michael would prefer to see someone other than her at his bedside. But although he'd noted the words as significant at the time, he hadn't had the head space to follow it through. 'Are you sure about him still being in love with Mum? He seems really keen to talk to you.'

His father had never taken him into his confidence when his mother had left. Not even mentioned it. But did parents ever confide in their kids about their relationship? Or kids confide in their parents? He certainly hadn't told either of them about Lucy, his girlfriend of six months, wanting to wait till they were both sure.

Rex had posited the theory, at the time of the split, that maybe there'd been an overlap with Anezka and their mum – she'd been on the scene earlier than was said – and that was what had driven their mum away. But Leo hadn't bought that about his dad. And his mother would surely have been angrier and let something slip, if that were the case.

Anezka didn't answer, just looked at him as if he was being disingenuous, a tight smile on her lips.

'OK . . . but right now his brain seems stuck in some sort of groove. Maybe he wants to apologize to you, or something,' Leo said. 'I'd appreciate it if you'd see him, anyway . . . sort out whatever it is.' The reluctance on her face was patent, but Leo stood firm. 'Please, Anezka.'

She sighed. 'I will come, if that's what you want. But I don't want to fight with him like we did that night.'

'Maybe ring him, then. Just make clear that it's really over, that you're not interested . . . and don't keep saying you love him, even if you do.'

His phone rang as he waited at the lights to cross Sloane Square on his way to visit his father. He smiled to himself as he saw who it was.

'Hi, bro,' Rex said. 'Thought I'd see how it's going over there.' He sounded annoyingly upbeat.

'If you're on the beach, I don't want to know how blue the sky is or how cool the water, OK?' Leo joked, although he was really happy to hear his brother's voice.

'Man, it's the middle of the night! So tell me about Dad.'

Leo sighed. 'Everyone keeps telling me he'll be fine in the end, and maybe he will, but it's really hard seeing him struggle to do even the smallest thing.'

Rex was silent for a moment. 'I feel so bad I'm not there to help.'

Leo was sure his brother did feel guilty. *But not guilty enough to come back*, he thought. Not that he blamed him.

'How is he in himself?' Rex was asking, as Leo weaved his way expertly round the crowded square, not waiting for the pedestrian lights to change to green before striding across the King's Road junction.

'Well, that's the odd thing. He's sort of mellowed. He's not nearly as scary as he used to be.'

'Like how?'

'It's weird,' Leo said, as he entered Symons Street. 'We actually had a real laugh together on Saturday. Can you believe that selfie I sent? *Dad* allowing me to take one? And he seems to be listening to me – even taking what I say seriously sometimes.'

'So his brain's definitely on the blink.'

'Very funny. It sort of is and isn't. He was able to quote some Supreme Court ruling without any trouble the other morning, but often he can't remember the name of a simple object, like his iPad.'

'So what does he do all day? Can he read and stuff?'

'Ah, well, wait for it . . . Dad's watching telly for the first time in his life! Mum's got a flat screen fitted on the wall in their bedroom where that gloomy bridge painting used to be and Dad's become a Netflix junkie.'

He heard Rex's disbelieving snort. Michael had spent most of their childhood ranting about television programmes being 'damaging, populist rubbish'. He'd tried to limit the amount the boys watched, but since he wasn't there most of the time and their mother didn't stress about it, they'd ended up with pretty much the same quota as their peers.

'You . . . are . . . kidding.' Rex was silent for a moment. 'And Mum?'

'That's another odd thing.' Leo paused as he stepped off the kerb, narrowly missing a massive white four-by-four with blacked-out windows. 'It's nearly a month now, and she's still there all the time – except one weekend – and they seem to be getting on better. I mean, sometimes really laughing together.' He hesitated. 'I've told her that with Daniel there she could probably go home and she says she will, but not yet . . . so maybe she's sort of enjoying being with Dad.'

'Hmm . . . interesting. You think this might bring them back together?' Rex yawned loudly. 'That'd be one good thing to come out of all this.'

'Well, let me tell you what Anezka said when I saw her just now.' Leo went on to fill Rex in.

'Do you think Mum knows? Because if that really is how Dad feels, it looks like the ball's in Mum's court now.'

Both brothers fell silent.

'Make sure you phone me with updates. I love our chats,' Rex said affectionately. 'I feel like I'm a million miles away and I miss you.'

'Bugger, bugger, bugger,' Michael muttered, as he sat in his armchair in the sitting room, struggling with the Velcro fastenings on his trainers, his breath coming in awkward gasps. He looked up at Leo and gave a resigned smile.

'You're doing well, Dad,' Leo encouraged.

His father snorted. 'For a cripple.'

'Yeah, for a cripple, obviously,' Leo ventured. This was new, the banter he and his father were establishing. His mother, setting a vase containing some tall purple irises on the coffee table, gave him a warning frown. But his dad just laughed.

'At least someone round here's being honest.'

'I don't think it's helpful.' His mother's voice was reproachful.

'Not helpful, perhaps,' Michael retorted, 'but refreshingly accurate.'

A moment later, Leo noticed his father staring at him intently, one eye on the door through which his mother had just disappeared to make coffee. He could hear the chuntering of the kettle in the kitchen, the rattle of crockery, the click of a cupboard door.

'You know your mother's got a boyfriend?' His father's voice was low and conspiratorial.

Leo's mouth fell open. He gave his father a sceptical look – he was not himself these days. 'You sure you've got that right, Dad?' he asked.

'What's more,' Michael ignored his son's condescension, 'she spent the night with him last week . . . Tuesday, was it? Wednesday?' A look of frustration crossed his face. 'People joke about not remembering the name of the prime minister . . .' Then he added, 'She didn't get back till nearly noon the next day.'

Now it was Leo's turn to glance towards the door. 'Did Mum actually tell you this? Maybe you're . . .' he didn't want to imply that his dad was an idiot '. . . confused about something she said.' *Mum with another man is ridiculous*, he told himself. Although, as he'd said to Rex, she did seem to be laughing more, these days, which he'd put down to her getting on better with his father.

Michael gave him an edgy half-smile. 'Ask her yourself,' he said, nodding towards the door as Romy walked in, carrying a tray laden with coffee, frothy milk and homemade lemon shortbread that one of Michael's visitors had brought.

Leo had no intention of asking her. He was embarrassed for his father. But Romy must have sensed the atmosphere because she turned a questioning look on Leo.

'What have you two been whispering about?'

'Your friendly neighbour,' Michael said promptly. 'The one you spent the night with last week. Leo doesn't seem to know anything about him.'

'Mum . . .' began Leo, intent on laughing it off. Then he saw the blush. Her head was bent over the coffee tray, but it was impossible to miss. '*Mum?*'

When Romy looked up, her expression was a mixture of defiance and irritation. She glared at his father. 'Thanks,' she muttered sarcastically.

Michael just shrugged. 'I assumed he knew.'

She handed Leo a cup of coffee but didn't look at him.

Leo frowned. 'Mum?' he repeated, for the third time, wondering what game these two were playing and wishing they wouldn't.

He saw her sigh as she sat down with her own cup of coffee in the chair opposite his father.

'I didn't tell you because there's nothing to tell.'

Leo took a relieved breath. 'That's what I told Dad.'

Then she went on quickly, 'His name is Robert Fincham – everyone calls him Finch. He's a neighbour in Sussex, retired from the army. And, yes, your father's right. I have been seeing him, but it's a very new thing. I didn't want to tell you until I was sure there was something in it.'

Leo was silent as he tried to digest this extraordinary piece of news. 'So is there? Something in it?' he asked eventually. His mother was blinking nervously, while his father's expression had reverted to a cynicism with which Leo was uncomfortably familiar.

'I don't know,' Romy said unhelpfully.

Silence fell, the three of them lost in their own thoughts. Leo didn't know why he was so shocked. He remembered when his father announced he wanted him and Rex to meet Anezka. That had been bad enough, both of them cringing at the implication their dad was probably having sex with someone other than their mother – having sex at all, in fact, even with their mother, *especially* with their mother. But this was somehow way, way worse. *Mum with another man?* It made him positively squirm and blew right out of the water Rex's

165

fond theory that their parents might get back together. Although he realized now that he, too, had been holding on to the idea that they might, ever since he'd been told they were separating.

'That's great, Mum.' Provoked into siding with her in the face of his father's obvious disapproval – something he'd done since childhood – Leo forced the words from between his lips.

He saw a pained look flit across his father's face. Then the bell rang and Leo leapt up from the sofa.

Later, while his father was being put through his paces by the physio, his mother took his arm and drew him into the dining room, shutting the heavy door behind her. Leo could still hear Imogen's monotonous exhortations from the next-door room.

'I'm sorry about that, sweetheart.'

Leo patted her shoulder. 'It's OK, Mum. It was a bit of a shock, hearing it from Dad like that. But I'm happy for you, really. It's your life and Dad has no right to make you feel guilty.'

'He does, though.'

'Yeah, well, he's jealous, probably.' He knew this now – courtesy of Anezka – although he hadn't yet mentioned that part of their conversation to his mother.

'It's early days. But I like him a lot.' She stopped, glanced away, clearly embarrassed.

Whoa, Leo thought, but said, 'Look forward to meeting him, then.'

'You do?' She raised an amused eyebrow.

He gave her a sheepish grin. 'Sort of.'

She laughed and hugged him. 'Love you for saying it, anyway.'

Leo felt oddly tearful as he retreated to Rex's old room 'for a read', as he told his mother. Why did things have to be so complicated with his parents? First the volatile Anezka and now some dodgy old soldier?

He couldn't really believe his mother was in love with this random guy. How could she do that to them right now, when everything was so horrible, so uncertain?

25

Finch huffed and puffed as he ran up the path through the woods towards Harting Down. Normally the route posed no problem, but this morning – a gorgeously bright-blue June day – his legs felt heavy and his lungs tight. Maybe the tension about Romy, stuck in that bloody flat with Michael, was making his body malfunction. He needed to be fit for the Irish marathon he was planning in the autumn. But somehow his previously pressing need, which Grace called 'compulsive', to run these gruelling distances – to prove himself again and again – had dwindled somewhat since meeting Romy.

He stopped as he reached the top of the hill and took a long, thirsty swig from the water bottle he carried on a belt round his waist, enchanted, as he always was, by the sweeping vista across the Downs. He could see for miles, the air so clear it was almost intoxicating, the soft greens and greys of early summer picked out by the spiky yellow of gorse. He pulled out his phone from the belt and took a photo, sending it to Romy with the caption: *Come with me next time?* x

The view always reminded him of training exercises in the Welsh mountains when he was in the army. But then he'd had to carry a massive thirty-kilo pack on his back. As he moved off along the crest of the hill, he adopted a gentler pace, his thoughts returning to Romy.

They'd had such a great night together after the dim sum. They jokingly called his club their 'love-nest', but it seemed to have become that for them – a place that was unconnected to their everyday lives, or their pasts, where Finch felt they could shut out the world and, for a few short hours, no one else existed.

It was the very unreality of their lovemaking that worried him, though. He didn't want to meet Romy for occasional sex, then watch her return to Michael. It was as if they were having an affair. The 'couple of weeks' she'd originally talked about had constantly been added to, and she was showing no signs of breaking free. From what she told him, she could easily step back, take on a monitoring role from a distance. *Why doesn't she leave?* he asked himself as he ran, hearing the bare resentment in his question.

He remembered her enthusiasm, when they'd first met, for the new start she was embarking on – before she'd even considered he might become part of that. *Would she give up on those dreams, go back to a life that clearly hadn't made her happy?* he wondered. But he had to face the fact – despite feeling that he and Romy were so good together – that the more time she spent with Michael, the closer they might potentially become. *All those decades of marriage . . .*

Finch got home around twelve and showered, flopping onto the bed in his towel and gazing up at the ceiling. This was the ceiling Nell had lain staring at for weeks on end while she was ill. The crack, which emanated from the central light fitting and weaved its way erratically towards the window, was still there, as was the damp patch in the corner — the result of a leak in the hot-water tank in the roof. *I should get the place painted*, he thought, knowing he wouldn't quite yet, because he still hung on to these small reminders of his wife.

His phone rang and he threw out a lazy hand to pick up the mobile from where it lay on the duvet.

'It's me,' Romy said, unnecessarily.

Finch sat up. 'Hey . . .' But before he could say any more, Romy interrupted, her voice flat with resentment.

'Leo knows about us. Michael told him.'

'OK . . .' Finch was not sure how to react. But if his own nervousness about the conversation he must eventually have with Grace was any reflection, then he could understand why she was irritated with her husband.

'So how did he take it?' Finch assumed badly, judging from Romy's obvious anger.

'He's a reasonable person, Leo. I'm sure he wants the best for me. And he said all the right things. But I know him well. He was shocked.' She hesitated. 'Maybe he's been hoping all along that Michael and I will get back together. It would be natural.' Finch heard a short laugh. 'And I'm his mum. It's not the same as Michael and Anezka.'

Did Leo think this was a realistic hope, his parents getting back together? Finch wondered unhappily. 'It should be, but I suppose it's not,' he replied.

'I just wanted to tell him myself. In my own time,' Romy said. 'And I would have, but Michael and his bloody stroke got in the way.' Finch winced at the harshness in her voice. 'He said he thought Leo already knew,' she went on. 'But in fact he was just being spiteful. Scoring points.'

Finch couldn't help experiencing a guilty surge of pleasure at her disparagement of Michael as he heard Romy add forcefully, 'Anyway, it's done now, and I'm glad he knows.'

'I'm glad you're glad,' he said, unable to keep the relief out of his voice. 'I should tell Gracie. She's coming down from Manchester this weekend. In fact, I was wondering . . . maybe it's too soon . . . but if you were here, perhaps we could meet up for a drink or something casual. I'd love you to meet her.'

'Me too. But it's your call. I was coming down on Saturday, anyway. I'm sorely tempted to just leave the miserable bastard to his own devices permanently, see how he likes that.'

But you won't, he thought.

'See how it goes with Grace,' Romy was saying. 'I won't be the least offended if you decide not to tell her yet. I've just been through the conversation with Leo, and you should think carefully about whether it's the right time or not.'

'I just want Grace to know how I feel about you,' he said simply, aware, as he spoke, that he wanted to tell as many people as possible about him and Romy. It seemed to him that the more public their relationship, the more it would cement it in everybody's eyes – including Michael's.

26

When she arrived on the doorstep later that afternoon, Anezka was clearly nervous.

'Come in.' Romy welcomed her warmly, but she was anxious about how Michael would cope with the meeting.

They stood in the hall in silence. Anezka handed her a fancy box from the patisserie in the mews off Sloane Square.

'He's in the sitting room.' Romy waved her hand towards the door.

Michael had put on a don't-give-a-toss act when Anezka had finally texted him earlier to ask if she could drop round.

'Nice of her to grace us with her presence, at last.' But Romy noticed his agitated blinking. 'I'd better get spruced up, I suppose,' he added, with the same studied nonchalance.

She'd helped him shower and dress – he'd insisted she shave his head properly because he kept nicking himself, then fussed about which shirt to wear.

'I can't wear those disgusting things.' He looked in despair at the grey jogging-pants Romy held out to him. '"Sweatpants are a sign of defeat," some wise person once said.'

'Maybe, but your others will be hard to get on and off . . . Peeing might be tricky.'

Michael's mouth pursed in an angry line. 'Bloody stroke. Bloody, bloody, fucking stroke.'

'Do you want to try your normal ones, then?' she asked, sympathizing with his loathing for the pull-on bottoms. Michael had always taken such a pride in his appearance: the traditional barrister's wig and gown, the beautifully tailored suits he'd favoured before the stroke, which shaped his slim frame so elegantly.

He'd thought about it, then sighed. 'No, probably stick to these hideous things. Don't want to piss myself because I can't get my flies undone.'

Now he was sitting in his armchair, his iPad on his knee, spruced up as best he could manage. Yet Romy couldn't help seeing her husband as Anezka would see him: old and frail. He was no longer the virile, successful, charismatic QC, with whom Anezka had fallen in love, swanning confidently into her restaurant with a host of important-looking colleagues.

Romy watched her hesitate on the threshold. Either Michael had not realized she was there, or he was pretending not to do so, because it wasn't till Anezka said his name that he raised his head.

'Anezka,' he said, holding out his good hand and beckoning her closer. 'I won't get up,' he joked.

Romy went to the kitchen to make tea and lay out the pink and green *macarons* from the fancy box. She could not hear anything from the other room at first because of the noise of the kettle. But once she'd poured the hot water onto the tea and left it to brew, she found herself guiltily creeping to the door, ear cocked. Anezka's voice, however – normally so strident – was quiet today and Romy could catch only a low murmur.

When she went through with the tea tray, the two were sitting in silence. Anezka had pulled up the leather pouffe Michael had brought back from a Moroccan trip decades ago and had taken his weaker hand in hers. But Romy caught the expression on her husband's face. He looked as if he were holding on to himself very tightly.

Anezka turned as Romy approached and she saw the tears in the woman's eyes. 'I should go,' she said, and jumped up from the pouffe, before Romy had even put the tray down.

Michael didn't move a muscle.

'Oh . . . I've made tea,' Romy said.

But Anezka pushed past her with a muttered 'Sorry, sorry . . .'

Romy hurried after her. Anezka was in the hall, searching in her bag for something. She stopped when she saw Romy.

'Are you OK?' Romy asked.

Anezka let out a long sigh and pressed the tissue she'd retrieved from her bag to her eyes. 'I love Michael so much.' She stopped and blinked at Romy. 'But I think he has what he always wanted now.'

Puzzled, Romy asked, 'What do you mean?'

Anezka said nothing, just stepped forward and gave Romy a brief hug, then turned and was gone, the door slamming behind her.

'It must have been the sweatpants,' Michael said grimly, when she went back into the sitting room.

Romy handed him his tea.

'The worst bit was seeing the pity on her face . . . remembering the man I was, the man she fell for . . .'

'I'm sorry,' she said, unable to deny the truth of what he said.

'Yes, well . . .' He shrugged and was silent for a moment. Then he seemed to pull himself together and gave her a charming smile. 'So, I'm footloose and fancy free again. Any takers?'

Romy forced a smile. She felt suddenly panicky and rose quickly to her feet, her tea still on the table, untouched. As she reached the door she heard Michael's voice behind her.

'I behaved like an arse yesterday, about Fincham,' he said, biting his lip. 'I'm sorry.'

Romy turned to see him staring at her intently, his right hand anxiously kneading his left in his lap.

'None of my business, what you get up to,' he went on. 'It was wrong of me to blurt it out to Leo like that.'

She nodded as she stood there, arms crossed. 'Thanks.'

Michael's expression was rueful. 'But I'll admit, I'm horribly jealous of your brigadier.'

'Colonel,' Romy corrected him.

He chuckled. 'I've just promoted him.' Then his expression sobered again. 'Anyway, the thought of him putting his hands all over you . . . It made me feel thoroughly sick.'

Romy suppressed a sigh. She didn't want Michael treading his muddy boots across her relationship with Finch, even in the privacy of his mind.

'Anezka got it right,' Michael was saying. His speech had much improved in the last week or so. He still spoke slowly, and often paused to find a word, but he was beginning to sound like a ponderous version of his old self. 'The reason I'm jealous is blindingly obvious.'

Romy barely controlled a sharp shake of the head. She didn't want to hear any more.

'I miss you. I miss our life together. I miss . . . all of it.'

However much she didn't want to hear them, his words sounded genuine and full of a passion he had latterly used only in the courtroom, never in relation to herself or their marriage. Tears rose to her eyes. *So that's what Anezka meant.*

'But I realize you're hardly going to plump for a miserable old crock like this,' he patted his chest, 'with Action Man waiting in the wings. And I don't blame you.'

'It's not about that, you know it isn't.' She sighed. 'I thought we'd put all this behind us.' She found her heart aching for the man, shrunken inside the chair opposite, and gave herself a mental shake. Going down that road would do neither of them any favours. 'You've always despised self-pity,' she said briskly. 'This is not like you.'

Michael blinked anxiously and visibly straightened up. 'I'm *not* like me, Romy. Can't you see that? I don't feel even remotely like the man I used to be. I . . .' He gave a gulping swallow. 'I feel pathetic, vulnerable, like I've lost a layer of skin. I keep seeing myself . . .'

Neither of them spoke for a long time. Thoughts churned in Romy's head, a jumble of the past and the present, of Michael, of Finch. None of it made much sense, except that she didn't want to be here, didn't want to be having this conversation.

'Are you in love with Fincham?' Michael's voice had suddenly found its strength again.

'I don't know,' she said, when he continued to stare, clearly waiting for her to speak.

But he wasn't satisfied with her response. 'Come on, Romy, not good enough. Speak up, you must have some idea.'

'We're not in court, Michael,' she retorted, remembering his habit of relentlessly picking away at a subject until he got the answer he required.

He gave an apologetic grin. 'Sorry, m'lud. Badgering the witness. But –'

'I said I don't know,' she interrupted. 'I like him a lot, but we haven't known each other all that long.'

Silence again. Romy was aware of the Circle Line thundering under the building. It was something she'd barely noticed when she lived in the flat.

She watched him as he picked up his iPad, lowered his head. He wasn't the man she'd married. Neither was he the man she'd left. This was – as Michael himself had told her – a whole new person she faced. And she wasn't sure how to relate to his uncustomary desire to emote, to apologize, to self-deprecate. His new-found appreciation of her was disturbing, to say the least. Disturbing, because she couldn't help but feel something tugging around her heart when he had claimed to miss so much about the life they had once shared.

Then swiftly on the heels of these thoughts came the words – involuntary and unwelcome – she would never forget: . . . *forcing me back . . . so I was pinned under him*, which no nostalgia – however genuine – was powerful enough to obliterate.

But through all this mental turmoil, one thing had become crystal clear: *I can't stay here with Michael any longer*, Romy decided. *I must talk to Daniel.*

27

Finch was sweating by the time he'd finished washing the kitchen floor. He'd been on a mission since early morning: scrubbing the toilet and shower, polishing the chrome on the taps until it shone, twitching the freshly washed duvet on Grace's bed until there wasn't a single crease, opening all the windows so that the mustiness of a man living alone was completely banished. Finch had been in the army too long to tolerate mess – the house was always in good order – but now he took it to another level. A jug of pink roses from the garden in her bedroom, an enticing pile of fruit in the bowl in the kitchen, surfaces wiped, cooker gleaming, cushions plumped – he wanted it to be perfect.

Grace had rung first thing to say that Sam wouldn't be able to make it till tomorrow. Finch was secretly pleased. He liked Sam – a mild-mannered surveyor with a neat auburn beard whom she'd been with for nearly four years now, married for two – but it was a treat, these days, to have time alone with his stepdaughter. It would give him a chance to tell her about Romy in private, gauge her reaction without an audience. And if it turned out Grace wasn't ready to meet Romy yet, then so be it.

She was due at six, but knowing Grace's slightly chaotic modus vivendi – and the Friday-night traffic – she might be much later. It was nearly six now, but he decided he had time to give Romy a quick ring and check she was still coming down.

'Definitely. I should be there by twelve at the latest.' She sounded, Finch thought, the most cheerful she had been since Michael's stroke. 'I've just been talking to Daniel. He says he's quite happy now to manage without me. Isn't that great?'

Finch laughed with pleasure. 'It certainly is.'

'Michael's really not going to like me deserting him, but still . . . this means I can pop in once a week or something, line somebody up for when Daniel has his days off and Leo can't make it . . . and I'm free.'

He felt his heart lift. 'That's brilliant news, Romy. I'm so happy for you.' *And for me too.*

She laughed, sounding almost drunk. 'OK. I'll text when I'm home.'

The lights of a car flashed through the sitting-room window. 'Better go,' Finch said, getting up. 'I think that's Grace.' As he closed his phone and went to greet his step-daughter, he felt a glow of optimism.

It was so good to see her. They had a delightful supper together: Finch cooked sausages, butter beans and baked tomatoes, added a green salad – Grace's go-to comfort meal from long before Finch had met her and Nell. It was warm enough to eat outside, and he brushed off the slatted wooden garden table, dug out the faded turquoise cushions for the chairs and lit three fat candles. It was not since Nell was alive that he'd had supper in the garden by candlelight.

Grace was in a buoyant mood. Nell had always worried about her, saying she was too neurotic to be happy and never settled at anything long enough to find out if it would make her so. But Finch had seen a change in recent years. Sam, he thought, was a steadying influence. Living with him had stopped her drinking so much – which Nell had worried about too – and given her a solid, loving base from which she could fly.

'To Mum,' Grace said, lifting her glass to chink against Finch's. Supper was finished, cherry stones lay on a saucer amid crumpled paper napkins, an empty dark-chocolate-bar wrapper and the remains of a bottle of Pinot.

'To Mum,' Finch echoed. And for a moment they sat in silence and remembered the woman they had loved so much. He smiled at Grace, thinking how beautiful she looked in the candlelight, with her thick corn-blonde waves tucked behind her ears and her mother's huge grey eyes. She was not like her mother in physique. Nell had been slight and fine-boned, while Grace was tall and strongly built, with long limbs and square swimmer's shoulders – her father's, he presumed, although he'd never met the man. Grace had had no contact with him since she was about ten – he just wasn't interested.

Finch had begun the evening nervously. He kept looking for a gap in the conversation – which wasn't easy, because Grace barely drew breath – where he could slip in his announcement about Romy. But gradually he relaxed and just enjoyed his stepdaughter's company as he listened to all the things that had been happening in her life since they'd last properly caught up.

'So how did the bathroom tiles work out?'

Grace pulled a face. 'Hmm. Not our greatest success. Sort of shed-work standard? But it'll have to do for now.'

'You won't notice after a while.'

Grace's eyes sparkled in the candlelight as she eyed him with a sudden directness. 'You seem in good form, Finch. Do I detect a bit of a glow about the cheeks?'

The perfect opportunity, plopping into his lap. Yet still he hesitated. Nell's presence was very strong this evening, with her daughter back in residence, but he couldn't let that put him off.

'Well,' he began, taking a steadying breath, 'funny you should say that . . .'

Grace leant forward eagerly. 'Go on.'

'There is someone . . .' *This is so difficult*, he thought. But Grace was staring expectantly at him. 'I've seen her around the village for a while, but then I met her properly for the first time when I did that charity 10K in March . . . and over the last few months, well, things have got a bit more involved . . .'

Grace's face was hard to read and he stopped, his worst fears coming to the fore.

She said, '"More involved", as in . . .?'

Another deep breath. 'Well . . . I like her a lot.'

'Wow. OK. That sounds serious, then.' Grace sat back in her chair. 'Wow,' she said again, almost in a whisper this time.

'I knew this would come as a shock to you, Gracie. And I was in two minds whether to tell you or not. But I don't want to be sneaking around behind your back.'

There was silence for a moment. Then his stepdaughter said emphatically, 'No . . . Listen, I'm really fine with it.' She gave him a wide grin. 'To be honest, I've been waiting for you to meet someone for ages. Just before she died, Mum told me she hoped you would . . .'

'She said that?' Finch was incredibly pleased to hear this. 'Well . . .' He felt almost embarrassed under his step-daughter's approving stare.

Neither spoke for a moment.

'We can't go on living in her shadow for ever,' Grace said softly.

'No, but nor will I ever replace your mum, Gracie. You know that. What I have with Romy is a totally different thing.'

'Romy? Is that her name? So tell me more about her.' His stepdaughter's voice had regained its usual bounce. She might be putting on a brave face, but at least they were over the first hurdle. Finch's breathing came more easily as he settled in to tell her.

'OK. Well, she's separated from her husband. Not divorced yet, but she will be. Or might have been, if he hadn't had a stroke a few weeks ago. She's gone back to London to help out until he's better, but normally she lives in one of those cottages on the harbour. It used to be their weekend place.'

Grace was frowning. 'Hmm . . . She's looking after him? And they're not divorced? Are you sure she's not spinning you a line, Finch?'

'I hope not. I don't think so. I've made it sound as if she's more attached to Michael – that's her husband – than she is.'

Grace seemed doubtful. He supposed it might all sound pretty unconventional. He couldn't expect her to be on board immediately.

'Romy's passionate about the environment, into conservation,' he hurried on, 'but not in a smug way. She volunteers for hazel coppicing and stuff, just because she loves doing it.' He realized he wasn't painting a very enticing picture of Romy. His stepdaughter had always made fun of the sandal-wearing vegans with grey ponytails whose territory she – and many others – considered environmental issues to be.

He tried again. 'She's not a hippie,' he insisted. 'She's led a sophisticated life in London – her ex is a successful QC. Michael Claire, he's often in the papers, defending some celebrity sex offender.' He knew he was being snide in defining Michael like that, but he didn't particularly care. It was Romy he wanted Grace to like, not Michael.

Grace's face, normally so animated, went very still.

28

As Finch cleared away the supper things, blew out the candles and filled the dishwasher, he was worried. Something wasn't right. *Her face*, he thought, *when I mentioned Michael's surname . . . That was when her mood changed.* Before that, she'd seemed quite happy to talk about Romy. But straight afterwards she'd said she was really tired, and rushed off, barely saying goodnight to him. *Does she know Michael?*

He lay awake for a long time. The moon was bright outside the window and he couldn't be bothered to get up and shut the curtains. He must have finally dropped off, though, because when he felt a hand on his shoulder, he had to drag himself up from a very great depth.

'Gracie?' He blinked, reaching for the bedside light, the figure of his stepdaughter in her pink childhood dressing gown – which still hung on the back of her bedroom door for when she visited – loomed above him, silhouetted by the moonlight. He heard a sob and instantly sat upright, swinging his legs out of the bed.

She plonked herself down beside him and he saw she was clutching a tissue in her hand, her face blotched, eyes red-rimmed from crying.

'Sweetheart . . .' He put his arm around her shoulders and brought her close. She was cold and shaking. 'What is it? What's happened?' He thought it must be something to do with Nell. Grace had always found it hard coming home since her mother had died. She'd said so, many a time. 'Are you missing your mum?' he asked.

But Grace shook her head vehemently. 'No, well, yes, I always miss her. But this . . .' She stopped.

'Tell me,' he said gently.

She began to cry again and he waited, just holding her until the tears had subsided. 'I've never told anyone,' she began, 'not in all these years. I didn't think I ever would.' She pulled away and blew her nose, clasping her hands tight together between her knees. 'But when you mentioned Michael Claire . . .'

'You know him?' Finch asked, his guts churning with an unnamed fear.

She nodded. 'I did work experience in his chambers when I was sixteen. For a week. James Bregman – the barrister Michael shares chambers with – was a friend of Mum's.' Grace was talking quickly now, and she barely paused before more words came tumbling out, her voice suddenly forceful and determined. 'You won't want to hear this, Finch, but Michael Claire assaulted me one night, when everyone else had gone home. He gave me wine and he assaulted me.'

Finch gasped, trying to take in what Grace was saying.

His stepdaughter's eyes were defiant. 'He sat next to me on this chaise-longue thing in his office and stuck his tongue down my throat and tore my dress, pinned me down, bruised my breasts and my thighs . . . It was brutal.'

'He raped you?' he croaked, the word stinging his tongue.

'No.' Grace's voice wobbled. 'But he might have, if the phone hadn't rung and I'd managed to push him off and escape.'

'Oh, my God.' Finch was horrified, stunned. *Romy's husband?* It made his blood run cold. 'What happened afterwards? Where did you go?' He was trying to get his head around what his stepdaughter was saying.

'I was staying with a school friend in town that week.'

'And your mum?'

'Mum was here. I didn't see her till the weekend.'

'But you told her?'

She bowed her head, looking defeated. 'No.'

Puzzled, Finch asked, 'Why ever not?'

'I was sure she'd say I led him on. Michael was such a star, so charismatic and charming. I'd been saying this to Mum all week so I thought she'd leap to conclusions.' She fell silent. 'And I wondered if I had led him on. Or maybe I'd imagined the whole thing, that it wasn't really so bad. He was just trying it on. Lots of men do that and nobody cares.' Another pause. 'He was so well connected, so admired, I knew if I told anyone they'd just think I was a silly girl trying to get some attention.' Her words had taken on an almost childish tone, as if she were speaking with her teenage voice. 'MeToo has become such a thing these days. Compared to some, my experience is minor league . . .'

Grace faltered and fell silent. Finch knew she would have repeated this account over and over to herself through the years as she tried to rationalize – unsuccessfully – what had happened to her. Tried to make light of it, to pretend it was no big deal.

'You poor, poor girl,' Finch said, wrapping his arms round the trembling figure. 'It isn't minor at all. Keeping it secret all these years must have been hell.' He looked down at her. 'So even Sam doesn't know?'

She shook her head miserably. 'I've never breathed a word to anyone till now. And I don't see the point in involving him. He'd only be upset. And he might want to make something of it . . . I couldn't bear that.' She raised her head. 'I will never, *ever* go to the police, Finch. So don't even suggest it.'

'I wasn't going to,' he said, although his blood was boiling with fury at the man. He should be made to pay, he thought. He should at least face some sort of public exposure. But the thought of what Grace would have to go through to achieve that end made him cringe. *What would Nell have done?* he asked himself. His wife's imagined opinion had been the benchmark for any problem in the past. She'd been so fearless when faced with a difficult situation, tackling it head on, never taking no for an answer.

'Your mum would definitely have believed you, Gracie. She'd never have thought you were to blame in a situation like that. You were sixteen, for God's sake.'

Grace looked almost sullen for a second. 'You don't know that. I was a bit of a crazy teenager, back then. I loved attention.' She gave an ironic smile. 'Not any more.'

'That's like saying a girl deserves to be raped because she's wearing a short skirt and has had a drink or two.'

'Yeah, I know. But it's different when it's you who's been attacked. It doesn't seem nearly so black and white then . . . I don't know, maybe he was going through a bad time – he was certainly working way too hard. Maybe he just lost it . . .'

'Nothing excuses what he did, Gracie. Nothing.'

Suddenly her eyes were pleading. 'You won't tell Sam? Please, Finch, he can't know. I wouldn't have told you if it wasn't for Romy.'

Romy . . . 'Of course I won't,' he assured her.

His mind, as soon as he was alone and Grace had gone back to her bedroom, began racing, unwelcome images flashing across his brain. He wondered what he should do with what he'd been told, how best he could help his stepdaughter. She had entrusted him with her biggest secret, her very soul, but just knowing it, Finch felt as if he'd been left balancing on a tightrope across a pitch-black chasm.

Suddenly the suspicion that had plagued him as soon as Grace made her revelation – a suspicion he was trying so desperately to evade – returned to smack him full in the face. *Did Romy know? Is that why she left Michael? Has she been covering up for the man all these years?*

29

Romy stood at the door of Michael's bedroom early on Saturday morning. She was itching to get back to Sussex. And intrigued to meet Grace.

His eyes flicked momentarily from the television screen, then back to what he was watching, a twitch around his mouth his only welcome. The room was in curtained darkness, although she had heard the noise of the TV through the wall since dawn. She glanced at the screen. A man lay flat on his back outside what looked like a small but elaborate mausoleum, a dark pool of blood spreading across the marble under his head. As she watched, the shot panned out, music swelled and the screen faded to black.

'Did he deserve it?' Romy asked, as Michael finally tore his gaze away from the television, a smile on his face.

'Oh, definitely. He'd had a child killed, so he had to go. A thoroughgoing bastard.' He sounded so satisfied that Romy smiled as she watched him pull himself awkwardly up in bed and glance at the bedside clock. 'You're early.'

'I'm off in a minute.'

There was silence as Romy saw Michael's expression fall. But since his outburst at the beginning of the week, he had not mentioned Finch, or his feelings for Romy, for which she was grateful. But she sensed them nonetheless, simmering hot beneath the surface, whenever she caught him looking at her.

'You're leaving me with Daniel, then?' Michael asked. 'Aren't you worried he'll neglect me? Starve me? Or, worse, make me eat that disgusting muesli mix he seems to dote on?'

Romy laughed. 'Probably be very good for you.'

He shrugged and did not reply.

'You don't need both of us any more, Michael. You're not incapable,' she said, more snappishly than she intended.

'Oh, thanks, good to know,' he retorted. 'Because from where I'm sitting – standing being a fucking nightmare, of course – it certainly doesn't feel like I'm in such great shape.'

She sighed inwardly, sorry for her impatience. 'No, OK. I sympathize, you know I do. But you seem to have forgotten you can make your own decisions. You just wait for people to do things for you – to you – that you're perfectly capable of doing yourself.'

'Such as?'

'Cleaning your teeth at the washbasin and not in that nasty plastic bowl. You can lean against the basin now. Washing yourself in the shower – you just wait for Daniel to do it. You even asked me to turn out your bedside light the other night.'

Michael glared at her. 'My bad hand is closest, that's all.'

'I know you think I'm being a nag. But I saw it with Barry. He just gave up after his stroke and Angie became his slave.'

'Ha! Is that what you're worried about? That you'll become my slave?' His tone was peevish.

'No, Michael,' she said, trying to be patient. Although it wasn't far from the truth. It did scare her that he wouldn't make enough effort to be independent. 'I just want you to get better. Is that such a bad thing?'

He turned his head away. When he looked back, his face was rigid with fear. 'You don't understand, Romy.' His voice rose. 'I get so bloody terrified . . . I don't even know what I'm terrified of, only that sometimes my heart pounds and I feel so scared I want to shit. But I can't even do that because I can't bloody get to the bathroom in time.' He gave a sardonic laugh, leaning forward, away from the pillows. 'Do you have any fucking idea what that feels like? *Do you?*' His eyes were shooting fire and she felt she must physically stand her ground or be blown away by his rage.

'No,' she said quietly, heart hammering. 'No, of course I don't. I'm sure it's absolute hell.'

His gaze softened and he muttered sheepishly, 'When you're here, I don't feel quite so scared.'

Romy cringed. Taking a deep breath, she said firmly, 'It's not good, getting too dependent on me or anyone else, however harsh it might seem to you right now.'

Michael closed his eyes. 'OK, OK.'

She sat down on the edge of his bed and took his limp hand. It was cold, as always, and she rubbed it between her own. Neither spoke for a while.

When he opened his eyes, he said, his voice pleading, 'I'm sorry I shouted. I know you're right, but it just feels so hopeless. I do the same sodding exercises every day, over and over till I want to scream, and nothing changes. Imogen keeps telling me – you *all* keep telling me – that I'm doing *so* well and there's *so* much improvement. But I can't see it.' His eyes gleamed with tears. 'I don't know what's going to happen to me.'

Romy's heart contracted. 'You *are* getting stronger, Michael. I can see it, even if you can't. And, yes, I know it's slow, but your walking is way better, and even your shoulder has got some strength back. It's only been a few weeks, remember.'

He nodded, wiping his eyes.

'I'll be back on Sunday evening,' she said, not wanting to emphasize, when he was so upset, that her stay in the flat was coming to an end. She would talk to him properly about it on Monday. 'Phone if you need me,' she added, hoping he wouldn't, because her mind was already off and away, back in her home by the sea, sitting in the sunny garden, pruning the climbing rose, seeing Finch . . . maybe even meeting his stepdaughter in the harbour-side pub for a chilled glass of something.

Romy was getting a takeaway coffee at Victoria station when Finch's text came in: *Hi. We'll have to postpone today. Sorry. Grace a bit wobbly. Talk soon.*

She stood amid the crowd around the departures board and reread his message. '*Wobbly*'? It seemed an odd word to use. She found she was disproportionately disappointed. And there was something about his text . . . Was it a bit peremptory? Finch was not a gusher, but this one felt different, somehow, as if he were subtly trying to pull away from her.

The worry haunted her all afternoon. *Is Grace having a problem with her stepfather moving on?* Or was Romy being paranoid and Grace was maybe just not well? 'Wobbly' could be taken in a number of ways, she realized. But if her suspicions were right, what did this mean for her and Finch?

She didn't go out, nervous that she might bump into them round the village. There was enough to keep her busy at home, anyway. The place needed cleaning and the garden was positively jungly, requiring serious attention, despite the two hours a fortnight she paid Susan, the gardener.

There was no word from Finch all day, even though she'd texted, asking him to ring when he had a chance. Romy could not help feeling rejected, however childish she knew that to be. She had been so looking forward to seeing him. But later that evening, as she sat with a bowl of tomato soup and her second glass of red wine – still nothing from Finch – she couldn't shake the feeling that something really wasn't right. By the third glass, she was reaching for her mobile to call him and find out. It went to voicemail and she didn't leave a message.

It was early afternoon on Sunday – Romy having all but given up hope of hearing from him – when her mobile pinged with a terse text: *Can I come over?*

30

The expression on Finch's face when she opened the cottage door was fixed like stone. Romy was taken aback. He looked as if he hadn't slept in a week, the circles beneath his eyes slate-grey and pronounced in his tanned face. But worse than that, his normally kind brown eyes regarded her warily.

'Hi,' he said, making no move to kiss or embrace her.

She stared at him, stepping back so he could enter the house before her, then closing the door. The atmosphere in the sitting room was heavy and still. Finch stood, arms crossed, in front of the empty wood-burner.

Romy frowned. 'You look awful.' She did not sit either, and they faced each other across the length of the coffee table in silence.

Suddenly his fierce demeanour crumpled and he covered his face with his hands. 'Oh, Romy. This is so terrible. I don't know how to tell you.'

Heart bursting, she crossed her own arms tight across her chest, trying, somehow, to still the cold panic rising through her body. *What on earth?*

Finch took a loud, rasping breath and began to pace up and down the small space by the stove. Then, as quickly as he'd started, he ground to a halt and faced her again, his look determined now, his eyes fixed on hers. 'It's Grace.'

Romy said nothing. Neither did Finch, for what seemed like an eternity.

'Right . . . Start from the beginning,' he said finally, his voice cracking with emotion. 'I was telling her about you, and she seemed happy for me. Her only worry was that you weren't divorced from Michael yet, and had gone back to look after him . . . She thought I might be being a mug.'

'I'd probably think the same,' Romy said.

Finch didn't seem to hear her, just twitched at her reply as if it were a passing fly.

'But then I told her more about you and mentioned Michael, used his full name.' He stopped and eyed her, as if this fact held some significance. But Romy didn't get it.

'So?'

'Grace knows Michael, Romy. From when she did work experience with him when she was sixteen . . .'

Romy froze. *Work experience, sixteen.* The words were so etched on her brain that Finch did not need to finish his sentence.

'There's no easy way to say this . . .'

She heard his next words as if from another universe and found her legs going from under her as she fell back on the sofa.

Finch's expression was tortured. She saw him swallow hard. 'Did you know?'

The letter. Romy blanched. *It was Grace who wrote the letter.* Multiple thoughts cascaded through her brain – but she was too shocked to make sense of them.

'*Did you*, Romy?' Finch's question was more strident this time.

'No,' she muttered, not looking at him. 'No, not at the time . . . and not that it was Grace.'

There was silence and she glanced up to see bewilderment on Finch's face.

Taking a deep breath, Romy went on, 'I got an anonymous letter . . .'

'A letter? When? What did it say?'

'Exactly what you've just told me.' Romy held her breath.

She heard Finch gasp. 'So you *did* know. You were actually told your husband had assaulted a sixteen-year-old child,' his emphasis on 'your husband' cut through her like a knife, 'but you did nothing about it?'

'It wasn't like that. I had no idea who it was from.' Romy, heart pounding, tried to gather her thoughts. 'And it only arrived three years ago. What *could* I have done when there was no name or contact details? And Michael flatly denied it, of course.' The words of the letter sprang before her eyes: *I just thought you should know who you're married to.* Romy could quote the letter verbatim, but that phrase, in particular, haunted her, pushing through her day-to-day thoughts at random intervals in the following years. It had only begun to fade since she'd moved to Sussex and distanced herself from Michael – since Finch had started to divert her into different waters.

'Do you still have the letter?' Finch demanded.

She nodded.

'Show me, please.'

She got up, shaking, and went to retrieve it, locked in her dressing-table drawer. Now she wished she'd torn it up when she'd had the chance.

*

197

Finch had tears in his eyes as he scanned the creased sheet of notepaper. 'It's exactly what she told me last night,' he murmured.

They were both on the sofa now. But there was no togetherness. Romy held herself stiff and scared beside him, the distance between them vast.

Lifting his head from the page, he frowned at her. 'So what did you do when you read it?'

'I – I showed it to Michael, obviously.'

'And what did he say?'

Romy twitched, feeling she was under interrogation. 'He said he didn't do it,' she replied. Although, in fact, it hadn't been his first reaction. 'He couldn't even remember who she was,' she added. But her own words made her squirm. They sounded so pathetic, such a huge lie, and she hurried on, desperate to make him understand: 'They have young people doing work experience in chambers all the time. There've been dozens of them.'

Finch stared at her in disbelief. 'You can't be serious, Romy. *Michael couldn't remember?*' He gave a derisive snort. 'Or did so many teenage girls accuse him of assault that he lost track?' When she didn't reply, he went on, 'So you didn't do a damn thing? You just put the letter – a letter that makes your hair stand on end – into a drawer and forgot about it, got on with your lives?'

It was damning. She tried again to explain. 'Michael insisted it wasn't true. And I believed him. He was my husband, the father of my children.' She took a trembling breath. 'There was no name, Finch. I had no idea who she was . . . and she said she didn't want to get the police involved. Why would I believe a letter from someone who wouldn't even give her name over the word of a man I'd been married to for nearly thirty years?' She paused. 'And the letter came thirteen years after it had supposedly happened –'

'*Supposedly?* Are you seriously telling me you still don't believe this? That you believe Michael over Grace, even after what she told me last night?' Finch waved the single sheet angrily under Romy's nose.

She pulled back, offended, feeling a spurt of anger at Finch's aggression, at his unquestioning assumption that his beloved Grace was telling the truth.

'Michael has always categorically denied it,' she said flatly. 'He was as horrified as you when he read the letter.'

'I imagine he was.' Finch snorted, breathing hard through his sarcasm, his face flushed with anger and confusion.

'And of course I didn't forget about it. It obsessed me. But what should I have done? He was my husband and I believed him. Would you really expect me to go to his chambers and ask around, find out if anyone knew who this girl might be, who was accusing Michael of sexual assault?' She wrapped her arms tightly around her shaking body. 'Michael is a barrister . . .'

Finch dropped his head into his hands. She wanted more than anything in the world to have him embrace her right now. But there was no way that would happen.

'But you knew, didn't you?' His voice was heavy and cruel and he would not look at her. 'You believed every word Grace wrote. That's why you left him.'

He's made up his mind, Romy thought, *but he's wrong*. She always told herself she hadn't left Michael because she believed the letter, but because of the effect the letter had had on her marriage. And even now, knowing who had written it, hearing the same accusations from practically the horse's mouth, she struggled to see Michael as the violent abuser Grace named in the letter. But, if she was being honest, she had to acknowledge that tiny sliver of doubt – born the day the letter came and Michael had reacted so strangely.

Her mind flashed back to the previous Friday, an image of him shuffling on his frame, like an old man, along the corridor towards the kitchen. 'Michael has many faults, but I have never known him to use physical violence on anyone in his entire life,' she said quietly.

Finch threw his arms into the air. 'If he didn't attack Grace, then why the fuck would she write this letter? Think about it, Romy. *Thirteen years* later? Why would she go white at the mention of the name "Michael Claire"? Why would she sob and shake with fear at the thought of anyone – even her mother, even dear, kind Sam – finding out what happened to her?' He glared at her. 'Tell me, does all that make sense if Michael didn't do it?'

It didn't. Romy accepted that. 'None of it makes sense, Finch, but you didn't know Grace back then,' she said, clutching at straws. 'You told me you only met when she was at college. So you've no idea what she was like when she was sixteen.'

Finch was frowning at her, apparently stupefied.

'You ask why Grace would say such things if they're not really true. But you must know people do, all the time.' She turned her head, unable to look at him any more. 'Listen, I'm not saying *something* didn't happen, but neither of us can be certain exactly what.' She took a breath. 'I just can't envisage Michael being violent.' It was as if the more Finch attacked her, the more stubborn she felt in her husband's defence. *How can Finch be so sure?*

Then, suddenly, the fight went out of her. She slumped on the cushions and swallowed the tears – she was not going to cry in front of him. After a shaky breath, she said, her tone conciliatory, 'Oh, Finch, I don't know, I honestly don't. Grace is obviously really traumatized about that night. But maybe it wasn't as black and white as it seems. I mean, Grace claims she saw Michael as a "bit of a god",' – the words were imprinted on her brain – 'and maybe she had a crush on him, maybe she sort of flirted with him, then things –'

'Stop right there,' Finch said, flicking his palm out to block her words, then sprang up from the sofa. 'I'm not going to sit here listening to you blame Gracie, just to save your miserable husband's miserable skin.'

Romy was shocked by the hostility in his voice. She had never seen this side to Finch. He'd always been so under control, so kind to everyone, not just to her. Although she understood why he was angry.

She watched him stalk towards the front door without another word. She wanted to call out to him, to pull him back, to find some common ground on which they might agree. But he was gone before she recovered her voice, and wouldn't have heard the pleading 'Finch!' that she croaked in his wake.

As she sat shaking on the sofa, no longer in the firing line of Finch's wrath, she tried to think clearly about what he had told her. And she was forced, unwillingly, to concede that Michael must have done *something* to that girl – she could not yet think of her as a real person, as Grace. But to what extent her account could be believed, Romy had no idea. Whatever the truth, her relationship with Finch looked to be well and truly over.

31

Finch strode through the village at top speed, his feet carrying him unconsciously towards his house, his brain spinning. He was devastated. He didn't know what to think, his mind a jumble of accusation and doubt. But what shocked him the most was Romy's intransigence in defence of Michael.

True, he hadn't known Grace back then – as Romy had been so keen to point out – but he'd known her for most of the sixteen years since and he thought he had a pretty good take on who his stepdaughter was and of what she was capable.

And, yes, she could be highly strung, but she was searingly honest, like her mother. And a very straightforward person. If she really had been flirting with Michael, as Romy suggested, and things had got out of hand, wouldn't she just have admitted it at the time? To her mother, at least – although Finch did remember Nell saying there was a lot of friction between her and Grace when she was in her teens, which Grace had alluded to last night.

He reached home and closed the front door behind him with a thud, relieved to be alone, relieved that Grace and Sam had gone, so he didn't have to face them in the state he was in.

There was still mess from brunch that he hadn't bothered to clear away. He'd been so keen to confront

Romy that he'd raced round to the cottage the minute he'd waved them off to Manchester, hoping against hope that she would convince him she had no knowledge of the attack. Or, if she did, that she'd left Michael the moment she found out. But those hopes were now dashed.

He automatically began scraping the bagel crumbs and smoked salmon bits off the plates, emptying the coffee grounds from the cafetière and putting the remaining half of a lemon into the fridge. It helped to do something practical and mindless. But his body was so pent up, he knew this wouldn't be enough to soothe him. He'd have to run it off later.

Grace had been pale and quiet when she came downstairs on Saturday morning. Finch wasn't sure how to treat her. *Does she want to talk about it?* She'd flicked him a half-smile, but otherwise didn't meet his eye, flopping down at the kitchen table, still wrapped tightly in her pink dressing gown, sleeves clutched over her hands, like a child. Last night's tears were not apparent, but her eyes were swollen and over-bright.

He made her a strong cup of coffee in silence, which she took with a sigh, closing both palms around the mug as if to warm them.

'I'm so sorry, Finch,' she said.

'*Sorry?*' he exclaimed. 'For God's sake, Gracie! You don't need to be sorry for anything. It's me who should apologize for bringing up the past like that . . . although I'm glad you told me.'

She gave him a sardonic smile. 'Really? Puts you in a bit of a tricky position with Romy, I imagine.'

Finch didn't want to think about that at the moment. 'It's not healthy to keep something so serious bottled up, sweetheart. You should tell Sam – really, you should.' He saw the immediate distress in her face.

She shook her head. 'I can't.' But Finch didn't think she sounded as definite as she had the night before.

'He would understand. And you know he'd do anything to support you.'

Grace didn't reply at once. Then she said, 'Maybe. But why put that image in his head? It's horrible.' She gave a shaky sigh. 'Especially when there's nothing he can do about it.'

'Still, now you've told me . . .'

She nodded and Finch decided to leave it at that. It was up to her, in the end.

'French toast?' he asked, knowing this was his step-daughter's favourite.

By the time Sam arrived from Manchester, Grace had showered and dressed. She seemed composed. If the hug she gave her husband was a little tighter than was usual, or her chatter less lively, then Sam didn't appear to notice. But Finch kept a close eye on her, his heart breaking at the struggle she must have had to live with the secret she'd chosen to keep since she was a teenager.

Later on Sunday evening, as the sun was setting, Finch changed into his running gear and set off around the harbour on his favourite loop. He had waited till this time because he knew Romy would probably have gone back to Michael by now. Michael, who had sexually assaulted his and Nell's adored Grace. He realized he was clenching his jaw as his feet squelched through the mounds of summer seaweed on the road, his stride breaking until he was clear of the slippery mass and round the corner on the southern spur of the estuary.

He had not heard from Romy since he had stormed out – and he'd made no attempt to contact her. Using the steady pounding of his feet as a metronome for his thoughts, Finch tried to make sense of what had happened, from Romy's point of view.

First there was the assault itself, sixteen years ago now. This was a fact, in his mind, whatever Romy chose to believe. Finch was pretty sure she hadn't known about it at the time, but what were her options when she received the letter? *Tell someone?* But this, as Romy kept saying, was her husband of thirty years, his record apparently unblemished . . . as far as she knew, of course.

He ran on, thoughts whirring. *So she shows him the letter and he pretends he doesn't remember Grace.* And, of course, Michael would only definitely remember her – given the number of work-experience girls in his chambers and the length of time involved – if he *had* assaulted her. When obviously he would lie.

Finch stopped and bent over, getting his breath. He'd been running for half an hour and veered away from the harbour onto the small road leading round the fields and back to the village. It was shadowy now, the sky lit to the west with a fading plum and primrose. *Romy didn't know Grace*, he reminded himself. She couldn't find out who the letter-writer was without implicating her husband – whose career at the Bar would be ruined if there were even a sniff of scandal. And she had two sons to think of. So she had no idea if Grace was telling the truth . . . Here, Finch's thoughts started to run round in circles.

It all boils down, he concluded, by the time he was back at the house, *to whether she believes her husband, or some random woman – some random* anonymous *woman.* And he knew which one he'd believe, if it had been between Nell and a man making similar accusations.

Finch found his heart was beginning to soften and he was regretting the accusations he'd hurled at Romy. But then, as he stood by the sink and drained the entire contents of a large glass of water, some of which dribbled down his chin onto his chest, he remembered the way in which she'd so pitilessly questioned Grace's verbal account. *People make stuff up.* Finch accepted this was true – but not Grace. *Isn't Michael – clever and so well versed in the lies people tell – the one more likely to be making things up?* he asked himself bitterly.

He showered, dressed and came back downstairs. He wanted to cry as he moved to stand in front of the photograph of Nell.

'Why didn't you know?' he demanded, choking back his tears. 'Why didn't you see how distressed Gracie was when she came home from London? You're her mum. You should have known.' It was the first time since she'd died that Finch had reproached his wife. But Nell just smiled back and, after a minute, he turned disconsolately away. Everything seemed broken and empty to him now: Grace's peace of mind, his possible future with Romy, even his consoling connection with his dead wife.

He wanted to talk to Romy so badly it made his whole body ache. He kept reaching for his phone, then throwing it back onto the worktop, composing speeches in his head, then quickly discarding them. Because he didn't see how things could possibly work between them now. How could he be with a woman who – however understandably – refused to accept her husband's obvious culpability? And how could he betray his stepdaughter, bring this same woman into their family and expect Grace to be comfortable around her?

He closed his eyes and remembered the last time he and Romy had made love. Those hazel eyes had looked at him with such tenderness, her body responding to his with such desire. Would he really never be with her like that again? Never hold her in his arms, laugh with her over chips and a cocktail? He felt close to despair.

32

'Mr Michael has not had a good day,' Daniel said, when Romy arrived back at the flat.

She nodded, although she was distracted. At this precise moment, she wished her husband in Hell. Because Michael had categorically lied to her. As Finch pointed out, no one in their right mind would make such a song and dance about an event so many years ago, unless there were at least some truth in it. So Michael *must* remember exactly who she was and what had happened between them.

Daniel continued: 'He would not eat his lunch. He has had only a small piece of toast all day. Then the physio came – not Imogen – and he slipped when she was walking with him on the frame.'

'Slipped?' The word impinged on Romy's scattered consciousness and she tried to focus.

'It was not serious,' Daniel said quickly. 'He just slid over and ended up on the floor. We picked him up, but his breathing was very fast and he make this moaning sound. I thought at first he might be badly injured or maybe he have some sort of attack.'

Daniel had her full attention now. 'Attack? What sort of attack?'

'I was not sure, but I thought, so soon after a stroke . . . So I ring the surgery and the locum doctor came out.'

'Wait – the doctor? Why didn't you call me, Daniel?'

Daniel gave her an apologetic smile. 'I did. I left four messages.'

Romy blinked. Then she remembered her phone wasn't on. She'd waited for a miserable agonizing hour for Finch to get in touch after he'd left. But she couldn't stop herself checking the bloody thing every two minutes, so eventually she'd turned it off.

'What did the doctor say?' she almost snapped, feeling so guilty for missing Daniel's calls.

'By the time he get here, Mr Michael was better. But when I describe what had happened, he thought it might be a panic attack,' the boy replied. 'He was very careful – he checked him out, but he couldn't find anything that was wrong, except his pulse was high.'

'A panic attack?' Romy said, but she was remembering a couple of evenings ago and her husband suddenly clutching his chest and breaking out in a sweat, his breathing laboured. It had frightened her, too.

'He said we must keep him as calm as possible for the next twenty-four hours and get Dr Beech to see him,' Daniel added, his young face searching hers for approval.

'Did somebody die?' Michael asked, his eyebrows raised as he noted her expression.

Romy stood in the doorway to his bedroom. Despite her concern for him in the light of what Daniel had told her, she found she couldn't bear the sight of the man. 'Not you, obviously,' she retorted, forcing a smile which probably looked more like a grimace. Her husband, whatever had gone on earlier, looked the picture of serenity as he lay back on his snowy pillows – the most cosseted man on earth.

'Sorry to disappoint you on that front,' he said, with mock-seriousness. 'I did my best. Had them all going this afternoon. But apparently it was just a bit of run-of-the-mill hysteria.'

Romy wasn't in the mood for Michael's banter.

He patted the duvet with his good hand. 'Sit down, tell me all about it.'

'Nothing to tell,' she said dully.

'Good weekend?'

'Not particularly.'

'Action Man playing up?' He was joking, and she expected to see a jealous sneer on his face, but all she saw was what looked like genuine concern.

Romy sighed. She hadn't moved from the doorway and had no intention of doing so.

'I'm tired,' she said. 'Is there anything I can get you before I go to bed?'

Part of her wanted to blurt out, then and there, what Finch had told her, finally force him to tell her the truth. But she knew she was too wound up, too exhausted to be coherent. Plus Michael needed to be kept calm. She didn't want him disappearing behind another panic attack just as she was getting to the crux of that evening with Grace. It would wait till tomorrow.

As she slipped into bed, Romy felt as if she'd been put through a mangle and spat out the other side. She still remembered her mother's mangle and could instantly recall washday and the delicious soapy smell of the laundry powder bubbling away in the steamy water of the twin tub, the clothes churning beneath the surface. Then her mother picking them out with wooden tongs and squeezing them briefly – the spinner bit of the 'twin' didn't work, like much else in the house – and feeding them through the two wooden rollers of the mangle.

Romy, as a small child, was allowed to turn the handle and watch the flattened clothes slide out the other side and plop stiffly into the waiting clothes basket before her mother hung them on the line outside. She felt like those clothes now: squashed flat, lifeless, devoid of her normal shape.

She could understand Finch's position all too well. If she were him, she would surely have reacted in the same way. But instead of sympathizing with Grace and being as appalled as he – which any decent person would have done – she'd gone on the defensive and virtually blamed the girl for Michael's behaviour.

That night, sixteen years ago, sat like a stone in Romy's stomach, as if she had been there too, as if she herself were also to blame: Michael's sleazy partner in crime. She knew it was ridiculous, but she felt like those mothers of serial killers who stand by their sons and say in all honesty, 'My Frankie's a good boy. He'd never do such a terrible thing.' She had seen it in Finch's eyes, his shock and bewilderment when she continued to side with Michael.

What did he do that night? she asked herself, as she lay there on the edge of sleep, eyelids drooping from tiredness in the stuffy bedroom.

But, whatever the truth, nothing would mend the chasm that had opened up between her and Finch. Apologizing for blaming Grace would not wipe Romy's words from his memory or hers. So even if she did say sorry, and she would, and even if he completely forgave her, which, being Finch, he might, Romy couldn't see him choosing her over his stepdaughter, over *Nell*'s daughter. And he would have to choose, because Grace was never going to be comfortable having Romy around for weekend visits or jolly family get-togethers.

No, her love affair with Finch – that beautiful, surprising connection they had – was ruined now. In her mangled state, she felt nothing, just completely numb.

She heard a thud from next door. The last thing she wanted right now was to have to face the man responsible for her current nightmare. She held her breath.

There was another thump, a loud groan, then Michael's voice calling her . . .

He had fallen out of bed and was lying on the floor, legs out at odd angles, head rammed against the bedside cabinet. He was clutching his reading glasses in his good hand, his eyes glazed as he stared in her direction.

'Can't move,' he muttered, straining to pull himself up. 'Can't move, Romy. Can't bloody move.' His voice became more and more strident as he writhed around, pulling at the bedclothes, scrabbling at the carpet with his fingers, his glasses flung away and being crushed beneath his body.

'It's OK. I'm here, Michael. We'll get you up. Stop – stop struggling.'

He blinked up at her and she saw the fear in his eyes as she knelt beside him and pulled him round until she could hook her arm through his and haul him up and onto the bed. He was gripping her with such ferocity that she knew she would have bruises by morning.

'I've got you, it's OK,' she kept repeating, trying to soothe him. But the way he was catching at her made them both almost topple over. It was a good few minutes before she managed to land him back on the bed, lifting his legs and swivelling him round until he was lying flat out. But he wouldn't let go of her and she lost her balance and fell down on top of him.

For a moment she lay there, unable to prevent the memory of the many times they had lain like this, naked, making love. Not for a while now, but the sex they had shared in the past – so different from her lovemaking with Finch – had been quick and fierce and hungry, Michael always in a hurry. *I enjoyed it*, she thought sadly, as she began to pull away – but not before Michael had laid his hand gently to her cheek, his eyes gazing at her with a sort of hopeless longing.

'Kiss me,' he asked, his voice no more than a whisper.

Romy instantly removed his hand, her body rigid. She was about to snap, 'Don't touch me,' but he looked so pathetic lying beneath her that the words died on her lips. She just scrambled off, wrapping her silk dressing gown more tightly round her nakedness. She shivered. He had been her husband, yet all she could see was Grace.

Michael turned his head away and she heard, 'Sorry . . . sorry.'

Pretending nothing had happened, Romy busied herself plumping his pillows, hoisting him onto them and hauling the duvet back onto the bed. Michael lay, eyes closed, so shrunken and pale. She could see his mouth working anxiously.

'I didn't mean that,' he said.

Romy nodded, but didn't reply.

'I'm all over the place. I'm sorry,' Michael went on.

'It's OK,' she muttered, not meeting his eye.

There was silence from the bed.

'You looked disgusted.'

Romy's breath caught in her throat. 'I was surprised, that's all,' she said eventually, looking directly at him. His dark eyes were unfathomable.

'I was discombobulated when I fell.' Michael's face twisted. 'And then you were lying on top of me and . . . it was like the past few years didn't exist. I thought for a stupid moment we were still together.'

Romy didn't know whether to believe him or not. It could just be him making up a clever excuse. 'It doesn't matter,' she said.

Michael leant forward. 'It does matter, Romy. I don't want you to think I'm taking advantage of your kindness. I got confused. Will you forget it ever happened? *Please?*'

The desperation in his voice hit home and she sighed. 'I said, it doesn't matter, Michael. Really, there's nothing to forget.' She gave his duvet a final tug and turned away. 'Are you OK now?'

'Yes, yes. I'm fine,' he said quietly.

She sensed he was waiting for her to give him some sort of sign, some indication that she had forgiven him. But she couldn't bring herself to offer anything but a brief wave of her hand as she turned away.

*

Romy pulled the duvet close round her body, holding her cold hands in a ball under her chin, her knees drawn up. *Tomorrow*, she told herself. *Tomorrow Michael will tell me the truth.* She was aware she could leave Michael in the safe hands of Daniel and Leo, just go home. But she would not leave quite yet, even though she could. Not before she had got the truth out of Michael about that night once and for all.

33

But the following morning, the freedom she'd begun almost to smell was yanked out of her hand, as if she'd been brutally mugged.

Dr Beech stood beside her in the hall. 'A man like Michael,' he said, 'used to being in total control, at the top of his professional tree, he's going to take this sort of setback hard.'

Romy could almost hear Michael scoffing at the word 'setback', but she didn't interrupt.

'I've put him on paroxetine. I'm afraid he's showing clear signs of depression. The panic attack was a symptom.' He handed Romy a prescription slip. 'It takes a while for it to kick in, so don't expect any improvement immediately, usually around a couple of weeks. Could be as much as six.'

But this was the third blow of the day. Before breakfast, she'd found Daniel in the kitchen, his eyes red from weeping. His mother, so his father had told him earlier, had suffered an escalation of the renal cancer she'd been fighting, and been told she had only months to live.

'I will stay until Friday,' he said, his usual pragmatic self, despite the devastating news. 'You will have time to get someone else for Mr Michael,' he said.

Romy hugged him, reeling at the news. 'For goodness' sake, Daniel, don't worry about us. I'm so sorry about your mum. You said she'd been ill, but I thought she was better.'

He gave a sad smile. 'I thought so too.'

'We'll all miss you so much. You've done miracles with Michael – I know it hasn't always been easy.'

Daniel shrugged. 'I will miss you too.'

'But it won't be long before he's able to manage on his own, with a bit of luck.'

He had smiled encouragingly, but the message she'd read in his light blue eyes told her it would need more than luck.

Then there had been her phone call to Finch. She desperately wanted to apologize for what she'd implied about Grace, in the heat of the moment, which, whatever doubts she still had about Michael, had been so insensitive.

'Hi, Romy.' Finch's voice was subdued, but the hostility from Sunday was no longer apparent. Now she had him on the other end of the phone, though, how to say what she wanted to say?

Before she'd had a chance to speak, it was Finch who was apologizing. 'I'm sorry for being so aggressive the other day, storming out like that,' he said, almost formally. But despite the apology, she couldn't hear any note of affection in his voice and the knowledge twisted her heart.

'No, please, it's me who should apologize. That's why I rang, to say how sorry I am for what I said.'

'Thank you.' Finch spoke the words softly. Then he went on, 'Have you talked to Michael?'

'Not yet. He had a bad panic attack yesterday . . .' Romy ground to a halt, but Finch said nothing, and she hurried on, 'The doctor said he shouldn't get wound up. So I plan to talk to him later today. I need him to listen properly to what I have to say.'

Finch did not reply.

'Finch?'

She heard him sigh. 'I can't do this, Romy. It's no good. You're so invested in Michael. You obviously care deeply about his welfare, which is fair enough, but I just can't listen to it any more.'

Romy held her breath, her heart thumping unevenly in her chest. 'He's a sick man, Finch. Daniel has to go back to Switzerland and I can't just abandon him.' She was close to tears.

'I'm sorry about Daniel. But this thing with Grace has been such a shock. I can't see how we can go back to how things were before, even if you do eventually get around to confronting him.'

Romy was offended. 'Are you implying I'm dragging my feet? That's not fair. I haven't done anything wrong here.' But even as she said the words, she felt a stab of conscience. Although she could in no way be held responsible for Michael's actions, she must accept some responsibility for remaining silent and passive about the letter all this time. But she was desperate to get her point across to Finch. 'I knew nothing whatever about any of this until her letter arrived, I *promise* you.' She cleared her throat, her voice croaking as she tried to finish what she was saying. 'But even if Michael did what he's accused of, Finch, there's nothing I can do now to make it better for her – short of going to the police, which Grace doesn't want to happen. You seem to think I can.'

'If, if,' Finch said quietly. 'You're still wondering *if* he did it.'

'Listen to me, will you?' she said, almost shouting with frustration. 'I accept something went on that night. But until Michael actually tells me, nobody can say for sure what it was.'

'Except Grace.'

'Yes, there's her version. But there were two people in that room. What happened to innocent until proven guilty?'

'Doesn't seem to count as far as Grace is concerned. You're obviously intent on only believing Michael's version – if you ever find out what that is, of course.' His voice was edgy with an uncharacteristic sarcasm.

'I'm sorry about Grace,' she repeated stiffly.

There was silence at the other end of the line. If Finch, at the beginning of the phone call, had had the slightest desire to mend the gulf that had sprung up between them, her seeming equivocation had just burnt that bridge to the ground. She was furious with him, but in that moment she felt her heart would break. Since the day she'd found the letter, she had felt its scattered contents spilling over her, invading her mind, her heart, even her physical body – always there, like a pernicious virus. She had never in a million years anticipated such a cruel denouement.

'Goodbye, Finch,' she muttered, and didn't wait for his reply.

Now, she gave Dr Beech a tight smile. *Six weeks . . .* the words closed round her, like a fist.

'Thanks, Guy.' Romy moved towards the front door, folding the prescription absentmindedly in her hand.

'He shouldn't be left alone. These panic attacks are very debilitating.' Dr Beech rocked back and forth in his polished brogues. 'But Michael's tough. The arm's not good, but getting his negative feelings under control will help . . . Another three or four months and he'll be a new man.' He patted her arm encouragingly as he added, 'Lucky he's got you.'

34

Jenny was already outside the pub when Finch pulled in on his bike. He regretted agreeing to meet up, but he'd bumped into his friend in the Co-op earlier in the week and she'd immediately put her head on one side, frowning at his appearance. 'Goodness me, you do look miserable.' When he hadn't offered any explanation, she'd gone on, 'Listen, there's the village art trail on Friday. Let's meet for a nice lunch and have a potter round. That'll cheer you up.'

Finch had been too slow to think up a good excuse. He wasn't in the least bit interested in local art – collecting stuff of any kind was not his thing – but he'd been slowly going crazy alone in the house in the three days since he'd told Romy about Grace and Michael. Running had helped – to a degree – in managing severe bouts of despair at losing Nell, but this thing with Romy was different. It wasn't clear-cut, like a death, but tormenting and infuriatingly complex. Finch felt only anger towards the man who had attacked Grace – but he couldn't avoid a reluctant sympathy for the man currently so disabled by a stroke. He was furious with Romy for siding so stubbornly with Michael – but he could partially understand why she did so in the context of her marriage. Every day he ran and ran, but all these contradictory emotions ran doggedly alongside him.

Jenny kissed his cheek and took his arm as they turned towards the pub door. 'There's a pensioners' lunch going on in there, I hope they don't think we're candidates.'

Finch laughed. 'Better sit outside, then.'

'Now,' said Jenny, as soon as they were settled at a wooden picnic table, with cider and a ploughman's each. 'Tell me what's wrong.' She gave him a knowing smile. 'Although maybe I can guess.'

'You can?'

'Romy's gone back to her husband?' She checked his face to see if she was right and obviously concluded she was, because she went on almost smugly, 'I was worried she might.'

Finch, embarrassed, said nothing. There was no chance he could open his heart up to Jenny about the real cause of his distress, no way he would betray Grace's confidence.

She took a hearty bite out of her bread and cheese while she waited for him to reply.

'It's complicated,' was the best he could come up with.

Jenny gave a sympathetic sigh. 'When are relationships ever not? I mean, look at Euan.'

Finch just nodded. He didn't want to 'look at Euan', not again. It was like plugging in a CD, the exact same bile flowing in a monotonous loop. What he really wanted was to ask Jenny something that had been niggling him, but which he had pushed aside in the face of Grace's anguish. Grace had mentioned – like Jenny previously – that her mum was a friend of James Bregman. But it was Jenny's sly expression when she herself had done so that came back to him now.

'So this James Bregman – Michael's partner,' he began. 'You say he's an old friend of yours?'

Jenny looked a bit sheepish. 'Well, we used to chat around the village sometimes, when he had a place here. I wouldn't call him exactly a friend.'

'But Nell was?'

Jenny hesitated, then gave a bright grin. 'Oh, you know Nell, Finch. She made friends with everyone.'

He smiled his agreement. 'I could never keep up.'

'Your wife had a very big heart,' Jenny added, her smile sentimental this time.

But there was something behind the smile that Finch found unsettling. He shook himself. He badly needed to get away from Jenny.

'Listen, I hope you don't mind,' he said, rising too quickly and barking his shins painfully on the wooden bench attached to the table, 'but I think I'll give the art trail a miss. I know Nell used to love them, but it's not really my thing.'

As Finch made his excuses to a clearly disappointed Jenny and rode off through the warm summer afternoon towards his house, he came to a decision: *I've got to get away.* Romy would be back in the village soon, maybe even for the weekend, then the next weekend, and the one after. He couldn't risk running into her. He didn't know if he could control himself if he saw her again. He might be tempted to forget Grace's problems ever existed.

No, he would search out an adventure, maybe travel thousands of miles and do something wild that would totally absorb his attention – the Amazon, New Guinea,

Alaska, perhaps. He was used to being on the move, good at being set down in foreign parts and adjusting.

Opening his laptop and settling to email some of his contacts scattered around the world, he started with his friend Paz – short for Pascal. Finch had met him in Bosnia, where Paz, employed by La France Diplomatie, had been involved in the United Nations Peacekeeping Force. It had been an instant friendship, the Frenchman's irreverence a breath of fresh air in such a grim environment. *He'll come up with something*, Finch thought.

For a while, he was buoyed up by action and the drama of his broken heart. But as the evening wore on and he trawled the endless multitude of travel options online, his head began to spin, his eyes to burn and the wine he'd drunk turn to acid in his empty stomach. Finch no longer felt intrepid, just bewildered and alone.

That night he woke with a start. It was a familiar flashback. At one time, back in the nineties, he'd experienced it on a regular basis. But now it seemed only to trouble him when he was under stress and vulnerable – like when Nell was dying.

The incident had occurred in Bosnia. Finch and his team were behind the lines. It was high summer and roasting hot. A black jeep pulled up in a cloud of choking dust and three fighters jumped out. All carried guns, the leader – dressed in black, his eyes cold and dead from too much anger, too much violence – brandished a vintage Winchester rifle, which Finch immediately identified. Finch and his men were there to negotiate – 'with the minimum use of force', went the orders. But the dead-eyed Bosnian Serb had other ideas.

None of these details are in the flashback. It is just a brief flare of dusty hotness, the man's haunted eyes and the pain of the cold, hard barrel of the Winchester being pressed into Finch's cheek. He knows he is going to die and the moment is freeze-framed for what seems like eternity . . . Then he wakes with a thudding heart, drenched with the sweat of relief.

When he occasionally told the story to people who had not been in similar situations, they would gasp and say how terrifying it must have been. But he did not recall fear, only his brain splitting in two. While the front half frantically sought a solution – which eventually resulted in the man being disarmed – the back half remained eerily calm. His thoughts were focused solely on the people he loved and how much they meant to him.

He saw the moment – however horrific at the time – as a valued part of his life experience, but he had no control over his dreams.

Finch turned over in bed. It was just past the summer solstice and the sky was already paler in the east – although it was not yet four o'clock. He got the odd feeling sometimes that the flashback was the universe's way of nudging him, reminding him that the only really important things in life were love and family. But tonight he felt aggrieved by the reminder. *I love Romy Claire*, he whispered silently, to the pale sky outside the open window. *But I love Gracie too.*

35

Daniel left. He cried as Romy embraced his slim figure and she found her heart breaking for him and his family – what a nightmare they all faced back in Switzerland. His quiet presence had been such a comfort to her in the last weeks. She didn't know how she would have coped without him. Didn't know how she would cope now.

Obviously she would find another carer. But whoever it was would need overseeing at first, to make sure they were settling in, that they were a good fit with Michael. And it would take a while for her to be able to trust them as she had Daniel. Nor could she rely on Michael not to be rude to them – intentionally or otherwise – even dismiss them out of hand.

As she poured the oats for Michael's porridge into a pan on Saturday morning – measuring the milk and stirring it in, turning the heat low – Romy was aware of a dull, throbbing resentment. She still hadn't confronted her husband about Grace. The whole week had been taken up with the doctor, with Michael's distressing anxiety, made worse by the fact of Daniel's departure.

Later, Michael sat opposite her at the table, his porridge bowl empty, his good hand clutched around his coffee mug. Now Daniel was gone, Romy insisted he eat all his meals at the table. He'd got used to being brought food in the bedroom or having it on his knee in the sitting room, when he was perfectly capable of walking – albeit painfully slowly – through to the kitchen. Daniel had too kind a heart.

'I talked to Blake earlier,' Romy said. 'He sent his best.' Her brother always rang, like Rex, around seven in the morning.

'How is he?'

'Same old, same old.' She smiled. 'I think he likes having Rex around, but he seems to think our son isn't exactly a grafter.'

Michael grinned back. 'Tell us something we don't know.' His face clouded slightly. 'Rex . . . I feel since the stroke . . . so disconnected from him, from everybody, Romy. I used to think I was such a player. But life seems to be going on out there quite happily without me.'

It was on the tip of her tongue to trot out the usual platitudes: it'll be fine, this won't last, you'll be on your feet in no time. But she realized that, to a degree, she was feeling the same.

The flat seemed to be closing in on them both, cutting them off from the outside world. Daniel was gone. Leo phoned every couple of days and visited at weekends, but was always busy. Blake and Rex were too far away to help. The visitors who had dropped by at first with gifts and encouragement obviously thought they'd done their bit, because they had not reappeared – except faithful Wendy, who still arrived dutifully at four most Sunday afternoons with something delicious for tea.

'I know what you mean.' She spoke with feeling and saw Michael's eyes soften, his gaze empty and sad. And despite her resentment, for a split second she felt an overwhelming sympathy for him. 'You'll miss Daniel.'

'I will . . . I do already.'

'I've been on to the agency. Hopefully, I'll find someone else quickly.' She stopped, not wanting her desperation to get back to her own life to show, with Michael in his current depressive state.

He nodded, but looked at her intently. 'So I suppose you're off with Action Man again this weekend?'

Romy felt her cheeks burn. She wished he wouldn't refer to Finch in that derogatory way. She swallowed hard. 'No, that's over. I'm going to Bettina's as soon as Leo gets here.'

Michael looked surprised. 'But . . .' He stopped, perhaps catching the warning in her eye.

She affected a shrug. Was this the moment to talk about Grace? But although it had smouldered in her mind for nearly a week now, the right words clogged in her throat. *Who am I protecting?* she asked herself. *Him or me? Am I just scared of what he might tell me?*

36

'You know how much I love riding,' Finch said, in response to Pascal's suggestion, when his friend rang. 'But a gaucho? I hadn't thought of that.'

Paz chuckled. 'It's tough. Believe me, I know. Cami made me do all that riding-across-the-pampas bollocks when we first went to meet her relatives. I was in love, so I didn't complain, but my butt's never recovered.'

'I really need to get away,' Finch said, trying to keep the urgency out of his voice. 'Argentina should be far enough.'

'Being chased by the taxman, is it? Or have you gone and made some gangster's moll pregnant?' Pascal was never serious about anything.

'Something like that,' Finch replied.

He heard Paz sucking his teeth. 'Hmm . . . in which case, might it not be wiser to choose somewhere the UK doesn't have an extradition treaty with – like Pakistan, for instance? Worked for our friend Osama for years. Or you could join the Foreign Legion! I've got contacts.'

Finch couldn't help laughing. 'I've had enough of being shot at, thanks. I just want a break – foreign parts, different scenery.'

'How's your Spanish, these days?'

'Bit rusty, I suppose, but I'll get by.'

'OK, then. If you're absolutely set on grinding your rump to ribbons, I'm your man. I'll talk to Cami and see which of her zillions of rich cousins can come up with an invitation.'

'I don't want to be pampered like a guest, Paz. If I'm going to do this, I want to be out there chasing cattle and wild horses, riding the range.'

'Being macho.'

'Getting so tired I can't bloody think any more.'

There was silence for a moment. Then Paz said, 'And her name is . . .?'

Finch was glad Paz couldn't see him cringe. 'It doesn't matter what she's called any more.'

'I see. Well, you know how much Cami loves you, Roberto, and Paris is only a train ride away. My area of special interest is currently Azerbaijan, but I'm sure I could mug up on broken-hearted soldiers, if required.'

Finch laughed and thanked him. When he came off the phone he still had a smile on his face: Paz always lifted his spirits. In fact, he was feeling better for the first time since Grace's visit. *I'll feel better still*, he thought, *when I can put some distance between Romy and me.*

When Grace called later that evening, Finch told her of Paz's suggestion.

'Right.' Grace's one-word response – after a very long pause – fell damply on Finch's enthusiasm. 'This is about Romy, isn't it?' she went on. 'I knew I should never have told you.' He heard an exasperated sigh. 'You see? This is what happens when people speak up about stuff like that. It ruins things for everyone. And you want me to tell

Sam?' Her tone was scathing. 'There are quite enough bodies under that particular bus as it is.'

Finch was silent. He'd been down the route of begging her to get the professional help she needed so often that it seemed pointless to reiterate it again now. He'd always tried to be honest with Grace. When her mother became ill the first time, Nell had wanted to keep the cancer secret, saying that Grace didn't need to know unless it was serious. But Finch had insisted she be told and they were both glad that he had. Grace had been such a comfort to them, especially at the end. She'd moved back into the Sussex house and helped Finch nurse her mother before the final hospice days. The girl's energy, her humour, her refusal to be maudlin about the future had kept them all afloat, for which Finch would always be grateful. But he knew he couldn't be honest about Romy now.

'You don't mind me going, Gracie?' he asked. 'It'll only be for a month or so, I think. But I won't if you don't want me to.' He found himself tempering his estimate, genuinely unsure how long he'd be gone and not wanting it to sound as if he were abandoning her for ever.

'Don't be ridiculous!' Grace's pitch had risen. 'Of course I don't mind. We don't see each other for months on end. I won't even notice you're gone.' She hesitated. 'I'm sorry,' she said, in a soft voice. 'I'm sorry I ruined things for you.'

'You didn't ruin anything, sweetheart,' Finch replied, with all honesty. None of this was Grace's fault. Michael was to blame for it all . . . and maybe himself, too, for being so aggressive towards Romy and pushing her into a corner with her contemptible husband.

Because he still wanted to believe in her. He still waited for the phone call that would be Romy telling him she'd been utterly wrong to side with Michael Claire. But in the end it wouldn't make any difference, he knew. Grace would always come between them.

37

Leo found his father sitting at the kitchen table when he arrived, his weak hand covered with a large, bright blue mitt – like a wicket-keeper's glove – with Velcro straps round the wrist, and a pile of coloured ping-pong balls in a box. Michael was slowly picking up the balls from the box and transferring them into an empty one a foot away. Leo watched in silence, his father barely glancing up at him, his concentration so focused on the task.

'Is that bionic?' Leo asked, when a ball skittered out of his father's grasp and went bouncing across the table, then the kitchen tiles. Leo bent to pick it up and return it to the box.

His father's face cleared and he smiled at Leo. 'Sodding thing.' He glared at his hand, as if it offended him, as if it wasn't part of him at all, just an irritating intrusion into his life.

'You couldn't have done that a few weeks ago,' Leo observed.

'That's because I didn't have what Imogen likes to call an "assisted device". She says it's the first stage. Apparently it's opening my hand and forcing it to do normal movements.' His dad started to laugh. 'Christ, Leo, what am I like? Sitting here like a big kid, shifting balls from one box to another. You were better at it when you were two!'

Leo couldn't help laughing with him: there was a comical side. 'Keep that up and you'll be playing for the county in no time,' he said, which was a poor joke, but it seemed to make his dad laugh even harder.

'Eat your heart out, Jimmy Anderson. Trouble with these balls is they don't have a seam. How's a chap to fast bowl if there's no seam?'

Leo gawped. 'Wait a minute! You've started watching *cricket*, Dad?' He loved the game, but he'd never known his father to be interested in any sport, ever.

'I watch anything that moves these days.' His father seemed in a high old mood today, which was encouraging, as Leo was in charge all weekend. His mum was just getting her stuff ready, and then she was off until Sunday night. 'In fact,' his dad was saying, 'I'm sure you're aware of today's one-dayer: India at Trent Bridge . . . if you're interested.' He gave what seemed to Leo to be an almost shy smile.

Leo grinned. 'Wow, Dad. I'm there! Hope the rain holds off.' He'd never in a million years thought he'd be sitting watching cricket with his father. He was touched that he'd obviously planned their day and didn't know what to say. This was so unlike the father he'd grown up with, who always seemed to hold him and Rex at arm's length, just homing in for the occasional lecture on working hard, getting good marks at school and being *ambitious*.

'Are you going to stand there all day with your mouth open? Or can you manage a coffee for your poor old dad?' Michael was still smiling as Leo went over to the pod machine his mum had bought – despite Michael's objections – because it was easier for him to manage. But as he unhooked the water cylinder from the back and filled it with tap water, he heard his name barked and jumped.

'He can do that himself.' His mother was standing at the kitchen door, looking fierce. 'Don't run around after him, Leo. He's perfectly capable of making *you* a cup of coffee.'

Leo pulled a face. 'Hi, Mum.'

Her expression relaxed. 'Hi, sweetheart. Sorry, it's just your father has become a lazy old bugger, haven't you, Michael?'

Michael shrugged. 'And you've become an annoying old harridan,' he retorted.

'Well, you're shot of me for a couple of days. You can bully your son to your heart's content.'

Leo held his breath. He didn't want to listen to his parents bickering. And whereas there didn't seem any real heat to their exchange – as if they'd both heard it all before – it felt as if there was something raw and uncomfortable between them today, the sparring merely a cover for a deeper unease.

'Are you going to the cottage?' Leo asked, wanting to defuse the atmosphere.

'No, Hastings. Staying with Bettina.'

'That'll be fun,' he said brightly, although his mother showed no enthusiasm for the plan.

She didn't reply, her gaze silently levelled at his dad. Leo couldn't work out what his mother's look meant. It seemed jaundiced, hostile . . . almost as if she were on the verge of saying something cutting to him.

But all she finally said was: 'OK, I'll be off. You know where I am.'

He nodded. 'Have a good time.'

His mother gave him a strained smile. 'Thanks.' Then she turned to walk away.

'Bye, Romy,' his father called after her. But she didn't respond, except with a brief backward wave.

Leo raised his eyebrows at his father. Both of them waited till they heard the front door shut, then a moment longer, before either spoke.

'Is Mum all right?'

'Not really.'

Leo continued to prepare the coffee – despite his mother's warning – slotting a blue foil pod into the machine, pressing the right-hand button and reaching for two cups. His father took it black. He, himself, liked a latte, but he couldn't be bothered to froth the milk.

'You heard about Fincham?' Michael asked, accepting the cup from his son.

'No. What's happened?'

'She says it's over. Didn't explain, but she's obviously fucking miserable, so I'm assuming old Action Man must be a bolter.' He shook his head. 'Never did trust those army types.'

'Really? Why not? I'd have thought a retired soldier would be the one person you could trust.' He sat down opposite his father, who was tugging off the blue glove with difficulty, his hand red and marked from the device and flaccid as he laid it gingerly on the wooden table.

Michael shrugged, said nothing.

'Do you even know any "army types", Dad?' Leo asked, amused.

His father gave him a sheepish grin. 'I've met a couple in my time.' He took a sip from his cup. 'But, no, I just made that up. He annoys me, for some reason.'

Leo didn't need to ask what that reason might be.

Michael leant forward. 'Listen, Leo . . . losing Daniel's been a blow. But I don't want your mum to feel she has to look after me now. She's obviously not happy being here, quite understandably. And since Daniel left she's been really snappish with me, just when I thought we were beginning to get on better. I wanted to talk to her about it, but this week has been so up and down . . . Please will you help her find someone else?'

'Of course. I'll do what I can.'

Michael sighed and closed his eyes. When he opened them, he stared intently at Leo. 'I love your mum, you know. I *really* love her.'

Despite what Anezka had told him previously, Leo was taken aback by the raw intensity of his father's declaration.

'I know I'm a wreck right now. And she probably isn't thinking in these terms, I've been such a bloody shit in the past . . . not something I'm proud of . . .' His father trailed off, seemingly at a loss. Then he went on, 'I'm determined to get fit again, Leo. It's probably a forlorn hope that she'd give us another go, but it might help if I was in better shape.'

Leo didn't reply. *Is this just Dad's fantasy?* A throwback to when his father felt Romy was always there for him? Because his mum's behaviour earlier certainly hadn't suggested she was on board with the idea.

'The problem is, she seems to find me revolting,' Michael added, in a musing sort of way.

Shocked out of his reverie, Leo said, 'That's a ridiculous thing to say, Dad.'

'Is it?' Michael turned away, apparently looking for his crutch, which was propped against the worktop behind him. He grabbed it. 'I need a pee.'

Leo jumped up to help him, but his father pushed him away. 'Didn't you hear your mother?' he snapped. 'I've got to do this myself.'

He watched Michael clumping slowly towards the door and had to restrain himself from rushing to his side. He listened intently as the step/drag, step/drag and the clunking of the aluminium crutch faded along the corridor to the loo, then heard the door slam shut. He folded his arms on the table and dropped his head to rest on them. He felt for his father. It was almost painful to hear him say how much he loved his mum – and it was the only time Leo had ever heard it. But there'd been something in his mother's face – he got the feeling she was ready to burst with pent-up emotion – something specifically directed at his father that she was hiding from them both. *This isn't just about Fincham*, he decided. *So what is it about?*

38

Romy held herself together on the Tube to Embankment, the walk up to Charing Cross, the hour and a half on the train to Hastings. She felt as if she needed to keep pressing down on a living presence in her body, leaning heavily on it – as you might the contents of a bulging suitcase – so that it didn't splurge out of her mouth in a horrific explosion.

She greeted Bettina, who picked her up from the station, and chatted inconsequentially on the short trip to her house in the centre of the old town, in a grand terrace close to the bakery she and Jost ran. She took her case up to her room and gazed longingly at the pristine sheets and plump duvet. She went downstairs and sat at the kitchen table, took the glass of cold Sancerre that her friend slid across to her. She took a large gulp, choked and sensed the presence inside her rumbling, then suddenly bursting its bonds. It was too late to stop it. Her cries thundered like the first waves of a massive tsunami.

Bettina, predictably, was calm, immediately enveloping her in a maternal hug from which Romy wanted never to be released. She clung to her friend, incoherent, wanting to explain so much that had happened and not knowing where to start. It was a long time before she could even catch her breath.

*

Later, Romy sat on the sofa in the high-ceilinged sitting room, the large sash windows facing out towards the sea. She was all cried out. Bettina sat beside her. She had listened intently, but said very little as Romy revealed the twists and turns of her story.

'Hmm,' she said eventually. 'It's unbelievably unfair, Grace turning out to be Finch's stepdaughter, to say the least.' Romy didn't reply and it was a while before Bettina continued. 'Walk away, is my advice. From the lot of them.'

'I don't have much choice. Finch will choose Grace over me every time. She's Nell's daughter. I should have trusted what she said from the start.'

'You've never met the girl. Why would you do that?'

'Tell that to Finch,' she said sadly.

'It's such a muddle.' Bettina let out a frustrated breath. 'I mean, if Michael came clean, explained what really happened . . .'

'It's pathetic, but I can't even bring myself to have the conversation with him.'

'Why not?'

'Because – because – I don't know. Maybe I don't want to hear what he has to say.'

Her friend absorbed this, then gave a shrug. 'Do you have to know? Can't you just leave it in the past, where it belongs?' She grabbed her hand. 'None of these people – including Michael – is your responsibility, Romy. Get a good carer-housekeeper person and move on with your life.'

'I'm trying, believe me. You saw the sorry bunch of candidates last time.' Romy felt suddenly fed up with herself and her whingeing. 'Listen, can we just go down to the sea and forget about the whole bang shoot? I want to drink too much wine and sleep like the dead and never let the names Michael or Grace or Finch darken my lips ever again.'

It must have been around midnight that Romy finally threw herself down on Bettina's beautifully laundered cotton sheets. Jost had come back from the shop in time for supper. Tall and lean, tanned, with a longish mop of fading brown hair, he was a man with a soft smile, who said very little. Bettina was the extrovert and it was she who wooed the customers, who knew all about their likes and dislikes, their ailments and allergies, their children and grandchildren, the names of their dogs tied up to the hooks outside. Jost did the baking, catering to the London crowd who had migrated to Hastings and craved pricey artisan loaves – stone-baked, sourdough, seeds, rye flour – and gluten-free cakes.

The day had been muggy, the temperature barely dropping as evening approached, and too hot to cook, so they'd eaten cold chicken and Caesar salad, no one saying very much, the silence easy between old friends. Romy, however, had been drinking for a large part of the day, her glass constantly topped up by Bettina. By the time she fell into bed, she was dizzy with it.

On a drunken impulse, as she checked for messages from Leo or Michael before plugging her phone in to charge, she pressed on Finch's number. Lying back, mobile to her ear, she listened woozily to the ring-tone, never expecting him to pick up. It was enough just to hear his voice on his answer message. So when he spoke in person, she shot up in bed as if the phone had delivered a powerful volt.

'Romy?' Finch's voice sounded wary, but she didn't care, it was such a joy to hear his voice.

'Hi.'

Silence, then, 'How are you?'

'I'm pissed.'

Finch didn't laugh, as, in her inebriated state, she had thought he might – as he would previously have done. He didn't respond at all.

'Finch?'

'I'm here.'

'How are you?'

'Umm, listen, Romy. Perhaps this isn't a good idea . . .'

Romy was puzzled. In her present mood she thought it was a splendid idea. 'Why not? I like talking to you.'

This provoked a sad laugh. 'I like talking to you too. But not when you're drunk and won't remember you called me when you wake up tomorrow.'

'Don't be stuffy, Finch.'

Another silence. 'So why did you ring?'

This seemed blindingly obvious. 'Because I miss you,' she said.

Finch did not reply. *What's wrong with him?* she wondered disconsolately. *Why's he being so unfriendly?*

'Romy . . .'

She was aware of her head spinning and she flopped back down on the cool pillow, her eyes closing as she listened to the strained silence. But closing her eyes made the spinning considerably worse.

'Finch, please, can't we meet? There must be a way to sort out . . . this stupid mess. It's crazy, us being apart when we . . . like each other so much.'

She waited for him to reply, then heard three short beeps. Checking her screen she realized with a shock that Finch had hung up. In her daze she wasn't sure if he'd said goodbye or not.

39

Finch was not asleep, or even in bed when Romy rang. He'd been packing. Cami had been in touch.

'Cousin Luis is delighted,' she'd said. 'I told him all about you and he's such a snob – he's dying to have a real live British colonel in residence to entertain his rich American clients.'

Finch had been alarmed. 'Entertain? My cabaret skills aren't exactly legendary, Cami.'

She'd laughed. 'He just wants to show you off. You're worth a few intelligent observations at the dinner table, no? And you can ride out with some of the more nervous guests. You always inspire confidence, Robert.'

'I do?'

'Don't worry. The visitors are only a small part of the operation. It's a proper working ranch – two hundred horses and five hundred head of cattle. Luis says you'll have the complete run of the place. I'm jealous – I haven't been home for two years.' She'd chuckled. 'Just don't mention the Falklands.'

Finch had assured her he wouldn't dream of it and thanked her profusely. He was excited. Luis, when he talked to him, had sounded charming and extremely welcoming. He told Finch he could stay as long as he liked. The estancia was two hours' drive north-west of Buenos Aires, and his host insisted he would be met at the airport.

It had all happened so quickly – almost too quickly – leaving Finch no time to think about whether this plan was a good one. He just went straight into logistics mode: booking flights, ordering online two pairs of khaki *bombachos*, the baggy, padded trousers the gauchos wore – Cami having told him the nearest town was not close – digging out the hiking boots she said were fine for riding, and getting his shirts washed, his jackets cleaned. It was the beginning of the season, still winter in Argentina, but the outdoor temperature would be in the late teens during the day and much colder at night.

Now, Finch was taken aback, completely thrown by the sound of Romy's voice. He found himself holding his breath. He so badly wanted her to tell him something new, to move the narrative on with an account of Michael's confession, or news that she had finally left the flat and stopped caring for her husband. But she was drunk, almost incoherent, although Finch thought he could sense the unhappiness behind her every word. And then she'd said she missed him and he couldn't bear it any more. He'd clicked off involuntarily, without saying goodbye, his stomach churning with the knowledge that he was going away, putting thousands of miles between himself and the woman he knew he loved, but with whom he could have no future.

Michael also began to chuckle. 'You malign me, my dear,' he said, with a dramatic eye roll, then added, 'I've been rehearsing that, too.' The pair of them were well away now, Michael's drawn face losing years in a second as he let himself go and laughed with her – about nothing, really – until both were gulping and wiping tears from their eyes.

Their son looked on, nonplussed.

'Sorry, Leo,' Romy managed to gasp before dissolving into giggles again.

But the exertion was too much for Michael, and Romy watched him slowly slide down the wall, then keel gently left, until his head was resting on the cream carpet.

'Dad!' Leo jumped to rescue his father, his face a picture of concern as he began to heave Michael upright. But Michael was unfazed. As he settled back on his crutch, he gave Romy such a wide grin that, for a second, she forgot Grace. It was just her and Michael, the two of them, making each other laugh.

Later that evening, after Leo had gone, she helped Michael get ready for bed. He was sitting on the edge of the mattress in his T-shirt and pyjama bottoms, clean and sweet-smelling from his wash, when he took her hand as she mechanically plumped his pillows, staring up into her face with a yearning that made her stomach flip.

'It was fun, laughing like that.'

Romy nodded, not wanting to snatch it away, but feeling uneasy, standing there, her hand in Michael's.

'Will you kiss me goodnight?' Michael asked. Then, perhaps seeing her face, he added, with a quick smile, 'No agenda.'

Romy hesitated. She would give him a friendly kiss – had done so on a number of occasions since the stroke. But she knew, from what Leo had told her earlier – and the softening of their mood since the laughter – that Michael might be angling for more than just 'friendly', despite his assertion to the contrary. She balked at the thought of anything that could presage a sexual invitation. Bending quickly, she dropped a brief peck on his cheek, at the same time withdrawing her hand from his grasp.

Michael's expression stilled, but he continued to gaze at her as she turned away.

'Not as bad as last time,' he said quietly, as he pulled his weak leg onto the mattress and lay back on the pillows. 'At least you didn't flinch.'

Romy was shocked, not so much by his words but by the obvious bitterness behind them. 'Michael . . .'

He waved his hand dismissively. 'Don't pity me, Romy.'

There was silence in the room. Romy busied herself picking up the clothes he had discarded and folding them, placing them on the chair. 'I'm not,' she replied briskly, although, to her own ears, her protestation rang weak and dishonest. *Michael believes I'm pitying him for his disability*, she thought. But her disinclination had nothing whatever to do with his current physical condition.

She took a deep breath. This was it. Leo's declaration had made her realize she couldn't continue in this no-man's-land with Michael for a second longer. Moving the clothes aside, she sat down on the orange armchair facing the bed. This was the moment she'd been avoiding for what seemed like two lifetimes.

'I've told you about my friend, Robert,' she began, 'and that we've broken up.' Michael nodded. 'Well, his wife died a few years ago, but he has a stepdaughter, who he's extremely fond of.' Romy swallowed hard. 'She's thirty-two now, apparently. And her name is Grace. Grace . . .' She realized she didn't know Grace's surname – Nell's before she'd married Finch.

Michael was watching her, impassively.

'She's called Grace Twiston now.' Romy stared back, searching his face for the tiniest twitch. 'I don't know what her surname was when she was sixteen.' Michael still didn't speak, but she saw a flicker of something in his eyes.

Her husband pulled himself up on the pillows, his expression hard to read. Romy waited. *He knows what I'm talking about*, she thought. *He knows.*

'Her name was Fleetwood,' Michael said. 'Grace Fleetwood.'

41

At the sound of Grace's name on Michael's lips, Romy felt the hairs on the back of her neck rise. The bedroom air was stagnant and suffocating, as she waited for him to go on. He was very still, propped against the headboard as if he were carved in stone, no muscle moving except the rapid blinking of his eyelids. But he didn't say a word for what seemed like an eternity, and neither did she – shaken, after all this time, that her husband had finally admitted knowing the girl.

When Michael began to speak, his voice was calm, his words measured. Romy was sure he had carefully rehearsed them – as meticulously, even, as he might his summing up to a jury. He did not meet her eye, just stared straight ahead towards the blank television screen on the far wall.

'I'm going to tell you exactly what happened. Please let me finish before you say anything. I know this is a she said/he said situation, and I want you to hear it as *I* remember it.'

Romy nodded, although he still did not turn his head to look at her. She clutched her hands in her lap, a shiver passing through her body.

Michael took a deep breath and exhaled it slowly. 'Grace was a very beautiful girl,' he began, 'not just beautiful, but also lively and charismatic, someone who laughed a lot. All those fraught clients and impossible caseloads . . . the atmosphere was heavy with tension most days.' He sighed. 'And Grace breezed in, like a breath of fresh air, cheering us all up.'

Romy waited for him to continue. His manner of speaking made it sound like the beginning of a fairytale. Not real life; not *his* life.

'She was keen as mustard to help, and she'd got this idea I was special in some way, I don't know why. James and her mother were having a thing at the time, so maybe James was boasting about our chambers and her mother passed it on . . .' He took a long breath. 'Anyway, as a result, when she was with me, she seemed overawed, almost tongue-tied. She used to gaze at me with these huge grey eyes as if I were a pop idol or something.' Michael glanced briefly at Romy, raising his eyebrows in a grim smile. 'It was very flattering.'

Romy did not respond. She heard the throwaway detail about James and Nell, but it barely registered, she was so intent on listening to what Michael had to say.

'I was in the middle of the Brigham case. I was stressed out of my mind, working every hour God sent. The man was such a devious bastard.' He stopped, as if he'd lost his thread. Then he shook his head, almost impatiently. 'Grace volunteered to help me sort out this mountain of papers for the following day. I was swamped. It was baking hot that week and the windows don't open properly in my rooms because of security, so the place was really stifling. I knew I'd be at it all night . . .' He took another deep breath.

Romy was listening in a haze of disappointment, realizing that some small part of her had still clung to the faint possibility that none of this had ever happened, that it was just some crazy fabrication on Grace's part. But he was speaking with too much gravitas.

'At some point I told her she should go home, it was late. But she refused. So I offered her a glass of wine and poured one for myself. She sat on the sofa and patted the seat next to her.' He paused, perhaps remembering. '"Stop that for a second," she said, "and come and sit over here."' He raised his head and looked across at Romy. She saw what she thought was almost defiance in his eyes. 'And, yes, I kissed her. I honestly thought she wanted me to . . . I'm so sorry, Romy.'

Romy heard a faint sigh and watched her husband press his good hand across his eyes. 'I thought . . . I don't know what I thought, I wasn't thinking at all. I was just . . .' He lifted his hand, palm up, as if, all these years later, he was still bewildered by what had happened that night. 'I know it was terribly wrong. She was a child. And, obviously, there was you . . .' He stopped again.

Romy frowned. *That's it? He's telling me it was just one kiss?* she asked herself, disgusted nevertheless as she pictured him pawing the teenager. 'She said you attacked her, Michael. Not just in the letter. She told the whole story to Finch.' She gulped, falling over the words in her head as she tried to make her point. 'When I got the letter, you denied even knowing her. You made me feel cruel and disloyal simply for asking you about it.' She heard the coldness in her voice, felt the quivering in her body. 'Why should I believe you now?'

Her husband's look was resolute. 'I absolutely was *not* violent, Romy. I wasn't. She responded to my kiss – I know

I'm not mistaken about that. And then the phone was ringing and she was pushing me off. She ran out before I had a chance to say anything.'

Michael spoke firmly, certainly with the appearance of honesty. But she knew her husband well and something wasn't ringing true. Could Grace really have embellished a single kiss into a drama of vicious assault?

'She was very clear, Michael. You tore her dress. Her breasts and her thighs were bruised, she said.'

He shook his head wearily. '*She said*. But that's utterly impossible. You know me, Romy, better than anyone. I am not a violent man.' When she didn't respond, he went on, 'I've been a selfish sod in all sorts of ways over the years, I'll admit, and I've got plenty of things wrong – not least that kiss and the lies I told subsequently. But can you honestly imagine me doing something so vile?' He shook his head in apparent bewilderment. 'I don't know why she's saying what she's saying. I can only suppose it was a moment she's remembered wrongly, something she feels she should be ashamed of for some reason.'

An edgy, breathless silence ensued.

'I really thought she was coming on to me, Romy. Not that that makes it OK, but . . .' His voice had risen plaintively. 'A pretty girl, late on a hot summer night when we were both slightly crazy with heat and exhaustion, accepts a glass of wine, then smiles at you with her huge grey eyes and pats the seat next to her. It certainly didn't feel as if I was forcing myself on her.'

Romy was thrown. She didn't know whether to believe a word of what Michael was saying. Yes, he'd had a stroke, but this was one very clever man. A man who was capable – brilliantly so, by all accounts – of manipulating the truth until the opposing barrister didn't know which way was up. Was this all just a crafty choreographing of events, worked out and nuanced over decades? Or was it true, and Grace – as Michael suggested – was suffering from misplaced shame?

'But why would she be suddenly motivated all these years later to write such an accusatory letter, if all you did was kiss her? And why be so traumatized?'

'*I don't know*, Romy,' Michael screeched. 'It doesn't make sense to me, either. I've thought about it non-stop since the day you showed me the bloody thing, but I can't square her account of what happened with my own recollection. I just can't. It's devastating, what she said.'

'Even now, she's still incredibly upset, according to Finch. Even after all this time.'

He let out an exasperated sigh. 'I'm sorry to hear that, but so am I. How do you think it feels to be accused like that? To see the doubt in your eyes, the contempt? It breaks my heart. And it destroyed our marriage.'

There was silence for a moment, before Romy answered. 'I didn't doubt you when I first read the letter, Michael. It was your reaction – refusing to engage with me about it, on any level – that helped destroy our marriage.' She took a breath. 'I never thought you capable of violence against anyone, let alone a young girl.'

'I would hope not. After a lifetime together, I think I deserve the benefit of the doubt,' Michael said, sounding hurt and slightly pompous.

Romy was too angry to reply.

Her husband slumped back against the pillows and closed his eyes as if he were defeated. She held on tightly to her fury as she straightened the clothes she'd scrunched up when she'd sat on the chair and turned towards the door. The whole sordid mess was like a cesspit opened to the air, the miasma choking everyone who stood too close.

Michael's confession, so long awaited, had left a bad taste in her mouth. True, he'd finally admitted his guilt about kissing Grace. Even said he was sorry. But he'd implied the teenager should also accept some responsibility. And he'd totally denied the violence that Grace had written and apparently spoken about in such graphic detail. *This cannot be the whole story*, she thought grimly, as she climbed into bed, her brain thumping restlessly with what she'd just heard.

42

Finch woke every morning exhilarated, with a feeling of purpose. Luis and Jocelyn's estancia was huge and wild and astonishing in its beauty. He rode the hills on the beautiful Peruvian Paso horses with such a sense of freedom, refusing to contemplate the people he'd left, the problems he faced, back in England. He knew it couldn't last, and he made a conscious decision just to live in the moment.

But his backside was agony, despite the padded *bombachas* and the famously smooth gait of the Pasos. Paz had not been wrong. The first week he was sore, but he'd expected that. He'd assumed it would get better, though, as his body became acclimatized to long hours in the saddle. But as he approached the middle of his third week in Argentina, riding for up to five or six hours a day sometimes, his bum had gone on strike. It was Marty – Jocelyn's nephew – who suggesting padded biking shorts under the gaucho trousers.

'Go get a bunch of them in town. It'll change your life,' Marty had told him. 'I always wear them if I haven't been in the saddle for a while.' Finch had done so a couple of days ago, and was relieved at the difference it made – although the raw patches of skin still chafed miserably.

Initially Marty had seemed quiet and shy. Wiry, with untidy light-brown hair and an almost bruised look in his grey eyes, his passion was horses. His father, Jocelyn's brother, owned a stud back in Wisconsin. But get him on a horse, and Marty came to life.

They had bonded over the thrilling gallops they'd taken together over the grey-brown winter hills, without the constraint of the more plodding guests to look after. Marty was confident enough to join the gauchos like a pro in the dusty, crazy, yelling-and-shouting mayhem of the round-up of cattle from the pampas. Finch was in awe. The American even rode like them, jamming his whole boot into the stirrup, tilting his heels up instead of just toeing the stirrup, and holding both reins in his left hand so his right was free for a rope or a gun. He'd earned the respect of the gauchos, big-time. Not an easy thing to do.

Finch, on the other hand, although in love with the Pasos, and considering himself, at the start of his visit, to be a pretty competent horseman, found the gauchos intimidating. Dressed at all times in sweaty shirts and dirty jeans, mostly unshaven, the men with their huge brown eyes and floppy *boinas*, their heavily accented Spanish, treated Finch with offhand suspicion at first. He was just another foreigner playing at doing their incredibly skilful job. But Finch's dogged perseverance impressed them and now he'd become friendly with one in particular – a young guy named José.

'You come with us today?' he said, one morning, to Finch.

'Sure he will,' Marty had answered for him, whacking him on the shoulder as they sat on their horses about to go out.

They spent the morning riding hell for leather as they chased hundreds of cattle into the valley where they began to separate off the young bullocks.

'Why are they doing that?' Finch asked Marty, as he drew up alongside.

'No idea,' replied the American, frowning. 'Helluva ride, no?'

They watched in awe and a certain amount of squeamishness on Finch's part as the men brewed up some strange black liquid in a rusty can, then expertly threw the bullocks to the earth and castrated them – lightning quick – then painted the wound with the black gunge. Finch saw the parts casually discarded in a metal bucket and hoped that was the end of the grisly drama.

But the men then proceeded to roast the bullock balls over the fire on a piece of flattened tin. Finch caught José's eye, noted his wicked grin, and spent the minutes while the things sizzled away wanting to run. But it was too late. José thrust a plate at him, on which a number of browned balls rolled merrily about.

'They tasted sort of sweet, a bit gristly. If I didn't know what they were . . .' Finch commented that evening to his friend. They had begged off early, immediately after dinner with Jocelyn and Luis's American guests, pleading exhaustion, and were now pleasantly drunk, lounging, legs spread, in fold-up chairs outside Finch's cottage, which sat on the edge of the red-roofed, sprawling ranch house, a half-empty bottle of Malbec on the path by their feet. It was a cold night, but neither felt like going inside.

'Yeah, made me heave.' Marty laughed.

'I've eaten sheep's eyes before,' Finch boasted. 'Maybe even sheep's balls. Same difference.'

There was a long, companionable silence between them. Then Marty spoke, his voice low. 'So tell me, Rob, what is it you're running away from?'

Taken aback, Finch didn't answer at once. The trip, so far, had been everything he'd hoped for: extraordinary new landscape, no one who knew him, and day after day in the saddle – which tired him out so he was asleep almost before he'd taken his boots off. He'd been so grateful not to think. But 'running away' seemed a vaguely pejorative term.

Marty was staring at him in the feeble light of the single bulb above the cottage door, those bruised grey eyes considering. 'You don't have to tell me, course, but I can see it on you.' He paused. 'I recognize it.'

'Recognize it?'

Marty shrugged. He seemed at ease with himself tonight, away from his doting aunt. Finch thought the wine was probably helping. 'My wife, Beth, she passed six years ago – a long struggle with her heart.' He looked enquiringly at Finch, as if he expected a matching confidence, but Finch was dumbstruck. *Is he psychic, a bloody mind reader?*

'I'm so sorry about your wife,' Finch said, rather stiffly, then added, 'But I'm not running away.'

Marty raised an eyebrow and grinned. 'You sure about that?' He reached for his glass and sipped, holding the wine in his mouth for a moment before swallowing as he looked up into the incredibly clear, starry night. 'Luis told me about your wife.'

And Cami told Cousin Luis, Finch thought. Suddenly all the stuff he'd been holding at bay swooped back, like a flock of starlings, to surround him. He sighed. 'It's not just about Nell.' And then, with the next breath, he was telling Marty everything about his wife's death. Every detail of those months when he'd watched her eyes become too bright as her face thinned and yellowed, saw her shoulder blades cutting through her delicate skin, the knobbled ridges of her spine as he washed her, the way she shook when she tried to stand. He told this stranger of the agonies he had kept hidden, almost cherished, since she died. Who else could he have told who might understand? And when he'd finished, there were tears pouring down his face.

Of course it's about Nell. Grace was Nell's daughter who reminded him of her constantly and whom he'd vowed to protect. Romy was a guilty pleasure, a betrayal of his perfect wife, the perfect love they'd shared, however much he told himself – and Romy – different.

Marty nodded intermittently, listened to his long and rambling account without speaking.

Finch thought of his endless chats with Nell's photograph. 'Just recently, though, I was beginning to appreciate things again,' he insisted, suddenly desperate to acknowledge Romy and everything she'd meant to him. 'But now . . .' He told Marty the bare bones of what had happened with Grace.

'Wow, cruel.' The American whistled. 'So you headed out, left them all to it?'

It sounded, as Marty said it, like the most craven thing Finch had ever done. He felt himself becoming hot with indignation. 'I needed a break.'

Marty held his hand up. 'Hey, I'm not judging. I did far worse when I lost Beth. Drugs, whiskey, self-pity, the lot.' He chuckled. 'Riding around the Gutierrez spread with a bunch of gauchos is tame by comparison.' He took another gulp of wine. 'But this stepdaughter of yours, doesn't she need your help right now?'

Finch thought of Grace, listened back, in his head, to the conversation they'd had about him going to Argentina. Heard, as loud as if she were talking right now, that she didn't want him to go. He was ashamed. He had known at the time but chosen not to focus, consumed with his broken heart.

When Marty eventually said goodnight and staggered off to his room in the main house, Finch found he couldn't sleep. He felt stupid and redundant in this estancia in the hills and knew he must go home. He had assured Jocelyn he would be there for her current guests from Chicago – both husbands had been in the Marines and loved to bond with Finch about their service days – but they would be leaving soon and, although she and Luis had made it quite clear he could stay as long as he liked, Finch knew he couldn't evade his responsibilities any longer.

But something else was keeping him awake: Romy. Talking about her to Marty had broken the log-jam he'd set in place before he'd left England, and his feelings for her had been let loose. Now, in his inebriated state, he sat down at his laptop and began to type:

Dearest Romy,

I hoped I could forget you, because the alternative will definitely send me mad. But I'm thousands of miles away right now, in a brilliantly distracting landscape of supreme beauty, among horses and cattle and new acquaintances who take up all my time, and still you haunt my thoughts.

I didn't say it, because we weren't quite there, and you might have been frightened off, but the truth is, I love you. I have done for some time. Maybe it's impossible for things to be right between us, there's too much in the way, but I wanted you to know how I feel – selfishly, I suppose. It's night here, and very quiet, the place is comfortable enough. But I just want to cry like a stupid baby.

Finch x

He stopped typing and hovered the cursor over send. *What have I got to lose?* But still he hesitated.

Marooned in this strange environment, where nothing related to his normal life, he could see how a person might slowly shed the past. Not from conscious choice, more from a lack of desire to deal with it. Easier by far to slip gradually into another familiarity, where new bonds would slowly begin to form – like his with Marty, or José and, to an extent, with the charming Luis. Perhaps it was merely a case of letting it happen. And maybe he would have, if he hadn't talked to Marty tonight.

Tired as he was, Finch felt the pull of home, of Grace and of Romy. Without another thought, he pressed the touchpad and the email was on its way. Slamming the computer shut, Finch ripped off his clothes. He fell onto the bed and into another dreamless sleep.

When he came to again, the sky was just beginning to lighten – he'd forgotten to close the shutters. Sunrise was around seven forty-five at this time of year and he thought it was probably an hour off, at least. So he lay on his back, eyes shut, and began to drift off again. Then he sat bolt upright in bed. *The email.*

Yanking the lid of the laptop open, he clicked on his account. *Will she have seen it yet?* He couldn't work out the time difference in his dozy state. But the email was still sitting in the outbox, undelivered – the connection to the ranch's erratic Wi-Fi obviously lost.

Finch stared at the screen, then opened the email and read it through. He could remember writing it, but he was unclear, this morning, as to what he'd actually said. *No,* he thought, cringing at the melodramatic prose. He deleted it quickly, then closed his eyes and groaned, muttering a silent thank-you to the universe for sparing him a terrible embarrassment.

43

'Happy birthday.' Romy pulled back the curtains in Michael's room with a strained smile. As usual, she'd heard the low murmur of the television and knew he'd been awake for some time. But she'd held off going in, the thought of the day ahead making her feel tired before she'd even started. Leo had arranged interviews at the flat with three more potential live-in Daniel replacements – the first crop totally unsuitable – and she knew she was now in the mood to hire the first person who walked through the door, even if he or she had two heads.

They had been sitting, subdued, opposite each other at the kitchen table again, with their porridge and coffee the previous morning – days after Michael had made his confession – when he'd apparently come to a decision.

'I know I behaved badly with Grace,' he began, his good hand roughly rubbing the weaker one on the table-top, his eyes fixed on her own. 'She was so young, and I was married to you . . . I was ashamed of myself. But I really need you to understand, Romy. Her version of events is just plain wrong.'

Romy, returning his stare, thought she could, indeed, detect the shame in his eyes. It spoke to her in a way his words – still hedged about with equivocation – could not. But she found her anger rising.

'You lied to me, Michael. For years.'

He nodded slowly. 'I know and I'm really sorry. I was terrified, Romy. Admitting to something so shameful? I thought everything would erupt. I'd lose my career, lose you, lose the boys' respect . . .'

Romy almost laughed at the order in which Michael categorized his potential losses, his career always number one. 'You did lose me, because you lied.'

She caught the flash of scepticism on her husband's face.

'So if I'd come clean when the letter arrived, you'd just have said, "Well, hey, never mind, these things happen"?'

'Don't be facetious, Michael.'

'I'm not. But are you seriously telling me you'd just have forgiven me and let it go – are you?' His tone was challenging.

'It's not up to me to forgive you.'

'Yes, *it is*. You're my wife. I cheated on you with a young girl.'

Oddly, Romy had never seen it as 'cheating'. That he'd violated Grace in a moment of madness was the issue. It was both more and less than cheating. She didn't reply.

'Look, I've let you down. I accept that. But I've apologized. I don't know what else I can do.' He picked up his cup and took a gulp of coffee, which, she thought, must be stone cold by now. 'Can we put all this behind us, do you think?' He let out a tired breath. 'It was a stupid, inappropriate fumble. One I will always regret. But certainly not a sexual assault. The whole thing's been blown up to ridiculous proportions by that letter. I did *not* attack Grace Fleetwood.'

Romy didn't move, didn't speak. His request paralysed her. His explanation was almost plausible, his contrition almost solid. Almost . . .

He wasn't pleading with her, thank goodness, when he said, his voice quietly firm, 'I've had the worst wake-up call anyone could imagine, Romy. I've lain in that bed all these weeks, confronting who I am and what I've done. And it's not a pretty sight. Yes, I've had a successful career – now over, I fear – but when you strip that away, what's left?' He shook his head sadly. 'Except the boys, not a lot.' He swallowed. 'But can't you and I find a way to move on from this, somehow?'

He smiled at her. It was a charmingly self-deprecating smile and Romy felt something give inside her. She suddenly had an image of the two of them waking up in that shabby London bedsit, which smelt of damp and something more sinister, the innocence of them both, the childish thrill of being in love, their optimism for the future stretching ahead of them, like the mythical Yellow Brick Road.

She noted the cautious relief that flooded Michael's face as she gave him a half-smile in return. But later, when she was alone, Romy realized she felt trapped by Michael's apology. He seemed to think that that was an end to it – case closed. The pressure was on her now, to get over her anger, to forgive him. 'Come on,' his smile was saying, 'you *know* you're on my side.'

All the love she'd ever had for her husband, though, was now muddled and muddied by the Grace issue, by Michael's lies and also by his confusing vulnerability – his change of character, post-stroke. Confused by Finch, too. The man who had gazed at her so ardently from the other side of the kitchen table represented only disorder, and an ill-defined barrier to her aching desire for independence.

But today it was down to her to make the birthday cake and prepare the sandwiches, get Michael into reasonable shape to receive visitors, then make nice to the guests they'd invited to the flat to celebrate. At any other time, this would be a pleasure – Romy always found baking therapeutic – but she felt so at sea that she doubted she could force herself into the jolly-hostess mode she would need in order to get through the afternoon.

She girded her loins, nonetheless, baked a coffee and walnut cake, and made cucumber sandwiches – the Claire family's favourite birthday tea. Michael seemed to understand that he couldn't push her. He'd been quiet and undemanding in the run-up to the party, thanking her for every little thing she did for him until she begged him to stop.

By four o'clock, he was sitting in his chair by the fireplace, clean and respectable, clad in normal trousers for the first time and a new white cotton shirt instead of the usual T, which Romy had had to button for him. He'd also managed to shave his own head, with only one nick at the back, where nobody would notice. She noted a new determination in the man – almost a spring in his step – and worried that he felt released by his assumption that they'd finally sucked the poison out of the secret that had been holding them back for so long.

*

'Hey, Mum.' Leo kissed her briefly, turning quickly to introduce the pretty, rounded blonde who stood hesitantly in his wake. 'This is Lucy . . . Lucy, this is Mum.'

Leo had asked if he could bring a 'friend' with him to the birthday tea and Romy had agreed, of course. Despite Leo rising thirty, Romy had never been introduced to any girlfriend before. She shook Lucy's hand and smiled warmly.

'Delighted to meet you, Lucy. Please, come in.'

Leo clutched at her sleeve as Romy ushered them towards the sitting-room door. 'Mum, wait a sec,' he whispered. 'Tell me how Dad is.' He seemed a bit on edge.

'Much the same, I suppose.'

Leo nodded. 'It's just . . . I wanted to introduce Lucy to you both but I don't want Dad . . . You know what he can be like or *could* be like.' He ground to a halt, started again. 'I thought maybe a thing where there were other people . . .'

Romy smiled, touched by her son's concern for Lucy. She was clearly not just a friend. 'He'll be fine, Leo, go and say hello.'

James followed Romy into the kitchen. He'd been late arriving, the tea party already well under way. Michael was more animated than Romy had seen him for a long time, including making an effort with Lucy. Leo, Romy could see, was beginning to relax. Romy had poured the tea, Wendy passing round the sandwiches that Micky, the chambers's long-serving senior clerk – dressed, as always, in a neat grey suit and matching waistcoat – grabbed two at a time and swallowed virtually whole.

'Great to see you looking *sooo* well, Michael,' James had gushed, as he greeted his old friend. 'You'll be back driving those judges to drink in no time, you old rogue.'

Romy had winced at the false bonhomie. Now she busied herself putting on the kettle for more tea and opening the packet of birthday candles, while James hovered silently in the doorway. She knew he had something to tell her and waited for him to speak.

'Romy, dear,' he began, 'I'm aware this is a little delicate, especially on the poor chap's birthday, but I thought maybe it's time for you and me to have a bit of a chat.' He hurried on: 'Now's not the time, of course, but I wondered if you might be free for lunch next week.'

Romy kept on twisting the multicoloured candles into the white plastic holders, then sticking them into the coffee butter icing in a circle around Michael's initial, which she'd doodled in wobbly chocolate script across the cake surface earlier. There were only twelve, but sixty-three seemed a step too far. She knew exactly what James wanted to talk about: Michael's ability to work again. She didn't blame him: the chambers were short of a famous silk, James the only senior barrister working alongside two junior colleagues, and things must be fraught. But she was still mildly offended on her husband's behalf.

'Shouldn't it be Michael you talk to, James?' she asked, glancing up from her task.

'Well . . .' James drew out the word '. . . thing is, I'm not sure how realistic he'll be about his condition. He's always been a cocky bastard.' He grinned, to take the sting out of his words. Then his expression became serious again. 'I thought perhaps you'd have the inside track on what you think him capable of, brain-wise.' His mouth twisted awkwardly in his round, fair face.

At least he has the grace to seem embarrassed, Romy thought. 'It's still early days. The doctor said another three months, minimum, and that was only a few weeks ago.'

James nodded slowly. 'I suppose I'm really asking if you think he'll be fit enough, down the line. Not physically, so much, but his brain.'

Romy couldn't help but picture Michael's dithering and insecurity about even the slightest task. The thought of him in court in an adversarial situation was unthinkable right now.

'I can't call it, James,' she replied. 'Stroke victims can make astonishing recoveries.'

'Of course they can! And I'm quite sure he will, my dear.' The man had clearly decided he was getting nowhere, and his demeanour changed back to one of forced jollity. 'Let's keep in touch,' he added, as if she were trying to sell him something he didn't want.

He turned to go, but Romy stopped him. 'James, I wanted to ask you something too, which is also rather delicate.'

James's eyebrows rose as he waited for her to go on.

'I hope you don't mind, but something's come up with Michael and I wondered if . . . I gather you knew Nell Fleetwood.'

James's face went still for a split second, then his cheeks coloured as only very fair-skinned people's do: the dull brick red that looks as if it will never fade.

'Michael told you that?'

She nodded.

'It was a long time ago. And Honor –'

Ignoring the fact of his marriage to the charming Honor – she wasn't here to judge – Romy said, 'It's just Nell's daughter, Grace . . .'

His eyes narrowed. 'Christ,' he said, the word thudding like lead into the silent kitchen. 'He told you that, too?'

Romy nodded.

'So what's your question?'

What is it? She felt flustered. Hadn't Michael already told her what happened? She went on with her task, but her hands were shaking slightly as she said, 'What did he tell you about that night, James?'

The silence made her turn. James was looking at her warily. 'You said you knew.'

She gave a small shrug. 'He told me his version . . . I'd like to hear yours.'

James hesitated, pulling nervously at his right ear lobe. 'I'm sure they're the same but, OK, yes, he came round that night, in a bit of a state. He was worried, because of her age. Obviously it wouldn't look good, if it came out – a schoolgirl and a senior barrister.'

Romy was aware of a small alarm bell going off in her head, triggered by James's split second of hesitation. 'But just a consensual kiss?' she said, as nonchalantly as possible, knowing there was more and wanting to flush James out – hoping the tremor in her voice did not betray her. 'Even given how young she was . . .'

James dropped his head. 'If you could call it that.' His voice was low and angry. 'He shouldn't have done it.' When he finally looked up, he'd got his features under control and said, with his usual bland delivery, 'I thought

273

Grace might run to her mother. So I put the feelers out, told her I thought Michael and Grace had had a silly moment. But Nell had no idea what I was on about. And I suppose I did make light of it then, because I was nervous of the repercussions for Michael if Grace spoke up.'

'Nell must have talked to her daughter, though, if you suggested there'd been some impropriety.' It was unthinkable she wouldn't. Yet Grace had told Finch her mother didn't know. Maybe Nell sounded her out and Grace denied it.

James shrugged. 'We stopped seeing each other soon after that, so I've really no idea. The whole thing put the wind up me, to be honest, Romy. My wife . . .' He didn't finish, just stood there in the doorway, looking – even at his age – like a guilty schoolboy.

Finch was so angry with me for protecting Michael, Romy thought bitterly. *But it seems everyone – Grace, Nell, James, even me – we were all bending over backwards to keep his nasty secret for him.*

'Long time ago,' James repeated. 'What brought it up?'

She could see his question wasn't as casual as he was trying to make it seem.

'Michael and I were just talking. Life-threatening illness can sometimes change a person's perspective.' She also spoke lightly, leaving James to assume she'd always known and wasn't fazed by it. But he appeared alarmed, crossing the kitchen to lean in to Romy, his voice lowered.

'Best he doesn't spread it about, my dear. Don't you think? Any *mea culpa* stuff, even in his condition, even after all this time, in the current climate, it wouldn't go down too well.' James checked her face to see if she understood. 'I'll maybe have a word with him.'

'Can I help in here?' Wendy's voice trilled in the doorway. She put the empty sandwich plate on the table. 'Oh, doesn't that look gorgeous!' she exclaimed, clapping her hands together as she peered at the cake. 'You're so clever, Romy.'

Romy glanced across at James, who seemed miles away, his fair face twisting almost as if he were having a bad dream. She heard again the anger in his voice when he'd said, 'If you could call it that', and wondered what he'd really meant, and what he was remembering now.

44

Of the three latest people who'd come for interview, there was only one, Janice – a middle-aged, lifelong carer-housekeeper whose last employer had just died – whom Romy considered even remotely suitable. She irritated Michael on sight, however, with her saccharine sweetness and mindless chatter. In her heart of hearts, Romy knew Michael would always find something wrong with every candidate. The whole thing infuriated her, but Leo had been investigating other agencies and she was determined that one would soon bear fruit, allowing her to leave and get her life back on track.

Despite these frustrations, Romy couldn't help feeling a creeping sense of hope. Michael was definitely improving. She could see it. He seemed happier, more energetic, apparently spurred on to get his body and mind back in working order. The probable reason for this change – getting the lies about Grace off his chest – almost offended her. But she was happy to see that he no longer lounged in bed with the television on and was up with the lark, washed, dressed and making breakfast for them both, becoming increasingly adept at a one-handed operation, his weak one now able to act as a pretty reliable anchor.

Some mornings she would find oats scattering the floor, milk spilt on the worktop, blueberries rolling about the kitchen table, but she didn't comment. He was trying so hard and her heart went out to him, despite herself. But when she caught him watching her sometimes, a brooding look on his face, she resolutely ignored it.

In the evenings, Michael insisted on Scrabble. 'I've got to chivvy my non-existent brain cells somehow,' he kept telling her.

'Bloody things,' he exploded one night, as he accidentally knocked the rack containing his letter tiles and sent the small plastic squares tumbling across the kitchen table, many face up. She and Michael employed very different tactics: Romy liked to hoard, wait till she could get something truly spectacular, using as many letters as possible – once she'd managed 'coquette' and scored nearly seventy points. Michael played to win – small, strategically placed, one-syllable words with ridiculous scores. He was much quicker than she to spot the opportunities. But since the stroke, he got muddled and sometimes flustered, tired easily. 'How the hell am I going to get on if I can't even play a stupid board game without fucking up?' He glared accusingly at Romy, as if she were to blame.

'Don't get antsy. I've often done that,' she said soothingly.

But Michael was not about to be soothed. He dumped the rack upside down and flung himself petulantly back against the kitchen chair, like a toddler contemplating a tantrum. It was hot and close in the room, the lingering smell of garlic and rosemary from the chicken Romy had cooked earlier still on the air. She saw Michael was sweating, her own cheeks flushed from the two glasses of red she'd consumed.

'I'd got "mazy" if you'd left that *y* open,' she complained to distract him.

'Mazy? What's that supposed to mean?'

She laughed. 'Sort of like a maze?' She thought for a moment. 'For instance, "My, that path looks very mazy, don't you think?"'

He grinned. 'Rubbish, never heard of it.'

'Shall I look it up?'

Michael shook his head and sighed deeply, running his good hand back and forth over his shaved head. 'You know James rang today,' he said despondently.

Romy felt a pang of guilt, remembering her talk with the man at Michael's birthday tea, a couple of weeks back. He'd made no attempt to lure her to lunch since then. 'What did he want?' she asked.

'Basically,' Michael replied, 'he wanted to know if I thought I'd ever come back to chambers. If I'd ever work again.'

'Right. So what did you say?'

He looked at her as if she were being disingenuous. 'I said I'd be up and running, ready to take on the world by Christmas, no problem.'

Four months, she calculated, alarmed. 'Do you think –'

'Joke,' he cut her off tersely. 'Of course I didn't bloody say that. For Christ's sake, look at me, Romy.' He shrugged. 'Imagine me standing up in court, for starters.' He shook his head. 'Then imagine me wading through a two-box brief overnight.' Another weary shake of the head. 'And, finally, imagine me putting together a coherent argument for my client against some of the sharpest minds in the land.' This time he didn't bother to shake his head, just gave her a level glance that said it all.

'You don't know what you'll be like by Christmas,' she said.

Michael didn't reply. He pushed his chair back and reached for his crutch. Then he turned back to her. 'Go home, Romy,' he said dully. 'You've done your bit.'

She stared at him.

'I'm fine on my own. You can stop looking for another bloody carer.' He glared at her defiantly. 'I may still be clumsy, but I'm perfectly capable of ordering food online. The surgery will drop off my pills. I can just about work the microwave, put stuff in the washing machine, shower and dress myself. It all takes me for ever, but I can do it.' He paused only to gather breath. 'I haven't told you, because she didn't confirm until tonight, but I've asked Theresa to come in for a couple of hours five mornings a week. So,' he added, almost nonchalantly, 'I don't need you or anybody else any more.'

Romy didn't reply. *This is just bravado*, she thought, although she was surprised he'd been so proactive with Theresa. She'd known from Leo – weeks ago – that Michael didn't want *her* being responsible for his care after Daniel left, but now he was suggesting managing almost completely on his own. Was he really ready? If she'd thought he was, she'd already have gone.

'Leave,' he went on, a martyrish note creeping into his voice. 'Go and find your brigadier, make it up to him. Get on with your life, Romy, while you still can.'

She frowned. Then she grinned. Michael looked offended. 'Another gold star for melodrama,' she said. 'Chart's filling up.'

'I meant every word,' he insisted, piqued.

'I'm sorry.' She tried, unsuccessfully, to stop smiling. 'It's just you sound like a bad Victorian novel. Doing the far, far better thing, setting me free to love, while you die a miserable death, all alone.' She knew she should shut up, stop making fun of feelings that seemed to have been genuinely expressed, but it had felt like just another of his theatrical moments of self-pity. It was hard to take him seriously.

Michael gave her a wounded smile and said quietly, 'You certainly know how to deflate a man.'

For a while they sat in silence. Romy heard Michael's phone buzz with the arrival of an email; the fridge wheezed and clunked; a door slammed somewhere in the block.

'Let's give it a go, then, if you're serious,' she said. 'I'll leave you for the weekend and see how you get on, OK?'

Michael's face stiffened. 'Bring it on,' he said, through clenched teeth.

So Romy went home.

45

The cottage seemed small and strange to her, after the high-ceilinged London flat, and somehow blank, as if it had lost her essence, finally given up on her. She felt like standing in the middle of each room and waving her hands, like a conductor, encouraging the place to life.

Later that afternoon she curled up on the bed. The clean sheets and her favourite pillow, the cool breeze blowing in from the harbour – just being home and in her own space, by herself for once – made the previous weeks' confusion melt temporarily away and she felt her body gradually relaxing, giving in to sleep. There was nothing she had to do, nowhere she had to be, no one waiting for her.

When she woke it was after six. She had slept for nearly three hours. In a panic, she jumped off the bed, dizzy and disoriented, then realized there was no reason why she shouldn't snooze all day if she wanted to.

The evening was too beautiful to stay inside, though. She pulled on her trainers and sunglasses, a peaked cap to keep the setting sun from her eyes, then walked purposefully down onto the sea road. There were families out in force, it being a Saturday, kids jumping off the jetty, or swinging from the tyre suspended over the small stream that ran into the sea, weekend sailors tinkering with their dinghies, students from the nearby college sitting in heaps in the meadow outside the church, barbecuing sausages in foil trays, their bikes thrown to the grass in a circle, like wagons in the Wild West.

Romy breathed deeply as she walked, swinging her arms wide to embrace the delightful familiarity. But all the while her gaze panned from side to side as each group of people approached her on the rutted road – *Was this tall outline against the horizon him?* – knowing that at any second she might catch sight of him, running towards her, his mucky trainers splashing in the edges of the incoming tide, cheeks glowing, arms pumping, then his warm brown eyes suddenly meeting hers. It had to happen sooner or later. The cottage, the harbour, the village were chock full of memories of Finch, which kept coming at her like missiles, relentless and hard to bat away.

When Romy found herself back at home, she felt desolate that she hadn't seen him. She wanted so badly to talk. Listening to Michael's protestations of innocence, she had had her doubts. But James's decided shiftiness at Michael's birthday tea had been fuel to the flames. Nothing might change in regard to her and Finch's relationship if she talked to him – although there still existed that tiny pinprick of hope – but at least she could voice her current suspicions, convince him that she wasn't the monster he no doubt thought she was . . . and tell him she was leaving the flat for good.

The following morning was drizzly but still warm as Romy walked determinedly across the village towards Finch's house. She had spent most of the night prevaricating. But she knew she had to try to make it right with him, or leave their memories of each other for ever stuck in that terrible altercation.

She wore her red anorak and cap – which she ripped off as soon as she turned the corner into his road, stopping on the narrow strip of grass opposite the solid seventies build that was Finch's house.

Romy spotted his Toyota, parked on the narrow concrete apron beside a small front lawn. *He's home.* Her stomach flipped. She was still wondering, in trepidation, how he would react to her impromptu visit when the front door opened and a young woman with bouncy blonde hair stepped out, calling over her shoulder to someone inside, 'Don't forget the book.'

Retreating behind a voluminous late-flowering ceanothus, like a spy in a fifties novel, Romy saw a man follow a minute later, also in his thirties or early forties, she gauged, clutching a glossy hardback. They got into a burnt-orange Kia, the woman driving, and pulled away from the kerb, passing close by Romy as she skulked in the bushes. She watched the man – nice-looking with a chubby, open face and beard – laughing at something as they followed the lane out of the village.

Romy knew exactly who they were: she'd seen a wedding photo in Finch's kitchen. The woman was unmistakably Grace, the man beside her Sam. She stood stock still, shadowed by the shrub, not knowing what to do. *Where's Finch?* The couple hadn't called goodbye as they left, in fact had seemed totally absorbed in each other and their mission, whatever that was. And the man had turned to double-lock the door.

She continued to gaze at the house. There was no movement, no sign of life at any of the windows – the house did not seem occupied now. After another couple of minutes' silent observation, Romy turned and walked slowly back the way she had come.

Grace – so real, so present, so huge in the insurmountable barrier she represented – had only brought home to her the hopelessness of any dreams she still harboured.

She quickened her pace in an attempt to get the blood flowing round her body and dispel the adrenalin that was making her buzz. The drizzle had stopped and the sun was out, but she barely noticed, she was so lost in regret. Tears for what might have been began to swim behind her eyes, mercifully hidden by her dark glasses.

Her eighty-something neighbour was snipping at the long tendrils of ivy spiking out of the privet hedge that sat along the low wall between her small front garden and Romy's. She was wearing her floppy flowered hat and round, very dark glasses, her body encased in a shapeless blue nylon housecoat – like the one Romy's mother had always worn. She peered at Romy and waved her gloved hand.

'Hello, Vera,' Romy said, moving quickly past to her front door. She was not in the mood for one of Vera's long conversations about either of her favourite topics: the proposed development along the top road out of the village, or the bins.

But her key wouldn't turn in the lock. She pulled on the brass doorknocker – which needed polishing, she noticed – to get purchase, but the bloody thing wouldn't budge. She could feel Vera's eyes boring into her back.

'It'll be the heat,' Vera commented, as Romy continued to sweat and struggle with the Yale key, swearing under her breath.

She was on the point of giving up and going round the back to the garden doors, when she heard Vera say, 'This is when you need that nice young soldier of yours.' Romy, still with her face to the door, froze. 'Shame he's so far away,' Vera added.

Romy swung round. *What does she mean?* She said, 'He's not *my* soldier, Vera.'

It seemed, from the politely raised eyebrows, that Vera knew this already. But she said, 'That's a shame, dear. He's such a charming man, a proper gentleman. And all those exhausting marathons he does for the hospice . . . Jenny adores him. She was showing me a postcard he sent from Argentina at the safari supper last week.'

Romy found herself rooted to the spot. She wanted to turn and run, to get away from her neighbour's inquisitive stare and the miasma of gossip that was clearly swirling round her relationship with Finch, but her feet would not obey her.

'What's he doing in Argentina?' she asked, almost against her will.

'Jenny says he's on sabbatical.' Vera chuckled. 'Not sure you can have one of those if you're retired, can you? But apparently he's having a high old time with all those gaucho people. Jenny says he speaks fluent Spanish, of course.' She leant on the wall with both hands, her secateurs discarded in her enjoyment of the gossip. 'I think she's a bit worried he won't come back.'

Romy tried to take in what she was hearing, but her mind was in turmoil.

'I'd better give this lock another try,' she said, turning quickly away, her breath fluttering in her chest as she stuck the key into the door. Miraculously, it twisted with only slight resistance. Waving a hand to her neighbour, she went inside and shut the door with exaggerated care, not wanting the distress she was feeling to be obvious to nosy Vera Boyce.

Hurrying through to the kitchen, she threw her cap and sunglasses on the table and sat down heavily. Finch had gone to Argentina and she didn't even know? And the postcard? He obviously hadn't left yesterday.

Romy knew she had no right to be upset. Finch was a free agent. But he had left without telling her, had been away without her knowing and was sending cosy postcards to the hostile Jenny. She couldn't help but feel incredibly hurt. The cold truth was that he had moved on.

46

Finch got back to his cottage on the Gutierrez estate around midnight, after an exhausting supper at which he'd earned his keep by recounting endless tales of derring-do to Luis and Jocelyn's American clients. It was only nine in the evening in the UK, and he was determined to get hold of Grace on WhatsApp. He'd tried on and off all day, but the mostly flickering broadband had been completely down and he had only a weak signal on his phone.

Grace picked up immediately. 'Finch!' She sounded so happy to hear him, he knew Marty had been right and kicked himself for being so blind.

'Hey, Gracie.'

He could hear the television in the background as Grace said, 'Hold on a minute. I'll go into the other room.'

'How are things?' he asked.

There was a pause. Then Grace replied, her voice lowered, 'Oh, I don't know. This thing . . . telling you . . . it's sort of churned me up. I can't stop thinking about it now.'

Finch wasn't sure what to say, but Grace went on, 'Don't tell me to get help, Finch. I'd feel like such a fucking loser, whingeing about something that happened when I was sixteen. It's just –' She stopped.

'Gracie, listen, I know about this. I had men in my unit traumatized by stuff and refusing to admit they were getting flashbacks, not sleeping, whatever, because they didn't think it was important enough, didn't want to appear cowardly or weak. They didn't get better on their own.' There was no response so he went on, hoping to drive home his advantage. 'What happened to you was real. It'll only get worse if you don't deal with it.'

'Yeah, well, telling you already made it worse.'

'That's probably the hardest part, opening up for the first time.'

He heard her sigh. 'I wish you were here, Finch.' She sounded on the verge of tears.

'Oh, Gracie. You should have said. I thought you were OK with me being away.'

'I was. I am. I'm totally OK. I just . . . Hearing your voice . . .'

He heard the crack in her words, and stifled sobs. 'Gracie, sweetheart . . .'

She cleared her throat. 'Come on, then,' she said. 'I want the latest on the roasted cow balls.'

Finch laughed. 'No latest, thank goodness. Listen, I was ringing to say I'm coming back. It's amazing here, but it's not real life.'

He heard Grace snort. 'Nothing so great about real life.' Silence, then she added, 'So you're really coming home?'

The cautious hope in her voice was too much for him and he coughed to get rid of the lump in his throat. 'I don't want to let Luis and Jocelyn down, they've been so good to me, but the current guests leave soon and I'll get a flight out after that.'

Grace gave a long sigh. 'That's great, Finch. Let me know when.'

Finch pulled up beside Marty on the bluff. The slopes of the distant hills were shaded purple, the pampas, stretching away down the valley, bleached sand-grey and shimmering, like a piece of silk, in the winter sunset. The emptiness, the sheer vastness and beauty of the landscape still awed him, even after the weeks at Luis's estancia.

'Thought I'd lost you.' Marty grinned, eyebrows raised smugly.

'Ha-ha.' Finch laughed. The American was so bloody competitive on a horse. And he'd found himself – against his better instincts – trying his best to match him, to beat him. But it was pointless: Marty was at one with the Paso.

For a while they sat there, the chomp, chomp of the horses as they lowered their heads to the grass the only sound. Finch breathed in the stillness, the silence. This grand wilderness seemed not to allow for petty concerns – which was probably why he loved it.

'I'm sad you're leaving,' Marty began, as they tightened their reins and turned their mounts back the way they'd come. 'Next time you want to take off, you should visit Wisconsin. Spend some time at the ranch. Daddy would love you and there's always a ton of work with the horses.'

'Thanks, I'll remember that,' Finch said. He smiled across at his friend. 'It's your fault I'm going.'

'How so?'

'Oh, you just reminded me of stuff I was trying to forget.'

'How thoughtless of me,' Marty joked. Then his expression became serious. 'But, trust me, it'll be a relief to stop running.'

47

When she returned to the flat after the trial weekend, Michael made his position quite clear.

'You see?' He waved his good hand, like an actor taking a bow. 'Still in one piece.' Looking triumphant he added, rather formally, 'So you can leave me with a clear conscience, Romy, and knowing you've done a spectacular job, getting me thus far. I can't thank you enough.'

Romy had heard from Leo, however, what a state Michael and the kitchen had been in that Sunday morning, how worried he and Lucy were.

'Honestly, Mum, the kitchen looked like the police had got a search warrant and popped by for a dawn raid. There was mess everywhere,' Leo said, when he phoned her on her journey back to London. 'Lucy wanted to clear it up, but I stopped her because you said not to do stuff for him this weekend.'

Romy had groaned silently. 'How did your father seem?'

'Oh, he was cheerful enough. He looked a wreck – hadn't shaved and had food down his T-shirt – but he seemed perfectly happy on his own.'

By the time Romy arrived at the flat, though – steeling herself to deal with the chaos – the place was relatively tidy. Michael had shaved and dressed in clean clothes. A ready-meal supper of fish pie for them both stood poised for nuking.

'It's great you feel you can manage,' she said now, watching as Michael balanced on the crutch and slung the pie confidently into the microwave, adjusting his reading glasses to peer down at the settings.

Romy was oddly discombobulated as she sat down at the table. The trial had worked. *I really can leave*, she thought. It was what she'd longed for, but she felt almost dithery, now the moment had finally come and she was no longer needed.

The following day Michael was subdued as he watched her gather her things together. Romy felt the wrench of leaving him, too. But there were people coming in: Theresa, Imogen, Leo on alert – Wendy, for Sunday tea. *He will be fine*, she told herself. She found she couldn't think about her own plans yet, as she wheeled her case down the corridor towards the front door. They were hovering on the horizon, just out of reach, like good weather after a storm. She would enjoy the sunshine later.

They stood together in the hall. *He looks so drawn and tired*, Romy thought, watching Michael manoeuvre himself until he was leaning against the wall. *Stop worrying*, she told herself firmly as she pulled on her jacket. But this felt like a huge moment, almost more significant than the first time she'd left him. Then, she had slunk off, not knowing what lay ahead, not even sure she was doing the right thing. But now she knew. Now she was quite sure.

'I'm really going to miss you,' he said, giving her a tender smile. His parting kiss lingered on her cheek for just a second longer than usual. She heard the nervousness in his voice as he added, 'You will keep in touch?'

'Of course I will,' Romy said, giving him a quick hug. But as she opened the front door her feelings were powerfully uncomplicated: she was free.

When she arrived back at the cottage, though, just as the sun was going down in a spectacular light show of pinks, purples and gold over the estuary, instead of celebrating her freedom she found herself giving in to the strong desire to cry – which had hovered like an itch she dared not scratch over the tedious journey in the hot, packed train carriage.

Romy had anticipated this moment for months – the moment when she no longer had to worry about Michael, or his prevarications, his frailty, the pressure of his unrequited feelings for her. She had thought she would be relieved, liberated to follow her own path. But there was no sense of freedom as she made her way up to bed that night, after too many shots of vodka from the bottle in the freezer. All she felt was drunk and exhausted . . . and overwhelmingly lonely.

Romy spent her first days at home mooching about, trying to summon the energy to begin again. But now, early on Saturday evening, she was hurrying along the lane to the village car park to meet the man who was going to fit a new windscreen in the Audi: she'd found a ten-pence-sized chip, sitting spider-like in the centre of the glass when she went to the car that lunchtime.

She no longer looked out for Finch, these days, knowing he was on the other side of the world, but the place felt empty and monochrome without him.

A white Transit, sporting the windscreen-repair-company logo, appeared at the edge of the car park and she waved him over.

'How long will it take?' she asked.

Darren, in overalls, examined the damage closely, narrowing his eyes. 'Forty-five for the screen. Can't drive it for another twenty or so, not till the sealant's gone off.' He pinged one of the wipers. 'These look a bit knackered. You want to replace them?'

Romy handed him her keys. 'OK, yes. Text me when you've finished.'

It was a warm, beautiful evening. Reluctant to go home, Romy decided to sit on the wall outside the waterside café and watch the world go by. As she rounded the bend from the car park, turning left down the slope that led to the harbour, she noticed a woman standing alone, to the left of the yellow ice-cream van – still plying its trade, although it was gone six thirty.

She had her back to Romy and was gazing out towards the sea, dressed in a white T-shirt and denim shorts, her blonde waves clamped under a navy cap, bare legs strong and tanned. But even from the back, even with the cap on, Romy recognized her instantly.

She stopped, almost not daring to breathe. She could turn and flee, hurry down the lane opposite and hide in her house until Darren texted her. Or she could finally speak to Grace, meet the woman who had, with that fateful letter, turned Romy's world inside out.

She hesitated, watching as Grace glanced around, then began to walk slowly along the shore, scuffing her flip-flops through the puddles left in the pitted tarmac by the outgoing tide, like a kid.

The sea was far out, the estuary a landscape of sandy-brown mud and vivid green seaweed, rivulets and pools catching the light of the descending sun, the boats – moored further out – stationary in the glassy channel of seawater. But as Grace disappeared behind the stone wall of the corner house, Romy found herself galvanized. She couldn't let this opportunity slip away – although she had no idea what she would actually say when she came face to face with the woman.

Quickening her pace, she caught up with the retreating figure, drew level, drew ahead and turned. Grace raised her head as she approached, but her glance was casual: she didn't know Romy.

'Grace?' Romy said, hearing the quiver in her voice. Her heart was thumping so hard she wanted to clamp her hands over her chest to prevent it bursting free.

Grace frowned, nodded.

Romy held her hand out. 'Romy. Romy Claire.'

The woman's face went still, then visibly paled, her beautiful grey eyes filling with apprehension. She ignored Romy's hand, crossing her arms firmly across her body and glancing around the harbour, as if in need of rescue. She seemed lost for words.

'I recognized you,' Romy went on, her voice wavering. 'Finch showed me your photograph. I thought . . . I wondered if we might talk for a minute. I don't mean any trouble.'

Grace stared at her, arms still pulled in tight, shoulders raised defensively. But she didn't speak and Romy begged, 'Please,' then held her breath.

'A minute, then,' Grace eventually replied. 'Sam's meeting me.'

Romy nodded. By tacit agreement the two women began to walk east along the road, the setting sun to their right, the ice-cream van and the remaining tourists behind them. But now Grace had agreed to talk to her, Romy did not know where to begin. It was Grace who spoke first.

'Sam doesn't know.'

'OK . . . I understand. Listen, I really don't want to upset you . . . I just wanted to say that I'm so sorry for what happened to you.'

Grace was silent. Romy could feel the tension coming in waves off the woman walking stiffly beside her.

'Have you asked him about it?' she said eventually, in a very small voice.

Romy hesitated. 'Yes.'

The woman stopped and turned to her, eyes defiant, but her voice faltering. 'I suppose he denied it?'

'No.' She took a long breath. 'But he remembers it differently.'

Grace shook her head, sucking her lips between her teeth as if to stop herself crying. Romy couldn't ignore the anguish in her eyes.

'I believe you, Grace.' Romy heard the words – sounding so purposeful as they spilt from her mouth – with a strange relief. Because she knew in that moment, witnessing her clear distress, that Michael – whatever expedient interpretation he'd placed on his actions – had done what the girl said he had done.

Her grey eyes brimmed over now. 'You do?'

She nodded.

Tears slid down her pale cheeks but she brushed them away. 'That means a lot,' Grace said, then turned her face away from Romy as she said the next words. 'I was scared. He really hurt me . . . He . . .' She didn't go on.

'I'm so sorry.' It seemed an inadequate response, but Romy was too shocked by Grace's words to find better. Spoken like that, with such a chilling lack of emphasis, they could not have been misinterpreted.

Grace shook herself as she dug out a tissue from her shorts' pocket and blew her nose. Looking at Romy intently, she said, 'You shouldn't apologize. You've done nothing wrong.'

'I did. I took Michael's side.' She lowered her gaze. 'I didn't want to believe he was capable of such a thing.' *But I do now*, she thought grimly.

Grace blinked rapidly. She seemed agitated, her gaze flicking to and fro. 'Sam will be here in a minute. Please, can you go?'

Romy – selfishly, she realized – didn't want to. She wanted to talk to Grace, to cling to this link with Finch for as long as she possibly could. But before she had time to speak, her phone rang.

'Tried texting you,' Darren said.

'I'll be right there.'

When she looked up, Grace was walking briskly back along the shore. She hadn't said goodbye and Romy was too choked to call out. She hurried round the corner to the car park, devastated for Grace, of course, but also furious with herself. The honesty in the girl's face had been painful to witness.

Romy listened with half an ear to Darren drone on earnestly about scuttle panels and primers. But her mind was elsewhere. *Michael is guilty.* It made her feel sick. All these months and years of wanting to believe him, her passionate defence of her husband in the face of Finch's testimony, the way she'd pointed the finger at poor Grace. *There was only one liar.*

48

James was already at the table when she went in, a breadstick in one hand – which he was chewing absent-mindedly – his sleek, big-screen iPhone in the other. The exclusive Italian restaurant on Aldwych was one he and Michael frequented. She had been there herself, in happier times, to meet her husband for lunch.

'Romy, my dear.' James threw breadstick and phone onto the starched white tablecloth and rose to give her his usual tentative cheek brush in greeting – he was not a man comfortable with hugs. 'This is a rare pleasure.'

Not when I tell you why I asked you to come, she thought, but smiled at him nonetheless as she returned his kiss and sat down, the maître d' pushing her chair in for her and shaking out her starched napkin, then laying it across her lap with a flourish.

'So how's the old rascal, then?' James asked cheerily, but he was clearly awkward with her. Not least because he had told Michael now that he was looking to take on a permanent replacement.

He probably thinks I'm here to plead Michael's cause, Romy thought wryly. 'I'm back home in Sussex now,' she said. 'But I hear he's doing well. Small improvements.'

James nodded, clicking his fingers to get the waiter's attention. 'They have a very serviceable Verdicchio here. You happy with white?'

Romy nodded, desperate for a large glug of alcohol – any would do – to calm her nerves. She was cold, although it was warm and muggy outside and the restaurant had no air-conditioning. They chatted about the summer – James had been to his house in Tuscany, then a wedding in Majorca – until the wine and bottled water arrived. Then Romy took a deep breath. But before she could speak, James held his hand up.

'I know why you invited me, Romy.' His fair, round face looked pained. 'And I understand why you're upset with me. But I honestly don't have a choice. Michael seems so . . . well, let's be honest,' he faltered, 'not himself. And we're inundated, as usual, working ourselves black and blue to deal with the caseload.'

Romy let his words hang in the air. She felt for him. 'I'm not here about that, James.'

His expression cleared. 'Oh, right. OK.'

She took a large mouthful of the chilled white, deliciously fortifying as it slid down her throat. 'I wanted to talk about Grace Fleetwood.'

James's eyes narrowed. But he said nothing.

'I'd like the truth. I'd like to know exactly what Michael told you that night when he came round to your house.' When the man still didn't answer, she added, 'Please, James. I saw you hesitate, when we last spoke about it, the day of Michael's tea. I heard what you said. I know you're hiding something.'

There was silence while James waved away the waiter who'd come to take their order and took what appeared to be a strategic sip from his glass. 'What's this all about, Romy?' He sounded nonchalant, but she knew he was not.

'Something isn't ringing true. And I think, as Michael's closest friend, you know what it is.'

James shook his head as if he were really puzzled. 'Why, though? Why do you want to know? It's decades ago.' He paused. 'Is the girl wanting to make trouble?'

His tone was chilly now and Romy could see how his bland, chummy exterior hid a very different persona. Michael had always told her, 'Don't be fooled by Bregman. He's a clever bastard. You wouldn't want to cross him in court.'

'She's a woman, James. And she's not going to "make trouble", as you put it. This is me who wants to know.'

James sighed. 'Romy, listen.' He reached across and grabbed her hand in his large, soft one. 'Don't do this. Don't torture yourself. Michael's a sick man. What good will it do to drag up the past now?' His look was entreating.

'Just tell me, James.' She heard the flat, uncompromising note in her voice, knew the look she shot him matched it, and saw James come to a decision.

Shaking his head slightly, he frowned. 'All right . . . What do you want to know?'

Romy didn't answer, just stared at him, waiting. For what seemed like an age, he looked away, eyelids blinking, mouth twisting. But eventually he gave a heavy sigh, leaning in towards her, his words barely audible above the muted hubbub of the restaurant and the churning hiss of the espresso machine behind the bar. 'If you really want to know the truth,' he began, 'Michael was not, as I told you before, in a "bit of a state" that night. He was in a dreadful state. So distraught he had to drink a large glass

301

of whisky before he could say a word. He gave me a garbled account of what had happened . . . Then he told me he was scared witless she'd go to the police.'

Romy swallowed, feeling a shiver go up her spine. 'The police?'

James hesitated, his eyes hooded. Then he nodded reluctantly. 'He said he thought he'd gone too far. When I asked what he meant, he said – and I quote, because I'll never forget his words – "I think I might have hurt her."' His cheeks puffed as he blew out a slow breath.

Romy held her napkin to her mouth, suddenly fearing that the wine she'd just swallowed might come right back up as her stomach clenched and pitched.

James, seeing her horror, went on earnestly, 'I honestly don't think he was in his right mind, Romy. You know Michael – he's Mr Cool most of the time, nothing fazes him. But that night he looked like he'd seen a ghost.'

Yes, thought Romy, bleakly, *the ghost of his real self.*

James was searching her face for a reaction. But all Romy could think about was Michael's dark eyes, full of bewilderment and hurt innocence, his anger that she should doubt him – *I absolutely was* not *violent, Romy. I wasn't.* She had tried so hard to believe in him. *He played me.* She shuddered at the thought. *He absolutely played me.* His wife of over thirty years and he'd looked her in the eyes and lied through his bloody teeth.

'I kept hoping I was wrong,' she said quietly, then added, 'Didn't you worry . . . that he was capable of doing such a thing?'

James sighed. 'Michael's not a violent man, I'm sure you'll agree. I was convinced it was just a very unfortunate one-off . . . maybe brought on by the ludicrous work pressure he was under.' He paused, and Romy saw he was sweating, his forehead pink and glistening.

He refused to meet her eye as, reluctantly, he forced out the next words. 'Michael said something along the lines of his being sure she wanted him, and when she resisted his advances, he just saw red. But he insisted he hadn't gone as far as rape and I believed him. I only knew the girl by sight from when I was still in the village. I'd been in Amsterdam all her work-experience week and Nell and I kept our thing quite separate so I had no idea what she was like. And I was thinking of chambers, what a potential scandal might do . . .' He finally looked up, his expression sheepish. 'Obviously I had something to hide, too.'

Rage whispered up through Romy's body. 'So you just left it, did nothing, hoped it would go away?' she hissed.

James shrugged. 'Pretty much. I didn't know what else *to* do.'

But as fast as the anger arrived, it ebbed away again as she heard the echo of Finch's furious accusation. She had not known what to do either, when she'd read the letter. So she'd also done nothing and hoped it would go away. As, perhaps, had Nell, when faced with James's no doubt sanitized tale of her daughter's assault.

His eyes were hangdog now. 'I'm ashamed of myself, Romy. Men have secrets together – I'm sure women do, too – but it honestly wasn't a secret I relished, being party to a sexual assault on a teenager . . . on Nell's daughter.'

Romy, against her will, found herself believing him.

'What will you do, now you know the truth?' James asked, his mouth twitching nervously. 'Will you go to the police?'

'It's not my secret to tell, James. If anyone goes to the police, it will be Grace.'

49

Grace and Sam had been holidaying in his house while he'd been away – Finch could almost feel their recent presence. They'd left butter and milk, some banana bread in tin foil and two apples in the fridge. And despite his reluctance to come back, he found himself giving a drawn-out sigh of relief as he imbibed the familiarity of home.

His stepdaughter was coming the following night, without Sam, who was attending a work seminar in Leicester on Saturday. Finch was looking forward to seeing her. He didn't know how he could help Grace, but as the only person she was close to who was aware of the assault, he could at least try. He could give her a hug and let her know he loved her. That was what he had come home for.

Finch wandered about, getting reacquainted with his home. He went over to the photograph of Nell on the kitchen wall and stood for a while staring at her face. But somehow the time away from his habit had broken the link. His wife's image was still powerful – he knew it always would be – but it was just an image now, a memory. He no longer sensed she was there with him, or felt the urge to talk to her in the way he had. And since his talks with Marty, he was all right with that.

*

It was late and pouring with rain when Grace arrived. She looked exhausted and bedraggled, her eyes round as saucers in the overhead kitchen light. Finch hugged her for a long time, then sat her down to a supper of watercress soup, bread and cheese. But he could see that she was struggling to eat, struggling to be cheerful as she went through the motions of questioning him about his time in Argentina.

'Finch,' she said, after a long silence, turning her mother's eyes up to him as he stood to clear the table, 'I need to tell you something.'

He sat down again.

For a moment she did not speak, just took another sip of wine. *She's drinking way too much*, Finch thought, watching the kitchen light cast shadows on her lovely face.

Another silence.

'I met Romy.'

Finch jolted. He hadn't expected that. Since being back in the same village, he'd thought of little else but her.

'Where?' he managed to ask, although he realized, stupidly, it was the least important detail of all.

'The harbour. She came up to me, introduced herself.'

Finch nodded, not daring to interrupt, not trusting his voice to do so.

'I didn't want to talk, but she insisted.' Grace was clearly wrestling with her thoughts. 'She told me Michael had a *different* version of what happened,' she gave a cynical roll of her eyes, 'but she said she believed me.'

'OK . . .'

'We didn't talk for long – I didn't want Sam to see us together so I asked her to leave.'

Finch tried to imagine the scene. *It must have taken a lot of guts for her to approach Grace*, he thought. He knew Romy would be sensitive – he could almost see those eyes of hers, full of determination, and his heart went out to her. It made him feel almost weak, the wave of longing that swept over him.

'I'm glad she told you she believed you,' he said.

Grace stared at him. 'Yeah,' she conceded eventually.

After another pause, during which Grace fiddled with the bread left on her plate, taking crumbs and rolling them into small balls between her fingers, which she then placed carefully in a pile, Finch said, 'Looks like things are pretty difficult for you at the moment?' He couldn't find a tactful way to say how distracted she seemed.

She nodded dumbly, head bowed. 'There's something else,' she said, and paused for what seemed like a very long time. Eventually she added softly, 'I lied to you, Finch.'

He held his breath. His heart was flapping like a flag in a storm. *No, no, please, no*, he thought. *Don't let this whole thing about Michael be some terrible invention.* He stared apprehensively at his stepdaughter, trying to fathom from her expression what she was about to reveal. But Grace wasn't looking at him. When she did begin to speak again, she simply sounded resigned and infinitely weary.

'When I said I didn't tell Mum, I wasn't being quite honest.' She drained her glass and set it down gently on the table. 'It was true I didn't, but she already knew at least some of it. From James Bregman.' Letting out a long sigh, Grace continued, her eyes filling with tears, 'But she didn't believe me when I told her my version of what happened.'

'*What?*' Finch spat the word out as if it were choking him.

'James must have said it was just a kiss, made out it was consensual or something.' Grace spoke very quietly, so Finch could barely make out her next words, the rest lost as Grace began to sob.

He got up and came round the table, sat on a chair beside her and put his arm round her shoulders until she quietened down a little. She turned her face towards him.

'It wasn't Mum's fault, Finch. James spun her what must have been Michael's account and she believed him. We weren't getting on back then, of course. She thought I was drinking too much, hanging out with the wrong crowd. I was judgemental about her having a thing with a married man . . .'

'A married man?'

Grace nodded. 'James.' She looked at him curiously. 'Didn't you know?'

Finch's head was spinning. *So that's what Jenny's sly comments implied*, he thought. *An affair with a married man?* Nell had always been incredibly disapproving – as a woman who'd been on the receiving end of infidelity with Grace's father – about people who did that. *No wonder she didn't tell me.* The biggest shock for him, though, was that Nell had known about Michael's attack. 'I can't believe your mum took James's word over yours,' he said, remembering the girl's heart-wrenching narrative that night. He blinked hard, as if trying to clear away this new image that was emerging about the woman he had always idolized.

Grace let out a tired sigh.

'So what exactly did she say?'

His stepdaughter hesitated. 'She said Michael shouldn't have kissed me. But then she asked if I was flirting with him. Said I got silly when I drank too much. Said Michael was a senior figure in the law and I should be very careful what I said because my accusations could ruin his life.'

'And you said?'

'I said I wasn't making any "accusations". I said I hadn't breathed a word and had no intention of doing so. I was just telling her what had happened because she asked. But James had got to her. She wasn't listening.'

She laid her head on his shoulder. 'We screamed at each other for hours, Finch, it was horrendous. I vowed after that I'd never mention it to another living soul.' She took a shuddering breath. 'Imagine telling Sam, and he reacts the same as Mum?' He felt her tremble. 'I'd die.'

Finch was struggling. He wasn't au fait with the metamorphosis of teenage years, when your beautiful communicative gem becomes a sullen two-headed monster overnight. He hadn't been there; he shouldn't judge. But still. Nell's response to Grace's account seemed so unsympathetic . . . her own daughter.

'We're going to get you some help,' he said, squeezing her shoulder. 'You can't deal with this on your own any more.'

This time, Grace did not put forward her usual objections. She just nodded and loudly blew her nose.

When the weekend was over, and Finch had time to think, it was to Romy – not Grace or Nell – he felt he owed an apology. Even Grace's own mother had not believed her: Nell, his perfect, gold-standard wife. James had brushed it under the carpet. No one, back then, had taken Michael's actions seriously. Just a foolish moment, oh, best forgotten. *Move away, everyone, nothing to see here.*

Now he grabbed his keys from the hook beside the door and his phone from the worktop. He needed to get some air – shake these people and their conflicting, bewildering behaviour from his tired brain.

50

After Romy had said a subdued goodbye to James on the pavement outside the restaurant, she had wanted to run, to go home to Sussex immediately and put as much distance as possible between herself and Michael. The thought of confronting him made her go cold. But she knew she had to do it. She didn't want another long drawn-out discussion with him about nuance – who had said what, done what, how or why or in which way things had happened – or to hear his smoothly calibrated excuses again. She just wanted to state what she'd found out. Let him know that she knew. Then leave him to stew in his lies. What she dreaded was his tears.

Michael did not respond to the bell, so she let herself in. He was in the sitting room, asleep, his shaved head lolling against the chair back, mouth yawning open. He looked so thin and frail that she had to remind herself of the conversation she'd just had with James. He opened his eyes as she approached and smiled.

'Hi, Romy . . . What are you doing here?' he asked, rubbing his hand over his face to wake himself up.

She sat down in the other armchair. 'I've just had lunch with James.'

'Oh?' He looked surprised.

She hesitated. She needed to get this right, not leave any loophole through which her lying husband could slip. 'I wanted to talk to him about Grace.'

The shutters instantly went up on Michael's face. *He knows what's coming.*

'He told me everything, Michael.' Romy spoke as firmly as she was able, her body like jelly, her breath catching as she waited for him to set off on his usual slippery, twisting mitigation for his behaviour.

But his expression hardened. 'Everything?' Michael gave a sardonic laugh. 'Is he dying or something? Wanting to clear his conscience?'

'It's not *his* conscience I'm concerned with.'

He looked defiant for a moment, then his features slumped and he raised his good hand in a gesture of defeat. 'I don't want to talk about it, Romy. I have nothing more to say.'

She knew there was a massive well of anger deep inside that one day she would need to address, in order to stop it poisoning her soul. But she couldn't access it now. All she felt, as she gazed at her damaged husband – on whose integrity she had so vehemently insisted – was an overwhelming pity.

She got up. 'You're a lucky man, Michael. That reputation of yours, which you value above all else, seems set to remain untarnished. It's more than you deserve.' Although Romy did not consider her husband lucky, not at all.

Michael clearly didn't either, because he harrumphed, made no reply. He was struggling to get out of the chair now, his face taut with effort. 'Need a pee.'

Her phone rang: Leo. She waited for Michael to leave the room before clicking on the call. Then found she couldn't speak, her throat closed with tears.

'Mum?'

Swallowing hard, she said, 'Hi, sweetheart.'

'You sound rough.'

'Just a bit of a throat thing.'

'Poor you. Are you at home?'

'No, I dropped in to see your father.'

'Great, how is he?'

'He's fine.'

'Good. I'm calling about Lucy. It's her thirtieth next week. She doesn't like fuss, but I thought it might be fun to go out, have a celebratory meal together somewhere. I wanted to ask if you thought Dad might be up for it.'

'Right . . .'

'So what do you think? Would he manage . . . even if just for an hour or so? We could do lunch, somewhere near the flat . . . Aragosta, perhaps? They love Dad there.'

'Which day?' she asked, trying to focus her thoughts.

'Saturday? Day after tomorrow. Short notice, I know. Her actual birthday's next Thursday, but she's seeing her family then.'

Romy didn't answer immediately and she heard Leo's voice, 'Mum? Listen, say if you think it's a bad idea, bringing Dad. We just thought he might enjoy getting out. Seems a bit mean to ask you and leave him behind.'

'Yes . . .'

'So shall I book for four?'

Romy didn't know what to say, so she muttered, 'That would be lovely,' just so she could get her son off the

313

phone. She wanted never to see Michael again. But she told herself she would do this last thing for Leo. She didn't even bother to call goodbye as she left the flat, just laid her keys on the ledge in the hall, slammed the front door behind her and hurried to Victoria to catch the train home.

51

Leo was nervous. He wanted Lucy's day to be perfect. But as they waited for his father to get ready, he had a bad feeling. His mother – who was meeting them at the restaurant – had seemed tense on the phone earlier, almost short with him. It was the way she'd snapped at him when he'd joked about his dad wearing his grey sweatpants to Aragosta that had unsettled him.

'I don't give a toss what your father wears,' had been his mother's terse response – almost as if she hated him.

'I'll just go and see how he's getting on,' he said to Lucy now, standing up from the sofa. 'The car will be here in a minute.'

Leo found he was holding his breath until his father was safely seated in the corner table of the restaurant, being fussed over by the owner.

'It is so good to see you, Mr Claire,' Antonio gushed, endearingly ignoring the change in his dad or his obvious disability. 'We have missed you and your lovely family.'

His father was making a huge effort, shaking the Italian's hand warmly and sitting up straight, smiling in a way Leo hadn't seen in a long while. 'We've missed you too, Antonio.'

Just like old times, Leo said to himself cynically, knowing it was nothing like the occasions when he and Rex had come here as teenagers, their parents bright and energetic, chatting to each other and to them. It was as if someone had come along with a paintbrush and a jar of water and wiped the wet bristles across his mother and father until the colour ran and they faded to the jaded pair sitting opposite him now.

Although his mother was being alarmingly over-bright – chatting non-stop with Lucy like a wind-up toy. She had given his girlfriend a lovely present of a silver bracelet, nicely wrapped in tissue paper with a ribbon and a card, but Leo sensed she was making a considerable effort to hold herself together. At first he'd thought she was ill with the throat bug she'd mentioned two days ago. But as the lunch went on, he knew it was something more fundamental than that. She could barely look at his father.

Things went reasonably well during the antipasti, the veal chop and right up until after the coffee semifreddo. Antonio had stuck a candle into Lucy's, written 'Happy Birthday' in piped chocolate around the edge of her plate, the waiters gathering round to sing to her – much to Lucy's intense embarrassment. Then, almost as if a switch had been thrown, his parents seemed to give up on the whole event.

'I need to pee,' his father said, uttering the now familiar refrain.

Which took for ever, as the Gents was down in the basement and Leo – who chaperoned him – was terrified he'd fall on the steep stairs, especially after two glasses of wine.

As his dad was peeing in the single urinal, Leo hovering nearby, Michael turned to look at him, stating baldly, 'I've upset your mother.'

Leo nodded as his father leant against the wall, breathing hard as he struggled to close his flies. 'I thought there was something up between you.' He raised an eyebrow. 'So what did you do this time, Dad?' His father appeared grim-faced but Leo couldn't imagine, in his current condition, that his offence was too serious. *Mum's probably just had enough*, he thought, mindful of the long and arduous months she'd put in, caring for him.

His dad didn't reply as he picked up his stick and began the slow journey out of the cramped toilet and up the stairs.

Leo, right behind, repeated, 'What did you do, Dad?'

'Don't ask. You really don't want to know,' came the caustic reply, as they reached the top of the stairs and were greeted by his mum, clearly impatient, and Lucy.

'We'll take you back,' Leo said to his father, assuming his mum would want to get home. Then he and Lucy planned to have a potter round the shops on Duke of York Square, although most of them were way out of their price range.

'No,' his mum said, directing a brittle smile at Lucy. 'I'll take him. You two go off and have fun.'

His dad shot him a knowing look and he found himself colouring. Leo was dying to get to the bottom of this row between his parents. His mum was clearly on the edge and he was loath to leave her like that. But he didn't want to spoil Lucy's day either. *I'll phone her later*, he decided, taking Lucy's hand and giving it a squeeze. *Maybe she'll open up about the problem when Dad's not around.*

'If you're sure?' he asked.

His mother nodded firmly, shooing them away with a smile. Leo grinned at Lucy. 'Come on then, birthday girl, let's hit the shops.'

52

Michael was curled up on top of the duvet, still in his smart trousers and shirt, already dozing when Romy entered the bedroom. For a moment she watched his face, sunken in repose, no trace of the deceit that now marred his waking countenance for her and was making her re-evaluate every one of the thirty years of their relationship.

Michael opened his eyes. 'I'm not asleep.'

She sat down abruptly in the stained orange armchair. 'We need to talk about the boys.'

He sighed, turned his face away.

Romy tried to calm her ragged breathing. 'Leo knows something's up. And I absolutely loathe lying to him. But I want you to know it won't be me who tells either him or Rex what happened with Grace. That's up to you.'

Michael's eyes widened. 'Christ! Are you joking?' he said, his voice suddenly high and weak. 'Tell the boys? They're all I've got – they'd never speak to me again if they knew.'

Romy couldn't help feeling a stab of sympathy. What a horrible dilemma he faced. 'Fine, up to you. But if you don't, Michael, I'm telling you it will haunt you for the rest of your life. Leo loves you . . . Maybe he'll come round.'

'You haven't.'

'You didn't lie to him.'

He looked away.

She got up. 'As I said, your call.'

Michael remained silent, his face still turned from her.

Romy stood for a moment, looking down at him. 'You know you can get back up to strength, Michael, if you choose. Face up to what you've done and forgive yourself. Be part of the world again.' The shadow of a cynical smile came and went on his face, but she ploughed on: 'Your arm might never be the same, but there are thousands of people out there who still contribute, lead a really good life, who aren't a hundred per cent fit.'

He finally turned to meet her eye, his own dark and unfathomable, his tone infinitely weary. 'I hear you, Romy. And I will tell Leo. Someday I will tell my sons what a bastard their father is . . . But not yet. I can't do it yet.'

53

As soon as Grace had left after breakfast on Sunday, Finch had contacted a psychotherapist he knew – the wife of an old army mate – and asked her if she had any recommendations in the Manchester area. He was waiting to hear back. Grace had assured Finch, when they'd said goodbye, that she was fine and that she would investigate professional help. But he had reservations on both counts. Her demeanour was too bright, too falsely compliant. He knew he would have to keep a pretty close eye on her, but it was so hard to do, when she was all the way up in Manchester. And this was making him think.

On his evening run around the harbour – avoiding the end where Romy's cottage stood, although he was sure she would be with that degenerate husband of hers on a Sunday night – an idea began to form. It had first crossed his mind on the plane coming home from Argentina, when he had sat, cramped in his seat – the rest of the cabin asleep – thinking how little there was keeping him in the village any more.

His time away had made it clear to him that he didn't want to go back to his old life of fundraising marathons and Jenny's coffee mornings – in fact, he hadn't contacted Jenny since he'd got back. He knew she would want to come round and see him immediately and he wasn't in the mood to have her clucking at him, to have his life taken over again. And as the dawn shone rosily across the billowing white floor of clouds outside the plane window, Finch had come to the unexpected realization that he wasn't, in fact, tied to his current lifestyle. He could change things.

Why can't I move up to Grace's neck of the woods? he asked himself now, as he jogged steadily past a couple walking their retriever in the brisk September dusk. *Find a little place in the Peak District – near her and Sam, but not too near – so I can keep an eye, be more involved in their lives.*

The idea really appealed. He wouldn't be burning his bridges. He could rent out his house, get somewhere for a year and see if it suited them all. His only real tie to this village had been Nell and, for a while, Romy. And both were gone from his life. He didn't want to spend the rest of his days keeping his eyes peeled every time he left his house, terrified of bumping into Romy and experiencing that thumping heartbreak all over again. By the time he reached home, he was buzzing.

'Shouldn't be a problem, Mr Fincham.' Haley, from lettings, with her strong Sussex accent, sounded eager. 'We're always on the lookout for properties in your location. If you're in such a hurry, maybe I could pop by later today and take some photos, get some details on the system.'

Finch had taken the bull by the horns first thing the next morning. Hearing Grace's shriek of excitement when he'd phoned her on her way to work and tentatively outlined his plan had been enough.

For the rest of the day, he was pinned to his screen, clicking forward and back, scrolling through wide-angle photos of sitting rooms, kitchens, bathrooms and bed-rooms – some of them probably no bigger than a cupboard – checking maps and transport links and noting broadband speed. It was a tiring business, but he didn't mind: he was on a roll and probably as excited as his stepdaughter. Now he had begun the process, he felt desperate to get going.

By the middle of the week the To Let sign had been stapled to the brick stanchion supporting the front gate and Finch was packing a spare shirt, boxers and socks in his canvas holdall, ahead of leaving for a few days with Grace and Sam in Manchester – and a slew of viewing appointments in the nearby Peak District.

54

The floodgates were open. As soon as Romy got home after Lucy's birthday lunch, she threw on her scruffiest jeans and a threadbare jumper and began to rampage around the cottage. She dragged out anything that reminded her of Michael: photographs with his coolly smiling, saturnine face; the pepper mill he'd given her for her birthday; his dressing gown, still hanging hidden behind the spare-room door; his stupid, shiny, designer wellies; his equally redundant Barbour flat cap on the shelf in the coat cupboard; his favourite white Wedgwood cup from which he'd liked to drink Earl Grey, the saucer broken long ago; and Simon Sebag Montefiore's *Stalin*, which he'd read to death one summer. She hurled the lot into a black bin bag to take to the charity shop.

As the last item fell into the crammed plastic sack, she collapsed onto the sofa, clutching a cushion to her chest, and listened to her tattered breathing. She was amazed to discover she didn't feel like crying any more – she was so sick of letting Michael Claire ruin her life.

Sitting there, she remembered her mother: arthritic and emphysemic – from all the cigarettes she and her father had consumed their entire life. Peggy had been dealing with recent memories of waking to find her husband dead beside her from a heart attack, struggling breathlessly to maintain her beloved vegetable garden and existing on a scant government pension. Bony, sweaty and blue-tinged, sitting in her chair with the oxygen mask clamped to her face, her mum still managed to smile. 'I'm a right old wreck,' she'd say cheerfully, between gasps. 'Knackered me in the end, all those fags. But I enjoyed every sodding one. I'd light up right now if this perishing oxygen tank wouldn't blow us both to smithereens.'

Romy compared Peggy's stalwart, unflinching attitude to Michael's . . . to her own. But both of them had been rendered weak and useless by the legacy of her husband's lies, while her mother was fulfilled, at peace with herself. And though Michael might choose not to be, Romy fully intended to grab her life by its collar and find her own version of fulfilment.

Tonight, she told herself, *I will open a bottle of wine and drink to me, Romy Margaret Turnbull.* Her maiden name sounded strange on her tongue after so long, but also comforting. It summoned up her parents' love, their strengths, their passionate commitment to a better planet and the values they'd instilled so solidly in her and Blake – all of which Michael had cruelly disparaged.

'To Romy Turnbull and a new start,' she said later, raising her glass of red in the air and smiling to the universe. Michael had bought the wine, but her anger was spent now, and she drew the line at giving away a very good Rioja, double standards or not.

There was so much to enjoy that didn't have to involve men. Finch had been someone who understood the life she wanted, who might have been a real soul-mate. But she tried not to think of him. She was sure she would find like-minded friends once she opened herself up to the possibility . . . once she knew more where she was going and who she was.

I'll continue up at Ebernoe. I'll chase a conservation job. I'll make an effort with people in the village. I'll try yoga. I'll paint the walls bright colours and make yoghurt like Mum used to in that jug in the airing cupboard. I'll take a trip somewhere interesting with Bettina. I might even get a cat. This last thought interrupted her manifesto and made her smile. Cats caused Michael's eyes to itch and swell up.

On Tuesday morning, Romy met up with Maureen at the harbour café. She wanted to pick her brains.

They sat for an hour or so, drinking tea and looking out across the water while they discussed progress at the common and various possibilities for a job for Romy. Maureen was enthusiastic. She knew everybody in the local conservation world and thought there might be something going in the Arun Wetlands Centre.

Later, as they stood by the till, waiting to pay for their drinks, Maureen commented casually, 'So sad about your army chap. We'll miss him.'

Romy started, her heart bouncing out of rhythm as she asked, 'Is he staying in Argentina, then?'

Maureen gave a surprised frown. 'No, no. Didn't you hear? He's not long back, but now he's off again, up to the Peak District to live with his stepdaughter, so Jenny tells me. She's terribly upset, of course, losing her loyal fundraiser.'

Romy made a sort of choked *hmm* noise that might have been agreement, might have been just her clearing her throat – she was incapable of forming a reply. And Maureen, having shared the latest gossip, said a brisk goodbye and took off on her rusty bike, which she'd propped carelessly against the glass of the café window.

Romy stood alone in the lane, blinking in the bright autumn sunlight. *That's it, then*, she told herself. *Finch has gone.*

55

In the weeks that followed, Romy found the miasma of the last few months gradually beginning to lift. Since leaving the flat, she'd seldom talked to Michael. And he never called her. At first she had checked in regularly with Theresa, who assured her he seemed to be managing, in a chaotic sort of way. Romy didn't know what that meant in terms of his mental health, but she felt it was no longer her business. The gaps between her calls to Theresa grew longer as she turned her focus to her own life.

This morning she got up early and dressed in her running gear, pulling on her woolly hat and gloves and walking out into the chilly, pre-dawn light. Sunrise was not long away, the sky to the east already softly luminous: it was going to be a beautiful day. The tide was as far out as possible, the autumn air so still across the undulating brown mud that Romy could hear her heart thudding in her ears as she ran.

She stopped to take in the scenery. She made herself do this every morning now. Instead of just running for exercise – making it all about effort and physicality – she tried to give the hour a meditative element, to appreciate the beauty around her and let nature expand her mind. She was determined to develop mental strategies, until eventually they would be habitual and she'd become strong like her mother, calm, and look to the future with enthusiasm.

As she stood and watched a large oystercatcher pecking at the seaweed with its orange-red bill, a figure coming off the back lane onto the harbour road caught her eye, jogging steadily towards her. She blinked hard, narrowed her eyes. *Could it be?*

He was still a long way off, but she knew his outline so well – that long, easy stride, the set of his head. She heard her breath catch as she froze, unable to do anything but watch, anticipation flaring painfully in her chest.

If he recognized her, he did not show it, his lope remaining regular and consistent as he drew closer. The sun tipped the horizon, blinding rays suddenly throwing the man into bright focus, like a theatrical spotlight. She could see his brown hair floating in the breeze, the triangle of sweat darkening the front of his grey T-shirt, bare arms jackknifing up and down as he ran. She pulled her beanie from her head and immediately regretted it – her hair was a terrible mess, as usual.

She watched as he finally noticed her standing there. He started. He stared. He slowed. Then he was in front of her, breathing hard, his face a mixture of surprise and acute embarrassment.

'Romy,' he gasped.

'I was told you'd left the village.'

Finch blinked, looked away. 'I'm packing up right now.'

He spoke as if he were in a daze and not really talking to her. She didn't know how to respond.

'How's Michael?'

'OK, I think. I haven't seen him for a while.'

Finch nodded. His face was flushed and covered with sweat, his hands hung loose by his side. He looked lost. Then he seemed to pull himself together. 'Good to see you, then,' he said, almost mechanically, but didn't move off.

She nodded, about to reply. But before she had time, he gave her a fleeting smile, turned and was gone. She listened in stunned silence to the slap, slap, slap of his trainers on the tarmac behind her. But she didn't turn.

After a long moment, she continued with her run, her pounding heart having little to do with the exercise. She was devastated. All these months she'd been worrying about seeing him, dreading it and longing for it in equal measures, and now it had finally happened and it was like . . . nothing at all.

The hurt lingered all day. Finch had treated her cruelly. She'd seen no sign on his face, as he pulled to a stop beside her, that he felt any more for her than he did for, say, Jenny or Maureen – just another middle-aged village woman with designs on his time. It was unbearable for Romy, as she tried to marry the strength of feeling she still had for the man with his astonishing indifference. He might as well have struck her.

But she had no time to mope; there was so much to do. Downstairs, the house was in chaos. She was halfway through painting the kitchen a vibrant primrose. She needed to put the first coat on today because the new cupboard doors were due on Friday and the paint had to be dry by then. So she climbed into her painting overalls, trapped her wild hair in a knot on the top of her head and turned the radio up loud, determinedly pushing aside the stabbing ache of her encounter with Finch.

She was still at it by early evening, stretched up on tiptoe, arm screaming, back protesting and paint dripping from the roller down her arm. Over the music, she heard a cautious knock at the front door. She sighed. At this hour it could only be Vera, complaining again. *Bins or top road?* Romy shook her head as she put the roller down in the tray, wiped her hands on her overalls and stepped barefoot to answer it, composing her face into a welcoming smile as she went.

'May I come in?' Finch asked.

Romy stood aside. She didn't care, this time, that she looked as if someone had stepped on her face, that she was spattered with yellow paint, that her hair looked like a rusty Brillo pad. She didn't care that her heart was being crushed to nothing in her breast, that her breath seemed trapped somewhere south of her ribs. She just walked ahead of him, back straight, without speaking, into the kitchen, and took up the sticky roller again.

Finch followed her, but also did not speak. He stood in the doorway and watched as she began the rhythmic rolling above her head again – back and forth, second coat, filling in any gaps where the old cream paint still poked through. The radio was playing a violin piece Romy recognized but couldn't name. She felt as if hours passed like this before he spoke.

'Looks nice.'

She stared at him, suspending her roller above the paint tray to catch any drips.

He gazed back and she heard him sigh.

She dropped the roller. Finch stepped towards her and she was suddenly in his arms, his mouth hot on hers, the tears running down her face as he kissed her again and again, until neither could breathe.

When, finally, they were both naked, back on the sofa where it had all begun, they lay very still, their bodies touching lightly, his skin like a feather laid against her breast. He looked into her eyes and all she saw was a longing so powerful it made her jolt with recognition at her own starved and pent-up need. She reached to kiss him again, savouring the beautiful familiarity of his mouth as, slowly, they began to make love.

56

Finch woke to find Romy beside him. He had to shake himself to remember how this had come about. He'd been furious with himself the previous morning. Walking away from her on the harbour road seemed, at the time, the only thing he was capable of doing. But as soon as he was out of sight, he realized he must be completely insane. *What the hell was I thinking?* he asked himself. She'd looked so beautiful in the dawn light, almost fragile in her confusion. Yet someone courageous enough to face up to Grace and admit she'd been wrong, say she was sorry – it was not an easy thing to do. He'd been appallingly, bafflingly rude. He'd run off as if she were toxic.

For the remainder of the day, as Finch cleared out the cupboard in his bedroom and packed his clothes into boxes to take up to Hawk Cottage – the pretty house with russet ivy clinging to the grey stone he'd eventually chosen, on the edge of the Peak District National Park – he thought of nothing else, cursing his stupidity, his boorishness.

Romy implied she wasn't caring for Michael any more, he thought. But what did it matter now? He had committed to tenants – a young couple and their small daughter – and Grace was expecting him. Nothing had changed for his poor stepdaughter.

But by the evening, his body was telling him otherwise, sweeping all obstacles aside and propelling him, unthinkingly, through the front door to walk – almost run – across the village to her house. If she threw him out, it was only what he deserved. He knew he would never forgive himself if he didn't at least try to see her and thank her for what she had said to Grace. But, in the end, neither had needed words.

Now he looked over at her sleeping face and his heart contracted. What had he done, coming here like this and making love to her as if they could instantly resurrect what they'd once had?

He slid out from under the duvet and began stealthily gathering his clothes from where they had fallen last night. The memory of their lovemaking almost stopped him in his tracks, but he knew he should leave before it became impossible.

It was already too late: Romy had opened her lovely gold-brown eyes and he was lost. Half dressed, he sat on the bed and picked up her hand, bringing it to his lips, where he kissed it softly and held it for a moment against his cheek.

She smiled. But he sighed and turned away. 'You know why I'm leaving the village?' he said quietly.

'To be with Grace, so I'm told.'

Now he twisted to face her. He didn't bother to ask who had told her. It was never one person, but a gossip-vine running effortlessly through a society desperate for anything new.

'She's been in a bad way. I worry about her, but there's precious little I can do when I'm so far away.' He searched Romy's sleepy face, but her expression was unreadable. 'Coming back from Argentina, knowing I didn't have you, I felt I needed to get away . . . I don't know . . . start again.' He realized he was gabbling and forced himself to stop.

She nodded, giving nothing away. 'So when do you go?'

'Couple of days.' He stood up. 'I'm sorry, I shouldn't have come here.'

Romy got out of bed in silence and picked up her blue dressing gown from the chair in the corner, sliding it over her naked body. She walked around the bed and stood close to him, arms akimbo, looking up into his face. He detected a new confidence in her eyes as he waited for her to speak.

'Are you *really* telling me, Robert Fincham, after what happened last night, that you're going to walk out of here and never see me again?' Her expression was not bewildered or questioning, but fierce in a way he'd never seen before.

When he didn't immediately answer, she said, less certainly this time, a tremor in her voice, '*Are* you?'

He didn't have to think. 'No. No, I'm not.' He pulled her close, smoothing his hand down the contours of her body through the silky rayon of her dressing gown.

Later they were back on the sofa, his arm around her shoulders, two mugs of tea cooling on the table in front of them. Romy had told him what James had said about Michael, the night he'd assaulted Grace, about Michael's reaction, about her own feelings for her husband now.

'Nell knew,' Finch began, when she ground to a halt.

Romy looked uncomfortable. 'James said.'

'She didn't believe Grace.'

'Oh. Poor girl.'

'Nell wasn't in full possession of the facts, so I'm not really judging her. But it's one of the reasons Grace didn't tell Sam till the other day . . . I never knew about Nell and James.'

They fell silent.

'There's always stuff we don't tell.'

'I suppose.' He shook his head in bewilderment. 'I'd always thought Nell was the most honest woman alive.'

'It was before you met. Maybe she thought you didn't need to know.'

Silence fell, as they were both dragged reluctantly back into the past.

Finch turned to look down at her. 'What about us, Romy? Where do we go from here?' She didn't answer immediately and he went on, 'The situation with Grace. When she's had the right help and feels better, I hope the two of you . . .'

Romy pulled away from him and sat hunched forward, her elbows on her knees. He put his hand tentatively on her back, but she gave an almost imperceptible twitch and he removed it.

When she turned, her face was resigned. 'You just have to do what you have to do, Finch.'

She got up, but he grabbed her hand, wouldn't let go as he also rose from the cushions and took her other hand, forcing her to meet his eye.

'I won't lose you again, Romy. I couldn't bear to. But Grace is in such a fragile state at the moment. I can't let her down.'

Romy eyed him. Then her face broke into a grin. 'This is exactly like listening to myself, persuading you how much Michael needed me.'

Finch laughed. 'And, like you, I don't feel I have a choice.'

'Will you tell Grace about us? If we keep in touch?'

He shrugged. 'Probably not right now.'

They regarded each other in silence.

'Well, we both have stuff to do,' Romy said, her voice firm. 'I need to sort my life out – Michael nearly finished me. You need to sort out Grace.'

They gazed at each other in silence, Finch feeling his heart contract at the thought of leaving her. 'I know we have to do this,' he said, 'but it feels really hard.' He stepped closer, his arms going round her and drawing her to him. 'I'm going to miss you so much.'

She reached up and kissed him, her mouth warm on his, and so familiar – like a beautiful memory. '*À bientôt*,' she whispered.

57

Michael watched his son carefully unpack the two chocolate eclairs from the white cardboard box and set them on a plate. The kettle was nearly boiled, the loose-leaf Earl Grey already spooned into the warmed pot: Leo took his tea seriously.

'No Lucy today?'

Leo shook his head. 'She's with her mum and sister. They're shopping for a sixtieth birthday present for her dad.' He poured the boiling water onto the tea leaves and knocked the metal lid of the pot back into place. 'She sent her love.'

Michael appreciated his son's Saturday visits, in fact looked forward to them so much he would become fidgety – like the silly old man he'd become – as the time got closer, in case Leo cancelled. Then the hour would go way too fast and the boy would be gone again, leaving him in such despair, drowning in such unbearable loneliness, he felt his heart might actually stop beating – although he would never dream of letting on to Leo how he felt.

There were people around during the week, of course – paid people – but Leo was different: Leo was family. 'Give her mine when you see her,' he said.

Michael watched Leo take a large bite of his pastry, the cream squidging out of the side in a fluted ribbon, which his son deftly caught and licked off his finger. He, himself, had no appetite, but knew he should make an effort – Leo bought them knowing they were his favourite.

'Any word from Mum?' Leo asked.

Michael thought he was fishing. Romy had made the decision – for which he was pathetically grateful – that the boys would never know from her what their father had done. But Leo was clearly baffled by his mum's total disappearance from his father's life.

'I think she's been busy, getting on with her own stuff. I'm happy for her, not having to cope with me and my annoying problems any more.' He smiled and spoke lightly. But Michael felt a leaden sadness.

His more sensitive clients sometimes used to say, when recounting the point at which their lives had taken a turn for the legally unsound, 'If I could just turn the clock back.' He'd privately smiled at their triteness. But, really, he understood.

Leo's phone rang and he watched his son glance at the screen then say, 'Got to get this, Dad. Be back in a minute.' He hurried out of the kitchen, leaving Michael wondering about Romy, wondering if she would ever be prepared to let him back into her life – in a limited capacity, obviously – for the boys' sakes. He thought back to the last time he had seen her and her stark warning that at some point he should tell their sons, or risk being haunted for ever by his crime.

Leo's intonation, filtering through from the hall, sounded as if he was winding up his call. *Is this the moment*, Michael wondered, his body shuddering fiercely at the thought, *that I do what I promised Romy I would?*

Grace Fleetwood. He turned the name over in his mind, where it lodged permanently, now. Such spirit the girl had had, with her youthful prettiness and bright summer dresses. It was just fun to be around her. And she had gravitated towards him – as if he were her special project – always the one to bring him coffee and offer help with even the smallest thing. Which he had really appreciated at the time: he was under intolerable pressure with the Brigham case.

Then that night . . . He had tried to make sense of it so many times, to understand how he could have done something so terrible. And finally, over the years, he'd come to the conclusion that it seemed intelligible only if he thought of it in terms of a perfect storm.

Grace had accepted the glass of wine he proffered, he remembered, drinking it way too quickly. The room was hot, so appallingly hot, it changed something for him, the stifling air, his overwhelming tiredness making rational thought impossible. She teased him about his work obsession. She gazed at him as if he were divine. He could still see her face as she beckoned him to sit next to her on the sofa. And, for that one crazy, stupid moment, he had believed she wanted him.

But as soon as he touched her skin, pressed his mouth to her young lips, his palm to her breast, he'd felt her flinch and pull away. He had known as clearly as he knew his own name that she did not want this, did not want *him*. And a switch went in his brain as he scrabbled to have as much of her as he could before she got away – something he remembered now with crippling shame. As he forced himself on her, her legs awkwardly splayed and pinioned beneath his body, her red dress rucked up, her breath jagged in his ear, he'd heard her whimpering, like the child she was.

It was then that the phone rang. It was a client, persistent and slightly unhinged, whom he quickly brushed off. But Grace had taken her chance and gone, *thank goodness*. Five minutes, maybe less, it was, since he had first laid his hand on the girl's bare thigh. But in that brief flash of time, he had done something totally inconceivable, an act of violence that it was impossible for him even to contemplate owning. Indeed, to this day, he could barely articulate his guilt.

That night, as he'd sat sweating and shaking, gasping for breath on the sofa in his rooms, he'd already found himself beginning to refute, to bury, to rewrite and smooth the edges of what had happened between him and the girl. It wasn't him. He couldn't have done it. So when he arrived at James's house, and his friend had asked him if he'd raped her, he had denied it with an almost fervent belief that it was impossible for him to have done so. But he had been *that close*. If the phone hadn't rung . . .

James had seemed to think that as long as it wasn't actual rape, it wasn't too serious. Which Michael knew was utterly wrong – and if he'd been in any doubt, the shocked and frightened expression in Grace's eyes, the way she flinched as he grabbed at her and began to kiss her made it clear enough. The revulsion in Romy's eyes made it clear, too – if he really needed to be told.

Michael had never stopped regretting that night. When he realized, as the weeks passed, that Grace might not speak up, he had determinedly buried the whole incident as best he could. But it haunted him, nonetheless. It drove him to work even harder, and, little by little, to take small steps away from Romy and the boys. Work was the only thing that blocked Grace's tear-stained face from his thoughts. But gradually, over the years, the images receded, the deed lodging in the dark pit of his consciousness, like a warning flag that occasionally caught his eye – until the letter.

Leo walked back into the kitchen, stashing his phone in the back pocket of his jeans. 'Sorry, Dad, stupid work thing.'

Michael felt sweat trickling down his back. He almost couldn't look at his son, fearing his excruciating memories might somehow be written on his face.

Leo refilled the pot and poured them both more tea. Then he settled at the table and gave his father a grin. 'So, Dad, have you thought some more about what you're going to do?'

'Do?' He tried to clear his thoughts, welcoming the chance to focus on something different, despite the subject being a contentious one.

'Yeah, Dad. We talked about this the other day. Work . . .'

Joke. Like the world was waiting with bated breath. 'I'm back!' he'd shout. And all his clients, the judges, court officials, his competitive colleagues – who'd probably been cheering from the rafters at his demise – would overlook the fact that he couldn't hold a pen and paper at the same time, could only type with one finger of one hand, couldn't remember if it was Monday or last year, had to pee every ten minutes and couldn't fucking stand upright without the help of a crutch. *Christ, I couldn't even put my wig on straight, these days, let alone fasten my bands or collar stud.*

He levelled his gaze at his son. 'Face it. I'm not going to be able to work, Leo, not even in a limited capacity, not for a long time . . . probably ever.'

He watched his son's face fall. 'Come on, Dad. Look at Andrew Marr. He's presenting one of the most prestigious programmes on TV and he had the same as you. You can't just give up like this.'

Michael growled silently. *Sodding Andrew Marr.* Held up as the poster-crock for every stroke patient from here to eternity. He loathed him for it. 'Being a television host doesn't carry quite the same level of responsibility as being a QC, all due respect to the man.'

Leo frowned. 'So . . . what? You're going to just sit here for the rest of your life and feel sorry for yourself?'

Michael nodded. 'Probably.' He didn't care what Leo thought – or anyone else, for that matter. They could harangue him all they liked, feed him pills he didn't want, make him eat vegetables and move balls from one box to another with that moron glove; it wouldn't mend what was going on in his head. Nor did it change the fact that Romy – even if they did come together for family occasions – would never look at him again without that veiled aversion in her eyes.

Leo's face cleared and he laughed. 'Hey, knock yourself out, then, Dad.'

'I might do just that,' he said, also smiling. 'Unintentionally, of course,' he added quickly, when he saw his son's alarm. That was the trouble with being in this state.

There was no room for irony or jest. If he said, 'I'm losing the will to live,' Imogen would look worried. If he said, 'Does it really matter if I drink too much at this stage?' he was being reckless. If he said, 'I can't go back to work,' it was defeatism. Any normal person said these things from time to time, but nobody took them seriously.

Leo got up to clear the tea plates. When he turned from the sink his expression was serious. 'Dad, this thing with Mum. She absolutely refuses to tell me what it's about.' He stopped, his eyes searching his father's face.

Michael felt himself go rigid. *No*, he thought instinctively. But Romy's words rushed back to him again with force. He'd always considered himself fearless, someone prepared to stand up and be counted under any circumstance, and ready to take any calculated risk. But here he was, cowering behind his toxic secret, like a craven sissy, still protected by Romy's stern compassion, despite his lies. It made him sick to realize what he had become.

Can I do it? he asked himself, panic building in his gut. Leo was watching him. *Can I?* Every cell in his body screamed, NO. But a persistent voice in his head was egging him on. *Go on, Michael. Stop being such a coward and do it. Now.*

For another endless moment he hesitated. Then he drew himself up and took a deep breath. 'Sit down, Leo.' He waited till his son was seated. 'I'm warning you, you're going to be horrified by what I'm about to tell you.' He stopped, trying to sort the jumble of words in his mind into some coherent package. It felt like a long time before he was able to speak. Leo's eyes continued to rest on him expectantly and he shuddered inwardly at the pain he was about to cause his son.

Bracing himself, he waded in. 'The fact is, I assaulted a girl one night. It was a long time ago . . . but she was young, only sixteen.' He swallowed hard, realizing he was twisting his bad hand painfully in the other. Leo was frowning. 'I thought, entirely mistakenly, that she was attracted to me . . . and I went too far.'

His son blinked, 'You mean . . .' He shook his head disbelievingly. After a long pause he added, his voice quiet with shock, 'Who was she?'

'Her name is Grace.'

Silence.

'You . . . raped her?'

Michael shook his head. 'No. But I might have.' He cringed as he spoke. 'I was unintentionally rough with her.'

Silence.

'And . . . Mum just found out?'

The story was long. Michael did not hold back as he had with Romy. And Leo did not try to interrupt. Sitting across the table from Michael, he seemed too stunned for speech.

When Michael finally stopped talking, there was an eerie silence in the kitchen, as if neither of them was actually breathing. He wished his son would say something. He had no hope of exoneration, of course, but he wanted to get this over with, to take the heavy blows of disgust and condemnation – the outrage – squarely on the chin. He was ready.

Leo got up in total silence, his face almost blank.

'Leo?'

His son moved towards the door. 'Can't talk to you, Dad. Not now.'

And with that he was gone.

Michael followed him, saw the door slam. He leant against the hall wall and began to cry tears of hopelessness. This, he knew, was his life now. Not just in his own head, but in his son's too – both his sons, when Rex found out – he was a pariah. He had no real friends. Romy was gone. And Leo would not be back.

But as Michael clumped his solitary way along the corridor to his bedroom, he was aware of the smallest, almost imperceptible lightening in his soul. For the first time in decades he had been completely honest. He was well aware, though, that that was not the end of it. There was something else he needed to do. And until he did that – the potential ramifications of which made him almost nauseous – he knew he would not be able to find even a modicum of peace.

58

Finch strode beside his stepdaughter as they climbed the hill behind his Derbyshire house. It was freezing, the easterly wind bitter. But the sun had shaken off the low clouds in the early afternoon, making Grace jump up from the lunch table and declare they all needed a walk.

Sam had grinned, but adamantly refused. 'You two go. I'll sit by the stove and trash my mind with the Sundays.'

'Snooze off, more like,' Grace said.

At which Sam had laughed easily and nodded. 'Hope so. But if you're nice to me, I might clear up first.'

So Finch had Grace to himself. Which was exactly what he wanted.

His stepdaughter, after opening up to Sam and then beginning her therapy, had got worse before she'd got better: the enlightened company she worked for had given her a month's sick leave, more if she needed it. So Finch went round to see her most weekdays. He'd sit with her, often in silence, make her lunch that she didn't eat, try to encourage her out, which she refused to do. She kept insisting he need not be there, but she didn't seem to mind his company.

So he stayed, ferrying her back and forth to the therapist on Tuesday and Friday mornings, finding anodyne movies on Netflix to watch in the afternoons, pressing treats on her – a lovely bath essence or her favourite chocolate – and telling her endless funny stories about her mother. In fact, it reminded him of those months when Nell was ill and he'd done every practical thing in his power to try to make things better. They never talked about Michael.

Finch missed Romy. But it wasn't a missing like the tearing heartache when they'd first split up. It was more a quiet, almost pleasurable knowing that she was still there, and a hope that soon they might be together. Though he worried that Grace might never willingly accept Romy's presence in her life.

He called Romy after supper every night, when he got back from his stepdaughter's house. He would pour himself a glass of wine and sit by the glowing stove in the sitting room. Romy would do likewise down in Sussex. And they would talk about everything, getting to know each other in a way their previous encounters had barely allowed for – so overshadowed had they been by their troubled pasts, by Michael's stroke, by Grace, and taken up with the powerful physical attraction that existed between them.

Romy told Finch she had secured a part-time job at the Arun Wetlands Centre, two days a week, working on a project to protect Bewick swans in their migration path. She said she and Cathy from the deli were becoming friends. Finch told Romy about Grace's progress, his plan to run a fundraising marathon in Russia next spring and his thoughts about getting a dog, perhaps a collie.

And, gradually, he watched Grace coming back to life. At first it was just the odd flash of her old ebullient personality, followed by troughs of silent despair. But the flashes were becoming more the norm, and both Finch and Sam began to allow themselves some hope.

Now, they climbed in silence. Finch was fitter than Grace, after her weeks of hibernation, and he heard her laboured breathing as they reached the top of the rise and looked out across the rolling hills of the National Park.

'Wow,' Grace said, when she'd caught her breath.

'It always takes my breath away.'

Grace laughed. 'It was that bloody hill took mine.'

After another moment during which they both gazed out at the glorious view, she went on, 'So do you like it here, Finch?'

'I love it.'

She turned a sharp eye on him. 'Honestly? You're not just saying that?'

'What's not to like?'

Finch *was* being honest. He felt at home in the cottage, even though he knew nobody in the surrounding area. This place was wilder, less manicured, less populated than Sussex, and he liked that. But he found he missed the sea, missed his harbour runs, missed his own house more than he'd thought he would.

Grace stroked his arm. 'You and Sam have been so amazing. I can't believe how patient you both are. You literally saved my life.' She let out a long breath. 'Mum would have been so proud of you,' she said, and Finch could hear the wobble in her voice.

They turned and walked east along the path that breasted the hill and dipped down towards a copse of trees in the distance. The wind was fierce up there, and they both shrank into their scarves and coats, hands buried deep in their pockets, noses pink with cold. Finch glanced sideways at his stepdaughter. The words were itching at the back of his throat, but he was so scared of tipping Grace back into the depths. He waited a moment longer, then took a deep breath.

'Do you mind if we talk about Romy?'

Grace immediately turned to him. 'Are you seeing her?'

'No, but we've kept in touch.'

She nodded slowly but didn't reply.

'What do you feel about her, Gracie?'

His stepdaughter's voice was tight as she said, 'She wasn't to blame for what happened.'

'But?' They'd turned back towards home now, the wind behind them.

His stepdaughter stopped beside him, kicking the loose stones on the path with the toe of her boot. 'She was Michael's wife.' Her tone was blunt. 'Which I know isn't fair . . . because she's a victim too.'

'She reminds you of him, obviously.'

'That . . . and I suppose at the time I saw her as the catalyst for me having to open up about Michael.'

They continued down the hill in silence.

'But I have absolutely nothing personal against her, Finch.'

He nodded.

She looked up at him. 'You still really like her, don't you?'

Finch was unable to stop a smile as he thought of how much he did like Romy, which Grace noted, her eyes flickering with amusement.

'You deserve to be happy, Finch,' she said, linking his arm in hers and squeezing him close as they arrived at the gate of Hawk Cottage. 'You've been the best father a girl could ever have.'

When Finch didn't reply for the lump in his throat, Grace looked up at him. 'Don't not see Romy on my account,' she said, her voice full of resolve. 'I'd hate that. Michael has already messed with far too many lives.' Her eyes blazed. 'It stops *right here, right now.*'

Finch, as he swung the wooden gate open, gesturing to Grace to go first, stood stock still for a moment and took what felt to him like the biggest breath he had ever taken in his life. He wanted to sing out. In that one sentence, Grace had served notice on the past. He knew nothing would be forgotten – abuse, he was sure, never was – but it was a signal of intent. *Michael's actions would do no further harm.*

59

That Sunday Romy and Leo sat on the harbour wall. It was sunny, not as cold as it was for Grace and Finch in Derbyshire, but there was a nippy wind off the sea, nonetheless. The two barely noticed, however, they were so involved in their conversation.

'Like a perfect storm,' Leo said, not for the first time. As if by repeating his father's rationale often enough, he might finally grasp the actuality of what he'd been told.

'Perhaps it was,' she said.

Leo turned to face her, his cheeks pink, his eyes troubled. 'I don't know what to do, Mum. Lucy says I should forgive him, but I think she's got more tools for that as a Christian. And Rex isn't much help. Dad asked me if I'd tell him, but I don't think Rex really took it in. Like, he's too far away for it to have an impact?' He sighed. 'God, how will I ever face Dad again? Knowing what he did.'

Silence fell as Romy struggled for an answer. 'I don't know, sweetheart. It's hard to forgive the deed, but the man who did it is not who your father is today. He would never have been brave enough to tell you, if he was.' She saw Leo considering this.

She had been surprised – and not without a certain respect – that Michael, after claiming he was not yet ready, had taken such a bold leap so soon. She could only guess at the courage it must have taken to confront his son with such a damning confession.

'Just on a basic level, it's cringingly embarrassing,' Leo was saying. 'He'll know exactly what I'm thinking, and I won't know what to say.'

'Then leave it for a while. Dad will respect your feelings. He won't be expecting you back, I imagine.'

Her son groaned. 'It's just so horrible, Mum. He's my dad . . .' His voice tailed off. 'I wish to hell I didn't know. It was my own stupid fault. I should never have kept pushing. I wish we could go back to how it was before. We were getting on better than we ever had in our whole lives.'

'Well, maybe what you've built with your father is strong enough . . .' Her son didn't reply, just leant in to her and laid his head wearily on her shoulder. 'You know you've been wonderful these last few months,' she added. 'You really stepped up to the plate in such a fantastic way.'

Leo straightened up and gave her a wry grin. 'Sounds like I surprised you, Mum.'

Romy smiled. 'Put it this way, I always knew you *could*, but it was a very big ask, for all of us, coping with your dad.'

Leo didn't speak for a moment. Then he said, his voice tinged with cynicism, 'Yeah, turned out to be a bigger bloody ask than I could ever have imagined.' There was a long pause, during which neither of them spoke. 'But Dad's obviously contrite,' he added. 'He even said he intends to write and apologize to Grace.'

Romy raised a sceptical eyebrow. 'Would he do that? It's evidence, and he's a lawyer.'

Her son shrugged. 'He sounded pretty convincing.'

As she saw Leo off on the London train, Romy really felt for her son. He'd looked so preoccupied, so bewildered as he'd tried to work out what best to do. But although she sympathized wholeheartedly with his desire not to know something so dreadful about a parent, she was convinced it was better this way. Better than allowing the secret to fester indefinitely, like a piece of rotting meat, sitting at the centre of all their lives.

Selfishly, she knew Michael's confession to Leo had cut the last thread that bound her to that secret. Despite Leo's distress, she couldn't help feeling an overwhelming sense of relief, realizing for the first time just how much it had cost her – since the letter – not to be honest with her sons. Now, at last, she could put Michael's crime behind her. She hoped, eventually, that he would write to Grace. She hoped Leo would come round – he was a kind man and he loved his father. But it was out of her hands now.

Thank God I don't have to go back to the flat tonight, she thought, as she walked briskly through the village – her village, now – and opened the front door to her cosy cottage. Tonight felt like a full stop on her past.

60

It was a few weeks since Finch had walked the steep, windy hillside behind his house with Grace, since Romy had sat on the sea wall, listening to her traumatized son. She and Finch were in her bright, newly painted primrose kitchen, Schubert playing softly on the radio, Romy rinsing out a blue metal Thermos at the sink. They were dressed in jeans and thermal tops, thick socks, ready for a morning on Ebernoe Common and Finch's first encounter with her conservationist friends.

'I always put the milk in with the tea,' she said.

'Perfect for me,' Finch replied. He was at the counter, where he'd neatly lined up four squares of buttered brown bread, which he was layering with slices of Cheddar, lettuce and pickle.

'Shame it's such a rubbish day.' Romy glanced out of the window. It was one of those still, grey winter mornings, where the damp air just hovers, as if it has nowhere better to go.

'Won't matter,' Finch said contentedly, as he packed the sandwiches in greaseproof paper and placed them in a Tupperware box, then in his black daypack. 'Do we need anything else? Apples, maybe?'

'Good idea. And Maureen always brings slabs of her delicious gingerbread.' Romy splashed milk into the Thermos, then swished the teapot a couple of times before pouring in the tea and screwing down the lid. She smiled to herself, surprised at the pleasure she found in sharing these simple domestic tasks with Finch.

He had arrived the previous Saturday evening. Seeing him, after their weeks apart, felt very different now. Romy was no longer insecure about his intentions, or hurt about the past, and welcomed him with a delighted hug, like a returning lover back from a short trip away. Because now she felt she really knew the man who walked through her cottage door – knew him so much better than before.

The intimate chats they'd shared on all those evenings since Finch's departure for Derbyshire – when they'd talked about everything from their childhoods to Nell and Grace, Michael, their hopes for the future – had given her a much deeper understanding of him and only served to strengthen her feelings.

They hadn't rushed to make love that first night, as they had on previous occasions. They'd just been content to be together again. Romy made beans on toast and they sat on the sofa in front of the flickering wood-burner with a glass of wine, Finch's arm around her shoulders, saying very little. There was an atmosphere between them that was fragile but also full of quiet joy, which both had wanted to savour. Obviously it would take time properly to dissolve the tensions that still lurked – with Grace, with Leo – but the logistics of how they would meld their lives and bring their two families together could wait until another day.

When they did finally make it up to bed, and Romy had felt Finch's naked warmth close against her, she'd let out a long sigh of happiness.

Now, she handed the Thermos to him and watched him fit it into the daypack. He smiled at her as he zipped it up, and in that moment her heart felt so full she wondered if she might actually be glowing. An energetic morning clearing bracken in the cold air; Thermos tea and gingerbread on a damp log; like-minded friends . . . Finch. *This is who I am*, she thought. *And this is where I want to be.*

Acknowledgements

I owe a large editorial debt to my three editors: Maxine Hitchcock, Clare Bowron and Tilda McDonald. Thank you so much. And thanks go to all the Michael Joseph team, including Emma Henderson, Hazel Orme and Lee Motley.

I would also like to thank my five-star agent, Jonathan Lloyd, and all at Curtis Brown.

For Finch's military background, I would like to thank Andrew Sharpe.

For Finch's sojourn in Argentina, I would like to thank Nick Davies.

For his help in so many ways, thank you, Don.

And Clare Boyd, without our numerous and encouraging fellow-writer conversations, I would be lost.

Reading Group Questions

1. How do you think *The Lie* approaches the theme of sexual assault and the 'Me Too' movement that was popularized in 2017?

2. '*Who am I protecting? . . . Him or me? Am I just scared of what he might tell me?*' What do you think leads Romy to lie to Finch about the circumstances of her marriage, rather than share the accusation made about Michael? Does she feel responsible? Is she embarrassed or ashamed for marrying a potential sexual predator? Or did she really believe the accusation to be untrue?

3. There is a contrast throughout the novel between country life in Sussex and the 'bright lights of London'. What role does this dichotomy play in *The Lie*?

4. 'Michael [is] a senior figure in the law and I should be very careful what I [say] because my accusation could ruin his life.' Grace's fear to speak up about the sexual assault due to Michael's status and the chance she may not be believed is not uncommon in real life today. Even her mother, Nell, thought Grace was lying. But did you believe her?

5. Finch uses running as a way of managing despair and frustration, even running away to another

country when things become unbearable. Similarly, Romy escapes to Sussex to get away from her toxic relationship with Michael. Is this healthy?

6. Discuss the dilemma Romy faces in being torn between the love, duty and sympathy she feels for Michael post-stroke, and the growing disgust the accusation generates in her. Did he deserve to be cared for so selflessly by Romy? Can you ever stop caring for someone you have spent thirty years married to, even when they do terrible things?

7. 'In that brief flash of time, he had done something totally inconceivable, an act of violence that it was impossible for him even to contemplate owning.' How did your beliefs of the accusation in the letter about Michael shift throughout the novel? Do you think Michael believed his own lie? How could he have acted differently, once the crime was committed?

8. What is your opinion on Finch's jealousy and frustration over Romy returning to Michael after his stroke? Was it warranted? What about the way he reacted to Romy after finding out about Grace's secret – was his blame and judgement towards her fair?

9. Discuss Romy's decision not to take action in response to the anonymous letter she received accusing her husband of sexual assault – was it wrong?

10. It is only through talking and opening up that Grace begins to seek recovery and Michael begins to find some sense of peace for his sins. What message do you think Boyd is giving here?

11. Does such an act as Michael's warrant forgiveness? If so, do you find yourself forgiving Michael by the end of the novel?

12. How does Romy's character develop throughout the novel? Is Romy's character one you found relatable or empowering?

13. 'Just as ripples spread out when a single pebble is dropped into water, the actions of individuals can have far-reaching effects.' *Dalai Lama*. Having now read *The Lie*, what does this epigraph used at the beginning of the book mean to you?

14. What do you think happens after the novel ends? Will Romy and Finch's relationship last? Will Grace accept Romy into her life? Will Michael's family be able to forgive him?

Hilary Boyd's new book

Coming 2021

Read on for the stunning
first chapter

I

Connie McCabe was an honest woman. At least she'd always considered herself as such. It wasn't something she prided herself in; it was just her default position, as another person's might be to slide away from the truth when it didn't suit them. But she was never brutal. If asked her opinion of a friend's new dress, she wouldn't say, 'That yellow makes you look as if your liver's packed in,' when the friend was stuck in the outfit for the foreseeable. So the events of that summer shocked Connie to the core and made her question everything she thought she knew about herself.

'On the 2pm xx' Connie texted her husband, Devan. They lived in a large village – almost a small town, or 'tillage', as the locals referred to it – south of the Mendips, on the Somerset Levels, and her journey from St Pancras would take close to three hours.

'See you at the station x' Devan texted back.

She sat back in the crowded train carriage, the heating turned up way too high for the mild April day, and closed her eyes, letting out a luxurious sigh of relief. For the past ten days she'd been on call, responsible for thirty-nine people's welfare – one passenger had cried off sick at the last minute – on a rail journey through the tulip fields of Holland. According to company guidelines, it was frowned upon to read or listen to anything – heaven forbid snooze – whilst accompanying her passengers across Europe. She should stay alert, poised to deal with any concerns her flock might have. So, despite loving every minute of her job as a tour manager, just sitting here, alone, with no responsibility to anyone but herself, was bliss.

Connie felt herself beginning to unwind as the train travelled west, past Reading and Swindon, the country-side awash with bright blossoms and deliciously pale spring green. It had been a good tour. Only one really irritating couple who'd picked holes in everything, from the pillows to the narrow steam train seats and rain on the day they toured Amsterdam. She'd been just waiting for them to kick off about the colours of the spectacular tulip displays. There was always one.

Now would be the time, she thought sadly, *when I'd ring Mum and fill her in about my trip.* Her dear mother, Sheila, had died in January in her sleep, at eighty-six, after barely a day's illness in her life. She'd been quietly independent to the last, living alone in her small South London flat with no fuss – miles from both her daughters. But Connie would ring most days and they would chat away. Sheila was wise, someone who really listened. But she also loved a good rant, a good gossip, a good laugh. *I miss you so much, Mum*, Connie whispered silently, her eyes filling with tears, which she quickly blinked away in the crowded car-riage. *And I really need your advice. I need you to tell me what to do about Devan.*

Her train arrived fifteen minutes late. But there was no sign of her husband, nor could she spot the red Honda in the semicircle of cars waiting on the station forecourt. She got out her mobile.

'Hi,' her husband said, sounding disoriented. 'Where are you?'

'At the station.' She tried to keep the irritation out of her voice, but she was dying to get home and take off her 'cruise wear' – as she called the outfits deemed suitable for her job – and have a long, hot soak in her own bath. She knew Devan had probably fallen asleep in front of some rugby match or other. It was all he seemed to do these days, since his retirement last summer as the village GP – a post he'd held for the past thirty years.

There was a moment's silence and she heard scuffling in the background. 'God . . . sorry . . . didn't realize the time. On my way,' Devan said, and clicked off.

'Good trip?' her husband asked, smiling briefly at her as she climbed into the car, but not removing his hand from the gear stick or leaning over to kiss her. His handsome face looked crumpled, his grey jumper had a large stain just below the crew neck and his chin sported a day's growth, the stubble sprouting silvery, although it was only the very edges of his dark hair that showed signs of grey. But Connie wasn't in the mood to comment or criticize.

'Yes, great. Weather was a bit rubbish the day we were in Amsterdam, but otherwise it went pretty smoothly, apart from the usual PPs,' which stood for Perfect Passengers and was their ironic acronym for any awkward customers on her tours. 'The wife kicked off because there wasn't a "pillow menu" at any of the hotels.'

Devan glanced round at her, his thoughtful blue eyes, deep-set beneath heavy brows – people likened him to the footballer George Best in his prime– coming suddenly to life. He had such a charming smile, which she'd instantly fallen in love with, that long-ago night in the festival medical tent. 'Is that even a thing?'

Connie nodded. 'These days, if you're in four- or five-star luxury, yes.'

He gave a disbelieving snort. 'Does it include starters and a main?'

'Well, I've seen buckwheat pillows listed – filled with buckwheat hulls, apparently – and one with herbs and essential oils. So you're not far off the mark.'

'Preposterous,' Devan chuckled.

They drove in silence for a while. 'How have you been?' Connie asked.

'Oh, you know . . .' Devan's words were lost in the roar and rattle of a passing tractor.

'Your back? Are the exercises helping at all?'

Her husband shot her a glance, his mouth clamped in a thin line of warning. He'd been plagued, on and off, by a degenerating disc in his lower back for the past couple of years, for which he'd been given a whole slew of exercises by the physio. But he never did them, as far as Connie could tell. 'God, Connie, don't start.'

His words were spoken softly, but she was taken aback by the veiled antagonism. She sympathized with someone in constant pain, obviously, but it was frustrating, watching him do nothing to alleviate the problem – Devan, a doctor who'd endlessly ranted about patients not being prepared to help themselves.

It was on the tip of her tongue to retort, but she took a deep breath instead. 'Hope it stays fine for the Hutchisons tomorrow,' she said, changing the subject as the atmosphere in the car grew thick with the unsaid. 'I got Carole a kitsch pair of clogs in Amsterdam and they painted her name on the side.'

Tim and Carole Hutchison owned an impressive Victorian villa at the top of the village, with spectacular views over the Somerset Levels. They always threw a spring party for Carole's birthday and although Connie wouldn't call them close friends – in fact she thought Tim, a retired fund-manager, pompous in the extreme – an invitation to the yearly bash was much coveted and a matter of pride in the village.

Devan didn't reply at once. 'I suppose we have to go,' he said, eventually, as they pulled on to the paved parking space at the side of their house and he turned off the engine. They both sat in silence for a moment, a weak evening sun breaking through the clouds and bathing their still faces in light pouring through the windscreen.

Connie frowned as she turned to her husband. 'You love their parties. You always say it's the best champagne in the county.'

He gave a weary nod. 'Yeah, well . . .'

Connie was about to remonstrate, but she heard Riley, their beloved Welsh terrier, barking excitedly and jumped out of the car. Biting her lip with disappointment at her husband, she pushed open the front door, bending to enjoy his enthusiastic welcome, to bury her fingers in his soft black and caramel fur and watch the perfect arc of his tail wagging furiously at seeing her.

Every time she went away these days – even if only for a week – she hoped, in her absence, things might shift for Devan. Hoped he might begin to shake off this pall of lethargy which broke her heart. Hoped to see the light in his eyes again. Her trips were like a bubble. She would escape into another world, swept up in the round-the-clock responsibility of the tour and its passengers, the extraordinary scenery, the diverse smells, the delicious local food – even the sun's rays seeming to fall differently abroad. Her problems with Devan faded into the background for those few short days. But coming home, however much she looked forward to it, forced her to face up to reality again.

The house was as messy as Connie had anticipated – sofa cushions squashed to Devan's shape, newspapers strewn, a dirty wine glass on the coffee table, some dried up olive stones in a ramekin. She took a deep breath as she entered the cosy farmhouse kitchen at the back of the house, where they'd spent a lot of family time when Caitlin – named after one of Devan's Irish grandmothers – was growing up. It wasn't bad, she conceded, casting an eye over the worktops and range, the oak refectory table. But Devan had never got a grip on surface wiping and the cooker was spattered from the endless fry-ups in which he'd no doubt been indulging; the worktop strewn with toast crumbs and greasy smears; tea and coffee stains ringing the area around the kettle; a pile of used teabags mouldering on a saucer.

She stopped herself from seizing a cloth and getting down to it immediately, knowing she was more pernickety than some and not wanting to wade in the second she was through the door in such an obviously censorious fashion. She would unpack first, have the bath she'd been longing for. She didn't want to pick a fight on her first night back.

'Think I'll go up. Been a long day,' Connie said later, pulling herself off the sofa and yawning as she reached for her reading glasses on the side table. They'd spent the evening with a bowl of ready-meal shepherd's pie, frozen peas and ketchup in front of the next episode of a Belgian police box set. Devan had held it over while she was away, although now she couldn't remember a single thing about who'd been bumped off or why – and was too tired to concentrate anyway.

Devan glanced up from his phone – which these days seemed to have become a physical extension of his hand. 'I'm sure it has,' he said absentmindedly, but made no move to join her. 'I might stay up for a bit . . .'

Connie felt a pang of disappointment. She just wanted to connect with him again, to be close. They had barely spoken all evening, except to catch up with trivial domestic news – such as the flush button coming loose in the downstairs loo and Rees, the gormless plumber's apprentice, coming to fix it. If she went to bed now, she would be dead to the world by the time he crept in beside her. Then in the morning, he would still be asleep when she got up.

'Please . . . come with me,' she said quietly and saw his face go still for a moment. Then he sighed and nodded.

'Sure, OK,' he said. But the reluctance was palpable, and quite upsetting.

Does he worry I'm after sex or something? she wondered, wryly, as she climbed the stairs to their bedroom, placing her glass of water and specs on the bedside table. But she'd stopped having expectations in that arena after a number of humiliatingly unsuccessful seductions on her part during the previous two years.

The last, months ago now, had been the worst – and such a sorry cliché. She had put on a slinky silk camisole in delicate lilac and matching knickers – saved at the back of her drawer from years back and barely worn – then waited for him to finish in the bathroom, heart knocking as she sat on the bed, hair fluffed and loose. When Devan saw her, he'd stopped short and stared, eyes wide, as if a woolly mammoth had landed on the duvet, his twitchy, but resigned expression reminiscent of an unwelcome appointment with the dentist.

He'd recovered sufficiently to force a smile and come over to sit beside her on the bed, picking up her hand and kissing it. But she'd seen the effort it took and she'd snatched it away, leaping up from the bed and shutting herself in the bathroom. She'd felt so utterly mortified – so unsexy, unattractive – that even the thought of it now made her cringe.

Although there had been many wonderful times in the past when they'd made love in this very bed, over the thirty-three years of their marriage. They'd always been good together, their attitude to sex one of relaxed mutual pleasure. No bells and whistles or swinging from the chandelier, neither of them trying to prove anything.

Just a light-hearted lust for each other, which she sorely missed.

She realized with a jolt that it was over two years since they'd properly made love – if you didn't count that night last summer when Neil, Connie's best friend, and his husband, Brooks, had asked them over, inventing this lethal cocktail of something green and sweet and fizzy, then burnt the chicken pie in the Aga. The only thing they'd eaten all evening was a handful of crisps and a piece of toast. Neither she nor Devan had known which way was up and they'd fallen into bed, heads spinning, and fumbled around in some half-hearted rendition of sex. Because although her husband had only retired last summer, things had been difficult between them for much longer than that, the strain Devan had been under at the surgery taking its inevitable toll.

Devan lay beside her now, his book – the usual weighty siege-and-massacre tome – propped on his chest. Connie tried to read, but sentences swam before her eyes and she knew she was wasting her time. She put down her reader and glasses and switched off the light, turning on her pillow to face her husband. Despite implying earlier that he wasn't tired, his book was swaying back and forth in his hands, his eyelids fluttering. A small fly was spinning in the beam of the desk lamp he read by, and she watched it for a while, then gently removed his book from his hands, turning down the page corner and closing it.

Devan jerked. 'Hey, I was reading.'

'You were almost asleep.'

He sighed and didn't object, removing his second pillow and slinging it to the floor, then turning off his own light. Their bedroom faced the main street of the village, and a car passed, headlights raking the ceiling in the semi-darkness. Connie placed her palm on his chest and stroked his warm skin. She just wanted some sign of affection, but he made no move to offer any. All he did was clamp her hand to his chest to still her stroking. She could feel the tension flowing off him like steam from a kettle.

'A cuddle would be nice,' she said.

After a moment's hesitation, Devan lifted his arm so she could lie against him, her head on his shoulder. She felt his hand pull her in, bringing her closer and she wanted to cry.

'Love you,' she said, softly.

'Love you too, Con,' he replied, automatically – she didn't sense his heart was fully behind his words.

Despite that, Connie luxuriated in his embrace. He smelt musty, but she didn't mind. His body was so comforting, so familiar, even in the state he was in, that she didn't want to let him go. When she woke around three in the morning to pee, she remembered that she'd gone to sleep in his arms, something she hadn't done for a very long time.